MM

HELPLESS BYSTANDERS IN AN INTERPLANETARY WAR

As the Krail and Earthmen prepared to do battle with space ships and futuristic weaponry, the natives of Eisernon took desperate steps to save their beautiful planet. Their only hope lay in finding and enlisting the aid of a super-race with unknown mental powers, believed by many to be on the verge of extinction. Other forces in the galaxy had failed in their own attempts to find this legendary super-race, but the Einai stayed with their search, knowing that failure would bring about annihilation of their planet. . . .

Simon Lang's
All the Gods of Eisernon

AVON
PUBLISHERS OF BARD, CAMELOT, DISCUS, EQUINOX AND FLARE BOOKS

To the Ancestor

ALL THE GODS OF EISERNON is an original publication of Avon Books. This Work has never before appeared in any form.

AVON BOOKS
A division of
The Hearst Corporation
959 Eighth Avenue
New York, New York 10019

First Avon Printing, June, 1973.

Printed in the U.S.A.

PROLOG

This is the First Book of the Han, that is, the books which concern themselves with the ancestral line of Priyam Hanshilobahr *Dom* Dao Marik, from the ancient times until the Now.

In those days there was the planet called Eisernon, which is to say, the Shining One. The legends of Eisernon and how it came to be are another book, but in the beginning there was Eisernon, and the People.

And the world was a green world, covered with jungles and forests thereupon, whose stems were as the girth of three men. And from these forests there sprang broad rivers, rushing to the sea. Eternal snows gleamed on the mountains, and the mountains were of purple and onyx, like unto neriosh and burnished obsidian so were the mountains of Eisernon.

There was one sea only, and the People had no other sea but that sea, of which the planet had but one; and the People took their ships down to the sea, to bring up all manner of fishes and scutlers and such creatures as the sea would surrender to them. And the sea covered half the world.

There were gods on Eisernon, and the People knew their gods and loved them with both their hearts. And the gods favored the People. And the gods were these: Roanouk, the Healer; Sibhem, the Merciful; and Quel, the Just. There were many smaller gods, who ruled the winds and protected the flocks; but the Three were the elder gods, and the people worshipped them and were made glad. And their storehouses were always full. For gods like the worship of men.

Now, it came to pass, in the fourth year of the Councilship of Thon the Huntsman (this was the Thon who slew

5

the gryphon at Allam-paila) that a ship came to Eisernon from the air.

It was not a ship of the sea and of the chalk cliffs, which men build with hands; but this was a ship that sailed stars, and fished the great deeps beyond the stars. The ship had no sail, that is, a sail to catch winds, but was full of wings which men could not see, as of a bird of prey stooping to its kill. And the ship was full of eyes, glowing with a light from within, as of a sun. And the People were sore afraid, for no one had seen the like of it before.

The ship was called *Argus,* that is, Thousand-eyed. And those who were in the ship, and sailed it, were called Earthlings, and they were as Men.

But Men, who were foolish, called them gods.

And Men forgot their gods, even casting the Three from their thoughts, and they opened their hands to the Earthlings, and gave them of all they possessed; of fish from the sea and of hennem pounded into cakes and sweetened; of gifts made by hands and treasures dug from the soil; of carven charis-wood and precious neriosh, so also did they give to them, for they judged them to be gods.

Then the Earthlings looked upon Eisernon, and saw its sea and its hennem, that they were good. They ate of its fruits, and slept soundly in the reed chisei, and they found it good. And they saw the daughters of Men, that they were fair, and they loved them and took them to themselves, and the daughters bore up sons who were not wholly of Eisernon, but were of the stars and the deeps between the stars. Then the People became afraid, and cast them out, for fear that this sin would be a curse to Eisernon, and to the People.

So the daughters of Men took their children to the chalk cliffs, and many of them cast the infants from the heights, that the curse of alien sons would not fall upon the People and anger the gods; for the children could hear the thoughts of Men, and their eyes were chalices of alien stars, and were not the eyes or the minds of the People.

But other daughters, forsaking the gods, nursed their children and raised them up. And generation after generation of children married, each to the other, until at last

6

there sprang up a third race, neither Earthling nor Einai (that is, of the People) but a race apart.

And there rose up from among them a dynasty of Kings, a line of Emperors, who were the servants of the People; and they were called the Han, after the name of their first father.

The Han ruled for a thousand years and half a thousand years. In the space of that time, the old gods died, and the true God revealed himself to Men. To all the People He revealed Himself, all of the People and the sons of Men knew His Name. And His Name was Tadae.

And Tadae was the sum of the old gods, and the grandfather in dignity over the Three, which were Roanouk, and Sibhem, and Quel; and He was more than all the gods, for this was the Living God, the Orderer and First Cause. This god *was* God.

All praise the Name of God, which is Tadae.

Everything which Tadae, the One, revealed to us is written in the Books of Fulfillment, which are the Books concerning the Word, who is T'ath.

T'ath lighted the shadows and the dark places, and the People cast him forth, and they killed him and were glad, for they had come to love the darkness and fear the light. Then Tadae was angry and turned His face from them and promised a dire judgment to them, a retribution that would come upon them, until they would cry to the mountains, 'Fall upon us!' and to the sea, 'Cover us, that we may be saved', but they would not.

But T'ath died, and in dying, pledged Tadae's word (for He was the Word) that the men of the people would be forgiven.

The suffering was yet to come, and men knew it not, for in their hearts they did not repent.

And men made unto themselves ships which stood on a column of fire, and they reached out and touched the face of Tadae. They stepped out upon new worlds and tamed them as one tames a d'injit and they ruled the worlds with the Peace of the Han, as commanded by the Emperor; for all were equal in the sight of Tadae. And the Emperor was the servant of the servants of Tadae.

The names of the worlds were these: Sauvage, our brother; and Minsoner, which is to say, the Dark Planet; and Krau. There were smaller worlds, which are not

7

named here, and the Emperor ruled them wisely, saying to himself, 'This would my Lord T'ath have me do.'

Then they made for themselves glass upon glass, cunningly contrived, until they could see into the interwoven secrets of life, learning for themselves that which Tadae had hidden there from the Beginning. As a father secretes sweetmeats under the eaves, and hides away jum in the tall grasses for his children to discover, covering his laughter with his hands, so also had Tadae hidden knowledge from his children, until men should find His knowledge and rejoice in Him.

But men forgot Tadea, and the judgment that was to come upon them. They became proud and strong, and peace lay no longer in the land. In the hennem fields there was no peace, and in the cities, strife. And men no longer carried Tadae about with them in their consciences.

The Han, who knew what was in their hearts, counciled them to humility, and in the marketplace exhorted them to love one another, as in the days of old. But the People's wickedness grew without bounds.

The old gods were revived and the People made for them great altars, which men had never built as far as men could remember and they set upon these altars stone images and carven statues of the old gods, and of machine and of currency and of evil, which men had invented unto themselves. And man looked upon the gods he had made, and he found them good.

And Tadae was forgotten, but did not forget.

Now, men killed the Han secretly and by stealth, saying to themselves, 'Let us be rid of these men, who can hear our thoughts, lest our evil be known amongst men.' For they feared them.

But the Han carried Tadae about with them in their hearts; and the Emperor (who *was* Han and remembered the prophecy of T'ath) forsook his golden pavilion. Neither did he stay within the Citadel walls, but took himself to a rude chisei made of reeds and woven with branches of wicker. And there he did penance for his people, that the judgment would not fall upon them. But in the day, he sat upon his crystal throne, that he be not accused of pride.

Many other Han did likewise, and they entered into the

8

Place of Peace, and became monks, and were subject to obedience. But the judgment had already been sealed.

The prophecy was completed; and judgment fell upon the People.

The Earthlings returned.

And the Earthlings knew their sons, and they hated them, and they vowed to kill them all.

Then the Earthlings let fall fire from the sky, as it was written; and all who were touched by it melted and burned. And the people wailed and gnashed their teeth, and cried to Tadae to preserve them. But Tadae turned his face away from them, and heard them not.

And the Earthlings brought with them a terrible weapon, which caused a new sun to shine above any city, and all who saw it were blinded; and all who touched the dust of that city, or drank its water, or stood in the rain from its sky, sickened and died. And the cities became lakes of glass.

Then the People fell down and wept and beat their foreheads in sorrow; and they pulled down the altars of the false gods and remembered Tadae. Repenting, they made sacrifice to Him, and sorrowing, repented their transgressions. And they freed their slaves, whom they had kept in secret, and loosed the bondsman from his debts. And Tadae forgave them, as T'ath had promised, for they were His People. And He was his God.

But when they searched for the Han, they could not find them. And the women of People wept for the Han, and for the lost glory of Eisernon, for the heel of Earth was heavy. And mothers begged Tadae for a child who could hear the thoughts of men, and whose eyes were chalices of alien stars, whose eyes and mind were not the eyes and mind of the People; that the Han could be preserved.

But they were no more.

In all the lands of the People, upon the sea and under the sea there were no Han to be found. For they were dead, or hidden. Until their name was a new name, and they were called Legend, and forgotten.

But the Han survived.

Chapter 1

MARIK

"I stand before the great god Quel, before Roanouk, and Sibhem, and all the gods of Eisernon . . ."
                                            Einai Medical Oath

Like all rocket strikes, this one gave no warning. One moment Priyam Dao Marik was bending over the field hospital's operating table, delicately probing splinters of shrapnel out of a man's left heart; the next minute the ground shook and roared, the lights shattered, raining glass, and Marik found himself plunging through a nightmare of screams and falling beams and powdery debris toward the brighter black rectangle of the door, his patient cradled protectively in his arms.

Two more rockets scored near misses in quick succession, throwing him heavily to the ground as he raced for the shelter of a low stone wall, and he recovered his patient only to find the man, not surprisingly, dead. Marik rubbed a quick hand across his eyes and pulled it away green and wet. He had picked up a nasty gash somewhere and the side of his face felt burned and raw. He stumbled to his feet and shouldered his way back into the shell of the hospital, through the deafening din of panicked ambulants and confused medical people, the cries of the injured and the dying, and the malignant tearing whine of Earthling skimmercraft streaking by overhead. Marik grabbed a blank-faced orderly. "The children," he shouted above the melee. "Where are the children?"

The man's eyes strayed out of focus, and little flecks of spittle foamed at the corners of his mouth. People

jostled them roughly and someone kept screaming "T'ath!
T'ath!" over and over in a thin, high-pitched voice.

"The *children!*" Marik insisted, shaking the orderly
sharply, and the man blinked a few times and waved an
arm loosely toward the devastated wards.

"Back there," he mumbled, beginning to weep. ". . . I
had just pust put him back to bed, and the wall . . . the
wall . . ."

Marik ran, clearing a path as he went.

He slipped and stumbled over a mound of masonry and
crushed cots, his progress sporadically lit by the flare of
rocket fire beyond the shattered roof; but sifting plaster
dust choked and blinded him, and for a precarious while
he scrambled along with only his hands and ears to guide
him, while the ground trembled and the building creaked
and groaned, sending down new showers of rock and dust.

After a dozen yards more it got better. Marik clambered
over a broken beam and saw Priyam Shari-Mnenoplan's white head bent over a cot in a far corner. The old
man was trying to lift a half-grown boy, supporting himself
weakly with a hand braced against the wall. Shari-Mnenoplan was bleeding from his nose and ears and mouth,
slim, fatal runnels of bright green arterial blood. Marik's
mind flung a wordless question of concern and felt the
answering wave of reassurance, of anguished compassion, and under that, a coldly growing absence from which
his mind instinctively recoiled.

He dodged a gout of falling masonry and, climbing
over the decapitated body of a nurse, levered the last
obstacle out of the way and snatched up the paralyzed
boy. Shari-Mnenoplan lifted another, smaller child and
Marik caught his arm clumsily, the boy sagging heavily
against his shoulder. The night roared and shuddered, and
Marik had to shout to make himself heard.

"Out here, sir! The back way!"

The old man nodded and staggered after him, and
Marik raced for the open door, huddled over the terrified
boy, deliberately blanking his mind to the raw panic that
poured from the child's eyes and mind and throat.

Outside in the darkness, people shrieked and rockets
swished by overhead and hit shudderingly nearby. There
was no sign of Shari-Mnenoplan. Then the hospital roof
slowly began to collapse.

12

Shoving the boy into the arms of a hysterical civilian and shouting futilely over the roar of the rockets, Marik gave the man a hard push toward a grove of fern trees and darted back into the building.

The old Priyam was kneeling in a tangle of wreckage, slumped forward over the baby in his arms. Marik couldn't see his face, but the old man's mind was conscious and serene.

He began dragging wood and bedframes out of the way, clawing through the rubble. He fought his way over and through the destruction, and had almost reached the old man when something heavy hit him in the back of the head, and he went down in a thunder of bricks and beams and roofing tiles. The last thing Marik was aware of was the old Priyam's dying thought, clear and sharp and aching.

He was regretting Marik's death.

There were no more rockets after that. Several out-buildings that had taken fire blazed brightly, lighting up the sky over the jungle, and a fuel shack blew apart with a brilliant blossom of flame and dark smoke, tossing minia-ture peasant figures gracefully into the air. The Earthling skimmers made several more low passes over the firelit clearing, but their pilots, seeing no motion below them, veered in formation and whined away toward the north, leaving only a quickly dissipating trail of light in the sky behind them.

The burned-out hangars and sheds flickered dimly for a while longer and then began to smoulder fitfully in the humid darkness. A night bird called and was answered, and small mammals, forgetting their fear, popped out of burrows and resumed their eternal foraging. Only the peasants stayed huddled in terror, their great, lambent cat's-eyes glowing yellow in the reflected firelight.

When the first glimmer of false dawn colored the eastern horizon, the peasants crept from their hiding places and sought out the living, bearing them away silent-ly on hastily-made litters. Several of the braver men dug half-heartedly through the rubble for survivors; but finding none alive in the thick, hot pre-dawn darkness, and being afraid the Earthlings would return, they buried what dead they could and went away, leaving no track in the jungle.

13

Sergeant Joe Garrett was a dogface, the kind of a foot-soldier who since time immemorial has spent his wars on his belly in a frozen foxhole, or slogging down some famous road through some equally famous mud. Garrett had seen action on Sauvage, on Canopus Five, on Krau; now he and his squad were on Eisernon.

Garrett didn't necessarily believe in this war, nor did he disbelieve it. He didn't think much about it one way or the other. Neither was he, basically, a killer. He was merely a fairly young man from Nyok, Earth—stocky, shaggy-haired, taciturn—who had grown up suddenly into a tough, resilient soldier who did what he was told and thought about it as little as possible. His duty, as he saw it, was to get the job done and stay alive, in that order. Right now the job consisted of wading into a Krail Command Post after the skimmers had softened them up, and doing the mopup, a tiring, necessary and thoroughly dirty job. Garrett did not anticipate it.

"Ci-pi."

Laj, their 'tame' Einai, squatted on the edge of the path and pointed one long arm downhill toward a sheltered clearing, where a few tendrils of white smoke wafted up from a circle of charred buildings.

"Ci-pi," he repeated. "Cigarek, shah?"

Garrett absently handed Laj a cigarette, studying the CP through narrowed eyes while Laj absorbedly lit up and began to smoke hungrily, dragging hard until his cheeks flattened under the high cheekbones. His slit pupils contracted to vertical lines as the tobacco's strong narcotic suffused his system.

"There she is, Sarge. Sum Chi T'ath." LaFarge handed Garrett the glasses. "That's six hundred years of Einai history standing there."

"That's a Krail CP, and we got orders to knock it out." Garrett adjusted the focus, but even under strong magnification, nothing moved. He swung the glasses in a slow, panning motion. Sheds . . . hangars . . . a half-gone brick building. A plank over the door was carved with one meaningless Einai word: 'ChiT'ath'. Garrett moved the glasses in a full arc, but the clearing was dead. Even at this range, he could sense the ancient stillness that hung over the place. Beside him LaFarge, with one quick thumb, reached under his transparent faceplate and flicked away

14

the sweat that had gathered under his stubbled chin. He blew out a soft breath, almost a sigh, and waited for Garrett's orders.

No one moved or spoke, and the sun beat down. A hot breeze stirred the grasses at their feet, and heat lightning flashed silently in a bank of slate-colored clouds at the horizon. Though it was just past noon, the jungle still steamed faintly, giving off the thick, fecund scents of myriad plant life. Small mammals skittered furtively in the underbrush, and high in the fern trees, memlikti caterpillared along on velvet bellies, patiently spinning their intricate spiderlike webs. Periodically, the younger memlikti would fall and dangle confusedly by one taut, golden thread, lazily turning first in one direction and then in the other, their colors brilliant in the smoky sun-shafts. The men had to be careful of the memlikti. Like many of the beautiful things on Eisernon—including the people—memlikti were particularly deadly.

LaFarge sighed again and Ross' boot thudded against a hidden root. He cursed under his breath, breaking the spell, and LaFarge shifted his weight.

"How far, Sarge?"

"I make it three hundred yards." He studied the clearing for a moment longer, then handed the glasses back.

"Sanders, Ross, you come in from the other side. Keep your eyes open. Take 'em alive if they'll let you." They ran.

"Connor's got the left flank, LaFarge, you've got the right. Doc, you come with me." He nodded shortly. "Move."

His men filtered away through the brush, the midday sun shadow-patterning their uniforms. Garrett pulled down his faceplate and thumbed the safety off his needler, feeling the familiar security of its fine, long, perfectly balanced weight. He set out at a smooth, dodging pace, straight up the main access road, Doc right behind him.

Running in a broken-field crouch and rabbiting across the last open spaces, Garrett's men converged on the Krail outpost.

At the back of the building a prowling carnivore, small and savage, slunk out of the jungle where it had been uneasily watching the ruins since dawn, nostrils

15

quivering and jaws slavering at the various effluvia hanging heavily around the place.

Now it approached the ruins on stiff legs, growling low and eagerly in its throat, for it was a scavenger and its belly was flat and empty. It snuffled and pawed at the broken bricks, causing a small avalanche of rubble and uncovering the head, shoulders and one arm of a man who lay buried beneath the tumulus. Its prey made no move and the scavenger got bolder, digging at the masonry, snuffling and whining eagerly, when suddenly its head lifted, ears forward, tense. An almost unheard breath, an alien scent, of adrenalin and Earthuman sweat, filled its nostrils and it sneezed, rubbing its muzzle against the bricks. The scent came again, stronger now, and after a moment's brief indecision, while its hunger warred with its caution, the scavenger skulked away.

The sounds of its presence and passage stirred numbed nerve centers inside a humanoid skull, set in motion synapses almost stilled. Ears began to listen, flesh to feel.

Priyam Hanshilobahr *Dom* Dao Marik, Chosen, moved his right hand.

Not far, but it moved. He encountered the abrasive touch of broken stone and the furlike softness of a child's hair. Pain grew cruelly and with it, cruelly, memory. The rockets, and Shari-Mnenoplan dying inside his mind; and he remembered hearing a voice, guttural and strangely his own, say "Tadae-", half a prayer. Then there had been blackness.

He lay still, his breathing painful and shallow. The Earthlikli would come, he knew. Having completed their destruction, they would want trophies of the kill. He moved his head carefully. Carefully. Turned it so that he could see devastation and bodies and part of the sweet green jungle beyond. He rested his cheek on the rough stone, exhausted. His uniform was torn and wet and sticky, and both hearts beat lightly and very, very fast. He tried to move, but the motion made him sick and he retched weakly and lay back, his face covered with a fine, thin sweat.

Gnats danced mindlessly around his head, and there was the heavy, low-key buzz of carrion flies. Far in the jungle, a memlikt trilled its heartbreakingly yearning song.

Marik lay still, thinking nothing, his ears hearing and

16

his body barely breathing for him. In a moment, he told himself with the euphoric logic of physiological shock, in just a moment, when I rest a little, I'll try again. But he didn't. For a long time he just lay there and let his body breathe.

Then there was a scuff, a crackle in the underbrush, a quick glimpse of combat boots, and he tried to raise himself up. The motion cost him his consciousness. High black walls closed around and over him, and he sank back gratefully into the darkness.

Garrett's men came into the clearing with faceplates down and needlers ready. But nothing moved, no one spoke. Fern trunks stood frozen against the hot blue sky and doors hung slack, ajar. A vagrant wind fluttered the toasted garments of those who lay in the road, and gently rearranged the dust about them, letting it settle softly, like a requiem. But nothing moved, and it was very still.

Only the Earthlings, cat-curious, tiger-deadly, investigated the empty windows and prowled the splintered sheds and peered between the charred bones of the hangars. In one of them, the blackened hull of an ambulance-skimmer still cooled slowly, making little metallic, creaking noises. But there was no life. Nothing moved.

The men came back empty-handed, all but Ross, who had found a bottle of tarangi. He took a great, sluicing swallow of it and offered it around, but nobody wanted any. They stepped over bodies and, unbelieving, kept searching for the enemy.

Garrett eased along the outer wall of what had been a large brick structure, whose sign 'ChiT'ath' had caught his eye from the ridge, and abruptly kicked the door open. It wrenched off its one remaining hinge and before it had rattled into silence, Garrett had flattened against the wall inside, sweeping his needler around in a quick arc. But the only life was small and vicious and rodentlike, that spat at him as it scuttled away.

Garrett shoved his faceplate up, pulled his canteen free and took a long swallow of the hot, stale water. It trickled easily, deliciously, down his throat and made his eyes burn and smart wetly.

"Sarge! Hey!—Sarge!" Ross lumbered across the clearing excitedly.

17

"Over here." Garrett stepped out into the open and capped his canteen, squinting against the sun and savoring the last drop of water that lingered on his tongue. Ross' bottle was half-gone and so was Ross. His speech was patently slurred.

"We foun' us a live one. Eye-eye officer. Collab'rator."

"Where?" Garrett crammed his helmet down on his head and crossed to Ross, who licked his lips and grinned.

"Back of the building." He tipped his head. "Looks like half the CP fell in on him. Doc don't think he'll make it."

The back of the building had been sheared off, a mass of wreckage and tumulus and stench, and the men made way for Garrett as he and Ross trotted up. The sergeant knelt down and got his first good, close look at an Einai officer.

And unaccountably saw Rome. Perhaps it was the color of the alien's skin that sparked the association, or the lay of the muscles of the neck, or maybe the gold sheen of him where he had sweat. And the hair, of course, black, close-cropped and curly, like an Italian kid Garrett had gone to school with when he was a boy. He tried for an instant to recall the little dago's name, with no success.

The alien's uniform was gray, suedelike, and fitted like a second hide; like the hide, it was ripped and bloody. But the insignia on his collar marked him out as a *Dom.* An officer. A second insignia meant nothing. Garrett glanced up at Connors.

"How long to get him out in one piece?"

Connors spat and rubbed it with his boot, considering. "It'll take a while," he said at last.

"He ain't got a while, Sarge." Doc sounded glum. "We don't get him up to a hospital ship right quick, we gonna lose ourselves a good eye-eye prisoner."

Garrett nodded shortly. "Get on it." He tugged off his helmet and wiped his forehead with his grimy sleeve.

As the men started clearing away the loose brick and rubble from the main beams that held the alien pinned, Garrett motioned to Doc.

"Can you give him something to wake him up?"

Doc thought about it. "I guess so. But it won't last long, Sarge. And it sure won't do him no good."

Garrett lit a cigarette and took a drag from it. "I've got to find out what he knows *now,* Doc. He might not make it

18

to that ship." He tucked his cigarette behind his ear and reached for his communicator. "If it's any help, I don't like it any more than you do." The unit flipped open easily. "Surface Control, this is SurCon Blue Seventeen, how do you read?" Doc's hypodermic hissed faintly behind him.

The unit clicked and replied metallically, "We read you five-square, Blue Seventeen. Go ahead."

"I've got an injured POW here. An eye-eye *Dom.* Collaborator. I need a medical assist, on the double. He's in bad shape."

"Understand emergency medical help, Blue Seventeen. Sending you a skimmer. SurCon off."

Garrett looked up into the full shock of gold-flecked alien eyes, slit-pupilled and gray, gazing back at him. If he had thought the *Dom* looked prosaically familiar before, he thought so no longer. The trapped man gazing at him was aware, intelligent—and *alien,* in a way unlike other aliens.

Snapping his compak shut, he snatched his cigarette down and offered it to the alien in a choppy lifting gesture, quick and interrogative; but Marik made a slight, almost imperceptible shake of the head and closed his eyes briefly. *No.* Garrett reached around and brought out his canteen, uncapped it and sloshed the water around so that Marik could hear what it was. Without waiting for an answer, he lifted Marik's head as well as he could and spilled some of the water into his mouth. Marik drank clumsily, thirstily, as little as he could to keep from strangling, and wearily rested his head against the cool, wet stone. Part of his mind was ferociously hating the Erthlikli, the child-killers, the destroyers; another, more detached part reminded him logically that water (*cool water, sluicing a parched throat, easing the rage of his fever, most desirable, sweet and yearned-for water, now that he had had far too much, or far too little*) had no nationality. He found, with objective surprise, that he was trembling violently, and considered the strong and meaningless probability that he was dying.

The sunlight grayed out and the wind rose a bit, cool and wet. Thunder muttered over the jungle.

Garrett poked a finger at Marik's shoulder and spoke

19

loudly and slowly, as if to a foreigner or a not-quite-bright child.

"You speakee Earthenglish?" Marik made no reply, and Garrett tried again.

"You Einai, yes? I—" he poked his own chest "—I Earthling. I get you *out*," he swept his hand, indicating Marik's predicament; "I help *you*—right?—*you*—" he poked Marik's shoulder again "—help *me*. Okay?"

Marik gazed back unblinkingly and Garrett frowned, not sure whether the injured alien heard him at all, or hearing, could understand. He searched his memory for scraps of eye-eye talk he'd picked up. Words, only, and insufficient.

"Alai?" he asked awkwardly, his accent deplorable. "Tu, uh, tu zo tek? Damn it, tu tek-zo?"

As Marik watched the Erthlik's face blur and green out, one lone fact came to him with ice-cold clarity, and he clung to it desperately.

Someone, he realized, had known about himself and Shari-Mnenoplan. Someone had betrayed them to the Erthlikli, that they were Han.

Earth and Eisernon had made their peace, and both were members of the Galactic Federation, whose allied forces now battled the invading Krail here on Eisernon. But there was a second war here, a guerilla war carried on in secret by the small, fanatical Purist Klan, whose membership numbered both Einai and Earthlikli. It was, said the Klan, against nature for the Han to exist at all; for, green-blooded, cat-eyed as they were, they carried Earth's genetic patterns, too. (A tiger-eyed Michelangelo? Not to be tolerated! A five-fingered Sho-Karolan? Utter nonsense!)

They called it 'purifying the races'. They called it 'insuring the peace'.

It was genocide.

The Federation outlawed the Klan, warned them to disband, imposed severe penalties on those Klansmen they caught. But the Federation was far away. The Han were here.

A handful of Han, like Marik and the renowned Shari-Mnenoplan, had dared practice their art as Priyamli, always with the same result. To reveal one's ancestry was to openly invite assassination.

Someone had betrayed them.

Not the peasants. The suffering peasants, and the few soldiers they'd gleaned from various battlefields where they had been left for dead, would not betray their one link with medical help. Besides, peasants were loyal only to the land and to their families. Earth, Krailim, and even Eisernon, as a planetary concept, did not exist for them. Only their land, their children and their hennem, growing ripe and ruddy in the fields, existed.

Who, then? Who stood to gain from the death of Han? Who would want power or revenge or status he could not otherwise have? Which Klansman would come this far into the outback to kill, to protect his name?

And then he knew. He knew who had brought down the wrath of the conquerors on his forsaken little outpost; and he knew whose men, directly or indirectly, these Earthlikli were.

With all the strength he could muster, Marik made himself focus on Garrett's face and said clearly, "Vartik!"

Garrett leaned forward quickly, solicitously. The alien had answered him, had said one incomprehensible eye-eye word. Now maybe we were getting somewhere. He thought he caught a flicker of—something, something, a realization hidden in the intelligent gray eyes; but La-Farge took that moment to try to move the beams pinning the alien's legs, and Marik's teeth locked and his pupils dilated until they were black caverns that glazed over and went blank. His one free fist relaxed and went limp.

Garrett lent a hand with the second beam, feeling a sharp regret at having missed whatever it was the eye-eye had tried to say. There was a brief, promontory splash of rain, hot as tears.

The beams slid off sideward, with a grating of rubble and wood, freeing Marik at last. Doc turned his head away, swallowing hard, and meeting Garrett's sick eyes, shrugged helplessly. Ross leaned over for a curious look and was violently, noisily sick.

The skimmercraft whined overhead and bellied in for a landing in the clearing, its skids tucked up against damage by rough terrain. Two medics met them halfway with a MAX tube and, expertly easing their patient onto its plastex slab, they busied themselves about connecting various contacts to strategic points on the alien's anatomy: cardiac monitors, long pressure sleeves, IV inputs, catheters, EEG leads. They eased a cryogenic 'cage' around the mangled legs. Garrett stood by, trying not to get in the way.

"Uh, Doc?"

The skimedic glanced over his shoulder and continued working, sliding the unconscious alien into the MAX, programming maximum plasma and automatic blood crossmatch into the computab on the MAX's flat stern. They closed the plastex hood and heard the faint sibilance of oxygen entering the cavity.

"Well, Sergeant?"

"Well, sir, I'd like to know if he's going to make it."

"He somebody special?"

Garrett explored a broken tooth with his tongue. "He said something a while ago. Before we dug him out. A word in his own language. I thought maybe you could tell me what it meant." The skimedic waited. "He said 'Vartik'. Just that. 'Vartik'."

The skimedic considered it, then shrugged. "No. Sorry. It doesn't mean anything to me." He hit the stud marked 'Readout', studied it, and muttered, "Probably delirious." He punched another series.

"Yes, sir," Garrett agreed, unconvinced.

They slapped the MAX into the aft skimmer compartment, confident in the knowledge that as they returned to the hospital ship orbiting high above, the MAX, of its own volition, would sustain and monitor their patient until the ship's staff of surgeons could take over.

Garrett watched the stubby craft shudder with the force of its engines, heard the pitch Doppler up until it crackled the eardrums and flung the craft upward into the low overcast.

"Well," LaFarge sighed, "there goes our eye-eye."

Connor pointed across the jungle, where a solid sheet of gray steadily advanced on them, making the vegetation tremble and hiss.

"And here comes the rain."

There was a dull rumble of thunder and they began walking to meet it along the water-pocked path. A dozen yards beyond the clearing Laj sat waiting for them, smiling and fawning, his palm out.

"Cigarek, shah? Cigarek?"

"Where the hell were you when we needed a strong back?" Ross asked him truculently.

"Holed up somewhere, high on cigarek, where else?" Connors chuckled. "Too bad it doesn't last 'em long. A few minutes flying time, and they come crashing down again." He watched Laj. "Otherwise, see, we could take the whole planet with a carton or two of Charlestons."

Rain whispered around them, slapping the leathery leaves as they ducked under them and making rivulets in the moss underfoot. It ran down them like sweat, hot and soaking, and made them thirst.

"It's that fast metabolism they got," Doc was saying.

I'm glad we got the eye-eye out, Garrett thought. *At least we got him out of the rain.*

"They got to eat more often, and medicine don't last as long for them as it does for us. Of course," he added as a generous afterthought, "they don't have to take as much, neither, just more often."

"Cigarek, shah?" Laj trotted along beside him, palm out as before. His eyes were desperate. "Cigarek?"

Vartik.

Garrett deliberately drew out a half-empty pack, tapped one into his palm and gestured with it to Laj. "Sure. Cigarette. Come on."

Laj fell in closer, watching the cigarette eagerly as Garrett toyed with it. The sergeant studied Laj out of the tail of his eye.

"Tell me some words, Laj. Eye-eye words, okay?"

Laj nodded enthusiastically, watching the cigarette. He wet his lips. "Eye-eye, sure. Okay words for Erthlik chum. Cigarek now?" He reached for it but Garrett snatched it away.

"Hey, Sarge," Ross offered, "according to Doc, here, all you got to do is give him half a smoke. I got to remember that, next time we hit town. That'll be good to remember, huh?" He nudged Sanders in the ribs and the silent dark boy grinned and rubbed the rain off his nose. "How 'bout that, Sarge? Ain't that something good to remember?"

"Shut up, Ross." Garrett tortured his tongue against the rough spot on his tooth, and showed Laj the cigarette, damp with rain.

"Cigarek," Laj whispered. "Cigarek for Laj. Laj *chum*."

23

"Yeah, for a price, Laj chum," Connors scoffed. "For a price, Laj cut Erthlik throat."

"Vartik," Garrett said quietly. "What does *Vartik* mean?"

Laj shrugged. "Vartik mean Vartik. Is name. Only." He smiled uneasily. "Cigarek," he insisted, half-pleading.

"One more thing. The word back there, the one carved over the door. Chay-"

"ChiT'ath. Is word, ChiT'ath."

"Right. That was fresh carving, a fairly new sign. What's it mean, ChiT'ath?"

"Mean House of God. Is what eye-eye call hostils. House of God." He moved around to Garrett's other side, nearer the cigarette, and watched it, absently licking rain off his face.

"Hostils? *Host*yles?"

"Num!" Laj put up both hands, shaking his head vehemently. Hostil. Eye-eye sick, eye-eye Priyam takit to hostil, make well or make die."

Realization hit Garrett with a sick knot under his ribs. "Hospital? That CP we blew up back there was a hospital? . . . " *Only one Krail body, plenty of eye-eyes, and children, children everywhere. Not collaborators, after all. A hospital!*

"Hospital. And that eye-eye *Dom*", he added tightly, "he was a medic, right?"

"Right, chum. Cigarek now? Laj get cigarek for all words?"

Garrett tossed him the pack and ignored his effusive thanks. He said very little for the rest of the day but then, he had a great deal to think about. And of one thing he was sure: no matter how long it took him, he would find out what 'Vartik' was—and what it had to do with the destruction of an Einai hospital, out in the middle of nowhere.

"House of God," he said, into the rain. "That goddam CP was a House of God!" But nobody heard him.

Doctor Danton Parks stood by the lee port of the *USS Pacific,* a small, dingy hospital ship, disinterestedly sipping a container of scalding coffee and watching yet another ambulance dart up from the planetary surface. He had been operating steadily for eighteen hours, three full shifts, and he was tired and testy.

"Here comes another one the eye-eyes took care of," he snapped, and Dave Lassai, changing into fresh surgical garments in the room across the way, chuckled at him.

"Could be your friendly neighborhood Krail had something to say about it, Doctor."

Parks made a rude sound in his throat. "Same thing. Half our so-called allies are collaborators anyway. We should've finished 'em when we had the chance. Then we'd only have the Krail to worry about!" He took a mouthful of his coffee and felt it burn all the way down. "I just lost that Captain from Base Five. Lousy peasant woman got him in the belly with a viith she'd saved from the War. Boy, when I opened him up—", he stopped. Lassai wagged his head, saying nothing.

"Leave it to me," Parks concluded, "I'd fuse the whole damn' planet. I guarantee you that'd settle 'em down!"

"New niggers." Lassai shrugged into his tunic.

"What?"

"I said, 'new niggers'." Lassai ran his pale palms over his crisp dark hair. "That's what my grandfather used to call people like the eye-eyes. Downtrodden people. Troublemakers. Losers. 'New niggers'."

"Yeah, but what does it mean?"

Lassai lifted his shoulders and pulled a grimace. "Who knows? Old men like to make talk, eh?" He glanced at his chronometer. "Hey, I'm due down on Level Five. See you later."

"Yeah, see you." Parks finished his coffee, thinking again of the endless line of men he had rebuilt and transplanted and pieced together today and all the days before; of the ones he had referred to the giant hospital ships and of others he had tagged for cargo shipment home. And he thought black thoughts of the Einai.

On the hangar deck below, two skimedics drew their craft to an abrupt halt, its emergency flashers still rotating, ejected the MAX into the hands of a team of orderlies and helped them swing it into a wall hatch, which they quickly dogged. One of the medics hit a stud on the hatch cover and the MAX was gone, whisked away at high speed on a cushion of compressed air. He leaned on the intercom. It piped and replied mechanically, "Emergency. Coe."

"Redblanket on his way, Coe. Tube One, Priority One."

"Acknowledged, Hangar Deck." Coe, unruffled at her Code Station on Surgery Deck, punched the series for on-duty medics and glanced disapprovingly at her fingernails, which badly needed a manicure. The computor set up emergency blinkers in the Orderly Lounge, the corridors and at the various nurses stations; then it selected several surgeons, discarded as non-available all but the last, which read out on Coe's screen: P-a-r-k-s, D-a-n-t-o-n. Simultaneously, Parks' armband signalled and Coe yawned, leaned forward and hit her intercom.

"Redblanket for you, doctor. Tube One, Priority One."

Parks regarded the band with distaste. On a sliding scale of one through ten, a P1 injury could be expected to give its surgical team a long, tough job and its victim, assuming he survived, a painful and difficult recovery. *If I ever get my hands on an eye-eye,* he thought . . .

"Doctor Parks," the armband insisted with mild asperity, "we have a redblanket, Priority One!"

"Coming!" He crumpled his coffee container and pitched it with some force into the receptacle; then he turned on his heel and stalked out toward the preop ward where Dao Marik, unconscious and barely alive, waited for his help.

Nurse Chaffee's face flashed up urgently as he stepped through the portal. "God! We're barely holding him!" A second nurse slapped a flat, transparent container of whole blood into the MAX's stern.

"Clear OR2 and get me an anesthetist. And Dave Lassai, down on Five," he added over his shoulder, as he flipped up the MAX's hood.

The sight jolted him. Try as he might to remain clinical, all he could think of, staring at the alien there on the scanslab, was a summer's day when he was a very small boy, and a sidewalk where a friend's trike had partly crushed a furry, black caterpillar. Mortally hurt, it had feebly tried to crawl away, and his friend had cried and said—over and over—kill it, Danny, it's suffering, kill it, kill it, kill it. He had stared in fascinated horror and then stamped once, leaving a green smear on the clean concrete.

The alien moved his head in pain, brushing Parks' hand

26

greenly, and he wiped it quickly on his smock, fighting down nausea.

"Doctor Parks, he's very bad off, sir . . . " Chaffee's voice was puzzled and urgent.

Parks slammed the MAX hood shut with an effort, his voice flat and unsteady. "What's he doing here? The *Repose*'s supposed to handle eye-eyes. We're not rigged for it."

"They're filled up, sir. Orders just came through. We've been assigned all the primary stuff."

Dave Lassai appeared. "What's happening, Doctor?"

Parks' face was strained and white around the mouth and nose. Ugly. He pulled the pak free of the MAX's stern and handed it to Lassai. "Eye-eye," he said tightly.

Lassai scanned it and whistled silently. "Looks like he's stabilized about as much as he's going to. We'd better get on it." Parks made no reply. "Doctor Parks?"

Parks met his eyes then, and the room clapped into silence. The floor rocked under Lassai's feet.

"No!"

"Look at him, Lassai! Goddamn it, look at him!" Parks tore the MAX hood open. There was a sickly sweet stench. "Now *you* tell *me*!"

Lassai passed his dark hand quickly over his face and head, swallowing hard. He punched continued cardiac pacemakers and an additional unit of whole blood into the computab on the pak and fitted it into the frame of the MAX. To the nurse, as he worked:

"Anything else on him, Chaffee?"

"Yes, sir. The skimedics reported he said 'Vartik' a couple of times." Lassai's quick hands froze, only for an instant.

Parks smiled contemptuously. "Still want to keep him alive?"

"You bet your sweet A, Dad," Lassai retorted crisply. "My racket is doctoring, not judging." He slapped the MAX. "OR2, MAX. On the double."

"Sure, Doc," the MAX replied flatly, and trundled itself down the corridor and into the operating complex, while Parks and Lassai entered an adjacent scrubroom and wordlessly prepared themselves for surgery.

The air between them was chill.

27

Still Marik moved not
A muscle, not a muscle
Moved, unmoving, moving
Not at all . . .

From 'The Lay of the Han' as translated by Sinuk
Ronhalovan the Younger, Colony Eden, 2217 G.F.T.

The prison ward was large and easily accommodated sixteen bunks, eight to a side. Because it had once been the
ship's brig, before the old vessel had been recommissioned as a hospital ship, its entire corridor face, from
deck to overhead, consisted of steel bars, with a heavy
door mounted in a sliding frame. Beside each bed was an
open basin for water and at the end of the room was the
nurses' station. A guard armed with a laser rifle was sit-
uated just outside the bars and another, similarly armed,
down the corridor. Once a day the medics made their
perfunctory rounds and the few nurses were brisk and
impersonal.

The one exception was Kraut Annie, a fortyish, blonde
Captain who had demanded that Parks transfer Marik immediately to Intensive Care. When he refused, saying that
they were all filled up, she reported the incident to her
superior and was flatly told to butt out. A call to the
Chief of Staff, Gordon Samstag, was put through channels. They would look into it.

Marik lay on his bunk and dazedly watched the endless
drip of blood through his antiquated IV setup, feeling the
fine, cold sweat gather at his ribs, his temples, on the
backs of his hands, and trickle into the meager, damp
mattress. They had dropped a nasotracheal tube and the
constant dry oxygen spray hissed in his ears and made his

28

throat raw. He would have sold his soul for the proper sedation, but the nurses, unfamiliar with Einai metabolism, gave him standard Earthuman doses, dangerously large for his species, at far-too-infrequent intervals. In between, Marik lay there dry-mouthed and watched the IV drip. There was water just beyond his arm's reach (light-years and an impossible three steps away) but it did not appreciably affect Marik's existence.

The man in the bed to his right was called Gates, a big, beefy Erthlik with a thick neck and a face like a jovial sun. Gates had spent Marik's first waking hours after surgery telling him the secret highlights of his past life, some of which were enough to fry the alien's ears. Then he had sat on Marik's bunk, playing the instrument he called a *mau thargan,* until Kraut Annie had chased him back to bed. Later, when she'd left, he came back.

Now, after another interminable concert, the *mau thargan* stopped and Gates beat it out against the palm of his hand and again eased his comfortable bulk gingerly onto the end of Marik's bunk. The room grayed out in a sick fog and swam back.

"—Annie see me sittin' here and she'll give us both hell, huh?" Gates was saying confidentially. "Lissen, you wanta hear a good one? I got this one from the quartermaster on the old *Alan B. Shepard.* Now that *Shepard,* she was a real home. Maybe she wasn't no, what you call star cruiser, like the *Missou* and the *Hope,* but she was one helluva ship, let me tell *you* . . ."

Marik let Gates tell him, while the oxygen hissed in his ears and time passed on lead feet. The big Earthling sat there telling Marik old Navy jokes until the dinner trays popped out of their chutes. Marik made no move toward eating, so Gates, with an apologetic grin, ate them both.

Dark. Very quiet. Marik opened his eyes and listened. A small sound, or possibly a swift thought, there and gone again, had dragged him from what might have been sleep. He had been dozing fitfully for—hours? Years? There was no way to tell.

It came again, a sound whispered so that only the sharp Einai ears could hear. Even Kraut Annie, at her lighted desk at the end of the ward, did not lift her head.

"Dom Marik."

29

Marik frowned. An Einai voice, familiar. The thought kept slipping away.

'In the Name of Tadae, *Dao*!"

Mennon! Domishan Kles Mennon, reckless and mercuric, violent and gentle; the son of a Han nobleman and one of his slaves. Mennon, the opponent when Marik, at four, had played with wooden viith; Mennon, with whom he had raced gryphons, shouting boyishly to each other high in the crisp, cold air; Mennon, his rival for the prettiest partners at the double-round dances; and the deadly serious partnership at the helm of Mennon's small, swift *Tsai*, fighting Krail, until the Erthlik allies made it dangerous for two Han to be in one place. Then Mennon disappeared into the bush country, and Marik, the disciple of Oman Shari-Mnenoplan, became a full Priyam.

Now Kles Mennon whispered to him from across the cell and he answered with difficulty: "Kles. Over here."

He closed his aching eyes and tears of weakness and relief slid down his temples. A wave of lassitude swept him and he was jarred abruptly up from unconsciousness to find Mennon next to his bed, the mane of straight black hair falling over the eyes, half the bony, green-gold face covered by a full beard. His voice was low.

"I wouldn't believe it until I saw you. What happened, Dao? We heard you were at Sum ChiT'ath."

Marik moistened his lips with a clumsy tongue. "The Erthlikli bombed us out . . ." Muscles twitched along his forearms.

Mennon sucked air between his teeth. "We heard that they'd missed their strike, but—"

Marik made a brief, bitter chuckle and winced. "They didn't miss." His head moved stiffly on the pillow, his jaw clenched tight. "They were . . . right on target."

Mennon doubled over suddenly, holding his side, and for the first time Marik saw the broad bandage around his ribs, freshly stained under his fingers.

"Kles? How bad?"

Mennon shook his head impatiently. "I'm fine. Tell me about Sum ChiT'ath."

Tell me about Sum ChiT'ath. Marik considered this, floating brilliant, electric, disoriented. Yes, it was important that Mennon know that he. And that the Erthlikli

30

came without any warning to. And, above all, that Shari-Mnenoplan, the Master, had.

"Dao?" A hand, slapping his face, stingingly, annoyingly. He jolted to the surface, head pounding, muscles straining at their moorings. His legs were an exquisite agony.

". . . where was I? Oh . . . my people, Kles . . ." He was too tired even to weep. ". . . I lost all my medics . . . and every . . . too sick to run . . . and the Priyam . . ."

"No!" Mennon burst out with the word. "Are you sure?—about the Master? *Think,* Dao! *Are you sure?"*

The memory was an old, old ache. ". . . I'm sure . . ."

"We thought—we hoped! —that he had taken Hennem-mishli away to the sea-cliffs." He raised his head. "We were at Allampaila less than a week ago. It was gutted. The summer pavilion, the servants' quarters, even the eyries."

"Mishli?" There was a long silence.

"It was Krail, Dao," Mennon said at last. "We didn't find her body."

Marik shut his eyes tightly. "I've got to . . . get out of here, Kles . . ." Savagely, *"I've got to get out of here!"* He reached for Mennon's shoulder to pull himself up, but his eyes glazed over and he made a throaty, strangled sound. A few hard tremors shook him and he stiffened, back arched, limbs rigid, breathing harsh and labored. His face, slick with sweat, turned a dark, dirty blue-green and his jaw clenched tightly in spasm. It was an eternity before he relaxed, apparently unconscious, and Mennon was frightened. He patted Marik's face gently, and then not so gently, making the jaw spasm, the limbs twitch. There was no conscious response for the space of ten breaths, then Marik opened his eyes. His lips moved and Mennon leaned close to catch the words.

". . . Kles . . . *you* get out . . . find Mishli . . ."

Mennon, frantic with concern and willing to swear to anything, extended his right hand palm forward, in the 'promise' gesture of old.

"By my life, and by the hands of Roanouk, I swear."

A faint smile touched Marik's face. ". . . done . . ."

It was a full minute before Mennon realized that Marik was no longer breathing. He shook him, with no response, slapped the nerveless face. He laid an ear to his chest and

31

could detect a beat from neither heart. His shout woke the ward.

"Nurse!" he roared. "Kraut Annie, quick!"

She came at a dead run.

Mephenocin and Levophed. Antibiotics, antitoxin, Seconal. Oxygen, external heart massage, respirator, defibrillator. They pumped him full of antitoxin and antispasmodic, brought his pressure to a believable level and even increased the CO_2 in his oxygen in an unsuccessful effort to force him to breathe for himself. Annie started a sterile water IV to combat dehydration; then she summoned the Surgical Resident from less critical situations in Intensive Care and through the small hours of the morning they fought convulsions, shock and fever, and watched helplessly as the tremors diminished due to exhaustion, and Marik's condition steadily deteriorated. By dawn he was moribund.

Dao was dying. Kles Mennon knew it and knew that Marik had known, yet he couldn't make himself accept it. Killing Krail (and an occasional Erthlik) was one thing; watching a man die who since childhood had been friend, surrogate brother, staunch ally despite Mennon's stigma of illigitimacy, was quite another. It hurt, desperately, and there wasn't anything he could do about it.

He stood pressed against the bars, holding his exploding side and turned wearily away from the busy, despairing medics at Marik's bedside, ignoring both the guard's indifference and the keen scrutiny of the Krail officer in the cell across the darkened corridor.

The guard stood up to stretch, yawned hugely and reached out as far as he could with both hands, easing his shoulders with a series of staccato grunts; then he went around with his hand torch to peer into each cell prior to leaving for his hourly break. Ostensibly, the guards at either end of the corridor would monitor the prisoners, but in practice it rarely happened. None of them actually believed that escape was possible, so security, even with Krail aboard, was lax.

The beam of the hand torch lanced into their darkened cell and the Resident, his face half-masked by infra-red goggles, wheeled on him as Marik made a strangled cry, back arching and teeth locked tensely, and signed the guard vehemently away. The beam swung away to a mumbled apology as the guard moved down the cellblock, and Marik's strained breathing lapsed into ragged sobs.

Mennon hit the bars with his fist again and again, scraping his knuckles raw, while the Krail stood clean and far beyond the safety of his own metal cage. After a moment he came to the bars, indicating Marik with a lift of the chin.

"You can help him, you know." His tone was confidential.

Mennon waited suspiciously. Marik, behind him, spasmed again, violently, and the Resident swore helplessly.

"I know the disease," the Krail continued. "We call it *Strecken*. They can last for more than a week like that, going from bad to worse—to dead." They listened to Marik gasping for breath. "I heard the nurses talking. Multiple compound fractures, they said. With *Strecken*, multiple fractures." He pantomimed sympathy with brows and puckered lips. "I wonder how that feels. And you could help him, if you would. If you were truly his friend."

Mennon said nothing and the Krail, after a moment's hesitation, shrugged slightly and started to turn away. Mennon hit the bars with his palm.

"How?" It nearly broke his teeth to ask, and the Krail knew it and felt he had scored a point. He returned, speaking conspiratorially across the corridor.

"If he stays here," he made a hopeless shrug, "you can see what lies in store for him. A lingering death, or at best—even if they save him—the life of a hopeless cripple aboard an Earthlikli prison ship." He rested both hands on the bars. Well-kept hands, tidily fleshed-out, and wearing a massive signet ring. Mennon mentally appraised its value, and was impressed.

"But we Krail have new methods, new techniques that could bring him out of that"—he tipped his head—"for hours at a time. And we are sorely in need of his Han talents."

"There are no Han—" Mennon cut in, but the Krail made a swift, sharp gesture that negated all argument.

"There—are—Han! Do you think me a fool, Einai? Do you think I could mistake the signs? Green blood, but gold skin! The strength of his mind!—even now, he touched my mind! What do you take me for, an Earthlikli

33

who hunts what he has in his grasp?" He pointed at Marik, his voice sibilant with contempt. "There is one of the few surviving Han! And I can save him if you help me!—or you can condemn him to death—or to a half-life of what you see there!—as a prisoner of your allies!" He paused, reading the twitch of the muscle at the corner of Mennon's eye, the whiteness of the knuckles gripping the bars. His tone became persuasive, sincere.

"We only need his mind for four hours. There is an Earthlikli convoy scheduled to come through here at oh-nine-hundred. Transports, heavy cruisers, destroyers and several subs. And most importantly, the Fleet Admiral's flagship. Now, I will not attempt to deny that the war is going badly for us. I will further admit that we are likely to lose it, if we do not have the information in that ship: battle formations, missile strength, the intricately illogical maneuvers of which the Earthlik mind is so fond."

"Dao can't get into that ship. He can't move!"

"His mind can. We can get him to the Admiral; your friend will listen to his thoughts for us."

"He cannot brainpick privileged information! It's contrary to our deepest ethic! He'd never do it!"

"You'll convince him." *Our* deepest ethic. And unaware of having said it. He made a mental note to check his mnemonic data for Han/Einai half-castes. This emotional link might indicate a powerful means of controlling them both. "If he can manage to stay alive for four hours—and aid us—I promise you his life—or at least a swift and merciful death at my own hand." It was Mennon's turn to smile crookedly, with derision.

"Easily said, Krail. But there you are behind your bars and here I am behind mine; and Dao is dying." For answer, the Krail plucked loose a strand of thread from the embroidered emblem on his sleeve, broke it off carefully and held it upright by one end for Mennon's examination. It was not a thread at all, but a wire, hair fine and metallic.

"Have you ever heard of a molecular splice?" he asked softly. Mennon's lips parted, his eyes shone. A molecular splice! The Krail, the clever Krail, could memorize a length of specially constructed metal wire, their fantastic, inhumanly accurate memories recalling the position of

34

each molecule; they could ravel the wire down to the molecular level and interweave it with another metal, (say, the metal of the prison bars that held them) creating false, weakened linkups and unnatural stresses. One sharp tug on the free end would collapse the entire structure.

A molecular splice! And here in the Krail's very hand. Mennon shook his shaggy head in admiration. The Krail were the enemy, cruel and cold and merciless; but, ah, they were clever. A molecular splice!

"It can get you out of here," the Krail offered softly, "if you agree to help us." He wove the thread unobtrusively into the design on his sleeve and waited for Mennon's answer.

Mennon thought fast. A way out, a way to get Dao to their own people, to proper medical help, to freedom! Whatever the Krail wanted, it was a small price to pay for Dao's life. And yet—

"He'd never forgive me," he replied, his face twisted so that it was hard to tell whether he was about to laugh or cry. "It's that simple." But it wasn't. It was an agony, listening to Dao die, knowing there was a way out. He leaned his head against the cold, uncaring metal of the bars, his side throbbing keenly.

Kraut Annie played her shielded hand torch over them. "Party's over, gentlemen. You, you Krail fellow, get back to bed, this patient's got to have his sleep." She showed impatience, herding Mennon back to bed. "Look at your side, it's bleeding again." She redressed the incision and gave Mennon a hypo; then she crossed back to Marik, her lifted brows asking a question of the Resident. He pulled down the corners of his mouth and shook his head.

"Another hour, maybe," he said.

Annie put in another call to Danton Parks—the fifth—and was patiently informed that Doctor Parks was still unavailable. The Resident gave up and went back to Intensive Care, rationalizing that Marik had the right to die 'with dignity and peace' and mumbling something about 'extraordinary means'. Annie, watching Marik in the throes of weakening convulsions, muttered an unprintable suggestion to the Resident's back and, taking matters into her own hands, punched the series for intercraft and rang Priyam Mykar Sharobi, aboard the USS Hope.

Kles Mennon woke to a sense of loss, an emptiness. *Alone.* He flung the blanket aside and steadied himself on the foot of the bed, staring at the empty bunk that had been Marik's personal rack. It had been stripped and was as yet unmade, a bleak symbol of loss. The remainder of the cell was empty. Loud, good-natured Gates had been released early last evening and had padded off amicably behind the orderly, waving a cheerful farewell with his *mau thargan.* Kraut Annie was nowhere to be seen; instead, at her desk there sat a thin, well-made-up woman with narrow features, who was writing on a noteboard. And Dao was gone.

"Where is he?" He stumbled to the desk and the new nurse surveyed his progress disapprovingly. "Mister Mennon, you must get back to bed. You'll hurt yourself."

"Where's Dao Marik? Where did they take him?"

She looked genuinely puzzled. "I don't know the name—" Mennon pointed at the empty bunk.

"Him. The Einai, the slant, the gook." He hit his chest. "The green one like me. Where is he?" A peculiar expression crossed her face and she quickly covered it with a professional pleasantness, supporting his elbow (he snatched it away) and mouthing platitudes.

"Don't worry about your friend, Mister Mennon, he'll be just fine, we're taking good care of him, you just get back to bed and try to rest." Mennon gripped her arms and shook her a few times until she subsided. "See here," she squeaked in a frightened little voice, "you can't . . . you get back to bed or I'll call the guard!" Mennon's grip tightened.

"He's dead, isn't he?" He shook her again, one time. *"Isn't* he?" Strands of her hair slipped untidily out of her bun, and her mouth trembled.

"Guard!" Weakly.

"Did you just let him die, or did you put him out of his misery, like a sick animal?"

"Hey, you, let her go! Let go!" Mennon threw a glance over his shoulder and straight up the muzzle of a laser rifle. A second guard, newly returned from one of the endless hourly breaks, stepped unheeding on half of a Hershey bar he'd dropped; the other half made an unchewed wad in his cheek.

"Drop the lady, Mac."

36

Mennon released her so suddenly she staggered, rubbing her arms and trying to regain her lost dignity. She smoothed her hair. "Now if you'll just get back to bed, Mister Mennon, we'll get you settled down and forget all about this little unpleasantness."

He shoved her fluttering hands aside and grabbed the bars.

"You! Krail!" The enemy officer appeared in the opposite cell. Mennon gazed at him with lambent yellow eyes, a tiger at bay. "I've changed my mind." The nurse prudently tiptoed away.

The Krail stared at him utterly without comprehension and deliberately ignored him, leaning casually against the bars and toying with the sleeve of his tunic. The guards lowered their weapons and stood about talking in low voices for awhile; then one of them resumed his post at the end of the hall. The other sat down, pulled a tape spool out of his pocket and plugged it into his ear, tipping his chair back and closing his eyes. The finest wisp of music spiralled out into the hallway and hung there in filmy patterns, like cobwebs.

Mennon glared at the Krail furiously at first, and then with growing comprehension. The white-skinned officer was absently—but thoroughly—plucking a lengthening fiber from his uniform sleeve, where the twin-star emblem was worked not in thread but in wire. He had several inches of it free; in a few moments, he would have enough for a complete splice. Mennon drew a deep, shuddering breath.

The Krail smiled up at him secretively. "Two hours," he said softly. "Be ready."

Mennon nodded grimly, thinking of Dao, of Hennemmishli, and of the vow he had made.

"I'll be ready," he said.

SHAROBI

"By the million eyes of Tadae, by T'ath, Hanshim-she'hai, and all my fathers' fathers, I take this oath . . ."

Sauvagi Medical Oath

To say that Mykar Sharobi was angry was to comment that Earth was a wet planet. It was so, but the observation didn't do justice to the fact.

Sharobi came storming through Emergency Deck wearing dirty surgical greens, a day's growth of beard and a black frown. Doors whisked open promptly as he strode toward them and the air around him all but seethed. Interns made way for him as he stalked down the corridor and nurses exchanged hurried whispers as he passed them by. Everyone either knew Sharobi by sight or had heard of him. He was a quarter-breed Sauvagi with a well-deserved reputation for irascibility and a genius that excused it. He was forty, tough, competent and not the sort of a man to accept any excuse but sudden and unavoidable death, the sort of a man who might have run a major hospital or an Air Force Wing during one of Earth's early pandemic wars.

Right now Sharobi stopped at Coe's Communication Station, surprising her at manicuring her nails, and slapped both his hands on the intervening counter.

"Where do I find Danton Parks?"

Coe, startled, dropped the open tube of polish into her lap, where it spread the newest yellow shade evenly across her uniform skirt. She reached for it, stammered, dithered,

38

and, checking her board, placed Parks in surgery. Nervously, she gave him the exact spot.

"Deck Four, OR2," he repeated coldly. "Thank you." He stepped into the lift and disappeared. Coe, viewing the mess in her lap, burst into tears.

Parks was cleaning up and exchanging pleasantries with several of the younger men and with Gordon Samstag, Chief of Staff who had been observing, when Sharobi came in. Samstag beamed.

"Mike! How are you? Good to see you, man!"

Sharobi ignored the outstretched hand. "Gordon."

Parks recognized him and smiled. He had a very personable smile. "Doctor Sharobi! A pleasure to see you, sir. I'm Doctor Parks. Danton Parks."

Sharobi sat heavily on the edge of a cabinet. "I know who you are, *Doctor*," he said in his calculated, unemotional monotone. "I came all the way over here from the *Hope* to tell you what I had to say in person."

Parks threw his disposable greens down the chute and shrugged.

"Here I am, sir."

Sharobi viewed him with contempt. "There you are." He sighed wearily. "I just finished an interesting procedure, *Doctor*. I thought I'd tell you about it, seeing that you have a vested interest in the patient."

Parks said suspiciously, " I don't think I understand."

"Man's name is Marik. Priyam *Dom* Dao Marik. That mean anything to you?"

"No."

Sharobi pursed his lips and nodded; he sighed again. "I got a patient this morning about six hundred, six-thirty. Pretty well mangled. Deep shock, several cardiac arrests . . . and he wasn't even in a MAX. What do you think of that?"

Samstag stepped in, even as Parks paled and started to speak.

"Come on, Mike. We're like every other field hospital— overcrowded and understaffed. We need those MAX's for our own people. Surely you can appreciate that."

Sharobi continued to ignore Samstag. "Seems the floor nurse kept trying to summon Marik's doctor and couldn't get hold of him, even when the patient went convulsive. Sound familiar yet, *Doctor*?"

Parks grew angry, his face pale and tight. "I don't have to stand here and listen to this, Sharobi."

Sharobi nodded slowly. "I think you do. I think you do. Because, Doctor, while my patient can thank his alien physique for bringing him this far, he might damn it by the knowledge that any Earthling with his kind of injuries wouldn't've lived to be brought here to you and butchered!" The other men in the room stood rooted, and for the first time, Sharobi allowed his gaze to rest heavily on them.

"As of now, this ship and its entire staff is on probation for the next six months. I'll expect your complete data bank, Gordon, to be fed into our computer direct within the hour, including a separate report on Marik's case. Please understand that another incident of this sort will subject this hospital's entire staff to a stringent security/ intelligence check and will result in the expulsion and loss of license of as many of you as are involved."

He got to his feet and got as far as the door before he turned around and impaled Parks on a frigid stare.

"Pack," he said.

Samstag caught up with him halfway down the corridor. "Mike, wait a minute." Sharobi didn't turn, merely paused and moved his head.

"Mike, come into my office for a minute. I want to talk to you." Sharobi hesitated, then followed him. The doors slid shut behind them. Samstag opened the wall cabinet and reached for a bottle. "Drink?"

"Scotch." Sharobi eased himself down into the one extra chair and buried his face in his hands for a moment, dragging his fingers down his cheeks. He blew out a weary breath, tugged off the surgical mask that still hung around his neck and tossed it onto the desk.

Samstag dropped a couple of ice wheels into a glass and handed it to Sharobi. "You were kind of tough on young Parks, weren't you?"

"Tough?" He thought of Marik, pieces lying on a table. "I don't think so."

"Well, I do!" Samstag leaned on his hands, facing Sharobi across the desk. "Now, Parks is a good man, and I need every one of my men! We've been swamped for the last three weeks, since the Krail started their big push! These boys have been working their tails off! All right!"

40

He took a turn down the cramped room, came back. "All right, so he botched the postop care on that eye-eye! That's no reason to crucify him! For God's sake," he shouted suddenly, "even if he killed him outright!—it's not as if that gook were human!" His face went ruddy and he stopped cold.

Sharobi narrowed his eyes thoughtfully, pursed his lips and regarded the amber liquid in his glass with intense interest.

Samstag sputtered, made a brief, indecisive wave of the hands.

"So I said it! It's the truth, its what we all feel. Just as well it's out in the open." He adopted a conciliatory tone.

"Mike, the boy was rash, I'll admit that. He should've done a better follow-up on that patient. But he was beat out! He'd been working for eighteen straight hours! Now, you can't blame him for being a little testy about being called out in the middle of the night!—when there was a Resident on duty."

Sharobi gazed at the Scotch, closed his eyes and drank. "No. You can't blame him for being a little testy." He looked up, hollow-eyed and grim. "Well, Gordon, my lad, I've been on duty for thirty-three hours, and I'm a little testy myself.

"Now let me straighten a few things out: if it was just the postop care that Parks had neglected, I might overlook it. We don't expect the field hospitals to pamper our people. But I got Marik with a full-fledged case of untreated tetanus! Fractures were left unset, some of them required initial debriding. We had peritonitis from Parks' leaky anastomosis, and thanks to that damned tropical climate down there!—and the fact that your boy neglected to order sufficient antibiotics!—I'm still fighting a roaring tetanus, plus an osteo that's going to cost Priyam Marik both his legs—and probably his life."

Samstag's mouth worked. "Priyam? He, ah, he's—"

Sharobi glanced at him. "A 'Doctor'? Oh, yes, Gordon. For your edification, Priyam Marik is a surgical officer with the Fifth Einai *Chosen* Regiment. A *Dom*. Check it out. He's registered on your own Medicomp, under 'Allied Surgical Personnel'." He leaned back wearily and steepled his fingers. "So what we have here, Gordon," he said slowly, "is a very sticky situation. It seems that you, as

41

Chief of Staff, have permitted the gross malpractice of medicine upon an officer and an ally, not to mention a medical colleague." He watched objectively as Samstag squirmed. "If the Surgeon General got wind of this, you'd be out of the Fleet so fast you wouldn't have time to collect your little wine cellar."

Samstag, in the middle of pouring himself another, stopped short, banged the bottle on the desk and yelled, "*You* certainly seem to enjoy '*my—little—wine—cellar*,' Doctor!"

Sharobi grinned drily. "We aliens can tolerate a great many things, Gordon. One of them is alcohol; another is being referred to as 'Doctor' when we are, in fact, something else entirely." He finished his Scotch as Samstag downed his drink and splashed another into the glass.

"All right," Samstag muttered thickly, "you're holding all the cards. What do you want me to do—beg? All right, I'll beg. I should've known about this, I should've kept closer check on my boys—but I didn't! I was too busy trying to save our own men!—Earthling men!—to check whether or not we were wet-nursing the eye-eyes! Is that what you want to hear? All right!—I've said it!" He swayed where he stood. "Want to record it?"

Sharobi rotated his empty glass, watching the ice slide and spin. "I want the offer of a position of dignity within the Fleet for Priyam Marik, in the event he lives; and suitable recompense to his survivors if we lose him. And I want a report of this to go to the *Hope*—to my hospital—no further."

"I can't do that!" Samstag shouted, reddening. "What kind of influence do you think I have? Chief of Staff of a rotten recommissioned tanker, trying to muddle my way through this idiot war—! What makes you think I can get your friend anything?—or would if I could?" he added recklessly. He poured another drink, spilling half of it over his hand, and gestured broadly with the glass.

"Besides," he yelled righteously, "this is blackmail, pure blackmail!"

"Gordon. Your brother is an Admiral with the Federation Sixth Fleet. Now, somehow—some way—you're going to have to make it clear to him that it's a fair trade: you for Marik. Your career for his. Incidentally," he added, picking up his mask and stuffing it into his pocket, "you needn't bother to tell him that your career has suddenly become a source of unending interest to me; in the event you make another mistake, we wouldn't want to embarrass him."

Samstag gulped a few times, like a netted fish. Finally, he wheezed, "That's inhuman, Mike! You can't mean it!" He slammed the glass down on the desk and it shattered in his hand. *That's not even human!*" he shouted shrilly.

Sharobi turned his dark, alien gaze on him and smiled a most deadly smile.

"How about that?" he said softly.

Then he walked out through the whispering doorway and Samstag was left alone.

Marik survived. That fact alone was miracle enough, but that he was able to walk (albeit with a cane), function normally, and take up his profession again was signal tribute to the *Hope*'s facilities in general and the genius of Mykar Sharobi in particular. When faced by a colleague with that observation, Sharobi was said to have grunted irritably and changed the subject.

There was no denying, however, the attention he had given Marik's case. For the first critical weeks, when Marik had hovered precariously between life and death, Sharobi had stayed with him around the clock. Had even ordered a cot brought into the room and slept there, if snatches of rest grabbed at odd hours could be termed sleeping. His concern was so profound that it was widely speculated among the hospital staff as to whether crusty old Sharobi and the handsome young Priyam might not somehow be related.

When it became possible that Priyam Marik might live after all, Sharobi had stationed Big Arty Michaels at the bedside, left a call for four hours later and fell exhausted into bed. It was a full thirty-two hours before anyone thought about waking him. By that time Marik had started to gain ground and they could begin talking about what was to be the first of many corrective surgical procedures.

What the next eight months cost Marik and Sharobi was drawn indelibly on their faces.

But Marik survived.

43

Sharobi came into the observation blister and saw Marik standing at the far railing, silhouetted against the glow from the planet's dayside. He was wearing Federation Navy dress blues, with twin gold stripes on the sleeve of his tunic. At his collar were the medical insignia, Federation and Einai, and on his left breast the golden dolphins of a sublight vessel. He was regarding his planet with a deep, brooding hunger, as if drinking it in. Rightly so, Sharobi mused, remembering Sauvage. It would be a long time before Marik saw Eisernon again.

"Priyam Marik."

Marik reluctantly pulled himself from the panorama and limped slowly across the polished metal deck to meet him. He skidded a bit on a slick spot and Sharobi put out an instinctive hand to steady him, but Marik shook his head almost imperceptibly, and said reassuringly, "No need."

They moved together down the corridor toward the transporter room, Sharobi matching his long stride to Marik's slower pace. He cleared his throat.

"Got everything?"

Marik nodded. A nurse passed them and murmured "Chom-ala, Priyamli," to which Sharobi muttered a curt "Chom." After a few more yards of silence, he growled, "You're sure."

"I didn't bring much luggage, sir," Marik observed drily, and Sharobi grunted. It might almost have been a chuckle.

"So you didn't," he agreed.

Marik paused in mid-corridor. "Priyam Sharobi—"

Sharobi kept walking. "We'll be late." He scowled at his chronometer and then back at Marik. "Your escort is probably waiting for us now."

Marik caught up to him with dogged determination and Sharobi obligingly slowed. Neither of them looked at the other. Marik's question was cool and sincere, and embarrassed neither of them.

"How does a man say it? I owe—"

"*I don't want to hear it!*" They passed several orderlies, who greeted them respectfully while Sharobi stared through them.

"There are only nine Priyamli left," Sharobi continued, in a quieter, more thoughtful tone. "Nine of us in the Galaxy. You tried for Shari-Mnenoplan, I tried for you,

44

it's that simple." He took a deep, shuddering breath. "The way I make it, I still owe you."

Marik pressed the stud for Identification at the transporter room portal. The communicator inquired, "Identification, please?"

"Sharobi and Marik," Sharobi growled. There was the quick metallic click of voiceprint match.

"We rendezvous in two years, Priyam. I'll have several weeks' free time. You can pay me off then." Marik smiled, but his eyes were hollow. Sharobi nodded, the lines in his face softening a bit.

"That'll be the last one, I promise you. Just so we can get you off those things—" He indicated Marik's cane. "Supports belong inside a man's legs, made of bone," he muttered. "If Tadae had intended Man to carry a cane in his hand—"

Marik laughed aloud as the portal hissed open, and the Transporter Officer gave him a quizzical stare.

A big, black Earthling officer crossed the room to greet them. He, too, wore the golden dolphins on his tunic.

"Mister Marik?" Sharobi scowled and Marik inclined his head. "I'm Simon M'Benga, First Officer of the USS Skipjack." He extended his right hand and, embarrassed, dropped it. Marik pretended not to see it. "If you're ready."

Marik turned to Sharobi. There were many things he would like to have said, but he said only, "Priyam."

Sharobi, understanding, nodded quickly and said unexpectedly, in a voice he did not recognize as his own, "He was my master, too."

Science Officer. It rankled. Marik, limping through the white-walled corridors of the USS Skipjack in tow of M'Benga, felt the same wash of frustration and outrage that had swept him when Administrator Barren broke the news.

"Impossible." Marik raised himself up on one elbow and stared earnestly into the face of the heavy-set, uniformed Earthling who sat uncomfortably next to his bed. "Science Officer? I am a Priyam, a—a physician. Surely my record is on file."

"Oh, yes." The Administrator lit a pipe and the thick, sweet smell of tobacco wafted up. It was an insult, a backhanded reminder of Earthling superiority, that they could inhale for hours what would narcotize an Einai in minutes. Marik knew it as such, and Barren knew he knew it, and didn't much care.

"Yes, your record is on file," he said at last. "Or at least, it was." He pulled a cassette from his inner pocket. "I took the liberty of removing it. Very interesting, very interesting, indeed." He casually dropped it down the disposal chute, where it would become fuel for the ship's nuclear converter. Marik blanched.

"I believe there are copies of that document available, sir," he observed stiffly.

"I think not. Shortly after you left the USS Pacific, she was scuttled by a group of prisoners, with a loss of all hands."

Marik's head spun. Kles! And Kraut Annie, and all those lives—! Kles! He frowned, indicating the chute. "If that is true, then why—?"

Barren cut him off. "The fact of the matter is, Mister Marik, you're proving to be something of an embarrassment to us. We don't quite know what to do with you. We can't send you back to your regiment—it's been so cut up by the Krail fleet that there's virtually no regiment left. And we can't have you in the Federation Medical Service, because you're not qualified. That leaves only the Star Service. Starfleet's agreed to take you on." He puffed on his pipe. "You should be grateful, Mister Marik. It's a high position, one many men would envy."

"May I—I would like to inquire, sir: in what way, in what subject am I not qualified?"

"History," Barren answered brightly, puffing on his abominable pipe. "Naturally, we understand that you people don't have the, ah, the cultural advantages that Earth has; but not to know Amerenglish history! We like our doctors to be, well, call it rounded-out, knowledgeable. We have a certain, oh, call it an image, eh? to preserve."

"I see." He saw, and shuddered inwardly.

"Under other circumstances, there would be no problem. A financial settlement, perhaps, a formal apology . . ." He made a futile wave of the hand. "But now Doctor Sharobi's in it, and he tends to be formidable, very formidable indeed. He wants you installed on a Federation vessel and out of here, and right now this is the

46

best we can do for you. You understand, if you were qualified, we could—"

"Thank you, Administrator. Earth has done more than enough for me." The words were gall and wormwood on the tongue, but the Administrator missed his meaning and stood up, his face clearing and relieved.

"That's good to hear. That's damned good to hear, Mister Marik. We—that is, some of us were afraid you might, er . . ." He laughed uneasily, dismissing the thought, and handed Marik a packet. "Your orders. You'll report to Captain Paul Riker of the *USS Skipjack*, on 22 November, that's, ah," he consulted his chronometer, "that's two weeks to the day." He extended a hand, which Marik took briefly. "It's been good talking to you, Mister Marik. Good day."

Mister Marik. *Mister Marik*. Rage and helpless frustration swelled in him unbearably, and he focused his anger on a point in the room that suddenly blazed incandescent, grew—and burst, disappeared, burned out, with a sound as of shattering glass. He lay back against his pillow, exhausted. *Mister Marik*.

"Mister Marik?" M'Benga was looking at him strangely and Marik started.

"Yes."

The door to the Captain's quarters was open—had whispered open before him, he realized—and he entered.

Paul Riker was seated at a table of carved charis-wood, dictating into a secretary, but at Marik's appearance he switched it off and came smoothly to his feet. "Mister Marik. Paul Riker." He did not offer his hand, as Earthlings were wont to do, but instead made a chom-ala sign, slickly, swiftly, as though he needn't think about it. Marik wondered coldly, as he returned the gesture, whether such courtesy was natural to Riker or whether he had practiced it before a mirror somewhere. The thought of it almost made him smile.

The Captain smiled, too, brief and businesslike. "Sit down." He punched a few tabs on his secretary and waited for the readout, studying it carefully, while Marik candidly scrutinized his Captain. Thick brown hair, long enough to brush his collar; frank, inquiring eyes; strong face and short, heavy hands. There was the feeling of immense power barely checked; in that way, he was much like

Sharobi. But Riker was an Earthlik—and Marik didn't mean to let himself forget it.

The Captain punched the tabs again and watched the screen, then lifted his eyes to Marik.

"We have almost no information on you, Mister Marik, so we'll have to be content with whatever you care to tell us." He grinned disarmingly. "This much we know, if you weren't qualified, you wouldn't be here. I'm betting on that. Coffee?" Marik hesitated and Riker added quickly, "It's been cleared for your species."

"Thank you, then. Yes."

It was black and bitter, a taste that Marik would always associate with his service among the Erthlikli, and it gave him a grim satisfaction. His leg ached hollowly.

"Let's have it, Marik." Riker was serious. "What about it? They send me a new man, no history, no recordtape on you, just 'here's a new Science Officer for you, Riker'. You're obviously not ready for duty; you could use another month on one of the whiteships." He tapped the desk impatiently with the edge of his hand. "Why now? Why you?"

"I was told to report to you, sir. I am here."

"But you don't like it—do you?"

"I was not aware that I was expected to like it, sir. I believe that I am expected to perform my function as this ship's Science Officer—and I am prepared to do just that."

Riker crossed the room and sat on the edge of a cabinet, pointing thoughtfully at Marik. "Somebody wanted you off-planet. Who?"

Who else? Marik thought. But he said, "I am qualified as your Science Officer, sir. And despite my . . . appearance, I am ready for duty."

Riker stood abruptly. "All right. You can log in anything you feel we ought to know about you. It'll be confidential. Only I, Mister M'Benga and the Computor Officer will have access to it." He hesitated as if waiting for some sign of warmth, of rapport, from Marik; but the impassive alien sat watching him with eyes like a winter sea, cold and unreadable. "That's all, Mister Marik," Riker said briskly. "The crewman outside will show you to your quarters. I'll expect you on the bridge at eighteen hundred hours."

He sat tapping the desk thoughtfully as the alien left silently and M'Benga sauntered in and slouched into the chair Marik had vacated.

"Problem?" MBenga rumbled, and Riker glanced up through his brows and shook his head.

"Who knows, Simon, who knows? I get this guy, he's been cleared through channels, but there's no record on him, no background, nothing. Obviously he's been through hell, but unless I'm judging him wrong, he's not going to open up for you, me, or anybody else."

"He's an alien, Paul. A gook. Let's face it, we haven't exactly given them a fair shake, and I guess they resent it. I mean, he is a man, even if he is a gook."

Riker toyed with his stylus. "Why don't we make a start by deleting that word. For some reason it bothers me."

"Sorry." M'Benga poured himself a cup of coffee and wrapped it in his big hands, savoring the warmth. "I don't think your boy wants babying, Paul. I think he'd resent coddling. Just—let him do his work. He'll come around."

"Maybe!" Riker moved restlessly around the room. "And maybe he won't. This is a sweet little ship, Simon, and she's mine; I won't have any grudge-bearers, any variable factors lousing her up!"

"Brass says Marik's at least a good Science Officer."

"He'd better be. He'd better be damn good."

"He'll work out. He's an Einai." Riker looked at him quizzically and M'Benga explained, "The eye-eyes are loyal the same way the Krail have that fantastic memory. It's part of the species, built in. If Marik swore the Oath of Fealty to the Federation, he'll be loyal even if he hates every one of us."

"That's something, anyway," Riker muttered. He felt bleak about Marik. M'Benga had put his finger on it: hatred. Marik hated every one of them. And there was no reason for it. No reason at all.

PAIGE

"I swear by Apollo the Physician, and Aesculapius and Hygaea, Panacea, and all the gods and goddesses . . ."

The runner came by noon.

Tom Paige had been expecting him. For the past two weeks, since the destruction of the city of Allampaila off to the east, there had been signs of trouble and unrest, even this far into the rain forest.

At first it had been only dark, oily smudges of smoke hanging heavily in the sky, where Krail and Federation skimmercraft battled like wheeling gryphons. They were usually too high—or too far away—to attract more than passing notice. But they got steadily closer.

Later, by handfuls and in frightened little knots of humanity, refugees began to trickle through Paige's outpost, growing to a steady stream of displaced people, bringing with them their children, their aged, their injured—and whatever pitiful possessions they had managed to save from the carnage at Allampaila. Most of them moved through during the night, from shortly before midnight until false dawn. Paige, taking time out between surgical procedures for a breath of fresh—jungle-hot, fog-wet—air, would regard them with compassion. Silent old men, women squatting by his watchfire, brewing weak stews made up of anything at hand; young mothers nursing thin, wailing infants; older children curled up like kittens to sleep against each others' warmth. There were never any older boys, or men young enough to fight.

50

The story was always the same: *Krail*. They said it with awe and terror in their voices, in tones of despair. They feared Paige for being an Earthling; yet they drank his water and submitted to his gentle help. But they dreaded the Krail, and fled before them, utterly panic-stricken, to run, and rest by day and run again.

The stream swelled to a river of refugees, some of them too ill to be moved, others who had died on the way, brought by hopeful peasant relatives, who wanted miracles because he was an Earthling, and therefore almost a god. Paige, who was only a man, turned them away in favor of those who still breathed, and heard their curses ring in his ears long after the jungle was still.

Last night—or this morning, in the small hours—Paige had seen a blossoming of burning lights on the night sky beyond the hills, a dull, red glare reflected against the overcast. He couldn't tell how far away it was, but it was there, it was too close, and it was deliberate. He stood musing in the doorway for a while, soberly contemplating it; then he went inside and began to get his patients ready to leave the outpost. His native assistant, Cox, asked no questions, nor was there any need for questions. He, too, had seen the ominous glow. He knew.

By dawn, Paige started sending his patients away. They left wordlessly, reluctantly, following the paths taken earlier by their relatives, filtering through the jungle and disappearing before his eyes, green on green.

By mid-morning Doctor Thomas M. Paige, *duli*, lately of De Bakey Memorial Institute, Denva, Earth, had only one patient left. That one was an old peasant named Jorn, who had been so imprudent as to oppose a Krail squad that came tramping across his freshly-planted fields.

Jorn had been unable to sit up since, or hear, or speak; but he was a pleasant old man and laughed a great deal, mostly to himself, as if relishing some delicious secret. Occasionally, he would snatch up Paige's hand and pat it, nodding and snickering conspiratorially.

Once he had carved a figure out of charis-wood (though where the material had come from, nobody knew, for charis-wood was rare in any case). The figure was of a cross with the horizontal member tilted askew; above it, and resting upon the lower, greater angle, was an S-shaped serpent, hovering protectively over the upright. He

51

had shoved it into Paige's hand, nodding and mewling; clearly a gift, then. So, to please him, Paige had stood it on the windowsill. The natives found it very impressive, and he thought he sensed a reverent change in their attitude toward him, although, he told himself, he might've imagined it.

Now, but for Jorn, the hospital stood empty. Cool, shaded, and very, very clean, it stood open to the winds. Poor as it was, Paige was inordinately proud of it, for he'd built it with his own hands, and it had served him well. He stood outside, bareheaded, his shirt open at the collar, and watched the runner approach.

It was not the usual man, but another native, stripped to a loincloth for speed; and the hair of his head had been ritually singed off in the manner of Einai messengers. Paige walked forward to meet him, for the man carried an *inau,* signifying that the message was from the Holy Ones, and that he was immune to all harm. Even the rudest peasants and the most determined criminals respected the *inau.* On the entire planet, it was the one inviolate flag of truce.

The man trotted into the clearing and gave him the chomala sign. *"Duli,"* he panted, "greetings from the Masters."

Masters? "Chom-ala," Paige replied, suspiciously. Something was decidedly wrong here. "Blessings on the Lifebearers."

"I do not speak of Shimshenli," the runner snapped. "I speak for my Masters, the Krail." His breathing had slowed and his voice was hard and sharp. "I bring the *duli* their commands. Hear the words of the Krail: the Earthling *duli* is under house arrest and shall not leave his station. The *duli* is forbidden to use his communication devices for any purpose. The *duli*—" His voice droned on and Paige felt a slow fury rising in him. So the Krail had taken Panormi; the monastery, too, he supposed. The Abbess, notoriously stubborn about such things, would never have surrendered her *inau* of office otherwise. He wondered whether she still lived.

The messenger's mouth moved on and on, and Paige marked the almost invisible notch along his jawline where one well-placed blow would render him non-combative; non-functioning for a respectable while, too, he amended.

52

Well, let them go, let them take the cities, he thought in a cold rage. They don't get this place; and if I can help it, they don't get me. There were stories about Krail slave pens—

"—*duli* is to preserve his records and make especial note of any Einai whom he shall see, who is not like other Einai, of the name and—"

"What's that supposed to mean?"

The man's mouth kept babbling rules routinely, and he shifted his weight to the other bare foot and spoke to a spot about three inches above Paige's head. Paige grabbed him.

"I said, what do they mean, 'make a note'? What do you think I'm going to do, turn these people over to the Krail? You've got to be kidding! I wouldn't turn a healthy hookworm over to the Krail!" He let the man go, and he jerked away from Paige furiously. "Go back and tell 'em they've got the wrong boy."

He turned on his heel to re-enter the outpost, but the midday shadow at his feet warned him of the heavy *inau* that came crashing down at his head. He whirled and caught the messenger's slick wrist in reflex accuracy, his free fist delivering a short, vicious jab to the native's solar plexus, momentarily paralyzing operations there. The man gasped for breath, found none and slumped to his knees, his face contorted. Paige picked up the *inau* and tucked it into his belt.

"Now you tell your 'masters', Charlie, that the next time they want to talk to me, they'd better have something better to say than 'heel'!"

He walked back to the hospital without a backward look, and Cox, Paige's native medic, ran stealthily out into the clearing and helped the wheezing messenger to his feet. By that time the man could stand alone, although his breath whistled through his teeth as his lungs dragged for air.

"*Duli* Paige does not know the rules," Cox explained anxiously. "He is an offworlder, and foolish. I will make him do as you say, only do not tell the Masters of this. Rakmaeli!—do not tell the Masters!"

The messenger pulled his arm free of Cox's solicitous hands, and took a few steadying breaths. "You tell your *duli,*" he spat "that we will see him dead. We will see you all dead."

Cox, believing it, stood shivering in the sun-hot clearing as the messenger walked arrogantly away.

Paige stepped into the sudden shadow of the outpost, but before his eyes adjusted to the light, a quick arm throttled him closely while the left hand held up a wicked-looking viith for his intimate inspection.

"Say nothing," warned a gruff voice.

A second form passed quickly between him and the doorway and poised beside it. Paige squinted and made out the shape of a small, shaven-headed man, who peered out at the compound.

"Gone?" asked the rough voice behind him. There was no answer. The pressure on Paige's throat was becoming uncomfortable, but Paige kept himself relaxed. It was not the first time he had been jumped by natives wanting his drugs, or his money—or his life. He could usually talk them out of it; and upon the isolated occasion when he could not, he merely offered them a casual cigarette—and watched objectively as they smoked themselves into a stupor.

"Gone, Ilai?" asked the rough voice again, and the small man nodded once. Paige's captor turned him slowly —still holding his throat—until he faced the open surgery door. There, half-sitting, half-leaning against Paige's makeshift operating table, was a tall, lean, bearded Einai. There could be no doubt that he was a guerilla, just as there was no doubt that he was the leader of these men. There was a certain discarded dignity, a military bearing about him; and he wore part of the uniform of the Chosen Regiment—that crack Einai squadron Earth had so hastily absorbed during the Takeover—and spacer's boots. The insignia, the color bands and the mesh spacer's helmet were conspicuously absent; instead, a grimy skimmer-pilot's headgear lay on the table. Paige, observing him camly, noted that in addition to his needler, he carried a viith slung over his shoulder and a honed-obsidian disc in a harness at his belt.

The man lifted his chin and Paige's captor let him go.

For what seemed a long time—but probably wasn't— he regarded the Earthling doctor out of intense, tiger-yellow eyes, his arms tightly folded; but when he unex-

54

pectedly dropped a hand to steady himself, Paige saw that his entire left side was soaked with blood. His right hand was gripping a wound, holding the edges together. He managed a wry smile.

"Duli," he said, in a surprisingly cultured tone, "I have a job for you."

Paige bent over the washbasin, rolling back his sleeves. "Up on the table," he ordered, beginning to scrub. "How long ago did this happen?"

The silent man considered the question while the shaven-headed one found a pack of cigarettes in Paige's shirt, lit one and placed it between his chief's lips. He pocketed the pack.

The silent man spoke. "Half hour, stretched."

"Flak?" He began cutting the soggy fabric away from the wound.

"I ditched."

Deep, uneven puncture, inflicted by a piece of jagged metal, probably still imbedded. He thought he could see a dark gleam along the rib when he pulled away the sponge. "I think there's still a fragment in there," he muttered, and the tiger eyes laughed at him. "There is." The leader took the cigarette out of his mouth. "I'm looking for a certain woman," he began, and the small man said heavily, "Mennon, she's with the old man!"

Mennon waved him to silence. "There was a girl—at Allampaila, small—perhaps this tall—" he drew her with expressive hands in the air. "She has dark hair and her skin is—more yellow, paler than mine. More like an Earthling's. Think, now—have you seen such a young woman? I'll reward you well."

How many young women had passed through the outpost, had come and rested and gone on, faces veiled against heat and grief, burdened unbearably with possessions and sorrow, yet staggering away toward what they hoped would be safety?

Paige shook his head. "Sorry."

The messenger's babbling mouth flashed before his inner eye, and the cold voice repeated for his ears alone, *any Einai he shall see who is not like other Einai.* A spark jumped in his brain, a synapse closed. But—a woman?

He lifted his head. "Is she the one the Krail are looking for?"

The leader brought his face around slowly. "What do you know about the Krail?"

"They sent a messenger. The *duli* will do this, the *duli* will not do that." He swabbed the wound as he talked.

"And they wanted Hennem-mishli?"

"Not by name. Just any Einai out of the ordinary. They didn't say why and I didn't ask." He clamped a few of the heavier bleeders while Mennon inhaled the tobacco deeply.

"And what did you tell them?" asked the even voice. The man watching at the window stirred, and it seemed Paige could hear his listening. Before he could answer, Mennon's shaggy head turned back, eye-level with the *inau* at his belt. His lips parted in wonder. "I see." He met Paige's eyes. "I think I like you, *duli*. Even if you are Earthlik."

"Yeah, I'm crazy about you, too, Charlie," Paige answered absentmindedly, groping for the fragment; his probe hit metal, and he breathed an 'ahhh' of satisfaction. He had it: a shard of alum-alloy about, oh, two centimeters by perhaps three and a half, it was hard to be sure. He palpated the rigid abdomen. From the bleeding, it had probably nicked the spleen. He didn't dare try to remove it here; the excision of a deep-set foreign body—and probably the spleen with it—required time he no longer had. Paige had no illusions about the Krail reaction to his treatment of their messenger. They would be here, down his neck, in a matter of minutes. He had no intention of letting them catch him in the middle of a procedure. No, Mennon's best chance was a hospital environment and prompt attention to his injury. Otherwise it was conceivable that he could simply lie here and bleed to death.

He tied off the troublesome bleeders, dressed the wound and crossed toward his communicator; but the shaven-headed man flipped a viith into the floor right where he was to have stepped.

"No radio," he said.

Paige was losing his patience. "Look, either you want him helped or you don't. Now, it doesn't matter to me one way or the other; but the Krail are going to be here in a couple of minutes to take this place. Maybe you want to be here when they show up. I don't."

The shaven-headed man looked to his chief for instructions. He, in turn, spoke to Paige. "Take the metal out of my side and let me go."

"Out of the question."

He blew a cloud of smoke around his head. "I could insist." He pointed. "Ilai and Jek, here, insist very efficiently." He smiled with the very white teeth of the Einai, and it was genuine and contagious. Paige made a grimace that might have been construed as a smile, plucked the cigarette from Mennon's lips and crushed it out.

"If you were going to play games, you'd have done it already. Now, what'll it be, Charlie?—the Krail or us?"

Mennon capitulating, spread his hands. "The easiest enemy," he said.

Paige made the call without any further difficulty. SurCon promised him a skimmercraft; they were sending down an emergency rig momentarily and had room for Mennon in the second aft compartment. Paige was relieved. This was better than he had dared hope for. Sometimes the wait stretched into hours.

By the time the call was completed, Jek and Ilai had faded into the jungle. Paige considered asking them to take old Jorn with them, but mentally vetoed the idea as unfeasible. Jorn would slow them down. They were guerilla fighters—not geriatric nursemaids.

Besides, Jorn was his own responsibility. The peasants had told him so when he took the old man in. Childless, and with no surviving family, Jorn had been left to the mercies of the wild d'injit that roamed the tender evenings of Eisernon. The d'injit would have settled the problem nicely. But the Earthling *duli*, for some explicable reason, had chosen to take Jorn in. Now the *duli* was stuck with him.

It occurred to Paige that Jorn might spell the difference between escape and death; but he could no more abandon the old man than stop breathing. He rubbed his tired eyes and massaged the back of his stiff neck. It was still and hot in the little room. Outside, far off, a jat barked a sharp, staccato call.

If he could get Jorn far into the junglebrush before they came, if he and Cox could manage to cover their tracks, there might be a chance. Admittedly, a very slim

57

chance, but better than nothing. Infinitely better than nothing.

The skimmer lighted down shortly thereafter, sweeping low over the hills, its hull wet with rain. Mennon was slipped neatly into the MAX tube, tied into the systems (Paige helping for the sake of speed) and the skimmer was gone. Paige was alone.

He ran back to the hospital hut, the need to hurry drawing his nerves out fine and thin. "Cox," he shouted, "see if you can dig up a stretcher the refugees didn't get." He began rummaging through a cabinet in the alcove that served as a pharmacy.

"Alai, dokta," Cox mumbled, and went back into the ward at a snail's pace. It was evident that he had been weeping: his eyes were green and puffy and his voice thick. The Einai were a highly emotional race, by contrast to their legends, which spoke of their being severely controlled. When Paige asked Cox about this, he'd laughed and explained, as if to a child, "But dokta, that were the Han; that were not us nor I."

Which was preposterous, of course; for it was common knowledge that the mythical Han were everything the Einai wanted to be and were not, much in the manner of some of the old Earthling gods. This Han fellow had probably been some chief, lionized and deified and finally bucked up the line until he assumed the stature of a legend, and his family with him. It had to be something simple. The Einai were a simple people.

He found the stretcher and brushed the dust off of it. It was in pretty good condition. One handle was missing, but they could manage. Jorn was light and frail. He was throwing a few basic instruments and medicines into his kit when Cox shuffled out of the galley with his arms laden with fruit. He put it down before Paige with a solemn, ritualistic gesture, and stepped back. Fruit, placed solemnly. Milai, for bitterness; the purple, faintly narcotic mung, for forgetting; and succulent, fleshy pij, for the sweetness of eternity. Fruit, the gift for the dead. Paige swept it off the table with one arm and kept loading his medikit.

"We'll take meat, Cox. Some of that smoked jat. We can pick up fruit as we go, the jungle's full of it."

Far off, and approaching steadily, Paige heard the thin,

58

distinctive whine of a Krail skimmercraft. Cox heard it, too, and whimpered.

Paige slung his kit over his shoulder and, with Cox's help, slid Jorn onto the stretcher with more haste then care. They were halfway outside when Jorn began a wordless howling, pointing a trembling finger toward the window. There on the sill stood the charis-wood carving, and the old man kept gesturing at it and making hoarse, inhuman sounds. Paige ran for it, impatiently shoved it into his bulging kit, and salved his exasperated conscience by rationalizing that it would take little room, and that it would keep the old man quiet. *What we need,* said his reasonable mind, *is less quiet and more running like hell.*

Paige patted the old man's shoulder and told him to lie down, that everything was going to be all right. He wished he could believe it.

The whine was a real and ominous presence. And there were still records to burn, names and descriptions to destroy.

They carried Jorn into the underbrush and Paige set Cox to watch him. He nodded, whispering to himself terrifiedly, as the *duli* raced back to the clearing. A broad shadow, kite-shaped and dread, swept him as he ran. He staggered under its weight.

Paige ransacked the hospital, pulled down the boxes containing his files, and dumped them in the middle of the ward. Down came 'Military, Einai', calmly mingling with 'Military, Krail'. 'Children, outpatient' tumbled headlong, and from the highest shelves, the snowy, fragile sheets marked 'Geriatric', sank wearily, halting and whispering, into the pile. 'Military, Earth' crashed onto the floor with a scattering of other lives drawn on paper. A few more boxes, and then the shelves were empty.

Paige grabbed ether containers and pitched one with all his might into the surgery, one into the ward, and, running out to the back, heaved the last two into the skimmershed where his lone, decrepit one-man sled stood sheltered.

He was feeling light-headed and giddy from the fumes, and even the loud approach whine of the skimmer landing seemed far away and of little moment.

Paige shook his head to clear it and scrambled for the galley, grabbed a lighter and a handful of bandage. Wadding it around the *inau* (may the alien gods forgive me!) he poured alcohol around it and ignited it. It bloomed up brightly and he barely escaped the several sudden explosive bursts of flame that appeared mere yards away, throwing him half out of the doorway and singeing his hair. The hut expanded into an orange flower, smokeless and brilliant, and Paige touched the *inau*-torch (a holy thing, surely) to the skimmershed and watched orange flowers devour his sled. It is to Paige's credit that he never considered the sled as a means of his own escape; and it would never have carried three men.

Behind him, cutting icily through the hoarse flames, came the snick-click of a needler, and he whirled, face flushed and skin scorched by the heat, to see the charcoal-and-ashes shape of a Krail killer as he brought the needler to his shoulder. In that reflex instant, he flung the blazing *inau* into the pale, featureless face and did not linger to hear the cry, but pounded back toward the jungle and safety. *If he could lead them away from Cox and the old man*, he thought, *and if he could put distance between himself and the Krail, maybe they would all stand a chance.* It was a vain and futile hope, and Paige knew that it was vain and futile, but it was all he had. The first green leaves beckoned.

The needle stung his back, and he grunted with pain. Another caught him in the neck, a third in the leg. A slow, burning warmth diffused up his body and into his shoulders and neck and head. He ran on unsubstantial footing, he balanced in null-G, toppling slowly. His eyes went wet and sandy and there was a ringing in his ears. Somewhere a hard, controlled voice gave an order, while the ground came slowly up to meet him, tasting sweat and salt. Then there was nothing left of Tom Paige but his head and his two hands and his blind, wet eyes as the Krail sedation took over.

Chapter II

He was lying on a cold surface. His head pounded and his face felt swollen and sore. He was vaguely aware that there was someone near, several people, in fact; but although he could hear their questions, he was unable to answer them rationally. Their faces were pale blurs, snow faces. Their boots were solid and real.

After a long while someone asked him—or at least he thought someone asked him, he couldn't be sure—where it hurt, and he remembered laughing, or thought he did, and then his face was wet. He licked the salty moisture greedily. Thirst had dried him out, crisped him, delicately dusted his nostrils and the mucosa inside his throat. Gentle hands probed his side painfully.

"*Duli,* where does it give you the most trouble?" asked the soft, feminine voice, and he answered obediently, in drug-slurred Eisernai, "The sixth intercostal, maybe, down to about the ninth . . ." Or thought he had said it, or dreamed he had. Nothing was certain any more but the consuming thirst. He thought he saw old Jorn, snickering and clapping until they killed him; but when he blinked his sandy eyes open, he was alone in a small monastic cell, lying on the stone floor. His hands were tied behind him, the fingers prickled and numbed. His shoes and shirt were gone and his ribs had been taped firmly, a professional job. He inhaled deeply, experimentally. There was almost no pain.

He maneuvered with chest and knees until he could sit up, but he came up too fast. Vertigo made his head swim, knotted his stomach. He held on until his vision began to black out; then he lowered his forehead to the cold stone floor and slowly, gratefully, stretched out full-length, waiting for the seizure to subside.

The flagging he lay on had a damp and earthy smell, the dust of centuries and bits of time settled through the ages, the musk of generations of Shimshenli who had paced the narrow cell through numberless dawnings, chanting their age-old jubilation. He recalled mere phrases, disjointed and meaningless:

". . . but the Day is come with a ringing of gongs . . . let the children be decked with flowers . . . for the Day, the glory of Tadae, is here . . ."

The Einai were great ones for the beating of small drums and the chiming of thousands of tiny bells. Their religious ceremonies, few and precise, were filled with the ringing.

There was a ringing in his ears too, a blurring of his vision, and Paige surrendered himself to the lassitude of the drug and lay quietly on the ancient flagging, waiting for whatever would happen next.

About mid-afternoon a small group of Krail entered the cell. They were alike, as were all Krail: tall, lean-muscled to the point of gauntness, and very fair. Their uniforms were black, the hair of their heads yellow-white, fine and thick; their eyes were ice-blue. It was said of them that they had no souls, and Paige, having doctored many of their victims, was prepared to believe it.

From his vantage point on the stone floor, they seemed vastly tall and ominous. Perhaps it was the drug. Surely, the drug. One of the younger Krail crossed to Paige and stood looking down at him.

"Behold the enemy," he said softly. The Krail never shouted, never raised their voices even in anger, or in battle. "Behold what protects a planet."

The others laughed softly, and one of the older men stepped forward. He wore the twin-star emblem on his wrist and when he spoke, the others fell silent.

"Earthlik. Where is the Han?"

Han? Paige frowned. The word kept popping up from unexpected places. First Cox, then Mennon, and somewhere in his drug-dream, someone else had wanted—very badly, too!—to know about the Han. The drug threatened to claim him again, and he shook his head to clear it.

The young Krail dispassionately kicked him in the face and Paige's teeth met through his lip; still, he made no sound, but lay there breathing raggedly, his eyes tightly shut.

"Pay attention, animal," the youngster said softly. "Beq nom-Pau speaks."

62

To hell with you, Charlie, Paige raged inside his mind. *Now I wish I knew something to keep from you.*

There was the faint 'shush' of boots on stone and Paige tensed, but there was only the cold sound of water running into a container just outside in the corridor, filling to a bubbled overflowing that gurgled down the drain. Paige swallowed once, convulsively, and shuddered.

"Earthlik."

He opened his eyes to the ice-and-crystal man who towered impossibly above him, the metal cup in his hand beaded sweetly with a trembling cool sweat. The Krail's brows lifted a notch, and he squatted next to Paige and proffered the cup.

"Will you drink?" The question was quiet and civil.

Paige's mind, numbed by the drug, moved slowly, mulling this new turn of events; and Beq nom-Pau, mistaking his dullness for suspicion, sipped from the cup himself. He smiled mirthlessly, showing long, blue-white teeth.

"You see? No poison." He offered the cup again. Paige drained it clumsily and lay back, immediately soaked with sweat. He indicated the cup with a lift of his chin. "Why?" His head cleared a bit and he was almost able to think.

"Perhaps you are a Han. We have need of Han talents."

Paige chuckled bitterly. "The Han are a bunch of fairy tales, a—a superstition, a legend. You're wasting your time. What would I know about your 'Han'?"

Beq nom-Pau smiled again. "Of course." He turned to hand the cup to a subordinate, and Paige seized his chance. A quick block (remembered from more athletic days on Earth) bowled the Krail commander over, sprawled him off-balance on the flagging. Paige twisted his hands around, ignoring the bite of the ropes, and grabbed the viith from the Krail's boot scabbard. He slashed at his bonds and was free in split seconds, lunging on his knees for the open door; but the youngster's knee caught him squarely in the mouth. There was an explosion of fireworks inside his head as another Krail struck him behind the head with the butt of his needler, and Paige went down like felled beef. The youngster, Charvin, hauled him to his feet and brought his arm up behind him to steady and immobilize him. Beq nom-Pau, patiently dusting himself off, laughed. Softly.

"Did you learn anything, *duli?*" Paige made no answer,

but stood there trying to keep his balance. Beq nom-Pau persisted, "Do you have a name, Earthlik? Or do we go on calling you *'duli'*?"

Paige licked his split lip and said tiredly, "Paige". His right eye was slowly swelling shut and he squinted at Beq nom-Pau through it, wishing desperately for the chance to square off with him, just the two of them with no gallery to lend aid and assistance.

Nom-Pau nodded acknowledgment of the name. "Now you will tell us, if you please, Paige, how you came by the *crux* we found in your medikit, and where you have hidden the Han woman. In return, I will answer any question you may wish to ask." *From the questions, I may derive answers of my own.* "No more of, ah . . ." He flicked away the attack with a gesture graceful for its brevity. "Agreed?"

There was no agreement in the Earthling's battered face or in the stubborn line of his body. Beq nom-Pau had not really expected an agreement, nor had he invited a truce; but a commitment could possibly have been useful.

Paige licked his lip. *Answers, eh? Well, he could do with a few answers. He'd been plunged into this Han-hunt along with Cox and Jorn and Mennon, and now the Krail, everyone searching for one lone Han, who happened to be a woman. Why? What made the Han—if there were such things as Han—so special? And what did it have to do with the destruction of Allampaila?* His head spun.

"Allampaila. Two weeks ago." Barely a whisper.

Allampaila. Beq nom-Pau was vaguely amused. How quickly a man's deeds follow him, he thought. He remembered with a keen satisfaction the plume of white smoke as Allampaila's great library went up like a crash of cymbals, all books, all ancient scrolls, all useless colored smears on whitebark and jatskin and canvas, all gone. At the command of Beq nom-Pau.

To destroy a nation, a Krail sage had written, *one need merely destroy its reverence for its gods, its arts and its aged; the rest will take care of itself.* Not difficult, theoretically; in practice, a perplexing task.

It had been impossible to make the Einai forsake their aged; the honor they did their old ones was inconceivable to the Krail mind.

And their art was intrinsic to the Einai nature. It was a pathetic Einai indeed who could not conceive life in a few strokes of charcoal, or make a canvas breathe at the flick of a brush.

They carried their gods in their consciences, making of themselves temples.

The Krail found that it was impossible to separate these green-gold upstarts from their treasures; so they did the next best thing. They bombed the storehouses of the arts, destroyed the poem-scrolls, divested the religious of their heads, and therefore of their gods. They turned the aged out to fend for themselves, and left them to die. Still Eisernon fought bitterly on; but the Krail had an insatiable lust for Empire, and they intended to win this war or destroy everything else along with themselves. *And we will win*, Beq nom-Pau thought, *gazing down at the arrogant Earthling, if it takes a thousand cities like Allampaila.*

"I know nothing of Allampaila," he said at last, and Paige, blotting his mouth with the back of his free wrist, stared back insolently at the lie and the liar.

"Of course," he replied, aping the Krail's tone exactly, and Beq nom-Pau betrayed his first sign of emotion, a subtle freezing in the lines of the thin, fair face, a chill passing over his gaunt frame. His tone remained civil.

"The *crux*. Where did it come from? And where is the woman?"

Paige licked his lip. "Jorn. The old man your boys killed"—he felt a surge of rage and frustration—"the helpless old cripple your warriors managed to subdue"—Charvin tightened his arm, and with it, his voice—"he carved it. As far as any woman—or a Han, if there are any such things as Han—I don't know anything about them."

Beq nom-Pau toyed absently with the twin-star emblem on his wrist. "And yet," he murmured, studying it carefully, "how strange that you would destroy all your records, if you had nothing to hide from us. Surely you had received your orders, you had no reason to distrust us."

"Perish forbid," Paige retorted drily, and Charvin twisted the arm sharply, making him catch his breath.

Beq nom-Pau was beginning to look bored. "You're certain you have nothing you wish to tell us, Paige?"

Paige hesitated. They were ready to kill him, he knew,

or to break his mind with torture. He had to buy time, to get away alone, even to the relative privacy of a cell, and think of a way out of here. And never, under any circumstances, must he let them know about Mennon, and the girl he had called Mishli.

"If you found the woman, what then?"

Nom-Pau's face flashed up, a glint of something feral and triumphant in the ice-blue eyes before he masked it. Behind him Charvin tensed.

"Why—nothing," Beq nom-Pau answered mildly. "We wish to ask a few questions, no more than that."

"You wouldn't harm her?"

"The Han are extremely valuable, Paige. Of course we wouldn't harm her."

Paige blotted his mouth again and laughed.

"Too bad I can't help you."

And for the first time, Beq nom-Pau struck him savagely, in anger.

When Paige could no longer stand, Charvin held him up, until the commander stepped back, spent and perspiring, his anger gone. Charvin let him go and Paige crumpled to the floor and did not move. Beq nom-Pau studied him for a long moment, regaining his composure, conscious of the cold, questioning eyes of his men; then he prodded Paige roughly onto his back with his boot.

"Charvin. See if he is dead."

The aide squatted next to the body and felt for the pulses in the throat. "He lives, Commander." He rose. "They say it is difficult to kill the Han."

Beq nom-Pau watched Paige, who was showing signs of coming around. No, this was no Han. The elusive gray-eyed telepaths would never have defied him, but would have other, more subtle means of attack. Paige was no Han; but he was brave to the point of stupidity, in the Krail's estimation, and admirably stubborn. When that was properly broken—

He must remember to have Charvin add Paige to his personal slave list, if it were not necessary to kill him first. He nudged Paige with his boot, kicked him lightly.

"Paige. Where is the Han who gave you the *crux*?" Paige made a smothered moan and shook his head. *No.* The commander lifted his brows. "Water, Paige. Cold water, and a medic for your cuts. It's only a name, Paige.

66

What harm can a name do?" His voice was low and monotonous, sleepy, a susurration of cadence and syllable, carefully trained in persuasion. "Cold water sliding down the throat, Paige, remember? It's only a name."

Paige rolled over and drew a breath that whistled past bleeding mouth and broken teeth. He dragged himself to his hands and knees and, lifting his head with an obvious effort, looked straight into Beq nom-Pau's face—and spat. It was rather an unsuccessful attempt but it made its point, and the commander's frosty smile faded quickly into fury.

"Paige!"—as to an unruly dog—"Heel!"

Then he let go of Charvin's arm.

Paige awoke sometime before dawn, in the damp, chill-smelling hours that under certain circumstances make stones and men weep. He tried again to get up, but his bunched, knotted muscles persuaded him to lie where he was. The darkness of his cell was thin and bitter, and tasted of blood and defeat.

Then he saw what had awakened him: a narrow band of light, a mere lessening of the blackness, level with his head. Inches away?—Miles? He tried to focus his aching eyes. Featherstep telegraphed through eons of stone corridor, mothtouch hovered at deaf door. Warm light waxed yellow under the door, wavered across the stone floor and stopped just short of him. Paige gathered himself for yet another onslaught of Krail persuasion. He promised himself that this time he would either escape or die, although he had no illusions as to which of these alternatives was more probable. At least he could gain a clean and honorable exit; the thought of lying here—drummed into mindless obedience, flogged into senseless cooperation—turned his stomach. Better to die swiftly and have done with it, while he was still his own man.

The door swung quickly, open, shut, and a heavily hooded-and-cloaked figure dropped down beside him, laying a small hand across his broken mouth. He winced involuntarily.

"Sh! We're going to get you out of here. Can you stand?"

He nodded briefly and hauled himself up painfully on one elbow. Immediately, his rescuer leaned down to help him with small, strong hands, and he realized that it was a woman. She got him unsteadily to his feet while the candlelight licked walls, lapped looming shadows, danced gargoyles across the ceiling. Paige put out a hand for balance against the unsubstantial wall. (It would have been hard enough for him to see, even had the light been excellent; for one eye was cemented almost shut with drying blood from a cut above it. He was afraid he'd lost the sight in the other.) The wavering candlelight made an already difficult situation nearly impossible. He stumbled and she slipped a slender arm around him, letting him lean heavily on her shoulder.

"Sorry," he mumbled. "I can't see—very well."

"Let me help you," she whispered. "The passageway is here—only a few steps more."

There was the muffled, sandy rumble of stone against stone, and a current of warm, wet air, an exhalation redolent of river and leaf-mold and morning, eddied around him. Far down the corridor, a Krail sentry laughed, his voice carrying lightly on the (soft!) pre-dawn air. The entryway grumbled shut behind them, and they were in a narrow alley between the inner and outer walls of the monastery. The long, angled passages made her voice rebound with strange, metallic overtones, like a small and perfect bell.

"These passages are as old as Time," she sang. *Ime, iim, iii,* sang the echo. "But only the Shimshenli—and a few fugitives know them.

She took his arm reassuringly and tugged him along; and after a moment he stumbled after her of his own accord, because there was nothing else he could do.

The room was small and clean and had rugged, metal-strapped wooden doors and several low windows opening onto dense brush outside. River water gurgled thirstily a few yards beyond and Paige fancied that he heard the cool splash of a fish jumping. His wounds throbbed dully and he lay there listening, and let them hurt, while the woman made busy glass-and-metal noises in the anteroom and the filtered light turned from black to gray. Then, high above in the monastery, the chanting began, as it had begun every dawn in the memory of man:

"Make a loud sound, the clapping of hands and the beating on drums, sounds of gladness to Tadae . . ."

Paige lifted his aching head from the thin mattress to the comparative luxury of his arm. Monastery. Riversound. Chants. He was alive. *Make a sound of gladness to Tadae, I'm alive.* Not a trap, after all. At least, not yet.

"*. . . for see, in the East, the sun shows his face. Play on the chukuri, all ye Shimshenli, cause the uala to flee the trees with a beating of wings AND loud cries. For the night has gone . . .*"

The door opened quietly and there were soft footfalls on the flagging; she closed his fingers around a metal goblet filled with a mixture of mung and pij juices. While he drank the sweet, pulpy liquid, she brought a pitcher and towels (ah, the circular music of a bumped basin!) and began bathing his lacerated face. The water had a faintly medicinal odor and immediately started to draw the soreness out of his stiffened cuts. The mung juice relaxed him, smoothed spasms and resolved knots of muscle into sleepy aches. Relieved, he took a welcome deep breath, opened his eyes—and saw! He could see!—even if the left eye blurred a bit, and danced with a radiant arc. *Swollen optic disc*, said the didactic little voice inside his head. *Nothing much to worry about.* He could see!

Far off, the chanting—monosyllabic in cadence, and in minor key where the cadence broke—continued:

"*. . . the eyes of Tadae have watched us through the darkness, but behold, the day is come with a ringing of golden gongs . . .*"

But Paige did not hear it; for now he could see the woman who had rescued him. And she was beautiful.

Translucent gold-green skin, almond gray-gold eyes, hair like dark music falling from her crown. The sleek sweep of the slope from rounded chin to smooth cheekbone left no doubt as to her alien-cat ancestry, a gift of the Einai. The even, white teeth, locked tightly behind parted lips, were human and compassionate. Paige breathed deeply.

"You're one of the Shimshenli?"

She nodded, carefully applying a towel to his cheek, where purpled bone had taken the blow meant for the eye.

"Charvin has heavy boots, *duli*." It was a quiet statement of fact, no sloppy sentiment, and Paige's estimation of her character went up another notch. Her voice was familiar. *Where does it give you the most trouble, duli?*

69

"You were here—with me—before—weren't you?"

"Yes." She changed the compress and added, ruefully, "So was Charvin."

"Charvin." The vicious Krail youngster. He tried a grin and thought better of it. "I thought those boots tasted familiar."

She dimpled and turned away quickly to discipline her smile. "You musn't joke about this, my friend," she told him soberly. "You're in terrible trouble with the commander."

Paige held the compress to his face. "I think I can get up now, if you'll give me a hand." He sat up slowly with the help of the little shimshen, and felt he had scored some kind of a triumph. At least he was vertical, if unsteady, and he sat shakily on the edge of the cot, grateful for the support of the stone wall behind him. She brought the basin closer and resumed her repair of his cuts as they talked. He watched her mobile lips with growing interest.

"So I'm in trouble with the commander. What's he going to do—have his hoods beat me up?" Her hands paused and she gave him a reproachful look.

"He was going to have you killed at the outpost," she confided, "but then—(I'm sorry, did that hurt you? There, that's better)—then they saw the *crux*—" she inclined her head reverently "—in your kit and decided to bring you here."

"What's a *crux*?"

Her eyes widened. "You must know what it is. I thought you . . . Dao might've given . . ." She started again, her face pale. "Please, *duli*—how did you come by the carving that was in your medikit?"

Paige stiffened suspiciously. "Why?" It would be like the Krail to use such tender and innocent bait.

Her eyes swam and she shook her dark head, as though hearing his thoughts. "I—I'm sorry, *duli*. I thought—you might've gotten the *crux* from—someone I know." Her eyes spilled over, gold on gold, and she wrung another cloth out of the basin, but Paige stopped her. His cuts were far less painful than his confusion—or her grief.

"From the beginning," he ordered.

"The *crux* saved you," she began, and Paige thought, strange word, *crux*. Like the old word for—

"A cross!" he blurted, catching her by the hands. "That's it, isn't it? The bent cross with the serpent on it! That's a *crux!*"

She retrieved her hands so gently he was scarcely aware of it. "It's the Han 'mercy' symbol, like your staff-and-serpents."

That's it, Jorn, Paige thought, *that was your delicious secret, your repayment. Safe passage, in case the Krail came. An eye for an eye. And a life for a life.* His eyes smarted and he began to laugh, a hurt, whimpering laugh that was mindful of his lacerated mouth. "My God," he choked, "I'm not even Jewish."

After a moment, while she watched him demurely, he blotted his face with the towel and prompted, "So the Krail thought I was a Han."

"You had the *crux.* What else could they think?"

"And what do you think?"

She turned to him, golden and damp, her lashes dark fringe on her cheeks, her brows upswept wings. At this close range, he could see the thoughts swimming like bright fish, golden flecks, in her serene gray eyes. "I think," she said at last, "that you are not a Han."

He marvelled at the fluid syllables formed by rounded throat and mobile lips. Lovely language, Eisernai, when spoken properly. Beautiful. The sun lines deepened at the corners of his eyes.

"I'm not a Han," he replied absently.

"And I think, too," she continued, "that we shall help each other get away from here. You to an Earthling base, and I—" her face softened "—I to Sum ChiT'ath."

"I take it there's something important to you—at Sum ChiT'ath?" Her smile was slow and introspective.

"*Everything*—that is important to me—is at Sum Chi-T'ath."

Beq nom-Pau stood motionless on the battlements of the monastery, the soft dawn breeze buffeting his cheek and rippling his tunic. He had been standing there patiently for almost an hour, knowing that the duli's cell was empty and that only the Han he sought could have helped him. A search of the monastery would have proven futile; nom-Pau knew enough of these Einai to understand that

71

he could have searched a thousand days and not found them, right under his hand.

So he had permitted them to escape, to taste the sweetness of being free, of feeling safe, the relaxation of letting down their defenses, while all during the night, even before the hoped-for escape, he had sent out patrols to establish themselves along the trails and high in the trees; for while it would be simpler to apprehend the fugitives outright (as they stepped out of the old wall-door, for instance) there were the Han to think of. The only way to catch a Han was to spring quickly, before he knew what he was about, and render him unconscious; otherwise one could suffer unexpected results. There were stories, rumors, only, but grave, about once-fine Krail warriors writhing and frothing under Han anger, while no hand touched them; or men suddenly glowing, shrieking, and bursting into myraid scintillating sparks that fell as gentle ashes. Such were the Han's mental powers reputed to be.

Beq nom-Pau shifted his weight uneasily. One need not believe these childish tales to know that the Han were not to be trusted. He gestured for Charvin, who appeared at his elbow wearing his throatset.

"By your leave, Commander?"

"Where are they now?"

He calculated quickly. "Approaching the clearing beyond the grove, Commander. Mathematical odds highly favoring a wish to rest."

"Contact the patrols. Begin closing in. I want them both alive."

Charvin saluted slickly and was gone, and Beq nom-Pau, remaining on the ancient parapet, permitted himself a cold smile at the thought of what prestige the capture of a live Han would afford him, and at the chagrin of his friend and associate, Neron Vartik.

By midmorning, the heat was heavy and oppressive. Trails had become tracks, and then paths, and finally had deteriorated into native bush country, densely grown with thorn trees and memlikti webs. For the last two hours the going had become increasingly difficult, for the saber grass was waist high and abounded with insect and other life.

Now Paige and the Shimshen emerged at the edge of an open glen, a natural hollow, rush-floored and mucky,

72

sparsely carpeted with purple flowers that floated lazily on the brack and gave off a thick, sweetish odor. The sun glittered on the needles of a gopher thicket and across the clearing a crystal tree shattered the light into a million colored splinters that riddled the eyes.

Paige paused, unbuttoning his borrowed shirt and blotting his forehead with the crook of his arm. There were dark maps of sweat on his ribs and along his backbone, and he saw that the Shimshen, too, tugged uncomfortably at the neckline of her coarse, peasant-boy's tunic. Tight tendrils of curly, newly-cropped hair hugged her forehead and stuck to her damp neck. The sun beat down, and there was silence.

There had been an abandoned railroad depot near Gram's house, Paige remembered, *with the rustymetal tracks singing silently to themselves under the molten sun, running off to nowhere anymore, and the weeds a dusty spume of green and the smell of tar and diesel oil and nostalgia drifting up from the rotting wooden ties . . . And the sun. And the silence.*

"Duli?" Earth hung suspended in the amber of a golden accent.

"We'd better rest for a while," he suggested, and they relaxed, Paige easing his stiff muscles down to the damp forest floor, and she sliding her back down a rock and plopping softly like a child, puffing out her cheeks in a smiling, weary expression that made him grin. "Just like a little kid," he scoffed, until the wide-set, fringed eyes glanced up at him reproachfully. *Not a kid, after all.* He picked up a twig and absently dug at the ground. The smell of chlorophyll—or what passed for it on Eisernon—was warm and drowsy. The Shimshen yawned behind her hand.

"What made you become a nun?" he asked abruptly, stumbling over the word 'nun' because it had no counterpart in Eisernai, and he had to say 'woman-who-promises-eternal-virginity-to-worship-Tadae'. She cocked her head to one side (the uptilted brows, eyes, ears, gave her an elfin look), and frowned.

"But I am not one of those. How could you think so?"

"Well, isn't a Shimshen . . . I mean, I've always thought the Shimshenli were . . ." He broke the twig in half and tossed part of it away. "I don't know, I . . . just

73

thought so," he finished lamely. *But if she is not a nun—* A hundred wild hopes danced in his head and chest.

She brightened. "Is an Erthlikli Shimshen called 'sister'? Yes?" she asked, trying to understand. "Because I once met an Erthlik officer and he called me 'sister' and the Abbess 'mother'; and after he was gone she studied the files for hours, trying to remember if she had borne him. But she had not."

He broke the twig again, with great deliberation, feeling the muscles sliding across the bones of his forearms, the sinews slipping inside his hands. "Then you are allowed to marry. Even if you are a Shimshen."

"Yes." For a moment, even the forest was breathless.

"In the beginning," she continued quietly, "before the Earthlik returned, there were many who feared for the quality of life of Eisernon, that it would diminish and we would become like the gameli, biting and clawing for space to live. And many women refused to bear their children, and said, 'I have children enough, let this one die.' And even the Priyamli, at that time, were forced to let them die, for it was our law, and the infants couldn't live outside the womb.

"But then there were many Holy Women—possibly much like your eternal-virgins-for-Tadae—who came forward and offered themselves for the unwanted children, and bore them. And these were the first of the Shimshenli. Afterward, others came forward, or were consecrated to Life. But all who wear the Blue Face must bear any child whose natural mother will not or cannot."

He gazed out unseeing over the clearing. "And the children?"

"Have gone to the stars," she answered simply.

"The monsters? The biological accidents?"

There was a long quiet, and the forest drowsed in the midday heat. She made no answer, and he turned to her and saw that she was absorbed in the progress of an insect, quite a large beetle, that was trundling up one side of her hand and down the other, endlessly. It was an ugly creature and looked as if it might have been poisonous.

"Rhysbeetle," she murmured. "For centuries they were considered useless, even a plague; for the new larvae devoured the crops every twenty-five years. Then a young Priyam by the name of Oman Shari-Mnenoplan discov-

74

ered that by studying these creatures, he could correlate research information he had compiled on a totally different problem, and come forth with answers. He studied them with love, as fellow creatures of Tadae, and that gave him great patience." She smiled at him. "Five years after Priyam Shari-Mnenoplan began to love the rhysbeetle, he found the cure for Jaffee's disease. The answer for one problem lay within the larvae of another."

"Typical Einai answer," Paige grumbled in Earthenglish. "Artistic construction of tangents and red herrings."

Her face turned upward, *pale metal sunflower tracking sound-source.* "Listen!"

One smooth motion brought him crouched, alert, every nerve singing, alive. The forest was so still he fancied he could hear the molecules bombarding his eardrums, valves sliding in his veins, lids snicking swiftly, open, shut, over his eyes. There was nothing. "I don't hear—"

She laid her fingers lightly over his mouth, still listening. "Uala," she whispered, and then he could hear them, too, the labored sculling of wings, the shrill cries of the big, clumsy, butter-yellow birds. Several of them lifted awkwardly from a grove of thorn trees about a hundred yards away and wheeled uncertainly.

"Krail." The word tasted sour in his mouth.

"It's me they want," she said dully. "If I surrender now, you can go free."

"No way, lady. They want me. They think I'm a Han, remember? Look, Bex-Elakli is only about fifteen or twenty miles farther on. If we should get separated, I'll meet you there." She nodded mutely. "Come on."

He snatched her hand and they ran, plunging out into the open, down the near side of the glen, making no effort to hide their presence. The Krail were too close for that, so close they could hear metal jingle, orders snap, heels thud behind them. They slid on the slippery rushes and plunged into the marshy ooze, knee-high and treacherous, splashing, wading, scrambling, wet, he lost her hand and grabbed it again, jerking her up from her knees, and towed her, floundering, to the other side just as the Krail charged noisily—wordlessly—through the trees and into the clearing. Paige stopped abruptly, shoving her ahead of him with all his might, a peculiar expression striking his face cold.

"Bex-Elakli," he repeated hoarsely. "Run!" She scrambled up the incline under the branches of the crystal trees, stumbling on prisms, and gained level ground at last. Paige was not with her.

The Shimshen glanced back. *Total image, landscape painted indelibly on the retina, of mellow sunlight and warm wind, bobbing bright flowerheads and Krail in black boots and needlers, frozen for an instant against the subtle browns and reds of thornbush and jasmin; while there in the hollow, still standing knee-deep in hyacinths, the duli gazed up with aching white face and blazing eyes*—then time ticked, hearts resumed beating, and the duli shouted savagely again, *"Run!"*

Reluctantly, she ran.

"Halt!" The voice was sharp, male, and carried the harsh Krail accent. Hennem-mishli stopped dead, afraid to breathe. *I'm old,* she thought desperately, winding the illusion about her, spinning the dream, *I'm old, old, old, with sunken eyes and cheeks like winter leaves and sparse hair touched with early frost . . .*

Hard footsteps waded through low fern growth behind her, a needler barrel jabbed the small of her back. She turned slowly, careful of her arthritic bones, her knobby, fragile joints, to face the Krail soldier. He frowned, glanced around, rubbed his eyes and frowned at her again.

"I thought—that is, I thought you were . . ." He straightened, his tone firming. "There was a young woman, dressed as a boy, who ran through here just now. Where did she go?"

Hennem-mishli shook her head dumbly, champing toothless gums.

"A woman," he persisted. "A young girl. Here, don't be afraid—" He reached into his pouch and brought out a sweetmeat, offering it to her. Hennem-mishli responded as an old peasant would. She backed away unsteadily, shaking her head and making the Infinity sign several times over her wrinkled forehead and wasted breast. Feigning fear, she pointed shakily to the road leading to Bex-Elakli. There were Earthlikli in Bex-Elakli, she reminded herself. Earthlik soldiers. They would be happy to direct him—

somewhere. He nodded his thanks and started off at a dogtrot, speaking a few low words into the air. After a moment's hesitation there were other footsteps, clipped monosyllables, the clink of metal, fading off into the forest. She stood motionless until they were gone, and for a long time afterward.

A bird twittered far overhead and an uala cried. She relaxed, her features filling and smoothing, her colorless eyes resuming their clear, even gray. Puffing out a relieved breath, she smiled to herself with white, even teeth and ran her hands through her cropped, black curls. It had been a hard disguise, hastily done. A little while longer and the Krail might have seen through it. She couldn't wait to tell them at the hospital what she had done. Dao would laugh and hug her close and perhaps even give her a little spank for daring it; her grandfather would merely peer humorously at her from the corners of his slanted eyes and chuckle. But they would be proud, both of them.

Picking a pij from an inner branch where they grew the juciest, she munched on it hungrily and started off cross-country for the road that would bring her to Sum Chi-T'ath.

It made a picture, the broad sweep of sunset-tinted water with thousands of small swords of rice reflecting blackly in its shallow expanse. Across the paddy, a silhouette of a peasant girl drove the silhouette of a low-horned bos toward the reed chisei in back of what must have served as a farmhouse. The hut was small and poor, but the smell of the evening meal wafted hungrily on the soft wind and made Hennem-mishli's stomach writhe. She sank wearily down on a grassy hummock and rubbed her sore feet. She was tired and hungry and unbelievably dirty. Two days of solitary travel through the fern forest avoiding Krail patrols, and two nights of fitful dozing crouched in treetops, did nothing for the muscles, not to mention the disposition.

It was lucky, she mused, that she'd come upon this place out in the middle of nowhere; it would soon be night and d'injit would be roaming in packs. There were no tall trees for cover here in this immense glen, not even ferns tall enough to climb. Certainly nothing like the towering conifers at home. She allowed herself a brief pang of homesickness for the high country of Pal Alden

Shali-Rho, for the pavilion she and Dao had shared so briefly, and for the chalk cliffs, sparkling with ice; then she stood up, brushed herself off, and started resolutely down toward the farmhouse.

At the back of the house, which faced steep hills and deeper fern forest, the man Asa stood stripped to the waist, washing himself cautiously. He had to be careful of his body. Today there had been several more hemorrhages under the skin of his legs; great blue-green bruises ached at his calves and swelled his thighs. Because he'd been born with the Bleeding Sickness, he expected this, just as he expected to die younger than his more fortunate friends, as his father and grandfather had died before him. His grandfather, who'd been in his prime when the Erthlikli returned, had farmed these very paddies, had seen the fireballs born over cities that now were only Glass Lakes where children skated.

After the fireballs' unholy winds and thunder, as from Quel himself, the rains came, months early, dark and ashen; and because he was a rice farmer and the crop needed planting, the grandfather and his sons had worked in that rain, knee-deep in the flourishing paddy. They had sickened. Some of them died.

Asa's father, being stronger than the others, lived long enough to produce several sons. Of these, Asa survived to adulthood, for gene-borne radiation was slow and deliberate in the Einai. Instead of a relatively swift death, such as Earthlikli endured under the same circumstances, an Einai with Bleeding Sickness lingered on and on, producing offspring that carried the same fatal gene in a fifty-percent ratio, and, grown weaker over the years, finally did himself and everyone else the favor of dying.

Asa wasn't afraid to die. Everything died, in its time. But he was afraid, and mortally so, of leaving his wife and daughter to the mercy of the Earthlikli or worse, the Krail. With money, they could escape when he died, could go to the fortress-like monastery to the south, where the Shimshenli would take them in. They would be cared for, would work for the Lifebearers, cooking and scrubbing and baking hennem-cakes on holidays. It would be like home.

But for that dream to become reality, Asa needed money. The Shimshenli would ask nothing for their help

78

and protection; but it was a long way to the monastery. His wife and daughter would need to buy food and lodging, and perhaps even (the thought chilled him) bribe thieves or soldiers to leave them safely alone. It was for this that Asa had sold his entire bos herd but one old cow, planted more paddies than he had strength to tend, and stashed his small savings away in the traditional hiding place no outworlder could hope to find. Now if he could find a hired man to help him with the extra work load—

The boy who came around the edge of the house was a mirage; a wish walking; the hand of Tadae. He was small but seemed healthy, Asa thought, and was, in the manner of boys, probably strong for his size. Also, his smile was friendly.

"Is this your house, chom-shan?" The tone was respectful. No one had ever addressed Asa as 'good sir' before and it made him glow a bit. Clearly this boy was a superior fellow. He put down the coarse brown towel and nodded solemnly. "It is my house."

"I wonder—" the long lashes dropped shyly "—I wonder if you would let me sleep here for the night—" he pointed quickly "—in the bos-barn, not in the house? I'll gladly work my way."

Asa turned this over in his mind and answered carefully, as if delivering a prepared speech. He spoke seldom, as a rule, and when he found it necessary to communicate, he generally looked upon it as an Occasion, and treated it as such. "We are honest people." He paused, and continued slowly, "We do not sleep humans in bos-barns like an Erthlik god. If you will work hard, I will let you stay and feed you with my family, even for many days."

"Only one day, chom-shan. I am on a journey."

Asa spoke slowly. "When the rice is planted, then you will go. Or go now." He picked up a wooden pail such as farmers used for milking bos, and silently offered it to Hennem-mishli. *Choose*, it said. You can't have it both ways. Out in the darkening forest a d'injit barked, and was answered in chorused yaps and howls. The stars sprang out like the many eyes of the legend, and Hennem-mishli considered the suicide of returning to a night-time forest. The d'injit yapped again, and she sighed, accepting the pail resignedly.

"My name is Ilen," she said.

The days passed easily, each the same as the one before it, blurring together at the edges. Ilen woke in the early morning hush and chanted her Jubilation, then stole quietly down the ladder and washed up outside before making her way down to the chisei to milk the heavy-bodied, split-hooved bos that only slightly resembled its Erthlikli ancestors. The Brahman cattle that had been imported to improve native m'lis herds had produced a hump-backed, low-horned work beast whose patient labor was worth ten motocats here in the outback. Splayed hooves plodded steadily on where metal-and-plastex treads would have broken down.

Mutants, Ilen thought soberly, swinging the pail a bit. That's what we all are. Changelings. She remembered her disguise of a few afternoons gone and smiled, biting her underlip. At least in her case, as with the bos, mutation served a useful purpose.

A furtive figure sidling past the chisei made her stop short, unmoving. There—and there. She leaned back into the dimness of the edge of the house and watched. Asa's daughter, a plain, lank-haired girl some years her senior, was stealing toward the house from the direction of the forest. But—the forest? At night? Ilen stepped into the light. "Good morning, *benklif*."

The girl jumped as if shot. "I didn't do nothing wrong," she whispered fiercely, defensively, throwing a frightened glance in the direction of the house. "You can't prove nothing."

Ilen swung the bucket idly. "I'm on my way to milk the bos," she offered. "All I see are the wind-ripples on the water, and the high white clouds in the sky, and the sun coming up over the forest."

The girl relaxed a trifle and tried a rusty smile. "I'll walk with you."

The *splish, splish, splish* of milk into milk made a sleepy sound inside the cobwebbed chisei. Fingers of early sunlight probed the spaces between the reeds of the wall and the fragrance of fresh hay was sweet and dusty and made Ilen sneeze.

"I love him," Asa's gaunt daughter said unexpectedly from her seat on a roll of hay, twisting a few strands of it in her work-weathered hands. Ilen was fascinated by

80

those hands: large for the rest of her, work-weathered and coarse, with knobby knuckles and broad palms, it was as though she had put on a pair of ugly gloves, and could shed them when she wished. *Splish, splish*, went the milk into the silence. "His family used to have a farm just over the hill, there. Raised a little hennem, not much, it's bad land. Had a mung orchard. We used to swim, down the way, when we's little; there's a pond, trees. You know?"

"I know." *Swim? We swam too, Dao and I, from the deck of the sleek ship Dao and Kles had helped the workmen build; swam out beyond the peach-and-gold shallows, with the chalk cliffs looming above us, glittering. He, like a young god, golden and white-laughing in the sunlight, and I? His eyes said all I ever needed to hear.*

Splish, splish, went the milk into the filling pail.

"You got to promise you won't tell, Ilen."

"I won't tell."

"I'm going off with him. He's gonna take me away, maybe even to Bex-Elakli, or—or—" her mind searched for grander horizons "—to Pal Alden Shali-Rho!"

Ilen said slowly, "It's a long way to the Capitol."

"He promised. He said he'd take me." She leaned forward eagerly. "Can you imagine, Ilen? Me, dressed like a lady? Wearing—" she made a helpless gesture "—silks and everything?" Ilen smiled but made no answer. "You don't believe me, do you? It's because you're a boy. You don't understand. Women can *tell!*" She scooted forward on her knees, speaking in a hoarse whisper. "And we tell each other everything. Everything. He's a soldier, and he can keep secrets just like I can."

"Secrets?" Ilen asked innocently, busily stripping the bos out.

"Never you mind." Asa's daughter nodded emphatically. "Just secrets, is all. And I told him my secret." Her voice dropped to a whisper and she leaned so close that Ilen could smell sour tarangi on her breath. "My father's got something hid away. Plenty of something. And I know where it is. 'Course—" she knelt back, lifting her brows condescendingly, "everybody knows *that;* but everybody never looked under the ashes, now, did they?" She laughed uncomfortably. "It turns up gone, now, we'll know who took it, won't we?"

"I'm very honest, *benklif*. I have never stolen money."

"You just better not, Ilen, if you know what's good for you. And you better not tell on me, either. Because I'll say *you* told the Krail where the money was."

Weakness tugged at Ilen's wrists. "He's with the Krail?"

"Do you think my Arv would fight with the Earthlik umbin?" She spat unprettily. "Look at my father and see what the Erthlikli do their allies! But the Krail gave Arv a uniform, and they feed him soldier food to make him strong, and one day he's gonna take me to Pal Alden Shali-Rho with him!" She got up to leave. "Don't you tell, Ilen," she warned. "Don't you ever tell!"

It never became necessary to tell.

That evening the Krail came. There was no warning. The door burst open upon their evening meal and a squad of Krail crowded into the cramped, badly-lit room. The leader gestured with a drawn sidearm.

"Stand against the wall." Shocked into stunned obedience, they all complied but Ilen, who crawled under the table and had to be dragged out by one leg, kicking and lamenting piteously in his coarse boy's voice. His captor flung him against the wall with the others, where he stood snuffling and rubbing his broad nose and big, round, yellow eyes. The leader stood before Asa, close and clean and smelling of space and death.

"Where is your money, animal?"

Asa cleared his throat. "We are honest people—"

"The money."

"I am a poor man, chom-shan, a sick man," Asa began again, and the Krail leader backhanded him with the weapon.

"You are a dead man," he corrected him. He signed his men and they began a search of the kitchen and of the rickety lean-to that served the family as a bedroom. Asa's wife moaned and wrung her hands as quilts and pottery flew, and the daughter's face lit up eagerly when an Einai, barefoot and wearing a conspicuously salvaged Krail uniform jacket and carrying a viith, entered uncertainly. He avoided the searching soldiers and followed the Krail leader closely, importantly, getting in the way as the leader took a besom of rice straw, swept the fire aside in one efficient stroke and wrestled a center stone out of the fireplace floor. It gave easily. He reached in

82

and pulled out a small homespun sack, spilling its contents onto his palm, counting it at a glance. Enough to buy a stout slave, he mused, impressed. The informer had been right. He tossed him one of the smaller cylinders—the equivalent of a coin—and stored the rest in his leather pouch.

"Why do these animals have no imagination?" he asked one of his men disgustedly. "It's always the fireplace."

Asa pulled himself up from the floor, leaning heavily on the table. "Chom-shan," he pleaded thickly, "it's everything I own."

Outside, the bos lowed uneasily, ending on a high, frantic note that cut off suddenly, and the Krail's eyes flicked to the window and back. "It is now," he agreed softly, smiling. He lifted his chin at Ilen. "How old are you, animal?"

"Three and twenty, chom-shan." He wiped spittle from his chin and neatly blew his nose on the ragged hem of his tunic. The Krail made a grimace of distaste.

"Why aren't you out fighting Earthlikli like the rest of your patriotic countrymen?" The sarcasm was lost on the dull-witted clod, who stared stupidly for a moment and slowly rolled up his sleeves and held his arms out toward the leader. The man who'd dragged Ilen out from under the table quickly wiped his hands on his trouser legs, and the leader wrinkled his face and made a sharp disclaiming gesture. Ilen slowly began rolling his sleeves down over the open sores of Storer's echthyma, a particularly virulent form of inflammatory skin disease that occurred in Einai living in rural areas. It was commonly known as 'sand sores' because of the granular encrustations it produced, and people scrupulously avoided its victims in fear of contagion. Asa's jaw dropped.

"You never said you had sand sores!" he accused bitterly, and Ilen replied stolidly, "You never asked me."

The leader signaled his men out and Arv trailed along behind them. They were hardly out of the door when the daughter broke and ran after them. "Arv," she called. "Arv, wait for me."

He paused in the middle of the road, somewhere between her and the Krail. "You can't come," he said.

"I can, too." She had thrown a few belongings into an untidy bundle and carried her father's flat, reed hat in her

83

hand. "You said we'd go away, remember? And I told you my secret, about the money."

"You can't come," he said again. "I don't want you. Go home." She put the bundle down slowly and carefully in the road, as if something might break at any moment. The corners of her mouth trembled and she caught his coat in both hands, patting and smoothing the collar and front of it.

"You *said*, Arv. Back in the forest, you said about nice things, and cities, and—and clothes . . . You *got* to take me."

"I can't." He felt uncomfortable in front of the mildly curious Krail, and kept disentangling her frantically grasping hands. He pushed her away, not ungently. "I can't," he repeated.

"You said you'd take me." She was beginning to cry, openmouthed and unbeautiful. "You said we'd go to Bex-Elakli."

"No." Just that.

She broke down and cried hard then, great, racking sobs; she clutched her belly. "I'm pregnant, Arv. It's yours. I can't stay here, you got to take me. I won't be no trouble." One of the Krail laughed softly and murmured to the leader, who laughed too, and motioned his men back the way they'd come. They started across the paddy in the summer dark, faceless apparitions disturbing starlit water. Arv hesitated.

"I can't," he said again, half-smiling, shrugging in embarrassment. "I can't." He walked away, leaving her standing there in the middle of the road with her face wet and streaming, the bundle at her feet, and her big, work-worn hands hanging down limply at her sides.

Long after their dispirited daughter had wept herself to sleep on her pallet by the door, Asa and his wife lay stiffly side by side in the tiny bedroom, listening to the night grow old. Neither of them could bring himself to speak of the Krail; the blow was too recent, too great. Nor could they discuss the coming child, or the bos that now lay dead in the rice paddy. Asa's frustration grew unbearably, an inarticulate rage that found its target sleeping above them, in the attic loft.

"He should have told me," Asa fumed impotently, his words muffled by his swollen cheek. "He should have said,

'I have sand sores'." He did not add, *chom-shan*, though it would have been good, hearing it aloud. "It would have been right, saying that to me."

His wife stared at the ceiling, saying nothing.

Asa frowned to himself in the dark, perplexed, trying to place the exact moment when his life had collapsed around him. He had worked his whole lifetime to build a herd and raise a crop that would get them ahead, just a little ahead of hunger, and of being afraid; and after those many years of working from first light until after dark, he'd at last accumulated four bos.

Finding a market for them, this far into the outback, was another story. The three he'd sold barely brought the price of his family's safety. Of course, the rice money —what little there was after the Protector had been paid —helped out; and the pittance he got from selling mung, in season, to the medicine-women.

He guiltily avoided thinking about the small patch of mutant tabac he kept, in a clearing beyond the glen, picked clean now and sold on the Black Market for native cigarek. Rationalizing, he'd planted it for those who, he'd told himself, would find it and buy it anyhow. His conscience had been clear and innocent. But now he didn't know. Nothing was the same, everything was changed or gone. Daughter, money, cattle, tabac. Even his absent neighbors' mung trees were not even in bloom, much less bearing. He'd nothing left to sell, no strength left to work. Now there would be a baby, too.

His wife stared up in silence, her breathing loud and terrified, clutching the blanket around her chin, though the night was humid.

Nothing left. Everything gone.

Not so, his mind suggested in a wee voice.

Nothing, he thought stubbornly, *nothing that is mine*.

But something, crooned the voice in his ears, the bee-buz in his head. *Something. Someone*.

He tossed his head to and fro on the thin pallet. *I don't know what you mean*. He lay gazing at the ceiling.

Yes, you do. And you need the money so badly, so badly, and how do you know it wasn't Ilen who informed to the Krail, and if he did, wouldn't it be right and just, wouldn't it serve him right—!

Asa sat up suddenly, holding his head in his hands, his

cheek aching. *I can't sell a person,* he argued desperately. *I can't take someone else's life, steal what isn't mind.*

How about the mung you've been stealing, queried the smug little voice, quite clearly. *How about the lives that tabac snares like birds in a net? Is this any worse? And you need the money so badly.*

Asa wet his lips. *He's sick,* he argued mentally, weakening, *Even if I wanted to sell him, I couldn't. He's sick.*

The little voice waited, humming behind his ears, lurked comfortably inside his head. It knew who would win.

Asa wiped his sweating face. *He's very sick. He really is.* He got to his feet righteously. *Here, I'll show you!*

Climbing the ladder in the dark was harder than he had expected, but by feeling for the rope rungs with his toes he managed to clamber partway into the loft and peer around, his head and shoulders sprouting like a skinny green plant from the old floorboards.

When his eyes became accustomed to the darkness, he made out the shape of Ilen, lying on a straw pallet not an arm's-length away. He pushed open the reed bull's-eye and admitted a wash of starlight. Asa stared and looked away and stared again.

She slept with her curly, dark head pillowed on a golden arm, black fans of lashes lying on her cheeks. The corners of her mouth drooped a bit, relaxed and vulnerable, and showed a white, wet edge of teeth.

Asa rubbed his eyes and scrubbed his face with both hands. He could not have been more astounded if he had gone to the chisei to fetch the bos and found instead a graceful jat, fragile and slender, tied in its place. He reached a trembling hand out and touched one finger to the sleek, rounded arm on which not a trace of blemish showed, jerking his hand back quickly.

The little voice laughed loudly in his head, in wonder and triumph, becoming a big voice, whose laughter and growing exultation deafened him and carried him along. He could scarcely climb down the ladder in his excitement, and in great and elaborate secrecy, woke his wife. She came up out of sleep like a flock of birds, shrieking thinly through her nose, but he covered her mouth.

"Shh, shh, be quiet!" he cautioned, glancing at the ceiling. "Wake up and listen to me, woman. I think I have a plan!"

Ilen woke with a start to a sound not quite heard, a sensation of guarded wakefulness. Even the pleasant, homely sounds of Asa's wife stirring (so early?) in her kitchen did nothing to assuage her uneasiness. Quickly rubbing the sleep out of her eyes and dusting away vagrant bits of straw, she slipped down the ladder and into the kitchen.

They were all there, crowded into the room with an atmosphere of whispered argument clamped off suddenly, of unspoken anger hanging thickly in the still air. Asa was sitting sullenly at the table, his hands spread open and flat on its top; he was studying them uneasily, finding it hard to meet Ilen's eyes. His wife's lips were tightly compressed and she radiated disapproval, especially of Asa. The daughter must have been crying again, for when Ilen climbed down into the room, clumsy and dull-faced, she began to snivel afresh; but when her father glared at her, she stopped as quickly as she had begun. Asa's wife slammed three flat hennem-cakes onto the bare table and angrily spooned a serving of thick gruel into the middle of each, splashing hot droplets of it on table and diners alike. She prepared a fourth for herself and stood by the stove to eat it, her stiff back to the room mute evidence of her disapproval.

Asa rolled his cake around the filling and deliberately began eating, making an obvious effort to appear casual. After an uncertain pause, Ilen sat down and picked up another, nibbling at the edges indifferently. The third cake lay before the daughter's place, hardening as it cooled, the filling turning watery around the edges and running in a rivulet onto the table. Asa's daughter twisted a lock of lank hair in her hand, and drew patterns in the runoff with one bony finger.

Asa cleared his throat. "Today we go to the town," he announced, chewing thoughtfully. "You will come with me."

Ilen looked at him curiously. "It would be better for me to stay here and plant the rice, chom-shan." *There could be Krail in the village, looking for a runaway Shimshen, and she was becoming exhausted from sustaining the illusion.*

87

"The women will plant rice today," Asa replied tonelessly. "You will come with me into the town." The daughter broke into a fresh spasm of weeping and ran from the table, knocking over her stool. Ilen watched her go, his round yellow eyes solemn; he sighed.

"Whatever pleases you, chom-shan."

They started for the town within the hour, for Asa always liked to get an early start, and his eagerness to sell Ilen and get the money blinded him to such subtleties as timing and camouflage. The wife brought out a large bundle and put it on Ilen's back. She tucked a cloth-wrapped package of hennem-cakes into his shirt, 'for hungry, later', she said, and stood rigid, her fist pressed against her tight lips. They turned their faces toward the forest, Asa wearing his brick-red pancake-shaped reed hat, Ilen burdened with whatever household possessions Asa thought he could sell, tied up in a quilt slung over his back. Asa's daughter threw her arms about Ilen's neck, weeping and sobbing apologies and blessings into his collar, and all in all providing a sorry business, until her father pulled her off. Then they trudged away, past the poor farmhouse, past the empty chisei, past the carcass of the bos, slowly swelling, stiff-legged, in the golden sun and hot green water of the paddy.

When they were lost to sight, the women took up bunches of rice plants and without a word began thrusting them into the rich mud under the water, stooping over, lifting and bending in a kind of awkward grace, stopping every now and then to make the Infinity Sign, at the forehead and at the breast, again and again, until evening.

The Columbia Eagle Bar was on a nameless side street, in a building that had once served as a fish-seller's stall and still stank of dead fish. An enterprising Einai businessman named Kahnet had rigged it out as a pub, installing a scarred opalwood bar, a few stools that bore suspicious resemblance to pieces that had been stolen from various on-base servicemen's clubs, and several long tables made from just about anything at hand. No one knew where Kahnet had gotten the idea, the furniture or the name (just as no one knew where he got his beer) but it was Earthling, and it was memorable, in a way, and after a while the Columbia Eagle Bar became the regular hang-out for off-duty Earthling soldiers.

It was midday, hot and muggy, with a school of thick, slate-colored clouds scraping their ponderous bellies on the low, tiled rooftops. A sullen, gray glare richocheted off the white house walls and spilled into the narrow streets; but inside the Columbia Eagle Bar, with its damp, stone floor and gurgling artesian well, the air was bearable. It could not have been more than ninety degrees in the cool stone room.

Sergeant Joe Garrett sat at one of Kahnet's long tables nursing his beer, only half-listening to his men as they talked of small and incidental things, of shore leaves and women and what home had been like and would be like and must be like now. Garrett tuned them out, tuned out everything but the taste of the good Earthling beer and the throbbing of his feet inside the heavy combat boots. He loosened his shirt, unbuttoned it halfway down his chest. He was hot and sweating and war-weary, and warm beer on a humid day on Eisernon, with the temperature outside standing at one hundred eighteen degrees Fahrenheit, was only vaguely reminiscent of home, and served best as a point of comparison.

Home seemed remote from his memory as well, with just a few isolated recollections standing out like mountain peaks above a layer of smog. Hot smog. He wiped his dripping throat with his sleeve. His mind turned over, revealing its harvest. *Winter's heavy, virgin, white snow turning to slush in the gutter; a newstand he'd had, on the corner of Thirty-Fourth and Eighth avenue, and pulling off the sheets of tall, red type as they printed out from his battered old Newsfax machine; playing stickball in the streets with Eddie and Lenny and Tom whatsisname, he never could remember, the kid whose ma used to wipe his nose on her apron, and little Gino. Gino Pietrosanto. Gino.*

He sat up straight. *Gino.* Gino, Gino, Gino. "Gino," he said aloud, to nobody in particular. The little dago kid with the million brothers and sisters, the kid with the curly black hair and the gold skin and the level gray eyes, who looked like the eye-eye Garrett had dug out of the ruins last month. Last month?

"Connors."

Connors swung his head around, a cigarette clamped in his teeth, and said, around it, "Yeah, Sarge?"

"How long's it been since we dug that eye-eye out?"

"What eye-eye?" He removed the cigarette and drank half his beer, his Adam's-apple bobbing, and belched noisily. "When?"

Doc cleared his throat. "Uh, that was about three weeks ago, Sarge, because, remember, we were at, uh, Chul T'ath, huh? Day before yesterday? And we dug him out three weeks before that."

They looked at Garrett strangely and he nodded and went back to his flat beer. Only twice had the war really gotten to him, reached him where he lived. Only twice in what seemed a century of fight and slog on and fight again.

The first time had been a couple of years ago, on the planet Krau, when he and his squad had come upon a village that had been sacked and left to die by the Krail. It hadn't looked too bad, until they found the people. They had been scalped. The incredibly luxurious, glossy fur that covered the natives from brow to shoulderblades was highly prized among Krail women; and therefore every villager, man, woman and child, had been scalped.

The second time was on his last patrol, when they had found the Einai *Dom* under the wreckage of his hospital. There had been an understanding, or the beginnings of an understanding, between them, and Garrett felt a sense of guilt, of loss, an unfinished feeling that kept nagging at him and wouldn't let him rest. He'd considered having a psych test run, but had changed his mind. What he felt for the eye-eye wasn't unhealthy, just miserable. If the damned guy had just yelled, or cursed, or tried to strike back, Garrett wouldn't have thought twice about him; but he had just lain there, with those quiet gray cat eyes staring at him—

"We're doing a terrific job on the northern front," Ross was saying to a friend. "We got a great body count, some Krail, but mostly eye-eyes."

Garrett lifted his head. "Not all eye-eye's are collaborators, Ross," he pointed out disgustedly. "Most of 'em are our allies, remember?"

Ross jerked a thumb at him. "What 'sa matter with him?"

90

"Ah, he's still stewing about that eye-eye back in the bush country." Connors drained his glass and motioned to the Einai waitress, a thin, green-gold old woman of perhaps nineteen, made up in red lipstick and false eyelashes in an effort to appear Earthuman.

"Hey, babe, get papa another one, eh?"

She smiled widely, trying too hard. "Sure, honey, Comin' right up!" But her accent made it sound like 'gummeen wry tupp', which made them laugh.

Sanders, the youngest of them, picked with his dagger at the mud caked on his boot. He had been at it for a while, and there was a scattering of mud on the damp floor, melting at the edges.

"I can't see what the Sarge sees in them gooks," he observed. "To me, they're kind of funny, you know? Weird."

"Yeah, I know what you mean," Ross' friend, a big, beefy man at the next table, interjected. "I just got offa hospital ship, and there was a guy in my ward with me that was a real weirdo. Eye-eye. He never talked or nothin', just stared at the ceilin' with them big gray cat-eyes." He blew the head off his beer and drank. "Boy! Talk about give you the willies!"

"Yeah, drink your beer, buddy," Connors answered. He leaned back to his friends. "Now, there's a guy's had too much to drink. Any damn fool in the service knows that eye-eyes have yellow eyes, eh? Not an eye-eye born but has yellow eyes. Right, baby?"

The waitress avoided his encircling arm and smiled widely, miserably. She put Connors' beer on the table and handed Sanders a second. "Right, baby. Unless you talk about Han, notso?"

Doc met Garrett's gaze, remembering, and Garrett caught the girl by the wrist. "What do you mean, *Han?*"

Ross snorted. "Aw, come on, Sarge, you're not gonna start being—"

The waitress shook her head. "Nonesuch. No Han, for real. Han legend, baby. Han damnfool pretend for tourist, notso?"

"Pretend for me." His grip tightened on her wrist. "Their eyes. What color are a Han's eyes?"

She wrenched her arm free and lifted a shoulder. "Who

91

cares? Momo not have time for Han-talk. Momo got job to take care of, you betcha, honey."

Garrett watched her walk away sulkily, rubbing her wrist where he had held it, and swinging her pitifully thin hips. He fished into his pocket. "Momo." She glanced back. He held a ten-credit note between his first two fingers. "What color?"

"Hey, Sarge, you're not gonna give that broad ten credits just for that, are you? *Just to tell you what color their eyes are?*" Sanders was incredulous.

"If *I* was gonna spend ten dollars, baby," Ross grinned, wagging his head.

Garrett saw her jaw muscles tighten, her throat work. *Hungry. That's what ails this kid, she's hungry.* He had time to wonder what Kahnet fed his girls, and then she was next to him, smiling as she had been told Earthling women smiled.

"You firstofall give to Momo, notso?" Her slender, three-fingered hand reached for the money, touched it, trembled. "Story say gray eye," she whispered. "Skin like you, but always gray eye." She took the money from his unresisting fingers and tucked it into her blouse. "Is only story, nobody talk about story, is foolish, for children." Her tone was anguished, begging him to believe her. "Han only legend now. All Han die, longtimego. Only story now." The truth lay plain on her face.

"Sure." Garrett picked up his helmet. The chair behind him was empty. "Ross." He gestured toward the empty chair. "Your friend. What's his name?"

"Gates. Ernie Gates." Connors scowled, and Doc stood up.

"Sarge," he ventured. "Could you sit down here a minute?"

He dragged a chiar up and sat backwards, his arms folded on the back of it, the helmet dangling from its strap. He waited.

Doc cleared his throat. "Sarge. Sarge, if this eye-eye we dug up ain't just a regular eye-eye,"—he pointed a finger at Garrett—"and you know there was something funny about him," he swallowed, "well, you might be in trouble."

Garrett looked at them. Ross had his muzzle in his beer glass, Connors' cigarette had a neglected inch of ash on it. Sanders was toying with his knife, not meeting his eyes. "What're you talking about?" Lightning flashed silently on the building across the street.

Connors spoke. "Sarge, we been your squad for a long time, right? We done a lot of fighting, we covered a lot of territory."

"All right."

Ross interrupted. "What he means is, we all done a lot of killing and we all came through it. Nobody got shook, no regrets, nothin' like that."

Garrett nodded, getting the idea. "And you think that I—"

"If he was one of them Han," Doc muttered, "He could've turned your mind. He could've just taken you over."

"Maybe he did." Ross finished off his beer. "You never can tell."

Garrett's jaw dropped and he would've answered them, but the storm broke with a gigantic clap of thunder, a torrent of rain, and another burst of thunder. Lightning threw a fiery reflection on the wet floor, and a chill current of wind eddied the sultry air. Cold rain blew into the open door. Their faces were remote, sullen, the faces of strangers. Garrett picked up his helmet and walked out into the storm without a word.

Gates was nowhere to be seen. The streets were flooded, the buildings streaming sheets of rain. An occasional Einai moved along the streets, heedless of the weather, but there was not a uniform in sight. Thunder boomed and a fresh torrent of rain beat down on Garrett's shoulders, soaking him to the skin, pouring down his neck and into his boots, which squished wetly with each step.

He followed the street for half-a-dozen blocks—if the twisting, winding, shop-clogged alleys that bisected the street could be said to mark off blocks—and saw only closed windows, lamps glowing warmly behind shuttered portals, and the steady downpour of the storm. Nothing stirred down the length of the street as far as he could see, only the rain, sluicing in great rivers over the cobbles, spouting hugely from stone gutters. He stood hesitating, half-ready to turn back to the warmth and light of the Columbia Eagle Bar, when thunder broke right above him, and the rain fell upon him in tons, great washes of it, as from gigantic waterfalls, making it impossible to breathe.

He ducked into a nondescript shop fronting on a narrow alley.

It was dark and musty inside, and as Garrett's eyes became accustomed to the gloom, he made out the figure of an old woman, bending over a stack of reed baskets. As he approached, she straightened with a little grunt and peered at him nearsightedly.

"Alai?" she croaked. She was much older than he had at first believed. Her face was a network of wrinkles and wrinkles and wrinkles, crosscrossing and coalescing, entrapping rheumy, colorless, old eyes. She sucked her toothless gums and regarded him with something less than kindliness.

"I, uh, I just came in here to get away from the rain." He jerked a thumb toward the door. "The rain."

She followed the thumb, then shrugged, shaking her head.

"Il' nu' myna," she muttered, half to herself. Garrett recognized the vulgar Low Eisernai. It was clear to them both that they weren't going to understand each other. The old woman shuffled through a curtained doorway leading to the nether regions of the shop, and after a brief muttered conversation, reappeared, pulling with her a man of late middle age. Garrett hovered uncomfortably near the door, but the little man crossed to him, bowing and nodding politely.

"I Quaby," he offered. "This my other parent, also have store same place. I find however you need, damnright." He bowed again and stood waiting expectantly, his watery yellow eyes gazing up like a pleading spaniel's. "Name of item?"

Garrett thought he had been introduced to Quaby's mother, but couldn't be sure. "How do you do?" he mumbled. "Look, uh, Quaby, I'm looking for a man, a soldier, an Earthling like me. Big. Fat." He pantomimed big and fat, to Quaby's sober and uncomprehending interest. "A soldier," he repeated. "Guy by the name of Ernie Gates. Have you seen a guy like that?"

Quaby brightened. "You want buy mattress? I give you hotcha deal."

Garrett drove his hand through his sodden hair and sneezed, while Quaby watched with polite interest. "Look, Quaby, I'm looking for a man, understand. I man," he hit his chest, "you man." He touched Quaby's chest, or would have, if the surprised little Einai hadn't jumped back as though burned.

"Sore luck to touch Earthlik soldier, notso?" he offered by way of explanation. "You need man? I man, you man, you want man, notso? Hotdamn, stand right where I am!" He disappeared into the back of the shop, and Garrett followed him a few steps, until the old woman started screaming something incomprehensible from behind the reed basket. So he stayed where he was, wishing the rain would slow down enough for him to breathe and get back to his men and the familiarity of the Columbia Eagle Bar.

Quaby reappeared, dragging a young boy with him, grinning from ear to ear. The boy's wrists were tied behind him and he stared down at the floor, so that Garrett could not see his face.

"You want man?" Quaby chortled. "I sell you man, dirt cheap, grantee to be hotcha man, work hard, shine boot, take care damnfine, yes?" He tugged the boy closer, and he came forward in a series of reluctant little running steps.

Garrett studied them both for a moment. He was not surprised by Quaby's possession of a slave; many Einai, especially the older people, could remember the dying days of the Empire, when slavery was the ordinary and accepted fact. But what surprised him was Quaby's offer to sell the slave to an Earthling soldier, when it was widely known that Earth supported the Federation edict against slavery in any form, and enforced that rule rigidly.

Garrett surprised them both by what he did next.

"What's his name?" Quaby's face lit up.

"Call this one Ilen. I sell him cheap for dirt, no better selling any store here."

"How long've you had him?" Garrett kept his voice level.

"Only a coupl'a day here. Him from Allampaila, walk all way. Him very strong like horse, bet you my life, shan."

At the mention of Allampaila, the boy's head came up sharply. His face was golden, his hair a cap of loose and silken curls. His face, aside from the strong cheekbones, was childish and very young, and his lashes were absurdly long, for a boy. Garrett stared at him, the hair prickling

95

on the back of his neck. The boy's eyes were gray, level and intelligent.

Garrett pulled himself away from the even gaze with an effort.

"How much?" he heard his voice ask. "How much do you want for him?" Quaby named an exorbitant price, grinning broadly.

He paid the money, throwing in an extra credit for Quaby's mother, and untied the boy's hands. The boy rubbed his wrists gingerly and murmured "Buchat ge."

"You coming to like boy Ilen," Quaby chortled, "you coming to big surprise, come soon, this day, watchan see, notso?"

"Sure," Garrett said. He glanced out the window and saw that the rain had settled to a steady downpour. "Come on," he told the boy, not unkindly. "Let's go."

Just outside the door, the boy caught his sleeve, pulling him around to look at him. "Earthlik." The voice was low, quiet, well-bred. "Earthlik, zo-ili ia Shimshen, 'a ze pavilion ili-Allam-paila. Teklif!" He was pleading, not without dignity, and yet as a child might plead. Garrett shook his head.

"I don't know what you're saying," he said; "I just wish I knew what you're talking about." He glanced around the street, prematurely dark because of the storm, and grabbed the boy's arm. "Come on, we'll find us an interpreter at the Checkpoint." He nodded encouragingly. "Come on."

The boy followed him into the dark, slippery streets, Garrett's boots slipping on the slick cobbles, the boy's light feet finding hidden security under the shallow film of muddy water that washed the streets. He slid not at all. Once, when Garrett stumbled, it was Ilen who slipped a small hand into his and led the way. They took shortcuts through back streets and reached the checkpoint ten minutes before Garrett had estimated they should. By that time they were both drenched, and Garrett was sneezing profusely. He pushed open the door of the makeshift sentry box at the checkpoint and a young PFC looked him over and grinned at him.

"Kinda wet out, eh, Sarge?"

"Yeah. Listen, you got a Translator in here? I just bought me an eye-eye and I have to find out what to do with him."

96

The youngster began rummaging around in a bin. "I got one in here somewheres, just saw it the other day . . . ah, here we go." He turned around to hand Garrett the translator, a slender cylinder of dull metal, when he glanced out into the rain and whistled appreciatively. Garrett turned and saw the Einai slave.

Ilen was standing in the rain, water sleeked over slender limbs, the coarse tunic moulded to a slim and girlish form. Her cropped hair, dragged down by the rain, clung to her shoulders.

The sentry nudged Garrett with a friendly elbow and winked. "Some guy you got there, Sarge. I wouldn't mind finding me one of them myself."

Garrett snatched the Translator and stepped outside long enough to pull Ilen out of the driving rain and into the sentry box. He hung the translator around his neck and said carefully, "Now, let's get down to the bottom of this: who are you, and why are you dressed as a boy?"

Her face brightened and blushed, a wash of green-gold under delicate height of cheekbone. "Zo-ili Hennem-mishli; zo-ili mutaph Sum ChiT'ath."

Garrett grabbed the sentry's arm. "Something's the matter with that thing. Why can't we understand her?" The word Sum ChiT'ath had hit a nerve, made him eager.

"I don't know, Sarge. I guess maybe a relay's out or something." He reached over and shook it and something rattled thinly. "Yep, sounds like a relay's out, all right. You want me to translate? I can talk a little bit of eye-eye."

Garrett thumbed back his helmet and wiped his mouth on his palm. "Tell me what she said just then. About Sum ChiT'ath."

"Looks like she wants to get there, Sarge. Looks like it's a hospital."

"I know it's a hospital. What does she want there?"

Before the sentry could translate, Ilen leaned forward, both hands gesturing expressively. She articulated a flow of musical syllables, her hands forming pictures in the air before her. The sentry muttered to Garrett, "She says—her grandfather and—somebody else, I don't get that relationship, a *Dao*—are there—at the hospital. She wants to go to them. She says—the Krail were after her —before a—a *Quaby*—found her—no, not found—

97

bought her. It's kind of mixed up, Sarge." He shrugged. "Anyways, she insists she wants to go to Sum ChiT'ath."

Garrett thought back to the destruction and the bodies and the sweet, thick stench of death lying over the hospital.

"Tell her I said no. Tell her I said I paid for her and she belongs to me."

The sentry gave him a dirty look.

"Tell her what I said." He explored the rough spot on his tooth. "Tell her I command a whole squad. She'd never get away."

Her shoulders sagged dispiritedly. A few syllables.

"She wants to know what her duties are gonna be, Sarge," the sentry repeated resentfully. His attitude was protective and vaguely indignant. Garrett heaved a deep breath and muttered, "*She* wants to know, eh?"

"And so do I!" added the sentry pugnaciously.

Garrett jammed his helmet down and squinted at him from underneath its rim. What was he, fifteen, sixteen, maybe? Old enough for talk, barracks talk, barracks jokes; young enough that the smell of soap and apples stuck with him. *Kid, when I was your age I'd already met the Krail and walked through them.* Then, *they never should've lowered the draft age; but with so few kids being born, and the Invader so many . . . How were we to know?*

"Houseboy," he replied in a monotone. "Just that. Not that it's any of your business."

"Oh. Well, okay, then," the sentry stammered glumly. He half-shrugged and didn't seem to know what to do with his hands. Garrett slapped the boy's helmet, half in reproof, half in rough affection, as he took Ilen's arm and led her off through the dark and winding streets.

The post passed them without a challenge and they slogged through the mud, the rain diminishing to fitful gusts under scudding dark clouds. A wet wind blew down from the jungle, promising more rain.

She tugged him to a halt just outside the barracks, where a warm yellow lamp lit the entrance to the bubble.

"Sarj?" She touched his chest. "Tu Sarj?" She nodded encouragingly.

"Yeah. Sarge." He unslung the Translator and put it around her neck. "Now, listen, this thing works one way, see? I can't understand you, but you can understand me,

98

or whoever talks to you. That way, we're fine. But the minute those guys hear that soft voice talking back, we're in trouble." He thought a minute, worrying his tooth around. "Maybe you can pretend to be a mute. You think you can pretend to be something you're not?"

She dimpled and nodded. "Alai," she murmured, as if enjoying a delicious secret.

"Okay, now, remember, no matter what, you're a mute boy, understand?" He tried to look stern. "No matter what."

She touched her chest. "Ilen ia shanklif." Soberly.

"That's right. A shanklif. A boy."

"Alai." She knelt quickly and began to unlace his boots, like any one of half a dozen houseboys the squad had picked up over the years, while Garrett stood there and felt that he ought to feel embarrassed, and did, and didn't know why. The door opened and Connors stuck his head outside. He indicated Ilen with a lift of his stubbled chin.

"What's that?"

Garrett worried his tooth. "It's an elephant."

"Aw, that's funny, Sarge. That's real funny. An elephant. Look, I'm laughing." He said it without rancor, both of them idly watching Ilen scrape the mud off of Garrett's boots with a broken piece of land-coral. There were patches of it all over the compound, and if you weren't careful, you could get a nasty cut that was sure to fester. Once in a while some joker would deliberately step into a patch of it to get out of going on patrol, or to avoid some unpleasant duty (backflushing the scrubber-vacs, for instance); but after a couple of them lost a foot or two from coral poisoning, the practice fell off somewhat.

"Hey, you, what's your name?" Connors nudged Ilen with his foot and the Einai glanced shyly at him and away again. "Gawd!" he expostulated. "He's pretty enough to be a woman!"

"To you my Grandpa's pretty enough to be a woman." Garrett indicated the Einai. "His name's Ilen. He's a mute, so leave him alone, you guys don't hassle him."

"A mute! Sarge, you're always bringing home stray cats! How much work is a poor deaf-mute—"

"I didn't say he was *deaf*, Connors!" Garrett interrupted. "Anyway," he continued, aware that he was being child-

99

ish and feeling absolutely justified, "how about that kid you dragged in off the street a couple of months ago, and you fed him and cleaned him up and when he got good and fat he beat it out of here with our chronos, that old pulsar Doc had picked up, and two hundred and fifty bucks belonging to yours truly! How about him?"

"Well, it wasn't bad for a kid with one leg!" Connors shouted defensively, his Adam's apple working. "And at least he could hear what you said to him!"

"Yeah, like, 'stop, thief!' Now, listen good, Connors. Ilen *can't* talk, but he *can* understand, he's wearing a Translator. Only, don't expect him to answer you, got it? Otherwise, he's fine, he can work and he'll take orders, awright?"

"Okay, okay!" Connors made a shrugging, innocent, palm's up motion, backing into the bubble. "Gawd, but you're getting touchy!"

Garrett stood there in his stockinged feet, feeling the mild buffeting of the wet wind, conscious of the frowning sky and Ilen's gray eyes on him surreptitiously, and he scowled. He *was* getting touchy. He missed the companionship, the comfortable old familiarity of the squad as it had been, before Sum ChiT'ath, before everything changed.

Sum ChiT'ath.

She had mentioned Sum ChiT'ath to the sentry, had been anxious (he said) to get there. Why? What did she know that he didn't know? He squatted down on his heel beside her.

"Ilen?" She looked at him brightly, tipping her head a bit as if to say, 'yes?' "What's at Sum ChiT'ath? Why did you want to get there so badly?"

She shook her head and patted her mouth and lifted a shoulder, signing that she was mute, and he snicked impatience between his teeth. Dampness crept in through his socks.

"Okay, you did a good job on Connors. But I mean it, now, it's important. Why did you want to go to Sum ChiT'ath?" She touched her mouth and throat with both hands and spread them helplessly. *I am mute.* He grasped her shoulders and spoke intensely, shaking her gently a little for emphasis.

"Okay, you're a mute! Awright! But I've got to know about Sum ChiT'ath—and you've got to tell me! Some

100

way, you've got to tell me!" She shook her head quickly, flicking a glance behind him, and he twisted round to see Ross looming above them, his belt sagging below his fat belly, his undershirt stained with beer from the can in his hand. He studied Ilen disrespectfully from head to toe and back again, marking Garrett's hands on the Einai's shoulders.

"Connors was right," he drawled thickly. "He *is* pretty enough to be a girl."

The jungle wind thumped them with soft edges, spilling dampness and the scent of the wild, eddying a rancid whiff of alcohol and Erthlik sweat. Ilen, without quite knowing why, gave a brief, involuntary shudder and looked away.

The sun. Whatever else Tom Paige had become accustomed to on Eisernon, he could never quite cope with the sun. After a fiery, spectacular sundown and a brief, black, tropical night that offered scant respite from the heat, it would vault up suddenly several hours later into a sky still thick with stars, shredding mists and pouring gold over the jungle, so that the leaves were not green alone, but were permanently tinted from straining the sun; and the Einai slaves, laboring on the Krail's accursed airstrip, seemed like metal men, like plant men, with their green-gold skins filmed with moisture, and their eyes like twin yellow suns.

Paige swung the heavy mattock into a sticky mass of wet clay and decaying fronds and heard the measured *slish-chuk!* of its impact at the precise moment his muscles stretched and recoiled, clean and easy. *Trapezius, doctor, and deltoid and teres major and triceps brachii and more.* Sweat ran into his eyes and he brushed it away impatiently, the scorched skin of his face and arms and bare back smarting angrily. He squinted at the sky, tasted salt on his lips, and swung the mattock again.

The sun beat down, and it was hot. More than merely light, it was a presence, an entity to be felt and seen and yes, even heard and tasted and smelled, if the saffron incense of dakan flowers and the susurrant murmur of aun in their treetop hives could be considered golden, and part of the sun. One week on Eisernon, Paige remembered, and you could think of them as nothing else. There was a

101

hive cluster of aun in a growth of giant fiddleheads near the airstrip they were building, and their endless undulating murmur was so familiar that once, when for some unknown reason the entire colony fell silent, every man of the work crew clapped his hands to his ears as if he had suddenly gone deaf.

The airstrip. He hefted the mattock, swinging freely. *Chuk.* Physically, he was healing. The open blisters in his hands had hardened to calluses, bruises faded, lash marks toughened to wealed scars. Even the painful puncture through his right instep, where he had stupidly impaled himself on a broken reed the day of his escape, had become a knot of numb white tissue. He thought of the Shimshen at odd moments and wondered if she had escaped, and to what; but the airstrip! The airstrip was the center of his life now.

The airstrip. *Slish-chuk!* It was a raw slash in the jungle, a humped and hillocky area of uprooted trees and mucky leaf-mold that gave off a fetid, swampy, wet stench of decaying vegetation. The stench clung to the skin. He awoke to it before dawn, before the grim wooden clappers summoned the work gangs, labored in it under the merciless sun until nightfall, and slept hating his own stink.

The brake offered other niceties as well. Fresh lash marks were open invitation to the larvae of several species of carrion flies; and tiny, wet, multi-legged things burrowed into tan and green flesh alike and festered there, causing abscesses and fevers. Boils and carbuncles were universal, and almost all the men were plagued by intestinal parasites, a difficulty Paige had so far avoided by shunning the slaves' stagnant bathing pond in favor of carefully rationed ounces of his own drinking water. Two slaves had died of an illness resembling cholera, and several were wasting away solely from that mortal soul-sickness peculiar to free men who, enslaved, abandon hope. Paige sometimes nursed men through weeks of this malady only to have them dragged off and executed as incurables just as he began to make progress.

"Build the airstrip!" someone hissed. He glanced around. Every head was bent, every back straining to its task; but a guard was eyeing him with more than casual interest, white hands restless at his weapon. *Slish-chuk!* Spatters of mud flew, and the sun fevered his brain and crisped the

102

delicate cartilages of his ears. When he looked up again, the guard had turned away and was watching a big mem-likt spin its web.

Build the airstrip. Among the slaves it was a watchword, the warning to a careless comrade, the reminder of the punishment that could strike from shock-collar or needler or even, in the hands of the Commander, a light-whip. Build the airstrip. Attend to business. Heads up.

Paige swung the mattock again. *Slish-chuk!* Ten feet to his right, another tool echoed, *chuk!* The airstrip. *Chuk!* Build the airstrip. *Chuk!* It became a rhythm, and he breathed to it. Build the airstrip. *Chuk!* Build the damned airstrip. *Chuk!* Damn the airstrip. *Chuk! Damn* the airstrip! *Chuk!* And damn Beq nom-Pau—*chuk!*—and his cold professionalism—*chuk!* and his insufferable smile—*chuk!* He paused, breathing hard.

And his light-whip.

Slish-chuk! Slish-chuk!

On Tenth-Day the slaves rested. They were free to do anything they liked, within reason, under the dispassionate watchfulness of armed guards. A few of the men played at Tiq', using crude, hand-made dice, arguing and swearing; others bartered meager possessions or sat staring at nothing, in a kind of stupor. Most of them slept.

For Paige, Tenth-Day meant holding a makeshift clinic, treating wounds and performing what minor surgery he could with the blade of a broken viith in impossibly septic hands, and a guard's needler trained on him less than ten feet away.

It was mid-morning his second?—fourth?—Tenth-Day. A *khamsin* was blowing, the hot, arid wind from the desert beyond the Glass Lakes, and the sun was thin and scorching. The seasonal rains were weeks late and great dry cracks had appeared in the springy soil, which shrank to the consistancy of crumbling sandstone. Deep potholes and dry rills appeared, with resultant bad falls and sprains where men, careless or merely numb, stepped into the unaware. Customarily, they would have been left in the forest for the d'injit, for the outlying Einai villages were full of potential Krail slaves; but Paige had engineered a deal with one of the guards to let him tend the worst of them in exchange for tutelage in the intricacies of chess.

103

Those slaves less seriously injured healed, or not, by themselves, or waited for the next Tenth-Day.

This morning Paige had reason to be grateful for the arrangement. Just after sundown yesterday, as the light was beginning to get bad, an Einai youngster running to answer the chow call plunged into a deep fissure, pitching sideward and snapping both bones nastily just above the ankle with an audible crack. He was unconscious when Paige reached him, his leg purpled and visibly swelling, the foot turned out and up at an unbelievable angle. Paige's hands flew, brown moth, brown feather on green and purpled skin. Classical Potts fracture, and a nasty one at that. Not only was the tip split off the lower end of the tibia, but—he felt carefully—the pinbone was displaced to the point where he could see the broken edge of it pressing up under the skin two full centimeters from its normal alignment. He tried to recall, as precisely as he could, the Einai venous setup, which differed from the Earthuman; but all he could hear, ringing in his ears, was "Build the airstrip, Build the airstrip." He swore under his breath.

Jackboots stopped beside him, the barrel of a needler visible at the corner of his eye. "Erthlik. The airstrip." He felt the presence of a third man somewhere behind him. "Let me help him. He's badly hurt, let me take care of him." It was as near a plea as Paige could come.

"You look very natural on your knees, Earthlik," one of them observed softly; then, "You left your work station. Is there any reason why I should not kill you?"

Paige ground his teeth and made no answer, and the guard laid the snout of the needler barrel at his throat, where a pulse beat slowly under the tan. "Beg, animal," he advised.

"Go to hell."

A second barrel struck him full on the side of the face, making the guards lethal needler charge go wild and harmless.

"Enough!" It was Paige's chess companion. "This one still has work to complete, are you aware of that? He is playing for time and you are permitting it."

The other's eyes glittered. "Your pardon, *Dirk* Powys."

Powys nudged Paige to his feet and muttered, "King's Pawn to King's Pawn's work." Their eyes met and Paige caught a fleeting glint of amusement; in his astonishment,

104

he almost laughed. Pathetic as it was, it was the first attempt at humor he'd ever heard a Krail make. Then the boy cried out in his insensible agony and Paige didn't feel like laughing any more.

"Let me go set that leg," he pleaded huskily. "It won't take but a few minutes." But *Dirk* Powys shook his head.

"You've used your good fortune for today." His face became a snow face, a mask, a totem, like every other Krail face, emotionless and cold. Paige wonderd if he'd imagined that spark or merely hallucinated. He felt utterly, ineffably weary.

As Powys nudged him past the line of slaves queued up for chow, the boy began to whimper; but none of them met Paige's gaze or paid the slightest attention to the boy in the rill. Upon looking closer, he glimpsed knots of muscle in a man's jaw, a telltale tic in another's cheek, and near the end of the line an old man stood staring fixedly at nothing in particular, his eyes full of tears.

The boy was left there until nightfall, when the obliging guard let Paige haul the boy, alternately howling and unconscious, back to the slave pen. There were no lights and no way to help him in the inky darkness, so all Paige could do was beg a blanket to keep him warm, and listen to him cry.

By dawn the youngster had rallied enough to drink some of Paige's water (his own ration had been stolen) and later he managed to down a little of the pounded-hennem gruel that constituted the main meal. Now, when the boy awoke, Paige had to set the ankle.

He didn't relish the task even under the best circumstances. A Pott's fracture in an Einai was tricky. Several important veins and at least one major nerve ran through the mess he'd been given; a wrong move and that twisted pinbone could perforate vein and skin alike, and he'd just have to stand there and watch his patient exsanguinate. Too, it could tear into musculature in the other direction and do considerable nerve damage.

What we really need, he thought dreamily, watching the boy stir fitfully in his sleep, is some really high-grade films, an AP, Lat and Tunnel lascan to pinpoint tissue damage, and facilities for an open reduction under anesthesia. Another, wicked, part of his mind added, *And a sixty-minute scrub to the elbow with industrial-strength detergent and a wire brush.*

He studied his hands. The creases of his knuckles were stubbornly grimed, the nails torn and blackened, the fine hairs bleached almost white by the sun. He turned them palms-up. Thick caramel-colored calluses, one of them pulling pinkly free at the base of his thumb. He caressed it absently with an index finger and grinned at the boy, who opened his eyes once, twice, and experimented with a smile that trembled to a tight halt.

Paige reached for a short length of hollow, small-bore pipe, an awning support that still had a few long tatters of tough webbing wrapped around it. He'd bartered tomorrow's water ration for it, thinking it would make a good splint. He'd been right, too. He tested the fabric. Strong enough. That, and his belt, would serve as lashings. He bent the stubborn pipe to a U-shape around his foot and he was ready.

A few of the other slaves had gathered and a couple of them squatted down interestedly, talking in whispers and pointing to the boy's deformed ankle. A guard stepped a few paces closer and craned his neck, made a grimace of distaste and moved away.

The boy watched Paige with trepidation in his cloudy yellow eyes, and the duli smiled at him.

"We're in business," he told him encouragingly. "Rai," this to a doubtful spectator, "you're pretty strong, you take his foot and when I tell you, you give me a nice, steady, hard pull, okay? Hold it like this . . . that's right." Rai nodded uncertainly. "And you men there, why don't you hold him under the arms, because we're going to be pulling pretty hard down here." Awkwardly, obediently, they held him. The boy, his face beaded with sweat, squeezed trembling hands against his face.

"*Duli*," his voice was muffled, will it be very bad?"

Paige squatted down and pulled away the boy's hands. His eyes were green-rimmed and wet. "What's your name, son?"

"Ronhalovan, *duli*."

"Does it hurt you now, Ronhalovan?"

He nodded, his face slick. "Yes. It is very bad, *duli*."

"Do you think it could be worse?"

"Only my Lord T'ath knows that, *duli*." He tried to

106

smile, then sobered. "No. I don't think so." His face was pale. Shock, pain, fear. Paige felt like a louse.

"I'll try to be quick," he promised. He felt for the bone ends as gently as he could, while Ronhalovan stifled a moan, his eyes tightly shut. A shadow fell over them, a needler rapped Paige smartly on his cheekbone and his face flashed up.

Charvin, expressionless. "Beq nom-Pau summons you, Paige."

His fingers probed, tested, *found it*! Ronhalovan tossed his head, crying "ahhh, ahhh—" and trying to lie still.

"He's got to wait. *Pull!*" Rai yanked the leg and Ronhalovan began to scream and scream. Paige expertly rotated the displacement, brought the bone ends into alignment, manipulated the slender pinbone until the delicate edges nearly touched.

Charvin struck him with the butt of the needler, a short, vicious jab back of the head that sent him sprawling across Ronhalovan, bleeding from the scalp. The Einai assistants backed away nervously and faded into the crowd and Ronhalovan's screams became a bubbled moan as he fainted.

Paige bounced off the ground like a cat, enraged, but Charvin swung the needler up and sighted down it, centering on him at point-blank range.

"Come, animal," he coaxed softly. "See what I have for you."

Paige knew. The needlers were tipped with curare, miserably uncomfortable for Einai and fatal for Earthlings. He stopped, his muscles bunched and ready. His heart was pounding, his skin flushed, and the air stirred cool and refreshing around him. *One chance,* he prayed, *oh, God, give me one chance at that bastard!*

"A splendid specimen, Father," nom-Pau Alain remarked interestedly, leaning his arms on the railing for a better view. The hot wind touched his tunic and ruffled the pale silken fur of his head. "What are you going to do with him?"

Below, in what might have been an arena, the injured slave stirred and cried out, and Paige made an abortive attempt to return to him, but Charvin's needler swung lazily, blocking him. Ronhalovan continued to cry, hopelessly, like a lost child.

"I don't know, Alain," Beq nom-Pau muttered, in a low tone. His eyelid twitched and his voice dropped, introspectively. "I should have him killed. He could have settled this war . . ."

The Imperator needed a Han. There was no way around it. Only the Han, with their insights and empathies, could winnow a man's mind for the tight-locked truth no interrogation could produce. There were Earthlik officers in other prison pens, their minds full of information, attacks and counterattacks, flanking maneuvers and strategic withdrawals; it would take only one co-operative Han to sift thoughts, calibrate ideas, win the Krail this war. Finding such a Han, he mused, would insure a man his choice of subjugated planets, a life such as no man had ever dreamed, and yes, even the favor of the Imperator himself.

Beyond that he dared not plan, although it was common knowledge that the Imperator was aging; might go suddenly any day, one never knew. Then the diadem would fall to the man strong enough to claim it.

Only one Han. And Paige had helped her escape.

Charvin, in the sunlit arena below, motioned with the needler and Paige padded past him, resentful and deadly, and slowly crossed the courtyard. Midway, he paused and regarded Beq nom-Pau with such implacable hatred that even at this distance he felt the impact almost as a physical sensation. He lifted his brows.

"One of the more useful facts to remember about slaves, Alain, is that they are capable of holding a grudge longer than any other animal." He watched them disappear into the black shadow of the stairwell entry, waiting for some response from Alain; but the incorrigible offspring of his first consort, apparently not having heard him at all, was sketching a quick study of the rebellious Earthlik and his tall, lean captor. The contrast was painfully clear: the immaculate, angular lines of the uniformed Charvin as opposed to the interrupted strokes delineating the filthy, sunburned Earthlik duli. In the background was the suffering Einai slave, also in redrawn lines, and Paige, although erect and tense in the picture, seemed somehow to incline toward him. The open hands, sketched and resketched well away from the body, might almost be held in supplication, but for the hatred evident in the face. Charvin, behind the needler, had virtually no face at all.

108

Beq nom-Pau disliked the sketch. It made Charvin appear the bully rather than the efficient aide he was. Art. What a waste. What utter nonsense.

"One might surmise that your sympathies were with the Earthlik, Alain," he offered silkily, and his son smiled absently.

"You know better than that, Father." He crosshatched shadows, regarded the picture critically, and, satisfied, put away the stylus. "No, I was thinking—and drawing—what it would be like to be down there—looking up at us."

Before Beq nom-Pau could formulate a reply to this astounding conjecture, Charvin appeared at his elbow. "Charvin."

"By your leave, Commander, the Earthlik has been brought under guard to your quarters, as ordered. Commander!" He braced stiffly.

"Well?" His annoying son was busily capturing Charvin yet again in stiff charcoal lines, expressionless white parchment sheets. *One must have another heir, one must produce a soldier.*

"An Earthlik skimmercraft approaches."

Beq nom-Pau wheeled. "Scan?"

"Positive. Three Krail, one Einai. It appears to have been stolen. Voice contact confirms Overlord Aper ser Nalm is aboard."

Beq nom-Pau brightened, his mind racing. Aper ser Nalm. The diplomat, the Emperor's right hand. If one could enlist his assistance, what an ally the man would make! And he had an unfavored daughter, young but probably old enough for childbearing. Perhaps, nom-Pau mused, he could hope for another heir after all, if everything went well. Good man, Aper ser Nalm. Very good man.

He started down the corridor toward the half-finished runway, Charvin at his heels. "Prepare the outpost for official welcome. Drummers in full regalia, honor guard. Notify the kitchen, and oh, yes, the Erthlikli wines His Excellency sent; have them served, chilled, I believe—"

"Father." Alain's voice cut cleanly through the summer air. "What of the slave called Paige?"

Beq nom-Pau made an abrupt gesture, stifling his vexation. "Do what you will," he retorted. "He's yours." He strode off to meet Aper ser Nalm.

The skimmer came bouncing in on the unfinished runway, skidding and slewing in the dry rills, tilting precariously around projecting tree boles and debris and jouncing to a sedate halt only a few yards from the monastery's broad stairs. With a complacent mental nod to the skill of Krail pilots, Beq nom-Pau came smartly to attention at the head of the stairs, above a double row of motionless black-uniformed men, Charvin at his elbow. A dozen drummers, black short-cloaks thrown back over the shoulder to reveal scarlet linings, began the traditional measured beat—beat—beat, a hollow, reverberating thunder that shook the bones and resounded like the footsteps of titans.

The Emperor's Emissary, Overlord Aper ser Nalm, stepped out of the skimmer, instantly flanked by a pair of subordinates who'd been cramped into the MAX holds, for Earthlikli skimmercraft were made to carry only two men, in addition to cargo.

The Einai was a surprise. Beq nom-Pau had expected the reported Einai to be a slave, or at best, a captive; but never this lean, confident, black-bearded man who was last to leave the skimmer—from the pilot's seat. In addition to a wide bandage around his ribs, he was wearing black uniform trousers and jackboots, his uniform jacket open. If he had any difficulty in navigating the stairs, despite his injury, it was not evident. Beq nom-Pau, thus observing him, was tardy in echoing Aper ser Nalm's artfully casual salute, and the Emissary noted it and followed his gaze.

"Commander Beq nom-Pau, may I present Kles Mennon. Mennon is one of us."

"Mennon," nom-Pau acknowledged stiffly, his lifted brows inquiring of the Overlord how we happened to have a native on our hands.

"Beq nom-Pau," Mennon drawled, sweeping him with tiger-eyes, "the Terror of Allampaila. Your head would have brought me ten thousand credits, Commander, had I brought it to the Commander of the Chosen."

"A remarkable observation, Mennon, considering your position here."

Mennon held his side unobtrusively. "Perhaps we had better make clear just what my position is, Noble ser Nalm."

Aper ser Nalm spread his hands. "And perhaps in more

110

suitable surroundings . . ." In a low voice he said to the Commander, "We will need your physician." Charvin left quickly, while the Commander ushered his guests down a waxed-tile corridor. Ser Nalm spoke hurriedly, half under his breath.

"The Einai lost a friend aboard the prison ship—a Han who died of *Strecken* and was removed while we were there. I have reason to believe that he has connections with others of the kind, or even that he is himself a Han. I need not tell you, nom-Pau, how valuable that makes him to the Imperator."

"Pardon, Overlord, but how did you—"

"Escape? I provided the fuse; the explosion was inherent in the Einai. Once I'd spliced the bars of our cells, set him free . . ." Puzzled wonder shadowed his face as he retraced engrams, reliving the experience. "They move so *quickly*." Another few paces and ser Nalm added absently, "They're descended from nocturnal hunting cats, you know."

Beq nom-Pau knew, but wisely said nothing. *Behind them, the tiger's spawn padded softly, following, following, down the long empty corridor.* The Overlord's bemused voice continued:

"He was everywhere—fighting off guards; on the Bridge, disabling the ship; the wards; the skimmerpods, holding them off until we could escape.

"He's fought beside me for months now. I've watched him kill. Were I a trusting man, nom-Pau, I would almost trust this Einai."

They entered an austere chamber of frescoed walls and hand-hewn beams. Mennon spotted every exit before lowering himself gratefully into a straightbacked chair. The Commander put a foot on an adjacent chair and leaned forward interestedly. "Well, Mennon. What do you think of fighting with the Imperial forces? A bit better than the Erthlikli, are we not?"

"You're quieter," Mennon admitted, making them laugh softly as Charvin returned with the physician, a slight, aging individual who was not so fair as colorless. Embarrassed by the presence of the nobleman, he saluted, rummaged fruitlessly in his medikit, and kept darting surreptitious glances at the door as if he would like to have fled but hadn't the courage. Aper ser Nalm, unaware of his discomfiture, strolled about the room scrutinizing the frescoes.

Just so long as he doesn't memorize them, Mennon thought, his muscles gathering unconsciously, *just so long as he doesn't realize that these frescoes are the code, the key, to the priceless treasures that lay slumbering, glittering, in the subbasement directly below. With that booty as a lever,* he reflected grimly, *the Krail could own Eisernon in less than a day.*

"They're not really bad," Aper ser Nalm pointed out, "if you like that sort of thing. Seems a monstrous waste of time." He continued his inspection of the walls, and the tension stretched out long and thin and elastic. "There's something about them that disturbs me, something I should remember . . ."

The physician made an abortive start toward Mennon, but realizing he couldn't examine him in the presence of the Overlord, headed for the door, stopped halfway, clearing his throat, and returned to the table where he had set up his equipment. His lips moved as if he was talking to himself, but his dry breath whispered away to nothing.

Beq nom-Pau broke the silence a little too heartily. "So! You helped the Overlord scuttle an Earthlikli ship—"

"He helped me."

The Commander's face was a chill mask. "Excellent!" He extended an antique, gold-filigreed cigarette case of Erthlikli manufacture, an anachronism he permitted himself. "How does it feel, killing your former allies?"

Mennon selected a smoke, lit it from Charvin's quick *feuer.* "No different than killing Krail," he mused. "Maybe a little noisier." He dragged luxuriously at the cigarette and glanced up, seemingly oblivious to his host's reaction. "Why do you ask?"

Aper ser Nalm chuckled mirthlessly. "Curiosity, my dear Mennon. We're eaten up by it." He clapped Beq nom-Pau's shoulder. "Come, nom-Pau, show me what you've done to this place. A monastery, wasn't it?" Beq nom-Pau reluctantly followed him into the corridor, rediscovering his hospitality with some effort.

We will deal with the Imperator's emissary now, and with the insolent Einai later. There were other Han about. The illusory telepaths were not nearly so rare as he had been led to believe. And one of them was a woman.

"—must remember, nom-Pau," the nobleman was saying, "his Han talents will repay us a hundredfold. He's already brainpicked several Earthlikli officers for us, with splendid results; therefore, the Imperator wants him kept content. He wanted to come here—in his stolen Earthlikli craft—and so we came—in that craft! He wants a certain woman purported to be here—and so we find the woman!"

"A woman, Overlord! But I know!"

"Don't anticipate me, nom-Pau. He isn't as free as one might suppose. Once his guard is down, we can get a shock-collar around his neck—then he's our animal."

"There may be some trouble about the woman, Overlord."

"Enough! There will be no trouble. You may regard that as an order!" He strode a few paces silently; then: "One woman cannot be very difficult to locate. I shall find her myself." Beq nom-Pau lifted his brows, amused. He'd tried, after all, to tell him. Now let the Nobleman fend for himself. He saluted submissively.

"The Fist of the Imperator," he murmured, acquiescing. Aper ser Nalm wondered why, for the rest of the tour, Beq nom-Pau seemed unusually cheerful and moved briskly, with great alacrity.

The jungle air, he thought. It must be the jungle air.

The physician watched them leave, standing uncertainly, half at attention, while their footsteps faded down the hall. Charvin remained outside the door. He wearily turned back to his erstwhile patient and found himself flat on his back with Mennon sitting on his chest, hands like vises around his throat. He shook his head, eyes boggling.

"I surrender," he squeaked. His face felt congested and it was hard to breathe.

"Weapons?" He shook his head again, gulping air past Mennon's hands, which mercifully let up a trifle.

"I'm not armed, brother. I'm a soldier, just like you. I'm a plain man, not like these noblemen, with their airs and graces. Just a country doctor, pressed into the service of his planet."

Mennon flung a glance at the door. "The soldier. Nom-Pau's aide."

"Charvin."

Mennon dragged him up, one arm across his throat. "Call him." The doctor took a deep breath and Mennon tightened his arm again, stifling the shout to a croak. "No signals, remember. Just call him."

No sooner had he called than Mennon felled him with a chop behind the ear. The door, swinging open, slammed shut with the Einai's full weight behind it, catching Charvin midway. He fell heavily against the jamb, trying to bring up the needler, but Mennon wrenched it out of his mashed hands and flung it aside, waving a viith under his nose.

"Quickly, now. I have no time and less patience." Charvin smiled and looked away. Mennon drew a thin red line, very shallow, on the fair throat, and snapped:

"A woman. Gold skin, gray eyes. Her name is Hennemmishli. Where is she?"

Charvin studied the junction of the wall with the heavy beams and sneered, and Mennon tossed away the viith, backing away and demonstrating his empty hands. "Krail umbin," he said contemptuously, "I am a Han."

Charvin cocked his head and studied him. "I don't think so, animal." He came away from the wall in an easy stalking awkwardness, typical of the Krail battle pace. "I think you're a liar."

"Then why are you afraid?"

Charvin, to prove that he wasn't, dove at Mennon and brought him crashing to the tiles. They were well matched and fought savagely, but Charvin gained the upper hand easily, as easily as if the Einai had planned it, and pinned his opponent to the tiles, reaching for the viith he'd discarded, reaching . . . he brought it down upon Mennon's right heart, but there was a blinding light in the Einai's eyes, a dazzling burst of brilliance in Charvin's brain, and black blobs danced in front of him, making his thrust go wild. He found that he couldn't see, and the realization terrified him as nothing ever had.

Mennon sprang up, snatching the viith away. "You see," he hissed, "I *am* a Han." Inside Charvin's head, pain grew with the brilliance, frighteningly, and he groped his way to a wall and up it.

"Yes." Charvin held his eyes, trying not to panic. *I am a Krail soldier. The Krail do not feel fear. The Krail do not feel pain. I am a Krail, the Krail do not feel fear, or*

114

pain, but— He could feel the Einai nearby, could sense his panthering back and forth, and his presence was both fear and pain.

"The woman. Where is she?"

"Gone." The word was torn from his throat. "She escaped."

"Where to?"

"I don't know. No one knows, I swear it. She disappeared."

Mennon's voice took on a faint overtone. "Was she well? Injured? Had she eaten?" Charvin was overlong in answering, and the pressure built up inside his head, making the black splotches dance sickeningly before his eyes. "Yes!" he ground out at last. "She was well. Dressed as a peasant boy." The pain grew.

"Where did you lose her?"

"I don't know. I don't know." He clapped his hands to his splitting head and staggered blindly, not knowing that Mennon's limited power made this inquest as agonizing for himself as for Charvin. He doubted he could keep it up much longer.

"Where?" He gave the Krail a last, desperate burst of anger.

"Bex-lakli! The road to Bex-lakli!"

Mennon released the pressure so quickly that Charvin fell to his knees and slumped to the ground, whole but stunned. The physician stirred, mumbling. Mennon steadied himself against the back of a chair for the space of two breaths and repeated, "Bex-lakli." Then, "Give the Noble ser Nalm my regards."

Slipping undetected out the rear exit was so simple as not to be discussed; reaching the nearest skimmercraft and setting its autopilot to impact in the near hills was another matter, which required the silent dispatching of two determined guards. Mennon found time to be grateful that the Krail were conditioned against loud noises and shouting.

In the confusion that followed the skimmers automatic liftoff, Mennon used the pulse-weapon a recumbent officer no longer needed, and fused the control panels on every one of the Krail skimmercraft, leaving them grounded. By the time he reached the Earthlikli craft, the weapon was almost drained, incapable of fusing the panel. He pulled the wires under the panel of the Earthlik craft, secretly glad that the weapon was drained, loath to destroy his last link with Dao, no matter how absurd. Besides, his practical nature reminded him that no Krail could repair the craft; their minds couldn't grasp the symbolism, didn't work that way. A mental blemish, Dao had called it. Whatever it was, he left the skimmer standing white and useless at the edge of the runway and plunged into the welcoming jungle before anyone could fully realize what had happened and who was responsible.

Several hours later, Kles Mennon staggered into guerilla headquarters, to the unbelieving delight of his men. They clapped his shoulders, hugged him in great, bear arms and pounded his head with joy. Somebody broke out a few bottles of terangi and popped the corks, sloshing the green bouquet of it all over hands, floor, faces. They poured it over Mennon's unprotesting head, pummeling him with delight. Ilai, his thin, bald lieutenant, touched the wicked gash on his upper arm where Charvin's viith stroke had fallen, unnoticed. "Mennon," he said in concern, you're hurt!"

Kles Mennon lowered the bottle of terangi he'd been draining, wiping his mouth on the sleeve of his Krail uniform.

"Hurt? No, Ilai," he laughed, "I'm *free!*"

Embers dreamed warmly in the firebowl, sighing golden reminiscence and gray ash. Sleeping shadows breathed, man-shaped, along the wall, and dampness seeped through the stone floor and cooled the small hours. A memlikt trilled in the jungle and one of the sentries, perched high in a fern tree, answered, the call passed from tree to thicket to rock outcropping and back again. *All's well*.

Mennon sat motionless, cross-legged, forearms resting on his knees, watching the fire. Ilai and Jek sat with him, asking nothing, requiring nothing, keeping the kin-vigil with Mennon even though there was no blood tie between him and Marik but the one they had fashioned for themselves as children, with cut wrists and fierce boyish vows of eternal brotherhood. Mennon did not speak to them, nor had he spoken to anyone since he had gotten up from the joyful meal celebrating his return, and poured a ritual palmful of tarangi, holding it high, at arm's length.

The men put down their bowls apprehensively, jokes and laughter murmured away and fell silent. Even the jungle was still. Mennon looked at each of them in turn.

"In the Name of Tadae," he announced distinctly, "let the Province be told: my Lord Priyam Hanshilobahr *Dom* Dao Marik is dead. I, Kles Mennon of Pal-alden-Shali-Rho, am witness." He spilled the tarangi slowly into the ground, letting it drip green as blood from his fingers and then, as tradition required, he ripped his garments to shreds. One of the men, an albino swamplander with emerald-green eyes, brought out a set of stoneglass rattles and crouched at the edge of the clearing, beating the old discordant native rhythm and pounding the hafts monotonously against the bars: . . . *ching-a-ching, thump, thump* . . . *ching-a-ching, thump, thump* . . . while Mennon, wearing a red band around his forehead, came out of the cave with the firebowl and set it on a high, flat rock. Ilai

117

grabbed his arm and whispered urgently, "Mennon—no," But Kles Mennon shook him off expressionlessly and joined the men who were already pacing off the circle for the Death Dance, absorbed in the rattles' insistant, hypnotic monotony, *ching-a-ching, thump, thump, ching-a-ching, thump, thump*. Their feet moved in intricate designs demonstrating events in Marik's life, here carefully constructing the spiral of a philosophy, there leaping the memory of a gryphon race. The rattles, warmed by the albino's hands, exhibited their own peculiar property: they became warmed, thinner, slowly losing their flat, declarative rattle and reverberated instead, bell-like, in deep, mellow echoes.

The albino began to sway in time with the rhythm, face half-hidden by his snowsilk hair, lost to everything but his hypnotic percussion, unaware of the looming trees or the dancers' shadows or the fevered and erratic breeze that made the coals breathe dragonfire and lick long tongues of flame at the starless sky; unaware as the dancers (so many of them, reliving Marik's life in reverent imitation) of anything but the sameness, the pattern, the hollow monotony of the repetitive stone bells. As they moved in unison through the complex visual narrative, the albino deliberately began to move them faster, degree by degree, sublimating their sorrow to motion, their grief to a pounding summation, until the mind anticipated the rhythm in an exquisite restlessness, an agony of expectation and exertion that brought a wet metallic sheen to the green-gold faces, the maximum pitch of tension to coiled and corded muscles. His bells were the meter to which their hearts hammered, the shallow measure of their breathing, the invisible wires jerking their puppet arms and legs, until over the hours the stately measures of the traditional death dance had accelerated into the wild, gyrating, bell-pealing, frothing frenzy of native ritual, and at its utter limit, when even the bells could evoke no more hysterical emotion, Mennon, slick and white-eyed and panting for breath, plunged both hands elbow-deep into the live coals and held fistfuls of them over his head, raining fire.

"*Dao!*" he roared at the top of his voice, "Dao!—come back!"

118

He stood frozen that way for an interminable moment, as if listening past the silence of the bells, the stillness of the men; then he flung the coals back into the firebowl and stalked wordlessly and with great dignity into the cave.

On the USS Hope, *light-years away, Dao Marik reluctantly opened his eyes and tried to focus on the faces that peered down at him through the MAX hood.*

" . . . Kles? . . ."

"Sharobi. You're in Recovery, Dao. How do you feel?"

Marik wanted to tell him about Kles, and the calling, but he closed his eyes against the light and the mist of sedation and heard—remotely—Sharobi tell him to rest, that he'd be in to see him later, and Marik let himself sink gratefully into the grayness wherein, somewhere, there were embers, yellow as the eyes of a friend.

Mennon was no sooner inside the cave than the men remembered to breathe, and quickly made the Infinity Sign at forehead and breast. Some of them bowed down to the ground and began the chanting which would continue intermittently for three days, while others, less religious, climbed signal trees and blew sonorous hollow tones through their cupped hands, a calling down a wind of time, a keening that would carry across the jungle. Waking villagers, hearing it and mourning, would pass it on to townsmen, who would pick it up, mourn, and climb dawn rooftops to blow their hands and thereby signal the next town, the next village, the next isolated shepherd.

Krail would hear it and dismiss it as illogical, and therefore meaningless, and the Earthlikli would laugh and wag their heads at quaint native custom; but before noon the following day, the entire province would know and be saddened that the last of the Mariks was gone.

For the Eight-day Time, street urchins would solemnly blow their hands through the alleys, and city women would go unbejewelled, their hair cropped short. Bars would close their doors and in every city, the House of A Hundred Delights would do no business, and its ladies would wear rags and dip their hands in white chalk to signify mourning. Village women would smear their faces with ashes in imitation of the Shimshenli's caste-mark and their men would bind their heads with sharlet bandeaux, even as Mennon wore now.

This knowledge comforted Mennon as he sat and stared at the embers. It was no small accomplishment to provide both the Mourning and the Eight-day Time in a state of war, during Krail occupation, and it was a deep satisfaction, a grim joy; but it had taken all he had. Now he was exhausted, his energy sapped. Chill tremors shuddered along the loosening muscles of forearm and thigh and shoulder, and his skin was icy. The burns on his hands and arms stung and were welcome, and he felt the overpowering need to sleep. Even big, silent Jek, keeping kin-vigil with him, nodded from time to time. Ilai, faithful, indomitable Ilai, sat erect, not moving a muscle. Mennon wondered idly what he was thinking.

Ilai was thinking of Marik—and of Mennon. He heaved a sigh. It was too bad about Priyam Marik, and he regretted his death; but he had mixed feelings about it, too. While he reverenced Marik, it was as a man admired a distant mountain, or believed in another galaxy. You knew it was there, but it didn't affect your everyday life. If it were destroyed, it was unbelievable, a heresy, a calamity; but it was everybody's calamity, and that made it easier to bear.

Mennon, now, was a different story. Mennon was alive and breathing, he could drink and fight and wench like a born backlander, yet his father had been nobility and he'd been brought up with them, and could turn a fair heel at round dances where ordinary folk were only allowed to watch. Ilai reverenced Marik—but he loved Mennon. Marik was the galaxy, important, remote, legendary. Mennon was his own personal sun. He cleared his throat and purposely broke the vigil with the question that no one else had dared ask, except with their eyes.

"With my Lord Dao Marik dead," he ventured, in the formal High Eisernai, "what of the Shimshen called Hennem-mishli?"

Mennon betrayed no sign of having heard him, except a line of muscle that tightened at his jaw. It was only when the eastern sky began to color that he looked up from cold eyes dead as gray ash . . . Mennon rubbed the burning from his yellow-ember eyes and answered Ilai's hour-old question.

"The Shimshen is somewhere in Bex-Elakli. Find her and bring her here to safety."

Ilai's expression was hooded, worshipful. "I will bring her here to *Mennon*," he corrected softly, and before Kles Mennon could open his mouth to protest, both Ilai and Jek had disappeared into the jungle.

The room was part of the guest suite of the monastery, now Beq nom-Pau's quarters, tastefully furnished, yet not without a certain austerity reminiscent, Paige thought, of the restrained opulence of Earth's Far East. Graceful arches opened onto one end of the gallery where Beq nom-Pau had stood, and a table of hand-rubbed bluewood served as a desk, virtually the only furniture in the room; but tall stands of various ferns and greenery softened the room's coldness and made it seem ethereal instead. The guard Powys (who had taken over in the corridor from Charvin when a message arrived) stood hard by the door, needler at ready. Unexpectedly, for the Krail were not given to unnecessary conversation, he said, "I will miss the chess games, Erthlik."

Blood from the scalp gash dried, itching, behind one ear. "Yeah." He listened for Ronhalovan but could hear only the dim quiet of the high, cool rooms. They were restful and clean, and smelled faintly of wool, of jasmin and of space. He took a few steps toward the open arches, shading his smarting eyes with his hand, but the needler snicked a warning behind him and he turned wearily back. "I'm listening for the boy," he said heavily. "If you'd let me help him last night, he wouldn't be down there hurting right now!"

"He lives, he dies . . . What is that to me?" Powys shrugged. "You are a strange people, you Earthlikli."

Brisk heels on flagging. A Krail youngster of about Ronhalovan's age stepped just inside the arches and hesitated, studying Paige candidly. Paige recognized the boy. He'd been following the slaves for over a week, sketchbook in hand, recording their motions, emotions and death, in his clean white pages. His uniform, predictably, was always creased and spotless, his boots shone, his manner was that of detached and superior interest. After he passed by, men spat.

122

Paige rubbed his watering eyes. He could no longer endure the contrast of shade to the brassy blue glare of sky, of shadow to the coarse, golden air outdoors. The deficient diet was beginning to tell on him: night-blindness, mucosal bleeding, the throbbing ache at the base of his skull.

"I am Nom-pau Alain. I watched you from the gallery," Alain said without preamble. "You're very quick." He sauntered into the room and paced a wide circle around Paige. "I did several rather good sketches of you and Charvin. Would you like to see them?" There was a boyish wistfulness in the question, just under the slick veneer of sophistication, but Paige chose to ignore it.

"You people didn't bring me up here to show me your etchings, Charlie. Get to the point."

"I miss the significance of 'etchiks', I'm afraid. Is this an art form?"

"Some people think so. Some people think *medicine* is an art form, and I was practicing a rudimentary version of that art when your gorilla Charvin yanked me up here. Now, what do you want? I've got a sick kid down there to take care of!"

"Down there? Oh, I see. In the pens. Ah, but you aren't going back there anymore, Paige. You're my slave now. Father gave you to me."

"Gave me to— You've got to be kidding, Charlie. I belong to *me!*—and I'm going to take care of that boy whether you like it or not!" He started for the door, but Powys swung the needler up to his shoulder in one smooth swing, sighting right on his throat.

Paige stopped, his eyes narrowed. "Let me pass, Powys."

"I don't want to kill you, Earthlik. You taught me the chess. We spoke together, long nights sleepless." His accent made the language sound ungainly, but the message came through. "Live—and let him die."

"*I can't!*" He whirled on Alain. "Don't you care if that boy dies?"

Alain crossed to the desk and picked up his sketchbook and stylus. "Boy?" he asked coolly. "Powys, do you know what Paige is talking about?"

Paige moved his head. The needler relaxed into port-arms, the face was masklike. "No, young Master." Alain laughed softly. "Tell me, Paige," he asked, trying a few

123

experimental strokes, "how can you bear to smell like that? Doesn't it disgust you?"

"Yeah, it disgusts me," Paige admitted evenly, "but not like watching you sit here, clean and full-bellied, when I know they're down there dirty and sick and needing the help you won't give them. How do you jokers manage to sleep nights?"

Alain glanced up and smiled thinly. "Perhaps we are merely well-disciplined savages, Paige. Perhaps we are barbarians." He put down the half-completed drawing and opened the lattices to an adjacent room.

Masculine colors, subtly blended; textures, forms, bound volumes and the smells of leather and sour alien spice. He gestured briefly at the score of masterful sketches matted on the wall, the portraits, the metal and stone effigies of great statesmen and nameless beauties that had graced half-a-score of planets. "And perhaps not," he finished quietly. "My personal quarters, can you tell?"

Paige's bare feet sank incongruously into deep, rich carpet. "So what's all this supposed to prove? That you're civilized? Guess again."

"You've no feeling for art, Paige." He sighed, shrugging. "Small wonder. Your entire culture is built on superstition and the neon light."

"We have a feeling for freedom, though, Charlie. We feel pretty strong about people—and freedom."

"Ah—freedom. But only adolescents believe in freedom, Paige." He slouched into a chair, then rose again, impatiently. "There can be such a thing as too much freedom!"

"Tell it to Ronhalovan."

The young Krail's long fingers caressed a *bun* tapestry, hand-knotted by The Keepers, an Order of congenitally blind monks who wove the Galaxy's music into their tapestries. A truly perceptive 'viewer', it was said, could trace the knotting and infallibly indentify the composition down to the last grace note. "My father considers art a weakness, Paige," Alain intruded softly. "What do you think?"

Grimly, "We were talking about prisoners."

Alain wheeled, his thin face animated. "Ah, but what excellent subjects they make! The lines of them, the colors! A certain sheen—have you noticed it about them? —where they sweat?—a golden film, a—"

"They're men!" Paige shouted. "You're not talking about daubs of paint on some moldy canvas, those are men! All right, so they've never painted a picture or carved marble!—but this isn't a war of art we've fighting, it's a war of men!" Ghosts of syllables reverberated faintly in the elegant room.

Alain strolled over to the bust of an ancient Earthling General that Paige didn't recognize, and regarded it soberly. "You're wrong, you know." He measured his words carefully. "It isn't a war of men at all. It's a war of *ideologies*." He fixed Paige with the same thoughtful gaze he had accorded the sculpure. "The last war of men was fought on horseback—and to the sound of trumpets."

"Excellent!" Aper ser Nalm remarked with amused sarcasm from their hidden vantage point. "How delightful, nom-Pau, that your son is a poet as well as an artist. Krailion has so few songbirds."

"My heir *must be* a soldier!" Beq nom-Pau ground out. "Alain is a bitter disappointment, a tragedy. Would that he had died in his infancy!"

Aper ser Nalm craned his neck for a better view of the Earthling slave. "Surely that could have been arranged," he replied absently. "You say the man's name is Paige?"

"*Duli* Paige, Noble. He'd kill me, if he could."

Aper ser Nalm was interested. The Earthlik was intelligent and showed a measure of breeding, standing out conspicuously above the usual run-of-the-mill captive Einai; his height, his fairer hair, the repulsive red-bronze of sunburned Earthlik skin. The color bothered Aper ser Nalm, had always bothered him, even during negotiations with the Earthlik diplomats. He could tolerate the restful green of the Einai, even find it somewhat pleasant, because he regarded them as animals, or at best, homonids; but this Paige obviously had a mind behind those (brown!) eyes, and Aper ser Nalm would like to have been able to explore it (and exploit it, if need be) without the offensive coloration distracting him. A pity, actually, he thought. Like being maimed. Part of his mind, obedient to its training, searched and replayed information regarding the effect of color prejudice in interspecies relationships; he clamped it off firmly and leaned forward for a better look at the Erthlik.

"How much?" he asked abruptly.

"The Noble Aper ser Nalm has a daughter—" Beq nom-Pau began, and the emissary cut him off coldly.

"I would not consider my daughter Favored by a poet."

Nom-Pau bit his lip. "Would you Favor her with a soldier, Noble?"

Aper ser Nalm narrowed his eyes, thinking fast. Absurd, of course, this common soldier Favoring his daughter. And yet—he reran nom-Pau's family lines and history with mnemonic precision—there had been several Tetrarchs, not too recently, to be sure, but the genes were there. Nom-Pau had risen rapidly from Armsman to Commander, and the Imperator had been keeping a close eye on him, worried, perhaps. Well, why not? Beq nom-Pau was ruthless and efficient, just the sort of a man to aspire to heights too far above his station, and just the sort to scale them, too, if he weren't closely watched. The genteel poor always felt they had something to prove, which made them extremely ambitious—and useful.

The heir, now combining nom-Pau's aggressive dominants with his own of diplomacy, deviousness and intellect . . . He lifted his brows. Perhaps it wasn't such a bad idea. One could always rule through an heir. And he could trade Paige into the bargain, brainpick him, hold him as hostage if things went badly in negotiation—as they almost certainly would—these coming weeks. The Erthlikli were insanely protective about each of their members; they would forfeit an entire city for one family. He wondered what, if anything, they would forfeit for Paige.

Meanwhile, he could enjoy flaunting an Erthlik slave before that fool, Vartik, who'd been trying to buy an Earthlik for five years. He realized that Beq nom-Pau was watching him, and he smiled.

"It is not common knowledge, nom-Pau, but I have several consorts, and daughters by each of them. Shall I suggest one, or will you choose?"

"I would not presume to make such a difficult decision, Noble. Your choice is mine."

Aper ser Nalm bowed, as to a social equal.

It was agreed, then. After dinner tonight Beq nom-Pau would pay the bride-price—which included the Earthlik slave known as Paige—to his kinsman-to-be, Aper ser Nalm, and together they would read the physician's report assuring the Commander of the girl's health, vigor and ability to bear offspring. They would hear the tapes of the character witnesses (although nom-Pau would normally have felt uneasy about taped interviews—tapes could so easily be altered—it was mathematically improbable that the Imperator's Emissary, with so many men eager to Favor his daughters, would bother.)

And at last, they would each sign the document the necessary three times. Afterward, they would be free to relax, drink and discuss the war. The girl would be notified when Aper ser Nalm got around to it.

Beq nom-Pau was secretly gratified that his consort was to be the younger daughter. The new heir was of paramount importance, and there was an old Krail saying, 'The younger the bride, the better the ovum'. It was a biological fact, honed down to a homey, sentimental proverb repeated daily in every Krail creche. It was heartwarming to the point of embarrassment to hear the children repeating it in their hundreds, in class. But it was a true and time-honored saying and Beq nom-Pau, anticipating his new son, was delighted by it.

Now there remained only the task of informing Alain. He wondered idly how his son would take the news.

As he might have expected, Alain took it badly. Instead of well-bred, calm acceptance of the fact that he was to be replaced as the heir, he'd paled visibly and become coldly formal, agreeing to sign the legal relinquishment documents, but balking stubbornly at giving up his slave of only a few hours.

"Will you leave me nothing, Father? My birthright, my status, my name, now even this slave is to be taken? I had outlined a series of sketches around him, planned a—"

Beq nom-Pau cut him off sharply, acutely conscious of Aper ser Nalm, examining Paige interestedly from a few yards distance, walking this way and that, thoughtfully rubbing his white, smooth-shaven chin. The Commander hissed, louder than he'd intended, "Your plans are of no consequence to me. The Paige belongs to Overlord Aper ser Nalm."

"No dice." It was Paige who had spoken, unexpectedly, and Powys brought the needler up alertly. "Paige belongs to Paige." He lifted his chin at Aper ser Nalm. "I'll make a deal with you, Charlie."

Beq nom-Pau laid a hand on his light-whip. "The Overlord does not bargain with animals, Paige."

"Hear him out, nom-Pau, this is interesting." The Nobleman sank into a chair with the grace of a mantis. "Proceed."

"All right, here's how it goes: I'm no good to you or anyone else if I'm dead or in chains. You let me set Ronhalovan's leg so he has an even chance, and I'll go along peacefully. Try to take me out of here by force, and I'll manage to get myself killed just to keep you from getting me."

Ser Nalm studied Paige calmly, considering the options, including a few the Earthlik hadn't thought of. "I saw the slave, down in the compound. He is not even of your species. Why the concern?"

Paige twitched his tired smile. "If you have to ask, I couldn't explain it."

"Even if I were to allow you to continue with this line of thought, my physician tells me that the Einai needs surgery to survive. Are you proposing to proceed without anesthesia, down in that filthy compound? Is this the mercy you Earthlikli are so noted for?"

Paige tried unsuccessfully to mask the hope that surged in him. "There is a surgical/maternity complex right here in the monastery. I've used it before. Sometimes the Shimshenli are delivered by Caesarian section, and the fetal transplants are always a sterile procedure. If I could—" He saw the cynical amusement in Aper ser Nalm's face and clamped off his eagerness, toning it down to an abrupt "—if I could borrow the equipment, I think I could bail him out."

The Overlord had intended to refuse him. These side jaunts into sentimentality always left him weary. But he admired science, knew that it had abundant military applications, and Paige had shown an interesting vulnerability in that direction, a lever, as is were. Besides, the Earthlik had offered to go peacefully, to, in effect, cooperate with the enemy. Whether or not that was what he'd intended, Aper ser Nalm was determined to take it that way, and hold him to it. He nodded.

"Very well. You have a bargain. Nom-Pau, have them fetch the slave. Paige, you will show me these operating chambers. The women of the monastery will get you whatever you need." To Powys, "See to it."

"But the prisoner, Overlord—!"

Aper ser Nalm watched Paige flex and limber his hands abstractedly. He smiled. "I don't think I have anything to fear from the prisoner."

The scrub, which extended from pate to soles, was an ecstacy. He washed half the swamp down the drain, scraped the stubble of the scissored beard off his face with a borrowed Einai razor, and slid into the familiar/unfamiliar surgical greens with a wordless prayer of gratitude to whatever God or gods protected the Einai.

The round, cream-walled operating theater was home territory. He'd often delivered for the Shimshenli when someone went sour, and routinely did their fetal transplants for them in exchange for the use of their facility (and assistance, for they were medically trained, the equivalent of Earthling physicians) when a difficult case turned up at the clinic.

He'd also done 'storing' procedures here, the delicate removal of a fetus from a biomother who could—or would not carry it, and the subsequent nitrogen-flashing that suspended its life, frozen—but did not kill or injure it—until an available womb could be found among the Shimshenli or adoptive mothers.

For a moment the 'jewel vaults', as the Shimshenli called them, flashed through his mind; deep below in the subcellar, row upon row of golden spheres glowing in the muted light, eternal Christmas (for was not Christmas the Celebration of Life and Light?). And in each of the thousands of ornaments (planets, mirrors), tiny people, from zygote to palm-sized miniature infants, ice-frosted, living fossil imprints of the parents, suspended in amber, ambiguity, amnionic ice.

He remembered (towelling off from his scrub beside the Krail physician) walking down one of the myriad rows where the babies who were wanted by their bioparents had been stored and tagged for safekeeping until after the war. Children with names and translated codons. This dark comma was to be a little red-haired girl who would love horses and be allergic to jat hair; that little boy, curled with vestigial hands near vestigial heart, would be very good at music and impossibly slow at chemistry, and would have a way with mechanical things. *Luvana, Boy,* read the tag on the next one, along with a list of characteristics. Paige's mind accompanied him down the line of golden spheres even as he moved toward the operating room doors.

Luvana, Boy; Luzk, Girl; Mai, Girl; Marik. Girl; Nux, Boy . . . So many of them, sleeping there; and he'd helped them live, had delivered them from the blind, seeking, plastex snake that would have sucked them cleanly from their mothers' wombs like marrow from a bone, and *flash!* into the incinerator, *whoosh!* up the flue, no blood, no guilt, the Ultimate Solution charred instantly into baby-shaped cinders, along with their music, their laughter, their tantrums and whatever potential for love and destruction slumbered with them.

He'd preserved them from the terror of birth during open warfare, too, from bombs and Krail and helpless, uncomprehending wailing on a shattered breast; husbanded them against the time of being wanted, of murmuring and womb-warmth and bright, squalling emergence into the morning of peace.

Now he had a chance to save Ronhalovan, too, from the agony of a world not of his own making. He chuckled, making the Krail physician, still scrubbing at the sink, glance at him quizzically. *But who among us makes his own world anyway? We take the one we've got and do the best we can with it.* He supposed he'd have ample opportunity to test that bit of philosophy in the next few —months? Years? Please God, not years.

He shoved his way through the ancient swinging doors and into the operating room. Ronhalovan had been prepped and sedated and was on the table, his leg elevated and draped. The leg was badly swollen below the knee, the foot cyanotic and dwarfed by the elephantine ankle; the fracture had perforated the skin, a result, he thought, of Charvin's insistent summons back in the arena. He felt for the pulses; they were light and unsteady, not bounding, as he would have hoped.

A Shimshen, masked and gloved, began washing the leg down with an antiseptic solution while another clamped a battery of X-rays and lascans of unusually fine resolution to a backlit, frosted-glass wall. The ladies really outdid themselves in technology this time, Paige thought; rarely did lascans show up so beautifully, pin-point damage so well. These films were the Shimshenli's passive approval, wordless support—and they couldn't be quoted.

While Paige was studying them, the Krail physician entered and said that he was ready. They decided to pin the tibia and splint the fibula—the pinbone—with narrow plastimetal bands which were tough, neutral and could be bonded to the bone with surgical epoxy. Nerve, tendon and soft tissue reconstruction would depend on the extent of damage once they got in.

Paige hesitated the barest fraction of a second before he began. He'd been away from it for a while and was un-easy. *Suppose,* his mind said meanly, *just suppose you've forgotten or gone sloppy.*

But then the training, the reflexes, the almost instinctive professionalism took over, and he was in and out of the ankle in just under three hours. Barring complications, Ronhalovan would have no further trouble, heal prompt-ly and be good as new.

He came out of the scrubroom feeling elated. He'd done a good job for a patient he liked, and the prognosis was excellent. Now he was ready for a thick steak, a stiff drink and twelve hours of uninterrupted sleep. He pushed open the door.

Aper ser Nalm was waiting for him in the hall, with Charvin behind him, needler lying easily, lethally in his arm.

Paige walked forward to meet them, with the feeling at the pit of his stomach of falling from a great height.

131

Behind the barracks there was a break in the fence, which opened immediately on a dirt road edged with grubby land-coral and heavily-travelled by vehicles carrying men and cargo to and from the war zone. Beyond the road, where the jungle grew dense and deep and thick, foliage screened away the Erthlikli and their world, there was a virgin stream of clear water, afloat with exotic spindly-legged blossoms and inhabited by several species of small fish.

Every day, when the work was done and everything had been set to rights, Ilen would slip away to lie on the flat rock overhanging the stream and watch the fish for hours, lost in thought. Once Garrett, having called several times, scouted the area and found Ilen lying prone on the rock, chin on her folded arms, the fish darting unnoticed below, but he had to tap her shoulder before Ilen—reluctantly dragging herself back from whatever far wanderings had occupied her mind—sighed pensively, gently patted his hand—and smiled.

Ilen smiled faintly again, recalling it, the rough surface of the rock cool and comfortable through the coarse fabric of her tunic and trousers. The tops of her bare feet stretched into damp, springy loam, and she wiggled her toes deliciously, lazily, and half-drowsed.

Things had gone well for her, even with the constant threat of Ross' smouldering watchfulness. The work was light, a low-key monotonous routine that fit well with Ilen's mood. She had been with Garrett's squad for a long time, a month, two, perhaps even four. Time slipped by, tasteless, too slow to measure, too swift to count. It didn't matter. After the jarring tension of Krail occupation and the reckless flight into the jungle with the Earthlik duli, it was comforting to lose oneself in the humdrum flow of everyday tasks, to blend with the scenery; not required to charm, to converse, to appreciate, but merely to vegetate

132

gratefully on a sea-floor level—she let her imagination drift idly—scudding slowly along with the crabs and other crustacea, hiding in her own welcome shell of enforced silence like a contemplative, wordlessly encysting: *nothing Else exists.*

She smiled softly. Ilen, boy crustacean. That brought a small frown. She responded to a masculine name, lived among men, even thought of herself as the boy Ilen. Soberly, she wondered where Hennem-mishli had got to, and if she'd lost that part of herself entirely. It occurred to her, as it did in infrequent low moments, that she might never again be fully Hennem-mishli. She wondered what her grandfather would say to that, and frowned again.

Grandfather.

And Dao.

It was strange; her mind could reach out to Dao and encounter a presence, no matter how pained or muddled (how like him to share his patients' suffering, and thereby diminish it); when she reached out for her grandfather, there was only an enormous emptiness, an absence, that sent her mind skittering back in fear and awe. There were Places even a Han's mind dare not go. *But how could grandfather venture there, unless he was. Unless he was.* Ilen bit her lip and said aloud, softly but clearly, "My grandfather, Oman Shari-Mnenoplan, is at Sum ChiT'ath."

She reached out to Dao again, feeling with a thousand tendrils, seeking, questioning discarding. She found him. Exultation now, *but he was far, far, a montage of agony and non-thought and raw id, struggling to survive.* It frightened her. She probed deeper, casting about and caught the tenuous edge of another, rational mind, *concern and intelligence and competence,* and for a moment she thought she might grasp the identity, too, but it was drowned by one coarse, blunt thought, nearby.

That ain't no boy.

Ilen leaped to her feet, aware too late of another presence, that of Ross, with his beer smell and his dirty fingernails, leaning against a nearby tree.

"You ain't no boy, baby," he repeated aloud. He disengaged himself from the tree and sauntered toward her with his easy, rolling gait, like a bear she'd once seen in an Earthlikli *zu.* She edged back along the rock and

133

made the mouth-throat-hand gesture that insisted she was mute, but Ross wasn't having any of it.

"Don't give me that stuff," he chortled. "I heard you mumblin' to yourself just now. I don't mind, see, if you're playin' footsie with Sarge, just so you be real nice to ol' Papa here . . . " He stepped up onto the edge of the rock, assuming a predatory stance, arms hooked, head low, making a playful feint toward her now and then to see her jump, and enjoying himself thoroughly. Ilen dodged him warily, agile as a jat, but her foot slipped over the lip of the rock and she plunged into the stream with a shrill yelp of surprise. Ross ran around the outcropping and into the steam after her, chased her a few foundering yards before he caught her, wet and bedraggled, and pulled her against him.

"Say 'uncle'," he smirked.

"Uncle," said the flat voice behind him, and Ross dropped Ilen as he wheeled to face Garrett, standing easy and empty-handed on the bank behind him. Ross shook his head and grinned.

"You don't understand, Sarge. Uh, she fell in the water —" Garrett hit him in the stomach and he staggered backward, holding his middle. "Sarge, for God's sake, she's only a gook broad, she—" The next one hit him in the eye, starting a quickly purpling lump. Ross swore and began to fight back, which was exactly what Garrett wanted; he had no relish for hitting a man who just stood there talking. Now it was on an even basis. He aimed mainly for the belly, which left no marks but did a lot of damage. Garrett regretted Ross' eye—and his own cut, under the left brow, that kept bleeding and getting in his way—but made up for it by concentrating on body blows that quickly tired Ross out. The burly man tried clinching, panting from the unaccustomed exertion, but Garrett finished him with a short left to the midsection and a blow to the chin that carried everything he had left.

He heard the crack in his hand before he felt it, before Ross hit the water and lay there without moving. Wearily, he caught the back of his collar and hauled Ross' inert frame onto the bank and sat down beside him, arms folded across his knees. He took a few deep breaths and looked up at Ilen.

"You okay?"

"Alai," she replied, kneeling beside him with a concerned air. She picked up his hand and felt it carefully, noting when he winced. Her lips compressed tightly and she held the hand steady. "Hankefish?"

"Handkerchief," he corrected tiredly, and handed it to her. She pulled a scale of bark off Ross' tree and bound his hand snugly to it; then she ripped off part of her sleeve and wiped his face clean, carefully avoiding the clotting cut over his eye. Ross shook himself and sat up snorting and grunting like a bull walrus.

"Ross." The big man scowled at him. "You open your mouth about any of this, I'm gonna tear off your ears and jam 'em down your throat, you got that?" His voice did not vary from its conversational tone, but Ross recognised its even monotony and the fury that could lie behind it, and he growled assent, shook himself like a big dog and tramped off toward the road.

Garrett watched him, troubled in his mind. Ross was sure to make an incident of the fight, especially since he'd lost; then it would come out that Garrett had been 'harboring a female alien in quarters', with all the problems and connotations inherent in such an accusation. He found himself wishing that he'd left Ilen where he found her. She tugged his arm.

"Tu priyam," she suggested softly, and he examined his hand ruefully.

"Yeah. My medic. I guess you're right. You go on back to the barracks; Ross won't bother you. I'll see you after I get this fixed and we'll decide what to do about you, okay?"

She nodded; then: "Sarj?" He paused. "Buchat ge."

Thank you. His mouth quirked. "Go on, get back to the barracks." He set off through the open woods toward the dispensary, thinking that he guessed having Ilen around hadn't been too bad and wishing, in a way, that she didn't have to go.

There were just a couple of men on sick call when Garrett got there, and the nurses and medics were talking and joking among themslves through the thin cubicle walls as they worked. There was one doctor no one spoke much to, a smallish, blond fox of a man with hair cut so short his scalp shone through a stubble of fine bristles.

After a while he motioned to Garrett, who followed him into a cubicle unknotting the handkerchief with his teeth and free hand. The scale of bark hit the floor with a small shower of noise and flakes, and the doctor pointedly picked it up and dropped it delicately into a waste chute. Garrett was about to apologize when the doctor snapped his head back and examined his eye with a rough thumb. "What's your name?"

"Garrett, sir."

"I'm Danton Parks. Here on TDY. I guess you've heard about me, haven't you?"

"No, sir." The antiseptic burned in Parks' brusque hands, and Garrett threw a look at him.

"Humh! Only man on base who *hasn't*—and talked about it, too! Hold still." He applied stitches with a portable hand suture, the intermittent pinpoints of actinic light like a welder's torch, reflected in his pupils as he bent close. "I'm the guy who was kicked off the USS *Pacific*, right before she was scuttled," he murmured, intent on his work, and Garrett muttered embarrassedly, "Oh. Yeah. I guess I did hear something about that. They, uh, thought maybe you, uh . . . "

Parks straightened and clicked off the unit. "That's right. I saw what was coming and took sanctuary with the Provincial Protector; and when the Brass read the spy-eye tapes and found out it was a Krail job—with a healthy assist from one of our *good—Einai—allies*, they graciously allowed me to return to the war, no hard feelings." He jerked his head toward the cubicle wall. "Try to tell it to those jokers. Here, let me see that hand." He felt it, noting Garrett's involuntary jerk as he manipulated the fracture; went to a cabinet and pulled out supplies. "Those damned gooks ought to be ripped off one by one until we wipe 'em out, right?" He paused, hands full of plastex cast-compound and solvent, waiting for Garrett's reply. The sergeant felt his rough tooth warily with the tip of his tongue.

"Sir, I go where they send me—and I do my job—and I don't think about it much, one way or the other. That's how I like it."

Parks laughed shortly as he dumped the plastex powder into a basin and watched it bubble into a viscous liquid. "Who'd you hit?"

136

"One of the men was hassling my houseboy."

"One of us for one of them, eh?" The plastex was turning into transparent gel. "Here, stick your hand in this—about halfway up the arm." Garrett complied; then:

"Look, Lieutenant, I don't know what your beef is, about the Einai, and I don't want to know. I just don't want to have to be a part of it."

"You're already a part of it, Garrett!" Parks snapped. "You were a part of it the minute you pulled that gook Marik out from under that Krail CP at Sum ChiT'ath!"

"It was a hospital!" The reply shot back of its own volition.

"And he was a Han! You rescued a Han and you didn't report it!—you concealed it! Do you know what the penalty is for concealing a Han, Sergeant?"

"That law's been obsolete for fifty years, Lieutenant. There hasn't been but maybe a dozen Han-hunts, all that time!"

"The law is still on the books. I checked it out."

Garrett said slowly, "Looks like you checked out a lot of things. Sir." *And just how much do you know—about Sum ChiT'ath?*

"I did my homework, Sergent," Parks smiled tightly. "I had six months to do nothing else but check on the Han—and you."

Garrett's jaw dropped. He wasn't worried about himself. His record was clean, and he felt pretty sure that old law wouldn't hold up. But the Einai, the one he'd pulled out of the ruins!—(what was it Parks had called him? Marik?)—could he have been a Han? He remembered with a rush the strangeness, the intellect in the level, gray eyes, and his men's concern that he might've been 'taken over'. He'd been so sure they were wrong, so certain of himself, and yet—he sat stunned. *Yet Ilen, too, had gray eyes!*

Ilen, who'd been quietly working, listening, perhaps storing information all these months. And she'd wanted to get to Sum ChiT'ath, too, in the beginning, he recalled, aghast, though she'd not mentioned it lately. He wondered why. A suspicion grew, small at first, but gaining ground. He pulled himself together as best he could, grasping for a few last shreds of loyalty to a people he had no real reason to be loyal to, a people he could not even hope to understand.

"But—he couldn't've been a Han! They're extinct—aren't they? Wiped out."

"You brought one in, Sergeant. You figure it."

Garrett worried his tooth. "Lieutenant, what does a real Han look like? I mean, aside from the monster and witchfolk stories, what do they look like? You ever seen one?"

Parks cleaned the remaining plastex off his fingers with a towel soaked in solvent. "Sure. I dragged one about two hundred yards last year. Truth." He grinned at Garrett's puzzlement. "A buddy of mine, gun collector, lives in the rain forest upcountry, where the Han used to be thick as thieves. Had me up for a weekend last spring, thought we'd get in a little shooting. It was a bust, from start to finish. First the beaters couldn't flush any game, and then when we got a couple on our own hook, we lost the beaters. Scared hell out of 'em when they saw those glassy gray eyes staring at 'em. They ran off yelling about 'alien stars', or some such rot. So we had to drag the damned carcasses back to camp ourselves." He paused and peered at Garrett closely. "You look a little pale. You want to lie down?"

"I'm all right."

"Well, I think you look shocky. Why don't you rest for a minute?" A hypo hissed and Garrett angrily jerked his arm away.

"I said I'm all right," Garrett insisted sharply. "You were going to tell me what the Han looked like. Sir."

"Yes." He continued, chuckling, "We dragged those damned stiffs back to camp in the midday heat, with about four billion flies and crawling things buzzing in our ears and the saber grass so tall you couldn't see over it, and you know what we'd brought down? After all that?" He chuckled again. "I bagged an old duffer whose bones creaked, if you looked at him crooked, and my buddy lucked out and got a young buck about seventeen who hung back to help *my* target. We had to leave 'em there, of course, with no bearers to haul 'em out; not that they would've made very good trophies anyway. We got some good tri-D pictures, though. Sure you wouldn't like to lie down?"

Garrett's head felt heavy with disgust and his mouth felt thick. "I asked you what they looked like." His ears were ringing and it made both their voices reverberate mildly.

"They're pretty much like your everyday gook, except for those gray eyes. Battleship gray, they used to call it, gray like a dove, like a cold rain." His image wavered before Garrett's eyes. "Some say there's a lot of difference in bone structure and build and skintone, but I can't see it. One gook looks just like the next one to me." He slapped the cast briskly. "Want to lie down? Tired yet?"

Garrett shook his immensely, heavy head. " . . . no . . ."

"Funny. Hypnine usually makes people want to lie down—and tell secrets. They always want to tell their secrets. Don't you have any secrets you want to tell me, Sergeant? Anything at all?"

Garrett scowled through a dark tunnel at earnest blue eyes that were a little too eager, a little too bright. " . . . no, sir, only . . ."

"Only what, Sergeant?"

"Only my houseboy, Lieutenant. My—my houseboy has gray eyes."

Parks shrugged elaborately. "Probably nothing. Probably nothing at all. But just to make sure, I'll give you a little post-suggestion, eh? You won't remember any of this, after I snap my fingers; but when you see your houseboy next, you'll bring him here to me so we can have a look, eh? Make sure he's not one of those filthy Han."

Garrett's head moved slowly from side to side. "I—I'm not sure, I" He was showing signs of coming out of it, and Parks barked, "Let's make that an order, Sergeant!"

"Yes, sir." The automatic, conditioned response. Good. Parks snapped his fingers and Garrett gazed at him blankly for a minute, and left looking puzzled.

When the room was safely empty, Parks pulled out his telecom and punched a private number, under a scrambler key. The Protector would want to know about the presence of another Han in this Province. It wouldn't do to have someone running loose who could control others' minds at will, and probe even one's most private thought, yes, and even their dreams. As the Protector had agreed, it was immoral and indecent. And Parks owed the Protector a favor. His Excellency had pulled strings to keep

139

him out of front-line duty, even after the flap that Sharobi had made over Marik.

Well, hell, he thought defensively, how was he to have known who Marik was, or what interest the name would have for the Protector? You win a few, you lose a few. If you have powerful friends, you didn't lose too much—and you might win quite a lot. He brightened as the connection came through.

"My name is Parks. Danton Parks," he announced confidently. "I'd like to speak to His Excellency, Protector Neron Vartik." He paused. "Of course, I'll wait. Thank you."

Ross occupied a barstool in the Columbia Eagle Bar, which was virtually empty, sullenly nursing his drink and his newly-blackened eye. He had poured some of the ice from his glass into a crumpled handkerchief and held it against the offending eye, while rivulets of dilute alchohol trickled down his neck and into his soiled collar.

"Damn' noncom ain't got no right to hit a man," he muttered to nobody in particular. "Ain't got the right to keep no dame around the barracks, neither." He raised his voice belligerently. " 'Speshly one of them eye-eye broads. Nobody gots the right." He nodded to himself. "Nobody."

There were few other patrons in the bar, only a few GI's, who occasionally called back derisive encouragement to the grumbling Ross, and a couple of Einai soldiers in their smooth gray uniforms and camouflaged overtunics, who ignored him. In one corner, two Einai bushmen sat, drinking little, talking not at all, as if waiting for someone.

"I knew Ilen was a girl," Ross burst out suddenly, and added, after draining half his glass, "I oughta report him, that's what. See how Mister Sergeant Garrett'd get himself outa that one, that's what . . ." He lifted his head and saw that the bushmen had taken seats on either side of him, though the other stools were vacant. One was a large, silent, burly fellow, with a worn viith slung over his shoulder; the other, the spokesman for the two, was small, bald and wiry. He gestured to the bartender.

"Kahnet. Get my friend another drink." He slid his gaze to Ross. "The same?"

"Uh, sure. Sure." Then louder: "why not? You guys

140

oughta buy us a few drinks. We're savin' your planet for you, ain't we? Sure. Buy me two, if you want."

The alien's face was unreadable. "Kahnet. Two drinks for my friend. Make them double."

Ross slapped him on the back, hard. "That's the kinda gratitude I like, buddy! I knew there had to be some eye-eyes that wasn't dead ones! Get it?" He laughed, slapping the silent giant, too; but the big bushman caught his wrist in a granite grip that made the bones creak. He shook his head ponderously from side to side.

"Don't hit Jek," he rumbled, and Ross found himself shaking his head along with him.

"Uh, no," he stammered, "no, I was, uh, I was kidding, you know? Kinda horsin' around." Jek dropped his wrist like a stone and repeated, "Don't hit Jek."

Kahnet sloshed Ross' two drinks on the bar in front of him and the small man paid in the slender, cylindrical money of the Einai.

"You mentioned that your leader had struck you, my friend," he offered. "Is that not against your rules?"

"You better know it!" Ross expostulated, and added ominously, "There's a lot of things against the rules, but I ain't gonna mention 'em here." He drained the glass and lifted it briefly in thanks to the little man.

"Of course not," his new friend agreed, pushing the fuller glass in front of him. "What pity that the man chosen leader cannot lead; while others, perhaps more deserving, were passed by."

"Yeah," Ross assented; then, "Yeah! I could've done a lot better job on some of them Krail we came up against, too, boy, and I wouldn't've wasted a lotta time babyin' 'em along, either. One sight of a Krail pelt and pow!—I would've brought in bazookas and cleaned 'em out."

"And your Captain—he could not see the wisdom of this course?"

"Aw, he ain't no Captain," Ross demurred. "He's a Sergeant. Maybe you heard of him? Joe Garrett, 369th?"

"Unfortunately—"

"Don't get me wrong, he ain't a bad leader. At least he wasn't 'till now. But, hell, if he's got something good stashed away, he can't blame a man for trying to get his share."

The small man signalled Kahnet for more drinks, even

141

though he had barely touched his own. Ross looked around for the quiet giant, but he was nowhere to be seen. He gestured with a thumb.

"What happened to your friend?" The Einai blinked solemnly.

"He left," he said, as if it was an explanation, and Ross felt that something was wrong but couldn't put a mental finger on it. He sipped the new drink experimentally and then dipped his whole muzzle in it. It was an eye-eye concoction, a beverage the natives had dreamed up, with mung juice and bourbon and lots of things he couldn't identify in it. The fumes rose up through his throat and nostrils and into his head and made him irrepressibly giddy. He put down the glass and started to chuckle at nothing in particular, the tears starting from his eyes, and when he looked around, the smaller man was gone, too; but he found that the only thing he was able to do was sit there and laugh weakly, with his wet face and helpless hands, until two very sober MPs came and picked him up.

The sentry at the West Gate fixed the two burdened Einai with a jaundiced eye and brought his needler to port-arms. "Halt," he ordered, and they obediently stopped, barefoot and innocent, in the middle of the bare road, under the pounding sun. "What's in the basket?"

The giant bushman put down the article in question, a four-foot, cylindrical basket woven of kalaree fibers, and unknotted the lid. Wordlessly, he displayed great gauzy, gaudy fistfuls of fabric so light and transparent it floated on the air in rose and green and gold wisps, dazzling the eyes.

"Silks, honorable," said the smaller man, also relinquishing his burden of gossamer to the hot glasphalt road. "We bring by request to Sarj Jo-Garet, three-six-ninth. This being the compound for three-six-ninth, notso?"

"Yeah, this's Garrett's unit. You guys got a civvy pass?" They looked blank. "A pass," insisted the sentry called Ramirez, gently. "A piece of the plastifilm with your thumbprint on it."

No, they had no pass. Jo-Garet had said nothing about a pass, but had spoken to them only of memlikti silks (they said), and how badly Jo-Garet wanted them for his aged and virtuous mother, whose hair was white.

142

A dark corridor of half-heard vehicles was building up behind them, rumbling and snorting at the silks that floated, capelike, across the road. A sleek two-man job at the end of the line presented a pointed horn, and the sentry stood dry-mouthed and let the sun pour its brazen air over his brown skin like a garment of lights.

"But without a pass, you can't get in," Ramirez reiterated. "I could get in a lot of trouble. You can see how it is." They saw. They looked at the men waving their hats and shouting, and smelled the warm gasoline sweats and sullen exhalations of tired beasts, and they nodded like sunflowers. The giant murmured, "My children do not mind hungry, one day more," but his small friend made a hushing motion and haphazardly stuffed the yards and yards of silk back into the basket.

"We understand, us," he assured the sentry. "Bad for soldier to see eye-eye coming to Base, notso? Jo-Garet must have maken mistake, ask for to come. Old mother not need silk, why for old woman want silk anyway? You tell, we go." He shouldered his bundle and the giant hefted the basket; smiling sadly and bowing, they trudged off dispiritedly down the road.

"Hey! You guys wait a minute." He grinned, shrugging. "If Garrett *told* you to come, you know? You guys go ahead. But don't get into any trouble, eh? Stay out in plain sight."

The small man bowed profusely. "Most kind honorable, gratitude in large containers. Now, if you will telling us of Jo-Garet's chisei?"

"Oh. Chisei. You mean his barracks." He stepped into the sun again, very straight, very brown, with his hair shining black as the bulls, and pointed his baton like a sword. "You take this road down to the flasher, make a left and it's the last bubble after you pass the PX. You can't miss it."

They walked for some distance in silence before Jek blurted, "You overdid your accent. And if Garrett *has* no mother—"

Ilai cut him off with a trace of asperity. "If your imaginary children are hungry, why do you eat so much? Why not save the food? I would have wept in another—"

"We lie too much," Jek finished sadly, and then

143

brightened, "But we are very good at stealing houseboys to bring to Mennon!"

Ilai reluctantly shared his broad grin. "Only when they are Shimshenli," he corrected. "Only then."

Within an hour they were back at the gate, and Ramirez greeted them with, "How much did he buy?"

"Not much, honorable. The small bundle."

A second sentry strolled up and rapped the basket with his baton. "What's in the basket, Joe?"

The small man brightened. "Jo, too? You are relative to Jo-Garet? How 'bout you buy silk, make old white-hair woman happy—"

"Silks. I checked them going in."

"You sure? I thought I saw that basket move."

"Plenty silk left. I show you—" He fumbled eagerly with the latch but Ramirez stopped him.

"No, thanks, friend, you go ahead through. Sure, I'm sure, Smitty, don't let them open it all up again. Please— go through." He held up the automatic gate with one hand.

"We not need pass to go out?"

"Well, *I* didn't see any silk—" Smitty's baton rapped the basket thoughtfully.

The Einai stood directly beneath the gate, uncertain, while Ramirez prayed his arm wouldn't fall off. "Get out!—please, huh?" They ducked through, smiling and bowing and waving goodbye. "Thank you. Goodbye, yes, yes." Ramirez turned to Smith, dropping the gate with a crash. "Even if I told you," he laughed, "you wouldn't believe those two guys."

Nor would they have believed Garrett's quarters, which by now were lighter by four chronometers and two hundred fifty-nine credits, plus several assorted telecoms, tri-V cassettes and shavers (which would be discarded in the forest) and one houseboy called Ilen (who would not); in return for which the barracks had been draped with Jek's whole basketful of silk, gauzy festoons of it sagging from window clips to light globes to furniture, minus only the quantity need to bind and gag an agile and determined Shimshen.

The men were cleaning it up when Garrett came back from the dispensary. "What's going on?" he asked thickly, steadying himself against the wall with his newly-cast hand. "Where's Ilen?" Sanders shot him a dirty look and Connors gave a short, barking laugh.

"Yeah, where's Ilen. That's what we'd like to know too, Sarge. Plus where's our telecoms and our money and our chronos, plus what the hell's this yard-goods doing all over the barracks?" He wadded up another strip, and Ross snatched it away and pitched it onto the growing pile on his bunk.

"Dammit, Connors, how many time I got to tell you? I want that stuff, it's worth money to me!"

"Then you clean it up!" Connors flared. Doc ambled over and indicated Garrett's hand. "What happened to your hand, Sarge?"

Garrett stared at Ross, with his puffed lip and purple eye, and Doc followed his gaze. "Oh." He disentangled his ankle from a loop of silk and continued, "Uh, Sarge, what do you suppose happened to, uh, Ilen? You think he really took that stuff?"

"I don't know, Doc, I don't know." Garrett threw himself down tiredly onto his bunk and covered his eyes with the crook of his arm. "But it's just as well she's gone."

He missed the realization dawning on Doc's face, the way Connors' cigarette fell unnoticed from his lips. La-Farge looked up from his tri-V and muttered, "Aw, no—ahn?" as if hoping he'd misunderstood.

Ross fiercely snatched up his silk and growled to Sanders, "I told you there was something funny about that kid—" he lowered his voice "—and I wouldn't be surprised if Ilen had something to do with that other funny gook, the one back at Sum ChiT'ath. I told you they took him over." Sanders nodded solemnly, as did the others, agreeing that there had been something funny about Ilen, and wondering just how badly their sergeant had been affected.

Garrett, weary and unaware, slept soundly as the fabric of his squad crumbled around him.

It seemed hours before the basket stopped its precarious swaying and its close darkness, shot through with points of dusty sunlight where the weave overlapped, gave way to deeper darkness, to damp stone air and cool cave echoes. There was a murmur of voices and footsteps, and Hennem-mishli (lately known as Ilen) felt the basket hit the

145

ground and heard a dear, familiar voice shout, "She's in the *what*?"

Kles! Hennem-mishli's face turned up mutely toward the top of the basket. *Kles!* She wriggled around as best she could to attract attention but it was unnecessary, for the top of the basket was abruptly jerked away and Kles lifted her out solicitously and supported her while he unbound her mouth and cut the silk that bound her hands together, her ankles to the backs of her thighs. She wincingly straightened her cramped legs and clung to him, weeping a bit in sheer joy, while Mennon smeared her tears with the flat of his palm and could think of nothing more intelligent to say than her name, over and over. At last she pulled free and dashed her tears away with both hands.

"Oh—Kles! Thank T'ath it's you. How did you find me?"

His voice was husky. "We knew where to look." They shared unsteady laughter and Hennem-mishli looked round eagerly.

"Where's Dao? Isn't he here?"

Mennon hesitated, sobering. "No." He forced a laugh and added quickly, "Gods, if you knew how long we looked for you! We heard wild rumors that the Krail had gotten you, that you were a farmhand, a houseboy, even that you had gone back to the monastery with the other Lifebearers!"

"I was, I did, all of it and more." She met his eyes steadily. "Kles, where is Dao?" Mennon drove a hand through his shaggy hair and avoided her gaze. "What is it? What's wrong? Has anything happened?" She paled visibly. "He was at Sum ChiT'ath—when it was destroyed —wasn't he? Oh, Kles, he didn't—*Dao didn't die at Sum ChiT'ath!*" She swayed where she stood and Mennon, his resolutions forgotten, caught her in his arms and let her sweet gravity weigh upon his hearts.

"Mishli, no," he insisted fiercely, protectively, "no, he didn't die—at Sum ChiT'ath! I—I saw him afterward, with the Erthlikli." He could feel her relax, limply, with relief, and continued softly, "But the Old Master, Priyam Shari-Mnenoplan . . ." She nodded wearily against his chest.

"I heard the mourning. It woke me in the night, and I

146

knelt and made the Chant." She raised her swimming eyes. "It's the first time, I think, that they've ever blown mourning for a Han who was not directly in the Imperial line." A smile touched her lips and trembled there. "Grandfather would have been pleased, I think. It's a very great honor."

"Yes," Mennon agreed, touching her cheek, "a very great honor."

Ilai sat high in the signal tree, the sun warming his hairless skull, thoughts warming the brain within. He was unable to hear what Mennon and the woman were saying, but he caught a glimpse of her in Mennon's arms, of Mennon touching her face, and he hummed a tuneless chant under his breath and surveyed the peaceful treetops with smug complacency. Nothing was so bad that some good could not come of it, one way or another. True, Lord Marik had died, and that was a terrible thing; but now the Shimshen would belong to Mennon, and that was very good indeed. The sun poured down slow and golden and viscous, and a hive of aun murmured sleepily in the jungle. Ilai sat humming softly and thinking how good it was that now Mennon had what he wanted most in the whole world: the Shimshen called Hennem-mishli.

The cave was a cup of darkness laced with cold green light, where Ilai sat huddled at a bench piecing together the combined components of several dismantled telecom units. Mennon paused in his pacing from bench to entrance to bench again, and asked, "Any luck?" Ilai shook his head.

"If only I had the ones we threw away," he mourned, and Mennon rapped his skull twice with his knuckles, lightly, much as an Erthlik might have slapped his shoulder, and stood at the cave entrance listening for the distinctive penetrating whine of Krail skimmercraft.

(Jek had brought him the sealed packet late this afternoon, saying laconically, "Slow courier." Mennon ripped the seal and queried, "No sled?" for Krail couriers always travelled by sled.

"Slow sled, too."

One of the men found the twisted wreckage later, and did what had to be done with the body.)

A thousand men, the dispatch read, one thousand foot-soldiers, trained jungle-fighters, were to be landed at the monastery on the River Elv tonight. Mennon's eyes narrowed. A thousand standing army could secure the province for Krailion, could enslave and murder and burn even as they had burned Allampaila and the house of Mennon's father.

The Federation had to be warned. It was as simple as that, and as complex. The problem was how to go about it.

A conventional telecom message could be hazardous. The Krail had perfected a nastily effective transponder that would pick up an 'unauthorized' beam and alter its echo resonance, converting the transmitter into a lethal subsonic device that spasmed the viscera, ruptured eyeballs, eardrums, heart, shook the very teeth loose from the skull. There were not many of them on Eisernon, but there were enough. There were more than enough.

Sending a courier was out of the question. Even if they had sufficient time, which they hadn't, Mennon's men were outlaws-by-association. Mennon had a price on his head. The spy-eye aboard the scuttled *Pacific* had seen to that.

The only recourse was a tight, closed-circuit beam that would permit no backtracing. Assuming, of course, that Ilai could build one in time, out of random parts; and assuming that the wildly fluctuating magnetic fields around Pal-alden-Shali-Rho, where the Federation was headquartered, would not distort the message beyond recognition; and assuming, at last, that the Erthlikli would believe the report of a man they called outlaw and pirate, and would send their lean, bronzed automatons trekking inexorably toward ancient Einai masonry and fresh enemy kills, on the fragile strength of his word alone. Ilai's voice was a welcome distraction.

"Mennon, it is a good thing that the woman is here."

A good thing, the gentle presence moving softly among them, a Shimshen to bless the table, a trace of mung and musk and dakan flowers that made the cave, oh, if not a hermitage, or anything quite so poetic, then at least the closest thing to a home that Mennon had known for a long, long while.

"Yes," he agreed warmly, watching the sky, "yes, it is a good thing."

"Mennon should have a woman who is not like other

148

women," Ilai continued obliquely. "It is good that she is here with you."

Mennon frowned back at him. "She is not 'here with me'. She's here where it is safe." Ilai shrugged non-committally, and Mennon continued, with some heat, "She belongs to Marik, Ilai. Before T'ath, Hennem-mishli belongs to my friend, to my *brother,* Dao Marik!"

"He is dead," Ilia persisted stubbornly, snapping the completed compak shut. "Now she belongs to Mennon."

"She will never belong to Mennon!"

Kles Mennon's voice was flat and harsh, and carried easily on the muggy stillness. Hennem-mishli, walking in the clearing in vain hope of a vagrant breeze, caught the sound and started back toward the cave, but the giant, Jek, standing nightwatch, put out a deferential hand to detain her.

"Shimshen, there is a place where night-flowers grow, over here," he offered loudly, hoping to drown out the argument. "You could pick some, maybe. Women like that." It was a long speech for Jek and he stood blankly after it, not knowing what to do with his hands. The Shimshen tilted her head, listening past him.

"They're talking about me—aren't they?" She stepped around him and moved toward the cave. She could hear them more clearly as she approached, all curiosity and caution, hushed by the leaf-mold under her feet and the whisper of an early autumn breathing in her ears. Jek followed her, helplessly.

"We brought her to you," Ilai was insisting. "You sent us to find her while you made mourning. Now—we found her. Now—she is yours!"

Mennon struck the table with his open palm. *"She belongs to Marik!"*

"Will she sleep with him in his tomb?" Ilai demanded. "What good is she to a dead man?"

Hennem-mishli reeled and saw her agony mirrored in big Jek's compassionate face. Her eyes widened and brimmed. "You knew," she whispered, and the massive head inclined.

"We danced his life a whole night."

"And no one told me . . ." She was white to the lips but she evaded Jek's sympathetic hand at her elbow.

149

"Kles let me believe Dao was alive . . . he lied to me . . . *Why?*"

"Because the truth would have done no good." The reedy voice wove a blurred patch of white in the jungle where the albino sat, strumming randon chords on a finger harp. His left hand was stretched and sewn and tendoned with fine silver wires, and it moved like a moth, like a memory, in the pitiless starlight. "Perhaps because he could not face losing both of you."

Silver traces on her cheeks, snail tracks on roses. "Kles had no right, no right—"

"He loves you."

She stood like carven stone from an ancient and forgotten age, webbed with starlight, her face terrible in its implacable serenity. The albino sighed and stood up, stripping the harp from his fingers, and peered at her with opaque jade eyes. His fine white hair webbed his face with silver wires, with snail track and starlight. He handed her the harp. A smooth, stone palm lifted emotionlessly to receive it.

"Remember only this," he advised. "You are alive. They are dead, but you live."

"Yes." Her voice was remote. "Yes. I live."

There was the familiar dread whine of Krail craft above them and someone shouted, "Here they come!" Jek ran for the clearing. Another whine, and another and another, beyond counting, rattling eardrums like windows, rattling windows like eardrums. Heads pivoted on slick sockets, faces lifted like searchlights. Mennon braced his hands against the sides of the cave door, teeth bared tensely as a swarm of twenty-man shuttles, visible only by the twin rockets, glowing sullenly at their kite-tips, passed over the jungle filling the air with their uproar.

"Ilai!" he shouted, and Ilai yelled back, "Ready!" Full-throated thunder reverberated in teeth and bone, and Mennon bellowed, "Let them hear this in Pal-alden-Shali-Rho!"

Ilai nodded quickly, squinting at the static through which microscopic men in Federation uniforms whispered and chittered in the honeycomb corridors of bone behind his ears.

The thunder overhead drummed like surf, one of a piece with wading through shoals of saber grass and skirt-

150

ing reefs of gopher thicket, and Hennem-mishli drifted with the pull of the tide, the unseen inner current that sluiced her inevitably back toward the monastery. She knew the Krail were there, knew that the shuttles weaving their endless warning pattern of *stop, stop, stop,* in twin red glows like marker buoys, would once have meant great danger to her.

But not anymore.

Now, with Grandfather gone and the anguish of Dao's death keen inside where she couldn't reach it yet (or wouldn't), she experienced a disembodied numbness, a sensation of invulnerability and imperviousness, and realized that nothing could ever hurt her again. This morning, when she was still a young girl, she'd been rigged full sail with the fresh spank of faith, trust, laughter and other childish things; now she was a tender, lighter, derelict, a fragile cockleshell washed ashore still whispering of Beginnings, and broken, pretending there had been no End.

She ran against the wind under quicksilver stars, following the rockets to their homeport, for it was her home, too; and in the fathomless deeps beneath the venerable refuge, in scarlet secret, subterranean caverns in the bowels of the earth, there slept in a frozen golden globule the one last thing that Hennem-mishli had to live for: Dao's child.

And hers.

It was barely dawn when she tapped at the old, wall door beside the river. She waited, ears straining for the light footsteps of the Doorkeeper, a friend called Sofyan, who could be trusted to help her spirit away her child. A tree frog barked faintly in the darkness. Hennem-mishli knocked again, heard—with relief—footfalls on flagging, and was unprepared for the Krail legionary who appeared in the doorway and appraised her with calculating interest.

"The Prodigal," Charvin smiled, like the premonition of death. "Welcome back." And before she could gather her wits about her, he drew her through the doorway and shut the door firmly behind him.

Beq nom-Pau spread the fingers of both hands as far as they could go on the top of his bare desk, and, inhaling deeply, sat down smiling absently to himself. He was feeling pleased with himself these days, everything had been going extremely well. Noble Aper ser Nalm was a frequent visitor to the monastery, the weather had been uncommonly fine, and best of all, his new wife was pregnant. The physician repeatedly avowed (on the basis of amniocentesis and multiple lascan) that it would be a son, an assurance with which even ser Nalm's rebellious slave, Paige, concurred.

To make matters even more perfect, Aper ser Nalm had brought him a thousand jungle-fighters last night, a thousand men who even now slumbered like pale wraiths in cool white beds in narrow cells cool as stone vaults, where centuries and centenarians had flaked away, falling in a dark snow, a fine and powdery dust. A thousand men breathing in lush, alien jungle, breathing out crisp, spearmint air, their snow dreams and sharp, crystal passions buried nine-tenths hidden under the blue transparent ice of the sleepers' wide and sleepless eyes.

Now the province was theirs. Once the last stubborn pockets of guerilla resistance were wiped out, and with Neron Vartik speaking eloquently for the Krail in the Einai Senate, a puppet government could be set up to rule not only the old Imperial Province but Eisernon itself. This was the best hope of Krailon, the fact that Federation Delegate Neron Vartik was willing to sell out his people for domination of the rich patrician territory. Of course, neither Beq nom-Pau nor anyone else had the slightest intention of letting a fool like Vartik rule the Province of the Han after he had served his purpose; but it was convenient to let him think he would.

And he was disgustingly grateful. Recently, when nom-Pau had made him a present of the slave Ronhalovan, Vartik had actually shed tears. Tears! Beq nom-Pau, sitting alone in his austere dawn office, curled a lip in contempt. Tears! What were these animals good for, other than slavery? There wasn't a man among the lot of them.

The door burst open and Charvin, his pale face flushed with triumph, flung him a salute.

"The Han woman, Commander. The one we lost. She is here."

Not a man among them, nom-Pau's mind echoed, and added, but ah, the women. She glided in, as slim as a ship

152

running before the wind, still as a ship becalmed. Beq nom-Pau rose instinctively to his feet.

"Shimshen." He bowed slightly, stiffly, and indicated the only other chair in the room. She sank into its cool green depths and regarded him with a gaze as flat and lifeless as that of those grotesque eyes the Einai insisted on painting on the bows of their vessels, from dory to warship. It made him somehow uneasy, as if her gaze stopped just short of him, resting on something he couldn't see. He lowered himself into his chair and opened a flat, gold case, extending it toward her. "Cigarette, gracious lady?"

Her eyes never left his face. "No," after a moment.

He selected one, lit it, and exhaled luxuriously. "Let us be candid, Shimshen. You are aware of the effort we put into your capture; and when you escaped, we had no way to find you, although we searched. Ah," he smiled briefly, "we searched. Now here you are, walking back into our hands, unarmed, unprotected." He flicked ash, delicately. "It makes me wonder why."

"There is something here that belongs to me," she murmured, her lips barely moving. He leaned forward to catch the words. "I came to get it."

He smiled. "And what could be so important that you would give up your freedom for it? For make no mistake, gracious lady, that is certainly what you have done."

She shook her head almost imperceptibly. "I don't think I want to tell you that."

"Come, now." His voice was growing less patient. "What if we should find your treasure, by some accident, and misuse or even destroy it, because we didn't know its value? You wouldn't want to have that happen." He dropped all semblance of persuasion. "You would do well to tell me what brought you back here."

She shook her head silently and closed her eyes (thereby releasing his soul) and he stood abruptly.

"Charvin." Softly. He was at the door like an apparition. "Take the Shimshen to one of the detention cells," nom-Pau ordered. "I understand that insane villagers used to be held there until they could be treated. We will see how such an environment affects our obstinate little telepath." He bowed again. "My lady."

She came up like a breeze from the south, a stirring and freshening on the air, and followed Charvin away, leaving behind her a wake of mung and musk and tamarind floating in the chilly room.

The borealis over the Provincial Capitol of Pal-alden-Shali-Rho began fading with the coming of the sun, and in FedCom Headquarters in the New City, a General rubbed his red-rimmed eyes and drawled, "What time is it, Carson?"

"Oh-five-seventeen, sir."

"Those damn' gooks kept us on the horn all that time?" He reached for a half-finished cup of cold coffee, smelled it, and set it down with a wry grimace.

"Yes, sir. Static can get pretty bad with that boreal—"

"Tell me again what they said." He hooked his thumbs under his cheekbones and massaged his forehead with stubby fingers. "It came in installments."

The young lieutenant summarized dutifully, "They want a detachment of ground troops sent in to cover a Krail buildup on the Elv River. There's an old monastery—"

"I know it. Go on."

"They want ground troops, they don't want an air strike. They were very definite on that point. They want ground troops. They're afraid an air strike will destroy their, ah, treasure, as they put it, sir. They want us to come by land, as fast as we can make it." He shrugged. "That's what they want, sir."

The General slammed his hands down, making the coffee cups jump. "They want, they want! Who the hell do these backwater gooks think they are, with *they want*? Who's this guy, what'd you say his name was?"

"Mennon, sir. He says he's a guerilla fighter."

"Mennon, Mennon . . ." He punched the name into his secretary and waited impatiently for the readout. "Here you go, Carson, here's your guerilla fighter! He's a turncoat, a traitor! Helped a Krail bigwig escape from a Federation vessel not six months ago! So he wants a detachment of ground troops, eh? We'll give him a detachment!" He hit his intercom. "This is General Howard. Get me Major Cline, over in the 41st Squadron." He glared at Carson. "Ground troops, eh? We'll give him ground troops up to his— Hello! Hello, Cline, this's General Howard. We've just got word that the Krail are building up steam along the Elv. Old monastery there, you know the

154

one I mean? Right. Scramble a few of your men and take care of it for me, will you? Good man. Right." He leaned back in his worn leather chair and pushed the nearest stale coffeecup toward Carson with the tip of a stylus. "Get rid of that, will you, Lieutenant?" He wagged his head and, remembering, gave a short, contemptuous laugh. *"They—want!"*

Overhead, a formation of jets, rockets tucked securely under their snubbed wings, made a sharp, tearing whine as they veered toward the south and the River Elv.

It was only imagination, Hennem-mishli told herself in the dense, disturbing atmosphere of the cell, imagination and the knowledge that generations of the hopelessly insane had gibbered here, drawing terror on the murky air with trembling bony fingers, and conjuring forth hordes of demons from the spouting volcanic fires that raged inside their skulls; imagination, surely, that caused enormous shadows to take on frightful, unwarranted shapes, at once strange and familiar. Imagination, that made a poke of dust move unnaturally, *so*, when there was no breeze to blow it, and only imagination that let mindless underground echoes quaver like low, monotonous laughter. *Among the murmurs, did Dao laugh, too, his low, husky chuckle mingled with the insane dead?*

She put her hands to her face and held them over her ears to stop the haphazard bombardment of thoughts that bounded and rebounded from the walls, floor, ceiling of the awakening cell; took a few steadying breaths and intoned carefully, *"Make a loud sound, the clapping of hands and the beating on drums, sounds of gladness to Tadae; for see, in the East, the sun shows his face . . ."* She faltered to a stop, listening, listening, certain that a mocking voice had sung the chant with her, only an instant late, half-a-note sharp. Still she was not frightened, could not shake off the numbing grief that insulated her even from this madness, and made her only mildly curious, vaguely interested.

Her face, staring up at her from the gelatinous green depths of a long-unused fountain-well, was not her face at all, but a montage of menace; and the cot, when she tried it, accepted her weight with a thousand tiny shrieks, reeking of fear and presence. She sat up, eyes wide, lips

155

parted. That was it—*presence*. A mental remnant of the many unfortunates who, interned, interred, here in this underground vault, this living burial, had awaited mercy and sanity and a return to life and sunlight. And cured, well, sane, had shed their sickness like dry snakeskin and gone on, leaving it here behind to rustle sibilantly, a residue of insanity, tangible enough to be scraped off the musty walls; a fine, ferocious mildew waiting to seep in through ears and nostrils and pores and work a kind of dryrot in the mind, a moldering decay, until the varnished veneer of civilization was corroded away and all that remained was the flayed bare flesh of the soul, the decomposition of the living mind whose parts fled screaming up axon, down dendrite, and off the edge of reason into the Abyss.

An apparition with yellow eyes and blue-painted face appeared at the barred doorway and said, "You're stronger than we knew, Hennem-mishli." The voice put the vision in focus, a familiar face, accustomed to peering through peepholes, the bright, merry, yellow eyes of Sofyan, the Doorkeeper.

"Sofyan! How did you—" She faltered to a stop. She'd almost said, 'How did you know where to find me?' but that brought back Kles, and loss and grief, and she stood mute.

The gentle, young-old face softened. "Through the night the monastery whispered of it, the wind sang and the stones breathed, and before morning, everyone knew that you'd come home.

"My lady, there isn't much time. The others sent me to tell you: we are leaving this place. I would take you, too, but—" she spread empty hands. "They took away my keys, Mishli." She bowed her head, and Hennem-mishli reached through the bars to touch her cheek.

"It's all right, Sofyan. It's all right."

Sofyan laid a hand against her rounded belly, as if listening. "I have to tell you something else." Her words came quick and breathless. "When the Krail came in force, and there was talk of a thousand men yet to come, we knew there was trouble afoot: so we went to the Erthlik duli, secretly, by twos and threes, and while his master slept, he took the children from the treasure vault —but, oh, Mishli, not all of them!—and with us helping

156

him, operating in the darkened theater, he directed the greatest drama of all, the Unbirthing; the little ones in their golden balloons, their sleek cocoons, going from light to dark, from cold to warm, from waiting to being wanted."

Hennem-mishli's eyes widened. "He implanted the children." Sofyan nodded solemnly and made the Infinity Sign.

"He implanted us. He husbanded the children against the destruction that is coming, who knows when, but soon. And when he was finished and there were more children but, oh, no more of us, and him celibate, us virginal, each of the Shimshenli carried three children, and will bear them to safety."

"What of the others?"

"We'll send back for them, after these are born safe, or when we can find more Shimshenli."

Mishli felt a warmth in her, and glistening, shimmering, gray ice melting, she tried a little smile. "And my baby? Who carries my baby?"

Sofyan opened her lips to speak, but a sudden gust of warmth eddied down the dank gallery, a wedge of light sliced from seashell morning groped its way along the musty straw.

"Sofyan, hurry!" The whisper snapped her head around. *"The Erthlikli are coming!"* Beyond, they could hear the spiteful bronze sizzling of metal wasps fevering the fragrant air.

"Sofyan—" *What of Dao's child, and mine?*

Sofyan stood poised, pulled two ways, answer half-formed on her tongue, running, already prickling, eager in her feet. Inside her, noiselessly, visibly, Life kicked. Hennem-mishli closed her eyes.

"—go!" she finished, breaking the spell. "Go, Sofyan, run!" Sofyan disappeared and the Shimshenli fled, a small, swift pattering of feet, an inundation of grunion, a splendid migration of plump partridges no man could conceive in his wildest dreams.

With the Shimshenli flown, safely deployed, Hennem-mishli realized fully for the first time her unique state, hapless, haploid, in her single lonely cell.

But not for long. There was the clatter of jackboots on the stairs, a hurried fumbling of keys at the lock, and

Charvin unceremoniously grabbed her wrist and dragged her up the stairs, half-running to keep up, and down the length of the crowded corridor, where black-uniformed men went coldly, quickly, about their duties and an undercurrent of excitement and anticipation permeated the air. As they passed what had once been the nursery, she could hear the smart slap of automatic weapons snatched from neat rows of open cases and thrust into waiting white hands.

Charvin pulled her after him through the arcade and out onto the airstrip, which was an anthill of taxiing kites and running pilots and gunners frantically setting up their beamers; and over it all, the stung-hummed parabolas of Erthlik aircraft as they dove and bombed and dove again, spouting up huge proliferations of flung earth and glasphalt.

Beq nom-Pau, Aper ser Nalm and a retinue that included serveral officers, the Krail physican, the Earthlik slave Paige and nom-Pau's young wife, the latter swathed in veils of many colors, came running down the stone stairs onto the far end of the landing strip, where a sleek, powerful launch stood waiting and ready. Charvin jerked her along at a dead run, and she raced after him, stumbling, dodging potholes and bodies, her lungs all fire and ice.

Aper ser Nalm leaped aboard and the rockets flared to life even as Charvin pushed Hennem-mishli into the tight knot of bodies scrambling to get into the launch. Paige saw the Shimshen, started for her with an exclamation of surprise and dismay; but ser-Nalm's aide, taking no chances, crowded the Earthlik into the launch with his hand-pulser, and Paige subsided angrily and looked away. A double concussion threw them abruptly against the bulkhead and nom-Pau's wife made a smothered moan behind her veiling; but then they were airborne, dragging themselves into acceleration couches against the pull of steadily mounting G-forces. Charvin deposited Hennem-mishli in a safe alcove and secured her straps in much the same way as he would have preserved a vase or a weapon Beq nom-Pau owned, and with as much interest; he strapped himself in beside her and began reloading his hand-pulser as the launch slowly looped over and the planetary surface, swung lazily around, and righted itself on a permanent thirty-degree angle.

The triangular porthole framed velvet: the tufted forest, the river's blue serenity, the weathered monastery; framed, too, the insectile scurrying of black motes scattering from a dark rain of metal, the placid convex hub of lapis lazuli that capped the cloister.

Suddenly, with a huge, convulsive shudder, the gracious rounded dome, the gravid egg, succumbed to the piercing of a single dart-like bomb, a silver seed, a mushroom spore, and nine months in an instant, Frankenstein reborn, it blossomed with a great blasphemous orange flower, scattering golden globes like pollen from the treasure vaults in the sub-sub-basement, withering and crisping them in an instant, gnashing stone, seething against the sky.

At the same instant, the turbulence hit them, a frenzied paroxysm that pitched them across the heavens with all the titanic fury of an enraged God, the agonized, full-throated scream of every woman who had ever witnessed such a prodigious miscarriage of mercy as the deliberate destruction of helpless Life.

Then they realized that the screaming was inside the ship, and Charvin, because he was efficient, reached over and slapped the Shimshen *hard* and *hard* and *hard*, until the screaming stopped, until she sat huddled there, shaking uncontrollably, the heartbeat fluttering in her throat, while the sleek, kite-shaped launch lifted effortlessly toward the Krail's Imperial flagship.

They almost made it unscathed. The looming bulk of the Imperial flagship was in sensor contact when from out of nowhere a light, maneuverable Federation ship, clearly of Erthlikli design, hove into range, closing fast. The launch was unprepared for battle with a warship, especially an Erthlikli sublight vessel, which could run silent until it was upon you, and then close in for the kill. Aper ser Nalm leaned anxiously toward the pilot.

"More power," he ordered quietly.

"On full, Noble."

"Elude them."

The launch swung sickeningly into evasive maneuvers and nom-Pau's young wife moaned again, gripping the

159

straps convulsively. She'd been in space only once before, when brought from the seraglio she had been raised in to her new husband. Then she'd been heavily sedated to stand the rigors of the voyage; now she was dizzy, very nauseated and petrified with fear. Her veils fell free and her hands, clinging the strap, could not move to replace them. A flare of light burst just outside her port and the launch veered steeply to avoid it, changing directions so quickly that she was disoriented. Before she settled, it changed again, and then again, veering, diving, climbing, until she could no longer bear it, but tore off the safety straps and started for the only security she knew.

"Father—" she began, and ser Nalm glanced back unbelievingly; but at that moment the pilot swerved to avoid a shielded torp, barrel-rolled the launch and dove so quickly that the girl was thrown violently against overhead, couches, bulkhead, deck, before anyone could move to save her.

The flagship, now in view, let loose a broadside that scored a glancing hit on the Federation sub and the predatory Earthlikli limped away toward atmosphere and safety.

Paige ripped out of his straps and was on his knees beside the unconscious girl even as the launch drifted cautiously under the shadowy bulk of the flagship and into the landing bay. Locks boomed shut behind them in the thickening air.

There was a great deal of blood. She was hemorrhaging from the nose and both ears and her conjunctiva and tongue were dead white. Her pupils pulsed and contracted irrespective of light stimuli and her heartbeat and breathing were faint and irregular. Paige felt carefully of her head, and winced. There, at the top of her head, under a wealth of yellow-white hair, an area some six centimeters in diameter was severely depressed.

He supported the bloody head in careful hands and looked up to find the Krail physician and Beq nom-Pau standing over him.

"Dead?" the physician wanted to know.

Someone cracked the hatch from the outside, and there were staccato voices.

"Not yet, but if we don't get her into treatment pretty quick, she will be; and the baby, too!"

160

Aper ser Nalm barked orders and a legionary purred up on a powersled that had obviously been used before for accident cases; another man ran for a wall communicator and spoke briefly into it. Paige climbed into the sled, still cradling the girl's head in his hands, while a Krail legionary jumped into the driver's seat and sped them to Sickbay up a series of tight, circular ramps.

They arrived to find an operating room already set up, its only illumination a wash of infra-red light. A surgical team, complete with special goggles, was scrubbed and ready. Aper ser Nalm, who'd taken the faster but more precarious lift with Beq nom-Pau and nom-Pau's personal physician, demanded of the company in general, "Where is the Han woman?"

"Under guard, Noble." Beq nom-Pau, rumpled and dishevelled, approached the sled, two spots of high color burning his thin cheeks. He regarded the girl with some discomfort but no sympathy, while ser Nalm gave orders to fetch the Shimshen and a legionary ran.

"Remove the fetus for transplant," he ordered, and Paige shook his head.

"No dice. No way. Among other things more important, she's got a broken pelvis."

"Surgically, if you must," nom-Pau ground out. "Dispose of her, if you must! —but save the child!"

Paige shot him a sour grimace and signalled an orderly to take her feet; to another: "You want to shove that gurney over here, Charlie?" Someone translated casually, and Paige, impatient, grabbed it with a free hand and jerked it into position. He began easing her head off his lap, noting that the bleeding had diminished perceptibly and realizing that unless the Krail helped him, in a hurry, the conversation would become a mere philosophical debate rather than a discussion of possibilities.

"Damn it, get them to help me!" he shouted in frustration. "She's got too little chance as it is!"

"My physician tells me that she is too badly damaged for salvage," nom-Pau persisted intensely, biting off each word individually, "therefore you will confine your attentions to saving the child. It is a vital political hybrid and is invaluable to me. *It—must—not—die!*"

Paige swore a mighty oath. "It is a *child*, and it must not die!" He jerked a long arm toward the sled. "That is a

161

woman, and she must not die!" He whirled on Aper ser Nalm. "Say something, man! This guy wants me to kill your daughter!"

Aper ser Nalm smiled thinly. "I have other daughters, Paige."

Paige swallowed, shaking his head. "Jesus," he muttered; his face flashed up angrily, and he licked his lip. "Okay, I try to save 'em both, or you can count me out! Do your own damn' killing!"

"We won't have to." The Krail physician straightened from the sled. "She has just died." There was a mild stir among the Krail and Paige's jaw dropped. Aper ser Nalm, noting it, commented coolly, "Now that we have concluded our discussion of Earthlikli medical ethics, would you care to save the infant?" He smiled toward the lift, which had only just disgorged Charvin and his prisoner. "Since we are all here." He made a mocking little half-bow. "Shimshen."

She took in the situation at a glance, her eyes puffy and swollen from weeping, and she paled. "You don't mean—me?" she asked weakly.

"You are a Shimshen, are you not?" Aper ser Nalm asked silkily. "Do you make a vow to bear Life, or do you not?"

"I won't do it," Paige barked. "You can't force her to live with you like some kind of a—" A Krail guard warned him back with a quick lift of his weapon, but Paige stood his ground.

"A container," Aper ser Nalm mused. "A jewel case for something precious. That is the Shimshen's function, nothing more. To be preserved, as long as it holds that which is valuable."

"Life-signs are diminishing, noble," murmured the Krail physician.

"And when the baby is born?" Paige snapped. "Then what?"

Beq nom-Pau spoke up. "She will be deposited on the nearest inhabited planet with all she needs for survival." He held up his clenched hand. "By the Fist of the Imperator." It was the nearest thing the Krail could come to an oath, and yet—

Paige scowled. "I still say no. Shimshen?"

She looked slowly around at the tall, forbidding, black-

162

uniformed Krail, at the man who would be her guardian for the six months remaining, at the still, pale shape of the dead girl, and last, at Paige.

And she remembered the treasure vault, sixty-thousand children strong, destroyed in a moment, and her own child, perhaps, among them. Now they offered her another child to fill the emptiness, an enemy child; and she wondered if a child could be an enemy. She decided not. The child was Life. She could not refuse it.

She moved quickly to a container that held a water-soluble, blue disinfectant, and, dipping her hand in it, painted the lower half of her face the traditional blue mask with two swipes of her hand, thereby accepting the child and the responsibility that went with it. She gave a long-drawn, shuddering intake of breath and said to Paige, in a small voice, "I made a vow, *duli*."

Paige's mouth quirked in a travesty of a smile. "So did I," he said softly, and, oblivious to the others, as if he were transporting an object of immense fragility and priceless value, he led her into the operating theater.

Kles Mennon lifted his pounding head from his arm and squinted at the elliptical brilliance of the cave opening. An insistent voice had summoned him from the welcome oblivion of a drunken stupor, and he resented it. He pushed away a few empty bottles and scowled. "Ilai?" he mumbled thickly.

Ilai padded across the cool stone floor and handed him a cold mug of pij juice. "There is one here to see you."

He let the cool, pulpy stuff slide down his swollen throat, drew a deep breath and drove his fingers through his shaggy hair, wincing. "Wha'd you say?" His head began to clear and he realized what he'd been told, and turned to look Ilai squarely in the face. The bald skull nodded once.

"Someone is here. From the monastery."

Mennon was on his feet immediately. "Not—"

"No. No word of her."

He struck the table clear with one reckless arm and demanded, "Why bother me, then!" Glass shattered on silence, and he muttered, after a moment, "Who is it?"

"A Krail." A trail-weary, blond youngster in a black uniform stained with mud and sweat dragged his heels across the floor and regarded the lean guerilla chief with

163

as much insolence as he could muster. "You're Mennon. I want to join you."

Mennon chuckled mirthlessly, holding his head. "Go on back to your Commander, boy. You don't have anything I want." He pulled the cork from a fresh bottle of tarangi and drained half of it in one draught. "Go on," he urged generously, noticing that he was still there. "Don't be afraid; my men will let you pass—this time."

"You need me, Mennon," the boy announced, and Mennon lowered the bottle and grinned wolfishly. He pulled his viith from its leather sleeve back of his left shoulder and flipped it cleanly into the table, where it stood quivering in the light.

"You see that viith?" he asked softly. "My men practice day and night with these, for the express purpose of killing Krail. And they're good. Very, very good. The only thing they lack is a suitable target." He drank again, cradling the bottle under his arm as he worked the blade loose from the table planks and sleeved it again. "Now why don't you run along home like a good lad before they get ideas about Krail—and targets—and how much we need you, after all?"

Standing, the boy was almost as tall as Mennon, and he smiled coldly into the yellow tiger-eyes. "I know where she is," he said.

Mennon put down the bottle in exaggerated slow-motion, studying the other's face as if to memorize every pore, every expression.

"If you're lying," he warned, dangerously soft, "I'll see to it that you never quite die!"

For answer, the Krail reached into an inner pocket for stylus and pad and made a few swift, adroit strokes. He handed the pad to Mennon.

The guerilla leader took it and sat slowly, drinking it in. The beloved face, with its terrible serenity, her cropped hair, even the silver finger-harp the albino claimed to have given her. He glanced up, swiftly, suddenly, burning bright.

"Ilai! Get glasses for yourself and my man, here." To the boy, "Now we will talk. What's your name?"

There was a pause. "Alain," he said at last.

"Alain. Just that?"

"Just that." He smiled briefly, bitterly. "Only that. Mennon's man—Alain."

INTERLUDE

The empty rice paddies brimmed with warm water reflecting the evening sky, and the farmhouse was a welcome sight to the man who had come so far to find this house, these paddies, and the one certain woman. The man, Laj, wearing new, clean peasant clothing and carrying a burlap sack over his shoulder, approached the darkened house diffidently, and with sudden embarrassment, started around to the back, when a sound of quiet singing from the deserted bos-barn turned him aside. He peered in through the partly open door. There, seated on a pile of hay, was a pitifully thin young woman, her lank hair falling forward over her face, her large, knobby hands cradling the baby she was nursing. She was singing, not well, but with a certain sweetness in her sincere, broken voice. Laj put down the heavy bundle and pulled off his flat reed hat, startling the girl to silence. She jumped to her feet, self-consciously covering herself.

"Who are you?" she demanded breathlessly. "What do you want?"

Laj stood flatfooted and calm in the doorway. "You are Arv's woman?" She hesitated and then nodded. "I brought you his bones, as he asked."

"You the one killed him?" She shifted the baby in her arm and pushed a lock of hair behind her ear.

"It was the war," Laj explained slowly. "My hand, but the war, you understand. There was a truce-time, and we ate together and spoke of women and food and which way was best to plant rice; and when the truce was over, I killed him." He shrugged. "It could have been the other way."

"War is a bad thing," she agreed, walking over and unwrapping the sackcloth. A few bones slipped and rattled drily, and she shook her head and covered them up again. "That ain't Arv," she said, holding the baby up to her face. "This here's Arv, all warm and breathin'. He

165

ain't got the Bleedin' Sickness, either." She chucked the baby under the chin and added, "I'll bury the bones after I'm done feedin' him." She sat on the hay and put the child to her breast, and Laj squatted on his heels beside the bundle, drawing absent circles in the dusty, straw-littered earth.

"Your parent would not bury him?" he asked, wondering how her thin arms could lift a shovel. She didn't look up.

"He's dead. We had a hired boy and my parent sold him in town after my muj told him not to; and on the way home, some bandits caught him and took all the money. So he came home with no hired boy and no money, and after a while he just died. The muj won't eat. She gives me her share to make milk for the baby."

Laj drew more pictures and said to the floor, "Arv said you are a good woman, a clean woman. He did not tell me you look like the drawing of every man's woman."

She shrugged and twisted a lock of hair around one finger. The baby blew little milky bubbles against her breast as he slept, and she wiped his mouth gently and buttoned her high collar, very conscious of Laj's careful study of the floor. They glanced at each other and looked away quickly and back again; and their glances held, permitting them to smile, shyly at first, and then more easily. She sighed, biting her lip, and patted the baby until it made a loud hiccup, and they laughed companionably.

"The war is over," Laj mused in the friendly quiet. "The offworlders who fought here will go away now, and talk of many things; and we will have our land again to plant rice—and other things." He dared not confess his addiction to this woman, but she remarked, as if guessing his meaning, "A little tabac is all right once in a while, I guess, so long's a man don't make a habit of it."

"You are a good woman," he replied warmly. "You are a good woman, and Arv has made a fine son. I have decided. I will stay here."

They were halfway to the farmhouse, with his hand protectively supporting her arm, before she remembered that she hadn't asked his name; and hard on the heels of that knowledge came the comforting realization that she could always ask tonight, tomorrow, next year. There was no longer any hurry, any desperation over food and helplessness and time. There was all the time in the world. Their hands slipped down, caught, and swung as they walked, like the hands of friends, or lovers.

Across the paddy, a restless flight of uala circled once, warily, and settled slowly into their nesting place.

Chapter IV

Dao Marik leaned his weight hard to the right and felt the gryphon bank with him, its brown-mottled pinions scooping the cold, fragrant air smoothly, easing into the level glide that would take them back to the eyries.

Below them, to the right, lay the planet's single great, tideless sea, stretched out green to the horizon, and above it loomed the snowy chalk cliffs, glistening with ice. A single, slant-rigged craft hoisted its orange sail as he watched and headed for the fishing lanes, far out to sea.

To his left, and as far as the eye could see, lay his father's vast Protectorate, a scenery of valley and hidden pass, of towering blue mountains folded in snow, and gently, rounded hills folded in Erthlikli sheep that grazed to the music of golden-eyed, green shepherds piping wild down the glens.

From his lofty height, Marik gazed down upon peace, from the busy eyries balanced precariously on the jutting rock to the west, past the bustle of servants at the field machinery—he half-turned in the saddle—to the colorful, flat headgear of women gathering miligachin in the marshlands, and the sweet-stark simplicity of his family's magnificent pavilion on the chalk cliffs high above the eternal sea. Peace.

He leaned forward and spoke to the gryphon, and the great wings began to beat, slowing, dropping. Marik felt the old familiar weightlessness of the calculated fall become different somehow, with the certain and irrevocable knowledge that something was desperately wrong.

The gryphon plummeted toward the spinning ground, the wind whining like a rocket, roaring like the rumble of falling masonry. There was an idiotic beeping in his ears and, suddenly, he was awake with a painful jolt, lying stiff and immobile on his bunk, his familiar bunk, in his Science Officer's quarters aboard the *USS Skipjack*. He was covered with a thin, cold sweat and lay there for interminable seconds, willing his hearts to steady, his breathing to slow, his memory under strict control. Moisture chilled the backs of his gold-skinned hands.

The communicator beeped again, and the precise feminine voice of the Communications Officer stated briskly, "Lieutenant-Commander Marik to the Bridge. Mister Marik to the Bridge."

Marik sat up, aware of the minutiae of sounds, scents and unconscious telepathic touches that marked an Erthlikli ship. His universe clicked together with an almost audible snap, and he got to his feet, shaking off the last remnants of the dream, and limped toward the portal and reality.

Captain Paul Riker sat easily at the helm, scarcely glancing away from the great forward port as Marik entered. In the endless, myriad panorama before them, one star burned with a steady splendor. Riker indicated it with a sweep of his hand.

"NGC5850. We've got orders to pick up a Galactic Investigation Team and transfer them to Federation Central. They're an interesting group: two Earthlings, two Einai. How do you suppose they'll look after two weeks in Eden?" Simon M'Benga gave him a slow smile from his XO's station, and Riker grinned up at Marik's lean height, but the gray, slit-pupiled eyes gazed through the port imperturbably, like a cat's, revealing nothing.

The Eden Project. It had been one of his honored father's fondest dreams, the terraforming of a worthless planet into a useful home to feed and free some of the galaxy's billions, to make fields of wildflowers and tall forests for people whose heels ached from pounding glasphalt and whose lungs had never known the scent of mint and honeysuckle on clear air.

The young Dao had been in the Senate gallery on the day his father put forth the suggestion for the pilot project, and he recalled with infinite clarity the uproar this new idea had caused. There had been cries of 'economic disaster', of 'total unreality' and 'fiscal irresponsibility', until the elder Marik, when the commotion died down somewhat, spoke in the quiet voice of reason, quoting in detail from government files the cost—in money, men and wastage—of Eisernon's most recent war. That conflict was the one referred to in history books throughout the galaxy

169

as the One Day War of the Han; and its mention was especially moving, Marik recalled, because everyone present knew that Aldon Marik was of direct Imperial lineage and was therefore accepting for himself and his ancestors the major burden of guilt. A respectful silence fell upon the assembly, and while spring breezes blew down from the high country through the magnificent Senate Pavilion, Aldon Marik spoke of man's responsibility not only to preserve life at all costs, but to provide for it. It was not enough, he submitted, to store infants if you were going to bring them into abject poverty. Life, once conceived, must come to fruition—but it must have hope, too.

Man had the technology, the ability, the tenacity, to live in hostile environments and make a home of them. He noted the delta folk, who had built dikes to hold back the sea, and were fishermen; he spoke of the nomads of the veldt, with their vast bos-herds; of people of the high crags, who lived where no one else could live, and who communicated through a series of whistled codes.

And he spoke of starships.

There was a universe full of homes, he proposed, and it took only the courage and imagination of man to realize that exploration, terraforming, immigration, were the only reasonable alternatives to war, and were little more expensive. There were new worlds, new homes out there, and we would find them as surely as Ingri discovered the fabled Northern Isles on his journey to buy spices on the Western Shores. What technology we lacked could be acquired. It was an honorable quest. It was a quest for civilized men.

The Senate conversation that ensued for the next weeks was overwhelmingly in favor of terraforming, of exploration. They would ask the help of the Erthlikli, who were widely known for their gadgetry, and were exceedingly industrious; in addition, it was generally felt that developing an altruistic interest in the energetic Erthlikli might divert their attentions from stockpiling ammunition, and train them to think in terms other than war, although no one was particularly optimistic on that point.

Upon the Senate's acceptance of the Eden Resolution, Neron Vartik, whose Protectorate was adjacent to Marik's, and Kel Patao, a weak-willed admirer of the tough and crafty Vartik, got up and summarily left the pavilion.

The resolution was passed without them.

Now, after both Earthlikli and Einai scientists, technicians, geologists, hydrodynamic engineers, botanists and countless others had spent ten years and untold monies on a barren, lifeless planet, that planet had been recreated into a copy of Old Earth, complete with seas, rolling green hills, evergreen forests and broad savannahs whose rich loam lay fallow under the sun.

There was another advantage that Aldon Marik, dead unexpectedly a few weeks after his proposal passed the Senate, could not have anticipated. The planet, renamed Eden after an Earthlikli legend, lay at a strategic point between Eisernon and Krailim. And while it would have been an easy prize, the Krail were cunning enough not to appropriate it during its formative stages, when it was of little value. Better, they felt, to let the Federation allies terraform the wasteland, and then claim it as booty once the war was won.

That had been a mistake. The war was going badly for the Krail, very badly indeed. Some claimed it was the fault of the aging Imperator; others that it was due to individual greed and intrigue. Whatever the case, the Krail had been driven off Krau and Minsoner, and only isolated pockets of them remained on Eisernon, where they had hoped to maintain a stronghold. Their last hope was the capture of strategic Eden, to hold this last hostage planet in hopes of winning gains in the inevitable peace talks ahead.

To do that, however, would mean running a blockade of Federation warships armed to the teeth with ingenious Earthlikli weapons, and murdering every living soul on the planet, which amounted to several thousand specialists and construction men. While it was possible to accomplish such a feat, Marik mused, it wasn't terribly likely anyone would try it. That ring of warships was a potent deterrent.

"Something wrong, Mister Marik?" The cool edge of Riker's voice cut cleanly through his reverie, and he stiffened.

"I was considering the Eden Project, Captain." Riker lifted his head with interest.

"Are you familiar with it, Marik?"

Before he could reply, the Communications Officer, Timmoni Jen, interrupted in her precise Earthenglish.

"Emergency dispatch coming in from Eisernon, sir. FedCom Headquarters."

Marik was busy at his station before she had finished the thought. "Patch me in." She complied quickly, with a minimum of agitation. Marik had the attention of the entire Bridge personnel, although he would rather not have had it. An emergency dispatch was a matter of concern to each of them, and they watched with keen interest the fleeting expressions flicker across his customarily impassive face, and tried to read their meaning; greater still was their evident surprise as he blanched even to the lips and his face took on weary lines of pain and fatigue, as if he were carrying an unbearable burden. M'Benga leaned toward him solicitously.

"What is it, Marik?"

The alien might not have heard him, for he replied to the message with a crisp, "Understood. Marik, for the USS Skipjack, clear." Before they could ask him their questions, he punched the 'attention' key and the computor replied mechanically, *"Ready."*

"Repeat message from FedCom Headquarters to USS Skipjack at—" he glanced at the fascia chronometer "—fifteen-twenty hours, this date."

"Authorization."

"Marik, Dao. Science Officer." There was the electronic chittering of voiceprint match and the tape coughed metallically and announced, "Uh, this' Major Dave Corwin, FedCom Headquarters, Pal-alden-Shali-Rho, on Eisernon." The voice was unmistakeably Earthling and hailed from the southernmost regions of North America. The message was brief. Federation High Command was informing the Fleet that Krailim had surrendered its hold on Eisernon and effected a strategic withdrawal, which caused a wave of jubilation to hit the Bridge with a pounding of shoulders and a smattering of applause.

Only Riker, noting Marik's haggard countenance, heard the reason for the withdrawal: the successful destruction by what was euphemistically termed a 'small, clean, nuclear device' of the key Krail outpost, the ancient monastery on the River Elv. He turned quickly. "Put it on intercraft, Jen. I want the crew to hear it."

The message began its replay and he sauntered over to

172

Marik's Science Station. "We'll be standing off Eden by sixteen hundred, Marik. Game of takkat while we wait?"

"If you wish, Captain."

Riker nodded curtly and moved away and Marik resumed his tasks, wondering how much the Captain had surmised about him, and the monastery at Elv, and hoping fervently that he would not ask questions it would be impossible to answer.

Paul Riker moved his jat-two figure to helix one, loop four, and grinned. "Watch yourself, Marik," he warned. Marik moved his hunter to level two, loop one and refolded his arms, studying the game which looked, to the untrained Earthling eye, like a section of antique bedsprings with odd chessmen caught in them. In reality, the hoary, venerable old game of takkat had been a planetary pastime with the Einai (who'd never invented bedsprings anyway) since time immemorial, and some takkat sets were worth small fortunes for their jewels and rare metals. Marik's was a simple bronze one of great age and beautiful patina worn smooth by loving hands over the centuries, its six carved figures—two jats, two gryphons, a hunter and a shimshen—intricately worked in stoneglass and delicately colored in the Old Way, which resembled Earthling batik only slightly, the way a Master's fresco might resemble his child's crayon drawing.

Riker moved his shimshen to block and observed quietly, "That monastery was important to you, wasn't it?" Marik studied the game for some moments in silence before he replied, moving his hunter to another helix, "There were sixty thousand children there when it was destroyed."

Riker winced. "Maybe they got them out before the bombing." But Marik shook his head definitely.

"Not these children." They sat for a time in uncomfortable quiet, occasionally moving a piece from helix to helix. Finally, Riker blurted, "I thought there might have been a more personal reason for your concern." Marik lifted his eyes to his, but said nothing, waiting. "You've been inquiring about a woman, Mister Marik, for the last six months. Every planetfall, every stranger, you ask the same question: 'A small woman with gray eyes, perhaps wearing the Blue Face of a Shimshen. Have you seen her?' "

173

"You're very thorough, Captain. Very astute. I'd thought myself discreet."

"Oh, you were, you were. But I make it a practice to keep tabs on my staff. Especially—" He stopped, embarrassed. He'd meant to say, 'especially, in your case', because he sensed a deep anguish, a desperation, in his impeccable Science Officer, and he hoped to be able to help. But his hesitation sounded like thinly disguised bigotry, and it flustered him. He was mentally groping for a graceful way out of the impasse when Marik offered, quietly, "Especially because I am the only member of my species aboard, and you would like to make me feel comfortable." He moved his hunter to helix four in an absent gesture that belied his even tone.

"Something like that." Riker's shimshen was at the Tower in one final move. "Game."

Marik gave the game his full attention, started to move a piece, paused, a bit surprised. Riker began to pick up the pieces and Marik took the shimshen from the tower and regarded it with single-minded absorption. Riker set up the pieces again, one by one, deliberately slow.

"Was she at the monastery?"

"If she was alive," he answered as from a vast mental distance, "she would have been there."

"Do you want to talk about it?"

Marik studied the takkat piece, his thumb absently caressing the tiny blue face. "No. Discussion would be pointless."

Riker wheeled on him, leaning both hands on the table. "Say something, Marik! Yell, throw things! Just this one time, show what you're feeling, get it off your chest! You can't afford to start brooding about it!" Marik made no reply, and Riker pushed the point harder. "Face it! Believe it, react! She's dead! You have the right to grieve—in public, if you feel like it! She was there!—and she's gone!—finished! Even the stones were turned to dust!" His bid to evoke a response—any response—failed miserably. Marik did not look up, and when he spoke, his tone was level and clear, betraying no emotion at all.

"You seem unduly concerned, Captain." He stood, his manner icily formal. "Is my efficiency impaired? Have you found errors in my—"

174

"You never make errors, Mister Marik! You are disgustingly accurate!"

"That is my function, is it not? As for anything else—" he put down the shimshen with precise care, as if it possessed enormous weight or importance—"I find it futile to resist the validity of a past event."

Riker would like to have continued his argument, but the wall communicator beeped and he hit it with some asperity. "Riker."

"Timmoni Jen, Captain," said the communicator primly. "Private launch leaving the surface on course for the *Skipjack*. Sensors report a crew of three."

"Three . . . there should be four." There was no response and muttering, "Riker out," he turned to Marik, who was standing at the shelves on the far wall, where he kept his various trophies. Both the alien's hands were placed flat against the sides of a large faceted gemstone, which glowed brilliant scarlet, and he was staring at it, transfixed. "That'll be the Delegates and their aides. Too bad we couldn't beam them up directly."

Marik kept his eyes on the gemstone. "Impossible, sir. The project's power sources are so delicately geared at this point, that even—"

"I know, I know. Not even ship-to-surface communications." He joined Marik at the shelves and casually examined an elaborately carved, reversible wooden rack some ten inches high, in which were stacked seven identical obsidian discs marked with a distinctive glyph. Each of the discs was, say, four inches by three-quarters of an inch, Riker supposed, measuring with the flat of his hand, and honed to razor sharpness on the perimeter. There was a scarlet silk tassel attached to the rack by a wide loop, and Riker moved it and tried to lift one of the discs. Marik wheeled.

"Be careful, Captain!"

Riker jerked away a bleeding hand, staring at it in disbelief. Marik examined the hand, mildly impressed by the injury, and tossed the Captain a towel. "On Eisernon," he noted, "it's considered very bad form to touch another man's weapons."

Riker wrapped his hand gingerly and gestured with the bulky bandage. "What is that thing?"

"An ancestral weapon. Handed down through my family from generation to generation for eight centuries. We call it shun-daki." He lifted it down ceremoniously with both hands. "Your race began with the throwing-stone. So did mine. But where your primitives added a shaft to make a spear and modified the spear to provide arrows—my race modified the stone itself. Later . . . we graduated to obsidian."

"After our mutual war?" The earnest, brown eyes held a trace of chagrin, and Marik almost smiled.

"The tenth Han Emperor," he told him, as if speaking to a child, "owned a shun-daki. That was almost a thousand years ago." He neglected to say that he was holding the Emperor's weapon. "It is thrown like this—" he lifted a disc expertly and made a feint as though scaling it at the Captain, in a predatory half-crouch "—at the sound of the enemy, to inflict fatal injury. Silent and efficient. We use them for hunting—and for duelling—" his impassivity slipped and he mused, as to himself "—and sometimes the shun-daki has another use . . . as assassins use . . ."

Riker looked at him sharply. "Assassins, Mister Marik?"

"Both my parents died slain by shun-daki. By the hand of a man named Vartik." Voice, like the eyes, cool and emotionless.

Riker was surprised and a bit shocked at the idea of such an assassination, and of Marik's seeming lack of vehemence concerning it. Somehow he had always thought of Marik as a total loner; it was extraordinary to think of him as having had a family. "I'm sorry", he said awkwardly. "I didn't know. This Vartik—was he caught?"

It was Marik's turn to be surprised. "Apprehended? Of course not. Why should he be?"

Riker folded his arms and leaned indolently against the table. "On our planet, he'd be interned in a penal colony. There was a time in our history when we would have executed a murderer."

Marik, who was putting away his weapon, turned back with a most alien expression, and just for an instant, Riker could see an echo of his ancestors, the jungle cats, burning behind his eyes. "That will be my privilege," he said softly. "Executing Neron Vartik."

The communicator signalled and Riker answered, careful of his bandaged hand. "Riker here."

"Jen here," said the communicator in proper metallic

176

tones. "Private launch heaving to alongside, sir. Crew of three request permission to beam across."

"Permission granted with our compliments, Miss Jen. Inform the Transporter Officer." He rang off. "Coming, Mister Marik?"

"Right with you, sir." With a last quick glance at the shun-daki, he followed him out. The portal whispered shut behind them.

The delegation was dressed according to its station, splendid in contrast to the starmen's uniforms. One of them, a white-haired intelligent-looking Earthling, looked decidedly ill; the others, both Einai, appeared well and healthy. The younger of the two was obviously subordinate to his companion, an arrogant, authoritative einai some twenty years Marik's senior, who was clearly the dominant member of the three. This man gave the assembled officers a perfunctory glance and made as if to step down, but Piet de Mies, Transporter Officer, intervened.

"Our sensors indicate the presence of virulent organisms, gentlemen," he said in his Nedelan accent. "Please remain in your places for decontamination." There was a high-pitched keening as several colors of lights washed them, and they stood quietly until all sound had stopped. The curved, transparent plastex doors slid back and the delegates stepped down. Their leader made a brief chomala to the assembled company.

Riker returned the gesture with the ease of a born Einai and offered his hand to the elderly Earthling, who shook it feebly with the tips of his fingers.

"Welcome aboard the *Skipjack*, gentlemen. I'm Captain Paul Riker. My First Officer, Commander Simon M'Benga—" the black man offered his hand to Vartik, who scarcely touched it, and then, with a good deal more warmth, to the old man "—and my Science Officer—"

The delegate interrupted smoothly, lifting a supercilious brow, "I am acquainted with Hanshilobahr *Dom* Dao Marik. His parent, the senior Marik, and I served in the Einai Senate together."

"At the same time," Marik corrected coolly. "Hardly 'together'."

The man gave him a curt, mocking little bow and con-

177

tinued, to Riker, "I am Senior Federation Delegate Neron Vartik. May I present my opposite number, Delegate Eugene Walters—"

The old man made a valiant effort to be congenial, even though his eyes were glazed with fever and his hands trembled perceptibly. Riker, torn between Marik's story, his concern for the elderly statesman and the obligations of his rank and responsibility, found it difficult to keep his composure. Vartik wasn't making it any easier.

Walters tried to murmur a few pleasantries, but Vartik cut him off with "—and my aide, Ronhalovan."

The deferential young Einai (scarcely more than a boy, really) made a respectful chom-ala to Riker and turned to Marik with profound admiration. *"Dom Marik,* the name of your parent, the Senator, was revered in our pavilion."

Marik inclined his head in acknowledgment and Ronhalovan started to make a deep chom-ala, but he caught sight of Vartik, who was casually toying with a signet ring on his left hand, and he faltered to a stop.

"It is unnecessary to chom-ala a half-caste, Ronhalovan," he admonished softly, and the boy assumed a formal posture.

"As you wish, delegate." He did not look at Marik.

Riker swept them all with narrowed eyes and the feeling of hackles going up on the back of his neck. *Curiouser and curiouser.* "Mister Walters. How does it happen, sir, that you have no aide?"

The old man seemed confused. He passed a shaky hand across his wet face, glanced at the expressionless Vartik, and seemed to shrivel as they watched. Riker stepped toward M'Benga and muttered, "Simon, get the surgeon up here, on the double." M'Benga hurried to a wall com and Riker took Walters' elbow. "Delegate? Your aide?"

"You see, Captain . . . my aide, Thomas . . . he became quite ill . . ." he gave Riker a travesty of a smile and swayed a bit, leaning heavily on the Captain's arm. ". . . you must understand, sir . . . we wanted to warn you, but . . . the *Project* . . ."

Riker thought he heard a change, a difficulty, in his breathing, when he tottered and slumped, his eyes rolling in his head.

"Marik!" The alien caught the old man just as his knees buckled and they eased him to the floor, still muttering.

". . . such a beautiful . . . you've never seen such . . . like Eden before the, before . . . it looks . . ." He was only semi-conscious, struggling for breath and clawing weakly at his collar. He focused on Marik and formed words with great difficulty, even as the alien ran through a brief, inconclusive examination. "He's trying to speak, Captain." Riker knelt close and Marik said, "One word over and over. Plague."

Vartik, and to a lesser extent, Ronhalovan, watched impersonally as Walters tried to form words through his delirious ramblings.

". . . verit'ble Eden, Captain, *plague!* tall green hills and *be careful!* flowers, you've never seen so many, *get them out! plague!* 'n your life, and bes' of all the lakes, *plague!* Cap'n, full of fish, an' . . . for'sts . . ." He trailed off, still muttering warnings.

Riker met Marik's eyes grimly and got to his feet. "What does he mean, plague, delegate Vartik? What's going on down there?"

"It is conceivable," Marik offered, "that rumors of plague encouraged our brave delegate to terminate his inspection tour."

"It is also possible," Vartik retorted, "that you give far too much credence to the delirium of a diseased individual."

"Ronhalovan? Do you know anything about this?" Ronhalovan's face lit up. It was obvious that he had something to say, perhaps of importance, but he caught sight of Vartik toying with the ring, and his face went blank. He shook his head and made no verbal reply. Vartik lifted a brow, examining his ring with pursed lips.

"Ronhalovan. Reply. Do you know anything about a— a *plague?*"

"No, delegate!"

The ship's surgeon, along with two corpsmen, appeared and began checking Walters over, and Riker crossed to the wall com.

"We'll see what the Project's medical officer has to say about this!"

"Impossible, Captain. At this point in Eden's development, all shields will have been activated. Sources of information from the surface are inaccessible." Marik's reasonable, even voice pulled him up short, tugged him around. "We will have to rely on the delegate's word that there is no disease on Eden's surface."

Vertik afforded them his superior smile, and said, "Shall we move to the Bridge, Captain Riker? I should like to see just how you run this ship." Until now, Riker hadn't liked the Einai delegate; he began to like him less.

"I run it very well, delegate," he retorted crisply, "with the help of an intelligent staff and an efficient crew. Incidentally, visitors are not permitted on the Bridge during warp. Yeoman Gomez will show you to your quarters, gentlemen. I'll expect you to dine with me at 2100 hours. Yeoman."

Pili Gomez stepped forward into the instant anger that crackled between the Captain and the green-gold Einai delegate. "If you will follow me, sir?" Vartik stared one moment longer, then turned on his heel, Ronhalovan trotting behind with his case, and followed her out.

The corpsmen, now that the surgeon had completed his work, lifted the unconscious Walters into a small lock in the wall, fitting him into a capsule slightly larger than his body and strapping him in snugly with restraints. They flipped a few switches inside the capsule, closed it and dogged the hatch. One of them pressed a stud and the capsule whisked away on a cushion of compressed air. The other corpsman touched the wall com.

"Kinney to Sickbay. He's on his way. Intercept at Tube Five."

"Sickbay. Affirmative," said the little metal voice. They followed its echo out of the Transporter and the portals *whished* shut. The surgeon, Neal Anderson, clapped Riker on the shoulder.

"It doesn't look too great, Paul. He's a sick man."

"He was muttering something about a plague. Let me know as soon as you have a report."

The doctor massaged his beefy jowls. "Right. And I'd like to put the other two through decontamination, too, just to be on the safe side." He pulled out his pipe and filled it lovingly.

Marik, who'd been prowling the Transporter Chamber itself, came out with an abstracted expression and left the Transporter Room without a backward look. Riker made a mental note to collar him at the nearest opportunity and find out what was going on. "Uh—Piet took care of it," he answered absently, and as Marik left, continued, "I want you to have a look at them, though. Especially the young one, Ronhalovan. Something wrong there. I can't put my finger on the trouble, but—maybe you can, eh?"

Anderson grinned at him around the stem of a pipe so omnipresent that at least one curious alien had been moved to inquire whether it was a symbiotic life-form or merely an artifact. "I take it they're VIP's."

"Federation delegates, Doctor," Riker assented, still smarting a bit from his encounter with Vartik. "See that you do a good job."

Pili Gomez glided gracefully through the door that adjoined Ronhalovan's comfortable quarters to Vartik's sumptious accommodations. Ronhalovan followed her, impressed and very pleased.

"We hope, you find your quarters satisfactory, Mister Ronhalovan," she dimpled, and Ronhalovan flushed.

"Most satisfactory, *benklif*. Many thanks."

"I think that's all, gentlemen." She indicated the wall com. "Oh, if there's anything you need, delegate, microbooks, entertainment tapes, refreshments—"

Vartik turned his back on her and strolled to the far end of the room. "Inform the Earthlik female," he ordered over his shoulder, "that I am acquainted with communications devices, and that I require neither her instructions nor any further service."

Pili stood as if struck by this colossal rudeness, and Ronhalovan waved the door open for her. "I believe you are aware of your dismissal," he murmured formally.

"Yes, sir." In a small voice. She stepped through and the portal closed behind her. In the corridor, she stood staring at it for a minute, then, not knowing whether to cry or rage, she combined a wordless bit of both, flung it at the impervious door, and stormed away.

As the woman exited, Vartik began to pace, evincing more interest in his surroundings, cracking his knuckles as he always did when he was excited about something. He picked up a table ornament, put it down again; waved a lamp on, and then off. Poured himself a little brandy from a nearby decanter and warmed it in his palm as he paced, smelling it occasionally. Ronhalovan watched him, alert and formal.

"It goes according to plan, Ronhalovan. By the time we reach Federation Central, the Eden Project will have been abandoned to the Krail—Marik's lands will be part of my Protectorate—and we can begin negotiations with the insufferable Earthlikli on our own terms!" He dropped into High Eisernai. "Chom! Sar-ili mishtai!" He sipped the brandy with keen relish.

"It is perfect, indeed, Delegate," Ronhalovan answered cautiously. "But one Marik is much like the other. The parent died denying you his lands. The son will not easily relinquish them."

Vartik set down his goblet carefully and opened his case, talking as he moved. "He has made that fact abundantly clear. However, if the Science Officer should die without offspring, the Marik lands become mine, by right of conquest." He pulled a hypodermic syringe from the case, held it up to the light to check its contents, and slipped it into an inner pocket of his sleeve. "I plan to fall heir to them."

"No!" Ronhalovan made an abortive move to protest, but Vartik pressed his ring, freezing Ronhalovan where he stood in an agony of shock, his hands at his neck. After a moment, he released him, the boy staggering a bit to regain his balance, breathing hard. He looked sullen and rebellious, but he was back on his leash.

"I will not permit you to do this thing," he muttered, still badly shaken, and Vartik smiled.

"Permit me, Ronhalovan? You are going to assist me."

From his Command Post, Riker gave the Bridge a last cursory check prior to warp. Marik was busy at his console, Rutledge stood by the helm and Jen was closely tracking the launch that, although homing naturally for the planet's surface, carried an unauthorized passenger—Simon M'Benga. If anyone could find out the truth, he could. Riker had unbounded faith in him. He only hoped M'Benga wouldn't get himself killed for his trouble.

"Prepare for warp, Mister Rutledge," he ordered.

"Aye, sir." Rutledge flipped a few switches. "Power Deck: stand by."

The prim Xhole glanced up from her Communications

182

Post. "Launch is on course for surface, sir. Homing in on standard drone band. She's cleared the shields."

"Good enough." Riker heaved out of his comfortable Post. "Take us out of here, Mister Rutledge." He crossed to Marik, who was sitting at his post watching first the planet, and then its star receded in his viewer. "Marik, you never cease to amaze me."

"How so, Captain?" He straightened and sat back in his chair, apparently disposed to conversation, and Riker half-sat on the edge of his console and folded his arms.

"This Vartik. Isn't he the man you said killed your parents?"

"That's right." His face was impassive, but the slit pupils contracted a bit, betraying him.

"And yet you gave no indication of it. Have you given up the idea of executing him?"

Marik turned back to his board and began coding patterns. "Not so, Captain. I am waiting for him to challenge me."

"For him—!" Riker gave a short, surprised laugh. "He'd be a fool to challenge you! Why should he? There's no reason for it."

There was a long pause while information fed back and Marik correlated it and disseminated it to various systems. He lifted his head. "Vartik is bound by honor to allow me the chance to terminate him."

Riker stood up. "Get this straight, Marik. You're not going to 'terminate' him on the *Skipjack*. If you have a grudge, you'll have to take care of it on your own time, where there are no general orders about mortal combat aboardship."

Marik, watching his viewer, coded in a few coordinates and the star pattern changed, and changed again. "Speaking of rules, Captain, there is an interesting regulation on file that refers to the transportation of known criminals."

"You mean the Delegate?" Riker said warily. "But Vartik is not a criminal to the Einai people—is he?"

"No, sir. But the Einai people do not command this ship." He placed his hands flat and quoted from memory, "Specifically, Regulation 6992b, amendment 4, states that in the event a known felon is permitted aboard, and/or transported from his last known planet of residence or

183

port-of-call, and this boarding and/or transportation shall be with the knowledge and/or—"

"—and/or consent of the Captain." Riker took it up testily, "said Captain is automatically relieved of his duties and command falls to the First Officer, or in his absence, to the Science Officer. In this case, you."

"Yes, sir." *Was that laughter just under his voice?*

"That smacks of mutiny, Mister Marik. Or is it blackmail?"

"Not so, Captain!" He looked up at him, keenly amused. "But you must admit that under the present circumstances, it is a highly interesting regulation."

Riker looked into Marik's viewer, in which he could no longer see Eden or even Eden's star, back at Marik's hidden humor. He was in a bit of a bind, and it annoyed him.

"There are other interesting regulations, Science Officer, governing, among other things, the safety and well-being of Galactic Delegates aboard Federation vessels. For which I am held responsible." Marik inclined his head in amused acquiescence, and Riker hit the com. "Sickbay!" To Jen, "Put it on the screen."

Neal Anderson appeared on the viewer, his face a picture of professional concern. Beyond him, they could see several nurses and another doctor—it looked like Ben Morrison—working over Walters, whose harsh breathing filled the room.

"What is it?" Anderson snapped, and then, "Oh—it's you, Paul."

"How's it coming, Neal? What's wrong with him?"

The doctor lowered his voice. "You'd better get down here. And bring Mister Marik with you." There was no mistaking the ominous glance the doctor gave the Bridge personnel as he rang off. Neal had something to tell him —but he wasn't going to make it a public declaration.

They had given Walters a private room, a rare luxury aboard the subs, where space was limited. The deference was due as much to the man as to his rank, and Riker suspected (wrongly, it turned out) that the fear of contagion had something to do with it.

Walters was unconscious, his face covered with a red rash and small, subcutaneous hemorrhages. His breathing was labored despite automatic assistance, his hands twitched spasmodically and he muttered occasionally in delirium. Anderson had him encased in a cryotherapy blanket, but it didn't seem to be doing much good. From Marik's unguarded expression as he checked the man over, it was anybody's guess just how long Federation Delegate Eugene Walters, would continue to be a going concern. Marik and Anderson exchanged a bit of desultory conversation and the doctor motioned Riker over to the portal, out of Walters' unlikely earshot.

"What's all the mystery, Neal? What's he got?"

"An ancient disease. I saw it only once in medical school, when I spent a year at Eisernon's Pathology Museum studying the history of human disease. It's called typhus."

"Typhus." Riker looked blank. "How bad is it, will he live?"

Anderson shook his head. "I'm afraid not, Paul. He's got pneumonia . . . kidney failure, brain damage from the high fever . . . and we don't even have a MAX aboard." He clamped his teeth on his cold pipe. "You see, mankind's outgrown a lot of its immunities. Even partial immunities we scarcely knew we had. Today a mild measles epidemic could wipe out a planet."

Riker repeated, "Measles?"

"Another extinct desease," Anderson explained. "Like typhus."

Marik added, as he joined them, "The entire Project may be contaminated. That may explain his reference to a plague—and the absence of his aide." To Anderson, "You're losing him, Doctor." Something in his tone, or manner, some indefineable air, made Anderson view him with new eyes for a moment, and Marik caught it and busied himself with his noteboard. Riker, continuing Marik's line of reasoning, mused aloud, "But it doesn't explain why Vartik and Ronhalovan haven't been touched. How does it spread, Neal? Is it contagious?"

"Not directly, no. Typhus is—was—spread by the bite of the rat flea." He regarded his pipe quizzically and began filling it from a soft, leather pouch. "And the last rat was exterminated two centuries ago, along with its fleas, or so we thought. Technically, typhus is impossible, but . . . " he shrugged.

185

"It *is* typhus," Riker persisted. "You couldn't be mistaken."

"Believe me, I wish I were."

The indicators on the various life-support mechanisms wavered to a stop, one by one, and Anderson started for the old man, but Morrison was there before him, hopefully listening for sounds they—and he—knew he wouldn't hear. He lifted his head. "He's gone, sir." Anderson helped him cover the mottled face.

"That's it, Paul. We've lost him."

The communicator beeped and the voice of Anderson's chief Lab Technician inquired with dispassionate urgency, "Doctor Anderson, will you have a look at this, please?"

They followed Anderson into the tiny Lab, where the technician, Donovan, was sitting at a console above which was a viewscreen. They watched as he cleared the image, that of an ordinary rat flea, magnified many times. Anderson made a breathy exclamation.

"A rat flea! Where the hell did that come from?"

"We found it in his clothing, doctor. It was obviously killed by the decontamination. I thought you'd better see it. It's infested with typhus organisms."

"It's on Eden, all right," Riker said grimly, and Marik, who'd been quietly listening and correlating, said suddenly, "Gameli!"

"Beg pardon?" Anderson removed his pipe from his mouth and grinned tolerantly, and the gray eyes blazed back at him excitedly.

"*Gameli.* Captain, when we terraform a planet, we completely decontaminate it. All useful life is relocated and the remainder destroyed. Not even a virulent micro-organism is left. This preserves the ecosphere and makes it safe for humanoid life."

"Go on," Riker agreed, encouragingly.

"Therefore, the only animal that could be on Eden— and carry this parasite—would be the gameli!" Riker's face brightened and Marik nodded once, conclusively. Anderson cleared his throat.

"Will someone enlighten my stupidity? What is a gameli?"

"Singular is 'gamel', Doctor," Marik corrected evenly, and proceeded to explain. "Gameli are angora rodents native to Eisernon. They are rare, valuable and uncom-

186

monly beautiful, and they are customarily presented as a gift when a Protector builds a new pavilion."

"Or a man opens a new planet," Riker put in.

"Just so," Marik agreed. "The Monitor of the terraforming Project on Eden is an Einai. Neron Vartik would have presented gameli as a matter of protocol."

"And the gameli carried the fleas," Riker finished. "Is there a vaccine?"

Anderson massaged his jawline thoughtfully. "We can program the Medicomp for one," he rumbled, half under his breath. He was speaking mostly to himself now, thinking fast. "Make a killed serum—*weakened* serum, maybe —of the organisms in Walters' bloodstream and duplicate what we need synthetically ... " He looked at Riker. "I think we can do it here. Too bad we can't help him." He indicated the old man's body.

"Well, maybe he can help *us*. Marik, get Ronhalovan and Vartik down here on the double. I want them checked for typhus. Neal, you'd better get on that vaccine. I have the feeling the Project's going to need a lot of it." He hit the wall com, and it squeaked, "Bridge. Rutledge."

"Riker here. Neutralize warp. Set return course for Eden."

"Say again, sir," the intercom begged.

"Set course for Eden, Mister Rutledge. Maximum speed. Riker clear."

Anderson took his pipe out of his mouth and wagged his head at Marik. "Angora rats," he chuckled. "You Einai have some of the damndest animals—" He adjusted the focus on the viewscreen.

Marik fixed him with that cool, gray stare and observed, "My initial reaction to the rhinoceros was not particularly favorable either, Doctor." Anderson blinked a few times, considering that bit of information and grinned to himself. One of these fine days, he thought, when Marik wasn't looking, he was going to turn into quite a human being. He was about to say as much to the frosty alien, but when he turned around, he found that he was gone, as silently as a tiger.

The door to Vartik's quarters hissed open at Marik's summons but he did not enter. Ronhalovan crossed to meet him, and Vartik, who was sitting comfortably in a reclining chair, put down his microfilmed book. Ronhalovan, knowing better than to make an obeisance, contented himself with bowing slightly. "Chom-ala, Dom Marik."

"Chom-ala," Marik replied, speaking chiefly to Varik. "You and delegate Vartik are to accompany me to Sikbei for medical examination."

Vartik got to his feet and sauntered toward them. "Notso, Marik. I am well. There is no need."

"But Walters is dead." There was a finality in his tone, a subtle accusation. Vartik scrutinized him with drawn brows and pursed lips. The tone was familiar, very like the father's had been. There was that same directness, and yet the undercurrent, so typical of the Han. He repressed a shudder and retorted, "So. Wait here. I will join you." He disappeared into the adjoining room and Ronhalovan seized this moment to act. He was tense, edgy, desperate but fiercely controlled, and it obviously took some effort.

"Dom Marik," he whispered, wetting his lips nervously, "It is imperative that I talk to you alone."

"We are alone," Marik observed crisply. Ronhalovan glanced at the door Vartik left through, and gritted, "*In the name of your ancestors—*!"

Marik caught his glance. "What is it, Ronhalovan? What—"

Ronhalovan fought to regain his composure. "Not here. It is unsafe."

Marik considered this. "On the lower levels, then. Near the Skimmer Pods. At 1900 hours."

"At 1900 hours," Ronhalovan agreed unsteadily. Glancing fearfully at the door through which Vartik had left, he said, "Then I will tell you what really happened on the planet called Eden."

Vartik, leaning on the inner wall beside the door, listened as Ronhalovan repeated the words he'd been taught, down to the very inflection. He smiled to himself, drew the hypodermic needle from its hiding place and held it up to the light, watching the deadly liquid inside bubble faintly as he tilted the syringe from one side to the other, and back again, and back . . .

Ronhalovan was still on the examining table when Anderson completed the check of Vartik, and told the dele-

188

gate to get dressed. Morrison, watching the vital signs on various mechanisms, gave a satisfied grunt.

"Heart rate 200, pressure negligible, all other vital signs normal," he reported, and added under his breath, "if you're Einai."

"You're lucky, Mister Vartik," Anderson told him, as Ronhalovan helped him with his jacket and struggled into his own tunic. "You're both in top shape. I can give you medical clearance as soon as I okay your lab report." He indicated a small computer which was chattering busily, tore off the emerging slip and read it. He frowned, studied Vartik's face and pocketed the slip, his expression clearing. He was disturbed and puzzled by what he'd read, but he wanted time to think, even, if necessary, time to check the report against facts that were only to be found on another ship, in another sector of space.

"All right, sir," he smiled. "We're finished with you for now. Crewman?" A crewman stepped forward and waved the door open for Vartik; let the delegate pass and escorted him out. Ronhalovan started to follow him, then paused.

"The time, Dokta?"

"Time? Oh!—the time!" He consulted the 'ticket' at his wrist, a convenient medical gadget that told not only time, but many things regarding the physiological condition of the wearer. Since the Great Epidemic of Ferret I, all Federation medical personnel were required by law to wear a ticket consistantly. Anderson walked toward Ronhalovan, still watching the time. "It's now—exactly 1855." He smiled. "Uh, Mister Ronhalovan, I wonder if you'd satisfy my curiosity for me?"

"Curiosity?" He appeared hesitant and wary.

Anderson pointed with the stem of his cold pipe. "I wonder if you'd roll up your sleeves for a minute. I'd just like to have a look at—"

Vartik appeared in the doorway, causing Ronhalovan to start visibly. "Further examination, Doctor?" He pressed his ring quite hard and the indicators on various mechanisms reacted as if to an electronic fluctuation. Ronhalovan's face became a mask of open-mouthed, silent agony for a long instant, and then he relaxed weakly as Vartik wheeled and exited; Ronhalovan trailed him without a word. Anderson stood staring after them, his mind racing;

189

then he pulled the lab report out of his pocket, reread it and tapped it thoughtfully against his palm.

The com signalled and he touched it lazily. "Anderson. Sickbay." The image of Riker appeared on the little screen.

"We've just made planetfall, Doctor. Get a team together and we'll send you down in skimmers. Not as good as beaming, but its the best we can do right now."

"Right. The vaccine's almost ready. We can take the first supply down with us. Paul—" he tapped the report a few times "—could you raise the Pathology Museum on Eisernon for me?"

"Sure, Neal. What's going on?"

Anderson waved a disclaiming hand. "Nothing. Nothing . . . just a hunch. Something that showed up in one of my reports. I'd like to rule it out."

The Captain nodded. "Will do. Riker clear." The screen went black and for a long while, Anderson sat contemplating his reflection in the glass, darkly, while he waited for the call to come through.

The Hangar Deck was a barren, comfortless, utilitarian area, dimly lit and presently deserted. Unlike the picture conjured up by the term 'hangar', the enclosure was relatively crowded. Row upon row of skimmercraft, most of them suspended on davits, hung ominously in the gloom like metal cocoons. Others stood neatly aligned on deck. Several sets of metal runners led to lens-aperture hatches slightly larger than the lateral measurement of the craft; each of these hatches opened onto a small airlock fitted with a second hatch which, opened, yawned into space. It was easier, the sub designers had felt, to pump the atmosphere out of a narrow airlock than it was to evacuate an entire deck that required refilling from a finite air supply. Such a task, it was felt, would be incredibly wasteful, expensive, and time-consuming, and would have the undesirable side effect (every time a skimmer arrived or departed) of driving Life Support personnel to the brink of insanity.

Insanity. A gargoyle's face, grotesquely reflected in the bee's-eye surface of a skimmer's flasher, leered back at Neron Vartik as he stole among the silent craft seeking a hiding place, a point from which to strike.

Vartik was no fool. He knew very well that the Krail

had no intention of granting him empires when and if they won the war—which was becoming more and more unlikely. That didn't concern him. He would make his own empire. He'd intended for a long while to gain the Marik Protectorate, a decision reinforced by Aldon Marik's 'Eden Proposal', which was to cost Vartik some tens of thousands of illegal slaves as colonists. His legal advisors had exhausted all forms of persuasion. Aldon Marik's son was as stubborn as his father. It was impossible to beg, buy or capture his lands. There was only one alternative remaining, the one his parents had required: he would have to assassinate Dao Marik. Today. Now.

He leaned back against the curve of a gleaming hull and permitted himself to dream a bit. Once he owned the Imperial Lands, he would be invulnerable, a world-mover. Krailim would court his favor because he had worked so diligently to help them gain access not only to Eisernon, but to the Eden Project; and the Federation would never suspect one of its own respected delegates, much less appropriate his lands.

Nothing stood between him and absolute power but one man—Dao Marik. The hangar doors shut with a muffled *boom* and he slipped into a niche between two craft and crouched motionless, waiting, hearts beating hard with hate and eagerness.

Marik.

He came softly into the Hangar, taking in the dim light and stifling shadow, the infinitesimal vibration of the deck under his boots, and the soundless music made by the fugues of curve and curve and curve again of skimmer-skimmerskimmer—he shut his eyes. Strange. There was the feeling, the mental scent, of another presence, and he walked up one aisle and down another between the craft, moving along slowly. Interesting. It was stronger here, an *inimical* impression. His sharp ears caught the sibilance of boot on decking, and he turned searching a bit, while Vartik cursed his own stupidity, hiding, waiting. Through the line of skimmercraft, the delegate could see Marik's boots move slowly toward him on the next aisle, and he slipped across in the darkness near the floor and crouched waiting as his enemy approached. The needle slipped easily out of its holder and he released the safety catch. And he waited. Marik strolled nearer. Only a few feet now. He

191

had to make certain. There would be only one chance. The boots moved closer, and he tensed. Ready, ready . . .

The hangar doors boomed and Ronhalovan entered. "Dom Marik? Zarik tu kelec imm?" he asked fearfully. *"Lord Marik, where are you?"*

The boots stopped, turned, moved swiftly, quietly, out of range. "An-an sōn," Marik answered, in Eisernai. *"I am here."*

Ronhalovan came hurrying through the aisles, disturbed, badly frightened, and trying to control it. He kept touching the base of his neck, absently, nervously, his face a careful blank.

"I must talk quickly. My presence must not be missed. Before he gets here, *Dom* Marik, go now. Leave this place!"

"You were going to tell me what happened to the Eden Project," Marik told him reassuringly.

Ronhalovan glanced around surreptitiously. "I was instructed to deliver that message." His words tumbled out, too quickly, in his eagerness. "Marik, listen well. Leave this place now. Never stay alone. Your life is in grave danger. Vartik desires your death for reasons—" Over Marik's shoulder, he saw Vartik's face gleam up at him from between two craft. In his hand, the hand with the hated ring-control, was the hypodermic needle. He became abruptly formal, and Marik noted this with keen interest. His ears, eyes, mind, became acutely alert, although his attitude remained the same.

"Continue," he encouraged. "Vartik desires my death . . . "

"I will tell you about the Eden Project," Ronhalovan stammered, as Vartik stealthily moved up behind Marik, the needle ready.

"The plague happened in this manner: delegate Vartik brought gameli to the Monitor, as is the custom. But the gameli carried a parasite that in turn—"

There was a small movement reflected in the curved hull of the skimmer behind Ronhalovan, and Marik used it as a mirror, coldly watching Vartik stealing up behind him. He tensed, poised, ready to move.

"—carried a disease that mankind had not known for—"

Vartik lunged at Marik, but he dodged aside nimbly and Vartik crashed into a skimmer. There was a wild scuffle, both of them trying to gain control of the oozing needle. Faces were obscured by the darkness underneath the skimmers, and as they struggled, Vartik got a hand free and, jerking a short stanchion free of its moorings, hit Marik with it, as hard as he could.

The Science Officer slumped into the aisle, stunned, and Vartik whipped the needle around to inject him, but Ronhalovan caught his arm. "No!" Marik got to his hands and knees, touched the side of his scalp and pulled away a green smear, shaking his head dizzily.

Vartik tried to pull free of Ronhalovan's restraining hands, whipping his arm savagely, but the boy intervened accidentally and took the full thrust of the needle. There was a loud, automatic, hiss, and Vartik fled down the darkened aisle as Ronhalovan grabbed the injection site and crumpled to the deck. Marik chased the shadowy running figure, but lost him among the aisles. Seconds later, he heard the portals *boom* softly, and he hurried back to Ronhalovan, kneeling beside him and flipping open his compak. He steadied himself with one hand against a skimmer.

"Security. Marik here. There has been an attempted murder on the Hangar Deck. Stand by to apprehend a fugitive." He touched his head, wincing. "Sickbay."

"Sickbay. Morrison."

"Corpsman to skimmer pods at once, Doctor. Emergency."

Ronhalovan writhed on the floor, obviously in great pain and mental anguish. *"Dom* Marik," he apologized raggedly, "I—regret I was—forced to—to participate— I ask your—pardon—"

Marik half-supported him with an arm. "Ronhalovan, was it Vartik? It happened so quickly—"

Ronhalovan covered his ears with shaking hands, his eyes wild and wide. Marik's quiet tone seemed to roar at him, the sound of his own breathing seemed like a hurricane, deafening him with intra-cranial resonances. Even the movement of uniform fabric against itself as Marik moved rasped unbearably in his ears. Light was intense, colors incredibly, painfully brilliant. He shut his eyes tightly, covering his ears as Marik queried again, "Was it Vartik?"

"Do not shout, *Dom* Marik," he begged, succumbing to

193

a growing tetanus; and, dropping into his own language, "Num sito. Rakmaeli Tadae, nun sito. Num sito . . ." A convulsive shudder ran through him and he trailed off into a repititious murmur.

Heightened sensory perception due to calcium lack, Marik's reasonable medical mind intoned, even as he repressed a black memory concerning pain and convulsions. Calcium lack. Someone was in dead earnest. They'd injected Ronhalovan with sulphates, meant for Marik. The boy had been right, Marik realized. Someone most definitely wanted him dead.

Vartik slowed to a walk when he reached a side corridor and threw the empty syringe into a disposal chute, where it would become fuel for the converter. He composed himself, brushed a careful hand over his clothes and by the time two security guards came racing down the corridor, he appeared no different from any other politician who might've been making an inspection of the ship. One of them stopped him respectfully.

"Excuse me, delegate, have you seen anyone run past here? Anyone at all." Big, solid men, these, and heavily armed.

Vartik pursed his lips and pretended to think about it. "No. However, there was some disturbance near the Hangars a short time ago."

"Thank you, sir. Come on, Kopicek." They raced down the corridor while Vartik calmly walked back toward his stateroom.

The atmosphere inside Sickbay was tense. Morrison and a knot of concerned nurses and medics were working over the nearly lifeless Ronhalovan, who, unconscious, labored in the throes of a prolonged tetany. Anderson detached himself from the group and stripped off the plastex gloves he'd been wearing, tossing them in the general direction of a waste chute. He spread his hands palms-up with an expression that told the Captain exactly nothing, and told Marik everything he already knew.

"Just like that," Riker said. "One minute he's about to tell us everything we want to know, and the next—" he snapped his fingers "—we're right back where we started. Is it typhus?"

Marik shook his head. "It's sulphate poisoning."

Anderson scrutinized him through narrowed eyes and slowly inclined his head. "Right on the button. Somebody really wanted you dead, Mister Marik." He pulled out his pipe and began filling it with tobacco. No one had ever seen him smoke. "You see, Paul," he explained, "The Einai's blood chemistry is based on a copper-in-a-calcium-chloride-base rather than iron-in-a-sodium-chloride-base, like ours. So that jolt of sulphates, combined with his calcium chloride plasma—well, its like giving one of us an injection of plaster of Paris. It's clogging his whole circulatory system. He's been showering emboli since we got him in here. So far nothing we've done has been much good." He stepped back to the bedside long enough to adjust the titration valve on an ancient robomedic and check the vital signs indicator, wagging his head ruefully. He tipped his head toward the bed. "This is our last bet. We're doing a complete blood transfer. His polluted blood is being removed and we're transfusing him with our reserve supply of Alpha R+. *All* of our Alpha R+. So, Mister Marik, until we can restock your own particular brand of green stuff, don't cut yourself, eh?"

Marik, closely scrutinizing the medical equipment, gave him a preoccupied nod, and Anderson wondered if the enigmatic alien had heard him at all. The communicator signalled and Riker leaned on it.

"Sickbay. Riker."

Timmoni Jen's punctilious voice replied, "This is the Bridge, sir. Skimmer 5 reports that the Eden Project *is* infected with typhus."

"How bad?"

She hesitated. "Epidemic proportions, sir."

"Riker clear." He wheeled on them. "Marik, get a Decontamination Team down there. Rig one of the lifeboats for the job. Make sure the Team's been immunized."

"Aye, sir." He was gone like smoke in the wind.

"Neal, how many of your personnel can you spare?" He was afire with impatience to get to the truth, and Anderson's slow consideration of the question annoyed him.

"Over and above what I have down there now," the doctor drawled, "maybe half a dozen." He put the pipe

195

back into his mouth and said, around it, "Of course, that's throwing in technicians, corpsmen . . ."

"Good," Riker assented quickly. "Good. We'll ship them down with the Decon Team." He paced a bit and stopped to stare belligerently up into the doctor's face.

"A perfectly safe planet, a *beautiful—planet!*—and then wholesale epidemic. And no one immune."

Anderson corrected soberly, "Almost no one," and Riker whirled on him, searching his eyes.

"What do you mean?"

"I mean that before this—" he jerked a thumb at Ronhalovan "—our two Einai visitors were in perfect health! Just off a plague planet, Paul, and they were in perfect health." Riker gave a relieved laugh, a weary bark of a laugh, and passed his hand across his brow.

"Well, that may not impress you, Doctor, but to me it's a huge relief that I can return at least two of my three charges to Federation Central in good condition." He regarded Ronhalovan somberly. "At least, I'm hoping for two."

Anderson stepped into the cubbyhole that served as his office, and Riker followed him to the door. The doctor rummaged a moment and came up with the Lab report that had earlier given him pause. He handed it to the Captain. "That's why they didn't catch the plague, Paul. Right there. The Medicomp found it. They were vaccinated! Before they came to Eden, they were both vaccinated against typhus!"

Riker found it hard to understand the doctor's excitement. "Well—they would be, wouldn't they?" he rationalized. "All communicable diseases? . . ." Anderson grabbed back the report disgustedly and tossed it into the chaos on his desk.

"Come on, Paul! They haven't included typhus in those shots for more than a century! That's like taking a vaccination for smallpox!—or—or cancer! It's just not necessary any more!"

"But," the truth started dawning on Riker's face, "but Vartik and Ronhalovan . . ."

Anderson stabbed at him with the stem of his pipe. "Right! They were immunized against this one ancient disease—no other. And another thing. I checked it out with Eisernon on sub-space, just to be sure." He bit his

196

pipe stem and grinned. "Where do you think Vartik got his 'gift of gameli'?"

His face clouded with disbelief. "You're not going to try to tell me——!"

"The Pathology Museum, Paul," Anderson finished, "where both of those beautiful, rare, valuable gifts that Vartik gave the Monitor had been used as hosts for one of the few remaining strains of rat fleas. The typhus carrier." He pulled the stem off of his pipe, squinted through it at the light, blew through it, and tapped it against his boot sole. He grimaced up at Riker from his bent position. "If I didn't know better, Paul, I'd say our boy Vartik deliberately sabotaged the entire planet."

Eden loomed blue and patchy brown under the broken cloud-cover, filling the viewer and lighting Marik and Riker's faces. Down there on the surface, perhaps on green hills, with winds and sweet rains blowing free over the land, Simon M'Benga and two skimedics worked among a plague-ridden population, hopefully with the help of Marik's Decontamination Team. There had been no word from M'Benga for several hours, and Riker was becoming concerned. A thought struck him. "Marik, do you know whether or not M'Benga was vaccinated?"

"I took the liberty of ordering his vaccination, sir, along with the others." He programmed for M'Benga's Life Glow, which burned with a steady white light on the panel; flicked it off. "He is well, sir."

Before Riker could answer, the portal opened to admit an angry Neron Vartik. Bridge personnel looked up curiously and Guns, the stocky, dark-faced Russian Weapons Officer, nudged the Helmsman.

"Captain Riker!" he called in a loud tone, and Riker started to walk toward him, but Marik's warning hand on his arm stopped him cold. There was a guarded stir, an electricity in the air.

"Delegate."

Vartik placed both hands on the catwalk railing and leaned hard on them. "I understand we have returned to the terraforming project."

"That's right. There is an emergency situation on the surface. We'll be standing by until we're sure it's under control."

Vartik laughed shortly. "There is a ring of warships around this system. Surely one of them could—"

"*No*, delegate!" Riker was fighting back now, hard and coldly civil, but in no way the genial host of a Federation Delegate. "They can't leave the system unguarded for one minute, because in one minute, the Krail buzzards could swarm in and settle on Eden. This is not their concern; this is *our* baby." He said over his shoulder, "Marik, any word from M'Benga?"

"No, sir."

Vartik lifted his head haughtily, nostrils flaring. "By what right do you disobey a Federation order and interrupt my journey?"

"By right of command. Mister Vartik," Riker retorted. "The *Skipjack* is my ship."

The Einai delegate came down the ramp, calmly drawing a pulseweapon of obvious Krail manufacture. "Not any more, Captain." There was an uneasy murmur among the other officers and Guns half-rose, but Vartik levelled the weapon at him and he sat slowly, his black eyes angry above the broad Kalmyk cheekbones. "I hereby commandeer this vessel for Federation purposes."

"The regulation is unmistakable," Marik said guardedly. "He is within his rights."

"Not with that weapon, Mister Marik," Riker clipped. "That weapon makes it piracy." Vartik strolled to the Command Post and sat comfortably in Riker's place, aiming his pulser at the back of Helmsman Rutledge's head.

"Captain, you will recall your people and proceed at once to Federation Central." Riker didn't move, and Vartik's voice became harsh and flat. "Any disobedience to my orders will be construed as mutiny and the offender will be pulsed out of existence. Clear, Captain?"

"Quite clear, Mister Vartik. May I also make it clear, sir, that I intend to file charges against you at our first starfall. For sabotage of a Federation project, attempted murder of my Science Officer, and piracy on the deep."

"Planetary sabotage, Captain?" Riker thought it notable that he ignored the other charges. "You would be well-advised to speak cautiously. To accuse a delegate of such a crime, without benefit of eyewitnesses . . ." he shrugged elaborately.

"We have Ronhalovan."

Vartik leaned back complacently and smiled, sardonic and unpleasant. He rubbed the ring and replied smoothly, "Not so, Earthlik. *I* have Ronhalovan." Then, tiring of this, "Begin your preparations for our journey. We warp at —" he consulted his elaborate chronometer "—2200 hours."

An hour from now, Riker thought desperately. And how can I get them all off the surface in one hour? "I can't warp until my people are aboard," he argued coldly. "If we leave them, they'll die with the people they came to save."

"Everyone dies, Captain," Vartik purred. "Not so, Dao Marik?" Riker realized that he was rubbing it in well that he'd killed Marik's parents; and he half-expected—even hoped for—a violent reaction from the unpredictable alien; but Marik replied, with a brief white smile that infuriated Vartik almost as much as it puzzled Riker, "Affirmative, surely, Delegate. A most astute observation."

The Captain realized three things with a rush: first, that he'd never seen Marik smile before, and a most dangerous smile it was; second, that, contrary to appearances, Marik was not being docile and stupid, but caustic; and third, that Vartik was being played like a takkat piece by the cunning alien. Marik's serene and deadly expression reminded him of a big cat stalking its prey. He decided to go along with him, praying that Marik knew what he was doing.

"Mister Vartik," he asked civilly, "what would you have us do?"

Vartik lifted his brows, pleased, and replied in a more dulcet voice, "We will have our meal. In your dining room, I believe, Captain?" Riker nodded shortly.

"Of course, sir." He crossed to the shocked Miss Jen. "Jen, send down to surface for all our personnel and anyone they can bring with them. Pack 'em in. We'll decontaminate and treat them here. Let me know when they report in."

"Aye, sir." Then quickly, "Captain!" He paused. "Is *he* running the ship now, sir?" Her blue skin paled and the ruff bisecting her hairless skull sagged, unhappily. He tried to be encouraging.

"Only temporarily, Miss Jen. But his pulser is set on destruct; so don't cross him, eh?" He crossed to the lift, where Vartik and Marik, whom he held as hostage, were waiting for him. The doors closed behind them. "Captain's Quarters," Marik said to the lift, and Riker hit the wall com.

"Galley. Riker here. Dinner for four in ten minutes. Sickbay, Riker. Anderson to my quarters." To Vartik, he explained shortly, "My Medical Officer frequently joins me on these festive occasions."

"Permission granted," Vartik purred, and Riker restrained a fleeting urge to hit him, very hard. He caught Marik's eye and saw that he was up to something. There was that hunting-cat expression on his face, and when he saw Riker watching him, he glanced pointedly at the corner of the lift, where some careless crewman had left a telecord. With a wash of hope, Riker maneuvered casually until he could slip the recording device into the tunic of his uniform: he managed it just as the lift drew to a halt, diverting Vartik's attention.

The delegate emerged first, motioning the others out with his weapon, and as Marik followed the Captain into the corridor, his cane caught on the hairline crack between lift and floor level, and he went down heavily, fetching up against the opposite corridor wall just beneath a wall com. Riker started to help him, but Vartik stepped between them.

"I think not," he smiled coldly, as Marik began painfully pulling himself up the wall. "Now, if you will come this way, Captain?—your Science Officer will follow, I think." He brandished the pulser and led Riker toward the second lift, whose lights showed it was about to emit a passenger. Marik's hand hit the wall com cautiously but it *beeped*, and Vartik, half-hearing it, started to turn; but Riker deliberately let the telecord drop with a resounding clatter, and Vartik wheeled on him and on Neal Anderson, who—by way of a second distraction, stepped out of the lift into the nervous sweep of Vartik's weapon. In the resulting cacophony of dropped telecord, Anderson's loud protestations and Riker's effort to quiet him down, Marik spoke urgently into the com, guarding his voice.

"Bridge."

"Bridge," said Miss Jen's prim voice metallically.

"Marik here. Raise the Federation High Council. Request an immediate hearing for high treason. We will be in Captain Riker's quarters. Transmit directly to Central. Clear." He was limping back toward the others before Vartik noticed his absence.

The Captain's Quarters were well appointed, with a few pieces of tasteful sculpture and several growing plants softening the clean, angular lines of wood and metal and plexiglas. A small visual communicator stood at Riker's right hand as he sat opposite Vartik, facing the large visual communicator set in the wall; Anderson and Marik shared the handsome table with them, and although the dinner steamed deliciously and was served to the accompaniment of old wines, no one but Vartik was very hungry.

On another planet, closer to the Galactic Hub, another large communicator stared down from the wall, this one in the High Council Chamber of the Galactic Federation. Before it, in the elaborately restrained decor of the room, stood a long table and seven imposing chairs, in which sat six Councilmen, one each from the known intelligent races of the Federation. The seventh chair stood empty. One of the elders lifted a hand and intoned, "The High Council of the Galactic Federation is now in session." He pressed a few keys on the panel under his hand and the screen flashed to life, closing in on the men at Riker's table. The Earthling Councilor tapped his ear and the elder brought up the audio. The men aboard the ship were deep in conversation, with the Captain holding the floor.

"You understand, Mister Vartik," he was saying respectfully, "that we could disarm you and try you for piracy. We have held legal proceedings aboard this vessel in the past."

"Quite so, Captain. However, a Federation delegate can only be tried by a jury of his peers, none of whom is present." He caressed the pulser with his free hand as he ate. "In addition," he pointed out, "any attempt to disarm me would prove fatal to many of you."

"But not to all of us," Riker retorted, and Vartik again showed his unpleasant smile.

"Small consolation to the fallen."

Neal Anderson pushed his plate back and folded his arms. "We don't need a jury, Delegate. We have legal computers that can sense what you're thinking and decide your innocence or guilt better than a human mind." He put his cold pipe between his teeth. "Faster, too."

201

"Not so, Doctor," Marik interjected quickly. "Legal computers can be altered by esper quality, and as you know, some Einai—notably the Han—are telepathic under certain conditions."

"Quite so," Vartik agreed smugly, and Anderson bit his pipe stem until it broke. He fumbled for the two pieces and glared at Marik.

"Hey, just whose side are you on, anyway?" he demanded. The cool, gray eyes were unreadable as they swung toward him.

"I am an Einai, Doctor, and thereby bound not only by Federation Law, but by the rules and customs peculiar to my own race. Not so, Delegate?" This to Vartik, who bowed an affirmative and tipped up his goblet, hiding his entire face. Marik seized this opportunity to tip his head toward the small, red-glowing indicator light half-hidden in the planting below the screen. Riker's face lit up when he realized they were being watched. Marik held up seven fingers briefly, and Riker leaned back a bit, more comfortable than he'd been in several hours. His disposition was vastly improved by this knowledge, and he felt expansive.

Vartik put down his goblet and Riker reached over to refill it for him. "You have an excellent cellar, Captain," the delegate told him, his face flushed with the liquor. "Native vintage?"

"Pure Earth stock," Riker replied cordially. "Our supply is limited, but we carry the best."

"'Pure Earth stock'," Vartik sneered. "The way you say it, reeking with embarrassing emotional pride!" He put down his goblet hard. "Does it never occur to you that another planet could equal Earth, could excel Earth? Its people, its products, its philosophies?"

Riker grinned boyishly. "Why, Delegate," he drawled, "I don't detect a bit of planetary pride there, do I? Embarrassing, emotional pride?" Anderson chuckled and Vartik laid a hand on his pulser.

"We are incapable of exhibiting pride," he boasted, and Riker leaned toward him intently, no longer smiling.

"And of hate, Mister Vartik? Are you incapable of hate? Because wouldn't it take a great deal of hate to deliberately infect a planet with a disease so ancient no one

202

remembers its cure?" He fervently hoped the Councilors had heard every word. Then Marik spoke.

"At one time, Captain, delegate Vartik was a bacteriologist of some renown. I don't wish to disagree with you, but I respectfully submit that it was pure scientific curiosity, not a base emotion like hatred or greed, that prompted him to infect the Project."

"Precisely," Vartik agreed quickly. "I merely—" he broke off suddenly, realizing what he'd agreed to, and retained his composure with some effort. His face flushed darkly and veins stood out in his temples. But if he controlled his emotions, Anderson did not. He broke into loud guffaws, laughing heartily until Vartik aimed the pulser at a spot directly between his eyes.

"Your humor is in very bad taste, Doctor," Vartik snapped, and Anderson, struggling to a choking halt, blotted his mouth with his napkin. He tried hard to ignore the nasty snout of the pulser.

"I begin to see it that way, yes," he chuckled, scowling, and Vartik turned his anger upon Marik.

"How clever of you to secure a confession of treason, *Mister* Marik—with no witnesses! Or did you intend to use this recorder—" he slammed it into the disposal chute "—to gather evidence against me? To use before the High Council, perhaps? Those poor fools know only what they are told!—and *I* tell them!" A vein pounded in his temple. "But you would have used it if you could. Another example of Earthlikli arrogance. Expand, absorb, assimilate! Convert or destroy! Colonize! If Earth has no more room, build a new Earth! Find a planet, give it an Earthlikli name, and terraform! And steal thousands of Einai to colonize it for you!"

"Those people were volunteers, Delegate," Riker retorted evenly. "I've seen the record. Earth didn't steal a march on Eisernon; we don't cheat anyone, even those thousands of farmers you claim you need to till your lands." He'd almost forgotten the listening screen opposite him, but on another planet, near the Galactic Hub, the Galactic High Council listened and weighed evidence, and sent electronic messengers searching secret files, each of them a delicate balance, sensing truth. In their huge screen, the image of Marik stirred and spoke.

"I was unaware that Neron Vartik owned any land not

riddled by mines and populated by his slaves." Vartik's head flashed up.

"*Tenants*, Dao Marik." Marik tasted the wine in his goblet.

"Wearing shock-collars around their necks?" He extended the beautiful goblet to Riker for refilling, and mourned, "Unfortunately, Delegate, you have always been a lamentably poor liar."

"Call it what you will," Vartik rejoined hotly, "I will not give up twenty-seven thousand workers to colonize a second Earth!" The communicator *beeped* and a picture flashed onto the little screen, that of Ben Morrison in Sickbay. Riker thumbed the stud. "Riker. Go ahead, Doctor."

"Message for Doctor Anderson, Captain." Morrison leaned aside and spoke directly to Anderson. "Ronhalovan is out of danger, Neal. He's awake, if you want to see him." Anderson put the stubby stump of the pipe in his teeth. "Let's have a look at him." Morrison keyed-in a sequence and the scene shifted to a private room—the only private room—in Sickbay, where Ronhalovan lay motionless. Anderson cleared his throat and the boy turned his face toward the screen.

"Ronhalovan. Doctor Anderson. How do you feel?"

"Tired, but otherwise well," the green-skinned youth answered weakly. "I am grateful, Doctor. Allow me to perform some service for you, in payment."

Anderson grinned around his pipe and rumbled, "As a matter of fact, m'boy, you can do us a favor. Will you tell the Captain, here, just who sabotaged the Eden Project?" Ronhalovan brightened and sat up, propped on his elbows and ready to speak, when Vartik sat forward where the boy could see him, casually twisting his ring.

"Go ahead, Ronhalovan," he insisted softly. "You have my permission. Tell them everything." The boy froze and turned his head away sharply, his eyes tightly shut; and Vartik smiled.

"Ronhalovan!" Riker struck the table in frustration and annoyance. "He can't hurt you, I give you my word! He'll never get at you!"

"Not so, Captain!" He turned away savagely and burrowed under the blankets until he was only a huddled lump.

"You see, gentlemen?" Vartik smiled, sipping his wine.

204

"Ronhalovan is *my* animal." He set down the goblet and steepled his fingers, making sure the pulser was within easy reach. "Now, gentlemen, my purpose for bringing you here. We will discuss land. Your land, I believe, *Mister* Marik."

Riker was surprised, and it showed. "I didn't know you were a landowner, Marik."

"Quite so, Captain. One of the largest Protectorates in our Province. Hereditary land that he permits common tenants to run." His voice was heavy with disdain and controlled rage, but Marik only nodded once, in agreement.

"And run well," he continued for him. "My steward is a most trustworthy individual." *'Steward'*, Riker thought; and then, *'What are we dealing with here?'* But Vartik jumped to his feet in a rage, his chair making a small statue behind him tumble and break, pounding both fists on the table violently in one great thud.

"Upon his death, the lands of the elder Marik were to have reverted to me! I killed Marik!—his lands are mine!"

Marik looked up at him, towering menacingly there, and slowly set down his goblet. "Only by right of conquest," he said evenly. "You still have to deal with me."

Vartik drew himself up contemptuously. "I will not enter battle with a *half-caste*!"

"Then you will live without my father's lands." He got to his feet, deliberate and deadly. "But I know you, Neron Vartik. You wanted more than land. I watched you come to our pavilion with your hands full of gifts and your eyes filled with the face of my Imperial mother. I saw you offer my father everything you possessed to put her aside, so that you—" Vartik backhanded him across the face with such force that his head rocked back. "Lies! Lies!" he yelled shrilly. "She was nothing but a filthy half-caste!"

Marik almost smiled, a savage and terrible triumph, and blotted the place on his lip that was bleeding greenly. He glanced at it.

"I consider the challenge valid. I believe the choice of weapons is mine." He took from the cuff at his wrist the scarlet loop from the shun-daki rack, and laid it across Vartik's right wrist like a slash, in a formal, ritual gesture. "I declare a shun-daki."

Vartik stared at it aghast for a moment and then shook

it off as if it were a snake. "No!" he shouted. "Not while I have—" He grabbed for the pulser, but the large screen suddenly flashed to life. "Negative, Neron Vartik!" a voice thundered, and he whirled to gape at the large screen, its light whiter still against his whitened face. His mouth went slack and he touched it with trembling fingers.

"The High Council! How long have you—"

"Long enough," answered the Councilor from Krau, inclining his white-maned head. "We are not so foolish as you imagine us to be. You will put down the weapon, please." The pulser slipped from Vartik's fingers and Marik picked it up and hit the com. "Security. Two men to the Captain's Quarters." Riker walked up to the screen.

"May I speak, Councilor?" The wrinkled, blue-skinned Xhole Councilor nodded gravely, and Riker took a deep breath. "Neron Vartik is a Federation Delegate. Now, I dislike the man. It's not going too far to say I could hate him with not much effort. He's a murderer and worse, the despoiler of a planet and the keeper of slaves. But I'm not a judge, I'm a ship's Captain; and I'm responsible for Vartik while he's aboard this vessel. I have to keep him alive. I respectfully request that the shun-daki be called off."

Marik thrust the pulser at him. "Then kill me now, Captain. Because if I live, he dies."

"Not aboard the *Skipjack*, Mister!"

"Here!—and now!" He turned to the Council. "I am an Einai! And we Einai are bound by rules other than those of the Federation, laws of honor and ancestry. The delegate himself agreed to this standpoint." He studied their faces soberly, as if he were in their physical presence and said, huskily, "I ask the High Council to permit the shun-daki."

The Einai elder, a green-gold legend whose image graced the Senate Pavilion, smiled briefly and folded his hands on the table before him.

"You are much like your parent, Dao Marik. We will confer, and give you our decision."

"You cannot decide!" Vartik shouted disrespectfully. "Seven sit on the Council, and only six are present!" There was a concerted murmur among the Councilmen, and the Kraun Councilor lifted a hand for silence.

"But we *are* all present, delegate Vartik. It is significant that you do not recognize the identity of the Seventh Councilor." He paused and meditated patience. "Before you retire, have you anything to say in your own defense?"

Vartik, closed in on the one side by Riker's starmen and his enemy Marik, and on the other by the highest court in the galaxy, breathed hard, his fear and hatred evident on his features. He was losing everything: status, credibility, power. There was only one thing left for him; if he had to go down to destruction, he would take the son of his hated enemy with him. He would kill Dao Marik. He wheeled on the Council and snarled, "Let the shun-daki decide!"

There was a pause, a bit of desultory conversation among the Councilors, and a silence; at last the Kraun Councilor lifted his white, thick-maned head and nodded once, impressively.

"So be it," he said.

Riker pushed the takkat set aside and half-sat on the edge of the table while Marik peeled off his tunic and opened a bluewood-and-lacquer chest. Kneeling, he removed its contents with great care and respect in a series of formalized motions that were as fascinating as they were incomprehensible.

"Why, Marik?" Riker demanded. "Why did you push this? They know he's guilty, he cut his throat every time he opened his mouth. Why did you have to make it personal?"

Marik stripped and donned a coarse, white ritual garment that consisted primarily of a long strip of fabric with a slit for the head, and which hung almost to the floor; he tied a cincture of scarlet rope at his waist and made much of knotting it, as though it were important, and carefully arranged the folds in order. He spoke as he dressed, grimly pondering his words, for he was not given to public displays of emotion, and they embarrassed him.

"Because the day Vartik killed my parents, I should have been killed, too. They wanted me to come riding with them but I stayed at the eyries to help birth a new gryphon brat. It was a thoroughbred, and we'd had trouble with the dam. So they rode out alone. Very high, very fast . . . very beautiful . . ." He fastened orange, brush anklets on

207

both legs and straightened. "By dusk they hadn't come back, so I took a mount and went looking for them. And I found them." The gray eyes narrowed reminiscently. "On the chalk cliffs. Their mounts' wings were cut to ribbons by Vartik's shun-daki. I can still see his symbol carved in them. And he'd used them well." He tugged himself back resolutely from that pool of painful reflection after a moment and continued, "They hadn't a chance. My beautiful mother, my father, had no chance to die honorably; it was a slaughter!" He tied a white bandeau around his forehead and fixed Riker with his level stare. "Now there will be another slaughter!"

"You told me you found it futile to resist the validity of a past event. This *is* a past event!" He was speaking to one of his ship's officers, a Federation appointee; but looking back at him out of unreadable, slit-pupiled gray eyes was an alien, barefoot and in ritual killing garb, and he realized that there was no way he could dissuade him.

"You're going through with it," he muttered, disgustedly. "You're going to be stubborn—and risk your life!—and for what?"

"For my honor, Captain." By way of explanation—for Riker seemed far from convinced—he added, quietly, "I do what I must. If I die, I will die well, which is no small consideration. If I win—if I win, thirty thousand slaves will be free of Vartik, and the honor of my family will be restored. I have no other choice—I must fight the shun-daki."

Riker searched his face with troubled eyes and saw, for the first time, a warmth and under that, a terrible purpose and need; and it both astounded and moved him to discover that Marik—impassive, aloof, solitary Marik—could be in need of his friendship and approval. What a pity to have found it out, he thought, when in a few minutes the man might easily be dead. And, since neither the Military Manual nor his own personal code of conduct covered the situation, he simply shrugged his acquiescence, smiled wryly and extended his hand, which Marik grasped firmly.

"Good luck, Mister Marik," he growled.

The door had hissed shut behind him before Marik moved. Then he lifted the *crux* from the highest shelf, lit incense before it and made a profound chom-ala; he clapped his hands loudly, sharply, together, elbows out, palms pressed tightly, his head slightly back as he prayed, in an all but inaudible monotone: "Chom-ala Tadae, zo varo rashaimon ze tarok m zo ronin shun-daki . . ."

Ronhalovan, weak but functional, stood between Marik and the Delegate, holding a footed brazier of hot coals in his hands, and a thin wisp of smoke drifted up and hung in the still air. The air vents had been shut off and the gym made as quiet as possible, for Ronhalovan had explained that the *dak* was thrown at the sound of the enemy; for this purpose, each contestant wore the orange bos-hair *mishge*—whisperers—on his ankles; and the coals, marking the center of the arena, gave a man his bearings. Riker thought, at the time, that in the lighted gym all this ritual was a bit much, but politely refrained from mentioning it. Later, he was to be glad that he had.

The contestants, each in his white raiment, stood facing the gymnasium, which had been cleared but for a shielded area at one side, behind which protection seating arrangements had been made for Riker, Anderson and the rest of the staff. Each man held his shun-daki rack by the top and bottom with both hands; each man glistened with oil, having anointed his limbs from a ceremonial vial. The screen behind them flashed on and the High Council, which was to witness the encounter ('A very great honor, Captain Riker', Ronhalovan had confided) appeared upon it. Ronhalovan turned to gaze up at them and the Kraun Councilor addressed him directly.

"Are you able to monitor this encounter, that it shall remain civilized?" Ronhalovan answered that he could. The question was rhetorical. Neron Vartik was widely known for this duelling skill, not only at shun-daki, but with viith; and Ronhalovan had always acted as his second, a nominal position only, he knew. There had never been need for a second. Vartik was too thorough a duellist for that. His affinity for bloodshed was so absolute as to prompt Aper ser Nalm to observe, in a rare unguarded moment, that had Vartik a talent for violin and a decent set of knees, he might've passed for an ancient Erthlik emperor, a remark which everyone but Vartik found rather droll.

The Kraun Councilor gave the signal to proceed, and Ronhalovan set forth the rules of battle.

"Behold the shun-daki, the Seven Birds. These, then, are the rules of Men:

'That no man remove his bandeau until one is dead.

'That no man, falling upon the coals, be cut until he regain his balance.

'That no man cut a fallen opponent, if he be wounded unto death.

'That no two men shall walk away from the shun-daki.' "

"Terasom!" announced Vartik, eagerly. *Ready!*

"Terasom," Marik repeated coolly. He seemed almost detached.

Ronhalovan placed the brazier squarely in the center of the bare room and backed away slowly as the combatants took up places on either side of the coals, each taking the other's meausre.

Riker studied them, too, and saw the reason for Vartik's enthusiasm. Marik was sleek, lean and compact, built like a young hunting-cat; under normal circumstances, he would be quick and dangerous, and could give a good account of himself in any ring. But the almost Earthuman gold of his skin was marred by wealed scars, some of them so new as to be a livid dark green, barely healed. Without his cane, his limp was more pronounced, and would seriously hinder him.

On the other hand, Vartik, the professional duellist, moved easily and outweighed Marik by twenty pounds, most of it about the shoulders and neck. Deadly, thick-muscled, crafty, he was the tiger to Marik's leopard, and the Captain began to understand the odds Marik had pitted himself against for the sake of his honor. He started to get to his feet and call a halt to this nonsense before somebody really got hurt, but Anderson's firm grip on his arm forced him back into his seat.

"They've started," he muttered.

"Tok!" Ronhalovan ordered, and both Marik and Vartik pulled down their bandeaux to cover their eyes.

"Terasom!"

They looped the top ring of the shun-daki rack over the center finger, left hand, and lifted out the first disc by its two flat faces. They both fell into a predatory stance, shifting a bit for balance, lifting their heads in quick, listening little jerks.

"Sahar!" he commanded them to begin, and stepped quickly behind the shield. He sat beside Riker and Anderson, who gave him a quick, professional scrutiny, even as the first sibilance of coarse, orange bos-hair whisks swished softly scross the floor.

Vartik spun the first disc. It narrowly missed Marik, who dodged its thin whine and spun his first, which hit the wall and caromed off with some force, rattling to the floor. Vartik's second was more successful. It drew first blood, slashing Marik's upper arm greenly; he slapped it, wincing and lifted his head blindly, listening, the invisible hairs inside his ears delicate antennae, sensing sound, and he scaled another *dak* at Vartik's infinitesimal sound, unheard breathing, oil-scent on the floating molecules of air.

The disc whirred through the intervening space, rebounding from the shield and striking Vartik's rack with splintering force, and Marik got off another and another in quick succession, grazing Vartik's ribs and gashing his shoulder. Furiously, Vartik ripped off his blindfold and touched his bleeding shoulder, unbelievingly, with groping fingers; it was evident that Neron Vartik had seldom been hit before, for his face darkened and he snatched a disc out of his rack, convulsed with rage, and began stalking Marik in earnest, oblivious both to Ronhalovan's protests and the commands that were signalled to him from the Council screen. Riker leapt to his feet, but Ronhalovan barred his way.

"You cannot go out there, Captain! They would kill you, from the sound of your walking!"

Riker leaned past him and shouted, "Marik! His blindfold is gone! He can see you!" To a crewman, he barked, "Douse those lights!"

The lights went down like a struck tent, leaving only the dubious glow of the brazier to light Vartik's way; the red glimmers reflected off slick muscles as they maneuvered for position, Marik listening, feeling, through his very skin, Vartik playing for time. Now that Marik's life was his, he felt no haste about taking it. He wanted to enjoy this killing, to destroy him piecemeal, without dignity. He made a sound and dove quickly in the opposite direction, and Marik got off a quick near-miss and spun a second disc at the involuntary explosion of a crewman's cough.

Vartik eyed Marik's rack: only one disc left. And he was

getting tired. His limp had worsened, he'd stumbled several times, not much, but enough that strain lines showed around his mouth; and the slash in his arm was bleeding freely, dripping off his dangling fingers and staining the white fabric of his robe.

The big man decided to make his move. Holding his breath so Marik could not hear even that, he cautiously removed one of the rustling *mishge* from his ankle and tossed it far to one side. And Marik—he almost laughed aloud in savage triumph!—Marik stopped, poised, his head cocked, listening—and with one fluid motion, spun his last disc with uncanny accuracy, after the *mishge*, and sliced it neatly in half.

But now his rack was empty.

And his enemy lived.

Vartik's face gleamed greasily in the flickering light as he closed in for the kill. Mari heard him come. His head swiveled even as he reached for another disc, but his hand closed on emptiness, and he fell into a feline half-crouch, willing to die if he must, but determined that Vartik would have to work at it. He had no intention of making him a gift of his life. Now Vartik started to talk, mostly to himself, soft and mindlessly.

"Like your parent, Hanshilobahr Dao Marik. Too honest, too trusting. Always believing that every man fights as you do."

He spun a disc that skimmed Marik's cheekbone, leaving a green streak, and Marik slapped it, dodged away, listening, feeling the floor for the impossible luck of a dropped disc.

"Believing that the only way to kill," Vartik continued in the same soft tone, "is face to face." He spun another disc, wounding Marik in the leg and bringing him down. Marik was hurt, bleeding and unarmed, and Riker shouted to the Council to stop the match, but they waved him to silence. Vartik advanced slowly upon his recumbent opponent and calmly drew his last disc, even as Marik dragged himself to his knees and fumbled for a disc nearby. Vartik aimed carefully, a classical offense stance, meaning his disc to bisect Marik at the throat, when with a quickness beyond belief, the celerity of a cat's-pounce, Marik whipped the disc at the delegate with all his might, the single motion of find, grasp, turn, throw, so swift and powerful that

212

the disc was driven—Anderson told them later—almost to the backbone.

Vartik clasped his arms around his middle and went down to his knees and then to the floor, his face blank and rather surprised. He lay curled on one side as the lights went back on abruptly and Anderson ran out to tend him.

Marik hauled himself up, slick with oil and sweat, and leaned against the wall for a moment, catching his breath. He pulled his bandeau free and tossed it away, and wiped the cut cheek with his arm. Riker hurried to him and asked anxiously if he were all right; Marik assured him quietly that he was. Then he walked to where Vartik lay dying and upended his shun-daki rack at the delegate's head, setting it firmly on the floor; then he stripped Vartik's scarlet silk loop from his wrist and racked both loops on it. He stepped back.

"The shun-daki is finished," Marik said formally, and Vartik sneered, with some of his old arrogance, *"Mishtai. And you have won. All my lands. All my slaves."*

A flick of Marik's hand disclaimed interest in land—and slaves. He said, instead, "You will require medical attention to stand trial. Doctor Anderson will see to it."

"Notso, Marik. I will not comply." A green foam showed at the corner of his mouth, and Anderson tried to persuade him.

"Mister Vartik, you're hemorrhaging. If you don't let us take care of it, you'll . . ." he trailed off, a peculiar look on his face. "Paul," he whispered hoarsely, *"Paul, we can't!* We used our entire supply on Ronhalovan!"

Marik, pulling his arm free of Morrison's patchwork, said quietly, "You may transfuse him from me." And, seeing Riker's disbelief, appended, "My honor has been satisfied, Captain."

But Vartik struggled to glare at him, and snarled, "The ultimate insult, Dao Marik? Not only to take my life, but to give it back again? Negative!" With great contempt, the dying man focused on the tight little group. "Transfusion? From Marik? All that foul . . . Earthlikli . . . blood?" To Anderson, he ground out, "Fool! . . . stupid . . . alien . . . fool!"

"Consider it well, Delegate," Márik interjected softly, and Vartik twisted about to look him in the face. Contemp-

213

tuously, with his last breath, he rasped, ". . . *Half-caste! . . .*"

He did not move again, nor breathe.

Riker and the others got up and stood quietly while crewmen removed the body; then the Captain turned to Marik pensively.

"He called you *'half-caste'*, Mister Marik." His inflection required an explanation, and Marik, wearied by his wounds and ordeal, decided to make a clean breast of it. Riker waited.

"Because I am one of *you* as well as one of *us*, Captain," he explained huskily. "I am the son of Moses, and of Isaac, and of Abraham, the brother of Christ and of Muhammed. Demosthenes was my teacher; I am the pupil of Aristotle, the kinsman of Genghis Khan, the victim of Hitler, the follower of Sun-yat-Sen. I am a Han."

Riker searched his face unbelievingly and shook his head almost imperceptibly. "Then—then the Han Emperor—"

"My mother, Miluae," Marik said softly, "was the Emperor's only daughter."

"It must have been some kind of a fight, Paul," Simon M'Benga rumbled, grinning. "I sure hate to have missed it."

"It was," Riker assured him fervently, while the Bridge buzzed and chittered around them and Miss Jen repeated the order to make ready to get under way.

"Ronhalovan was the surprise," Riker remembered, absently examining the shock collar. "After Vartik died, he went up to the screen with a whole new attitude, that subservient shell cast off somewhere and the new man shining out, eh? and he volunteered to testify at the hearing." He smiled reminiscently. "And when the Kraun Councilor asked him why he'd refused his help before—and was willing to testify now—he showed them Vartik's control ring—and this monstrosity"—he indicated the shock collar —"and threw them both on the floor—and said—proudly, Simon—'Because now I am my own animal. My own man!' " He sat lost in a brown study for a bit, while in the silence, voices reported in-ship status, secured lifeboats and personnel, made ready to get under way.

Then M'Benga, a frown creasing his broad, silver-black forehead, asked puzzledly, "Paul, there's just one thing I

don't understand. Six men were on the Council, right?—
and seven chairs?" When Riker nodded, he continued,
"Who was missing? Who was the Seventh Councilor?"

Riker smiled pensively. "Why—justice, Mister M'Benga.
That's what the Council is—six men—and justice." He sat
toying absently with the collar, deep in thought for a moment; then he tugged himself back to reality and ordered,
crisply, "All ahead one third, Mister Rutledge."

"All ahead one third, sir," the Helm murmured, and the
ship moved, like a gull, like a shark, its belly flashing and
fading against the deeps, and homed for the stars.

Chapter V

The State Banquet marking the cessation of hostilities between the Federation and the Krail was a political necessity, and was to be held on Xholemeache, which was as neutral a planet as anyone was likely to find. The Xhole themselves, although members of the Federation, sustained diplomatic relations with Krailim, and, typically both eager to please their distinguished guests and anxious to be recognized as an upcoming galactic community, had provided the week-long ceremony with all the luxury at their command, which was considerable. Athletes, folk-dancing troupes and entertainers were summoned from three entire sectors of space, for the end of an interplanetary war concerned everyone. Snow beds were imported from Krailim, Beluga caviar from Earth, thoroughbred, racing gryphons from Eisernon. Sauvage contributed singing stones, and Krau, Ksatriya, the dancers of their military caste, tough, swarthy, male and maned with the familiar, russet fur that covered their heads from brow to shoulder blades. The sedate Xhole had ventured the suggestion that Krau send an alternate representative group, as everyone had seen enough of war, and the Ksatriya, with their fierce beards and stamping dances and whirling swords were not necessarily conductive to peaceful contemplation; to which Krau replied bluntly that they were sending the Ksatriya as their planet's contribution to the celebration, and if Xhole didn't like it, the Kraun ambassador and his entourage would be happy to call upon the Xholian embassy to discuss it. The suggestion was summarily withdrawn. The Ksatriya would dance.

In their zeal for hospitality, the Xhole had gone to the extent of enlisting the aid of a committee of Earthlings to handle preparations for an informal gathering to be held before dinner around the Vice-Chancellor's sumptuous pool.

Sheila Mallory, wife of the Senator, was nominated head

of the committee, just as she'd planned. It had taken a bit of dexterously applied political pull, a judicious bribe here, a veiled threat there; but now she was running this part of the show, and she meant to make the most of it. The real dignitaries, busy at their intrigues, wouldn't arrive until just before dinner, which left the early evening free for cementing relationships and making new contacts, and provided an excellent opportunity to meet this Doctor Marik everyone was talking about. She was curious to see what kind of a man he was, this crippled, alien physician who could declare a shun-daki against master duellist, Federation Delegate Neron Vartik—and win. Dying, the Delegate was said to have named Marik as a Han, and all hell broke loose. The Purist Klan demanded his execution, the Einai people hailed him as a hero, and the Federation Star Service considered him an insoluble problem.

The duel had been witnessed by no less an august body than the Federation High Council, which abrogated the necessity for a trial, although there had been a closed formal hearing on the matter. Although Marik was officially innocent, he was alien, he was a Han, and he had killed, all of which left the Federation in the uncomfortable position of not knowing quite what to do with him. One could only surmise the chagrin of his fellow officers, having to order about the last living descendant of the Han Emperors, and a telepath to boot.

Sheila wondered idly whether or not he had a woman —dozens of them, probably, she thought—and whether he could find an Earthling attractive. Probably so. Half his ancestors had been human. She smiled to herself and touched her high-piled hair, nodding pleasantly to the Gruk Senator and his daughter, who was blossoming into an absolute beauty. Something would have to be done about her; an engagement, perhaps. A discreet affair. We would see.

It had been months since Sheila had met an interesting new man, and anticipation lent her a flush of excitement, a brittle, nervous good humor. She even managed to tolerate a few moments of non-stop sermon from the Reverend Kaiser, who disapproved volubly of cocktail parties in general and cocktail parties where one gave 'spirits to the heathen' in particular, but who found it essential to be

217

present because he was pronouncing the invocation before dinner; and had a few kind words for Rhonda Littlehorn, who was an utter bore. Mainly, she watched the crowd, trying to catch sight of Marik; for the party, abundantly successful, was in full swing.

Faced with varying tastes, Sheila had provided a pleasant middle-ground situation. She'd planned an Earthling cock-tail party and set it in nearly perfect Eisernai surroundings. The pool-houses were decorated as pavilions, their sheer hangings, tinted green and cerulian and rose, were authentic 'silk' as spun by the velvet memlikti. The pool water had been dyed peach and golden, and was faintly effervescent; and coreliae, Eisernon's wild, fragrant trumpet vines, twined tall columns that mimicked perfectly the ruins at Pal-alden-Shali-Rho.

Sheila herself, a tall, cool blonde who'd once been a fashion model, wore an exquisite copy of a museum piece, a gown made entirely of irridescent bands of flowing fabric hanging straight from her shoulders and bound only by a thin chain belt, a costume permitted only (although Sheila had no way of knowing it) to Shimshenli of the Second Rank. The effect was breathtaking. Of all the guests present, only Marik—and perhaps Sharobi, one never knew—found it incongruous, as though an Einai woman, in an effort to please her Earthlikli guests, had attended a party in a nun's habit.

Sheila caught his eye and came toward him confidently on long legs. She was very beautiful, and she knew it, and she knew that most of the men in the room thought so, too. She tipped her head back and regarded him with candid admiration.

"So you're Doctor Marik," she said in her throaty murmur. "I'm Sheila Mallory. Your hostess."

"Mrs. Mallory." He inclined his head briefly and she took his free arm proprietorially, smiling across at him almost at eye level. *He'd had to look down at Mishli.*

"Everyone's just dying to meet you," she confided, steering him around a group of dignitaries in evening dress. Their conversation faltered to a stop as Marik passed, then took up again in a different tone. He was aware of surreptitious eyes on them and would have extricated himself if he could have done so; but she clung to his arm and filled a plate for him with more Earthlikli delicacies than

218

he could have ingested in a week, introducing him around as 'that fascinating Doctor Marik, Pooky's been telling us about'. Everyone made a point of being polite, extremely polite, and talked and laughed a great deal, and tried to make Marik feel welcome, whether he was or not. Sheila overfed him, or tried to (Marik declined the plate—Sheila immobilized his one arm, and the other was busy with his cane—even though the faint fish scent of caviar had possibilities), Rhonda Littlehorn went into gory and tedious detail about her gallbladder surgery last year (Marik was properly sympathetic), and Frank Littlehorn, Rhonda's husband, told him a string of locker-room jokes in particularly bad taste; but Marik retaliated by feigning ignorance of some of the more uncommonly common terms, which sent Frank off, in a red-faced dither, after more punch for the ladies.

It was at this point that Senator Burdett 'Pooky' Mallory put in an appearance. He bellied into the group, scooped up several canapes on one pink palm, and beamed at Marik, his eyes twinkling shrewdly behind the cherubic mask.

"Sorry to be late, folks," he announced heartily. "Been busy inside with the Policy Makers, trying to elect another Delegate to replace Mister Vartik." He chuckled and wagged his head. "You sure did us out of a good man, there, Doc. Not that you weren't justified, I'm not saying that." He chuckled again and put a canape into his mouth. His eyes gleamed up at Marik, and when he could speak, he continued, good-humoredly, "But it would've been a damn sight easier to elect a new Science Officer!"

"Science Officers are not elected, sir," Marik replied neutrally. "They are appointed."

"That's right, that's right." He nudged Marik with a pudgy elbow and gestured at the group around them. "Now—we're all friends here, Doc; we know what happened on the *Skipjack*, saw it on the Tri-V News. Tell us, now, Doc, you're a medico: just how does it feel to kill a man?"

"Professionally, or otherwise, sir?" Marik inquired evenly.

Mallory threw an arm about the alien's shoulders, much to Marik's evident distaste. "Well, just how many men have you killed, now, Doc—professionally or otherwise?"

219

"One does not keep count, sir. There isn't time. I was stationed at a field hospital in a particularly dirty war. Men die—in a war. Remove your arm, sir."

Mallory dropped the offending arm. "And on a duelling field? How does that feel?" He leaned forward, wetting his lips, his eyes feverishly bright. *Faces at a Roman circus,* Marik thought bitterly.

"Approximately what one would expect it to be like, sir."

"And what's that?"

Marik's eyes were gray ice. "That would depend upon what one expected, would it not?" he retorted crisply, and Mallory retreated a step or two, nodding several times.

"That's right, that's right, good answer, there, Doc. 'Course the more civilized worlds outlawed duelling centuries ago. Called it barbaric. Barbaric. Well, folks, no accounting for taste, eh?"

A few of the group smiled embarrassedly, but no one ventured a comment; least of all Marik, who might not have heard Mallory at all, or might have thought the comment unworthy of a reply. There was no way to read his impassive face.

Pooky Mallory eyed the crowd alertly, though Marik was sure that he would already have counted and categorized every individual present.

"Looks like we'ge got all kinds of celebrities here tonight, Doc. You. Doctor Sharobi, of course. Aper ser Nalm, inside, and Beq nom-Pau and his lady. Captain Riker. The Vice Chancellor. We're just overwhelmed, Sheila and me. Overwhelmed." He waited for Marik's reaction. There was none. Marik just stood there, courteously attentive but being no help at all. Better let the little man have his say. This smooth and chubby politician had more in his paws than velvet. Sheila tugged at his arm.

"I'd love a drink, Doctor. I wonder if we couldn't—"

"Of course." Marik inclined his head at the senator and his audience and started away; but Mallory refused to break the thread of conversation, and pulled them up short by it.

"Seems the hostilities are just about finished on your little planet, Doc," he continued in a louder tone, attracting attention. "I'll bet you're glad to see it all over, eh?" Marik (quietly, from where he stood) allowed that, yes, it was always a relief to see war end, most especially on one's own planet.

"Always good to see the Federation annex another world, too, Doc, no matter what the cost, eh? Bring a backward people the advantages of civilization. Life, liberty and all that?"

Mari shifted his weight restlessly and observed stiffly that life and liberty were admirable and valid goals for any planet or people. The audience was becoming uncomfortable; several people edged away and sauntered off, talking in low voices and glancing back uneasily. The Senator pushed his point harder.

"I mean, now, I'll bet you're glad to see Ay-ser-noun finally cooperating with the Federation, instead of holding a fifty-year-old grudge. I mean, being a Federation officer and all that. Am I right?"

Marik fixed him with a level gaze. "My politics died with the Emperor, sir. I have no politics. But my sworn loyalties are with your Federation."

Mallory pounced. *"Your* Federation, you say. *Your* Federation. Well, now." He chuckled. "What do you know about that?" He picked up an intricately-fashioned morsel and examined it from all sides before biting it evenly in half. He had the attention of a growing assembly of guests and he was having the time of his life. "I would've thought it was your Federation, too, Doc, from that uniform you're wearing. We've lost sixty-three thousand men on Eisernon, Doc."

We've lost a third of our population, Senator. And many of them elders and children. He remembered the furlike softness of a child's hair, the crushing weight of roofing beams. His legs ached dully.

"Well, never mind. Never wait for gratitude, they say, eh, Doc?" Mallory ate the other half of the canape and selected another, stepping confidentially close to Marik. "I'm not questioning your loyalty or anything like that, Doctor, but surely you have an opinion—off the record, now—as to which bloc you'd like to see Eisernon belong to: the Federation or the Krail?"

Marik's pupils dilated, making his eyes glitter blackly. "I'd like to see it given back to the Einai," he said quietly, and Pooky Mallory choked on his canape, whooping and spluttering. People pounded him on the back, and

221

when he could answer, he wheezed hoarsely, "Why—that's absurd! Impossible!" His face was purple.

"Yes," Marik replied drily, "isn't it?"

Sheila Mallory announced tartly that she wanted that drink and she wanted it now, and dragged Marik away from her husband's solicitous friends, her eyes snapping angrily, hugging his arm so closely that he could feel her warm contours. He wondered absently, with mild scientific curiosity, whether Sheila was in season or whether her species' females were always so demonstrative. If the latter were so, he reflected, the Earthlikli were to be commended for accomplishing so much under unusually distracting conditions.

"I think it's just terrible of Pooky to put you on like that, Doctor," she was saying. "Believe me, Pooky's going to hear from me!"

Marik assured her that Pooky had done no harm, and she wasn't to fret about it. She smiled at him gratefully and slowed her steps as they brushed through the silk hangings of a pavilion.

"You're a nice man." She traced the stripes on his sleeve with an absent forefinger. "Do you have a first name, Doctor?"

"Several." It sounded curt, almost rude, and he tried to soften it by adding, "Some of them are ancestral titles. My given name is Dao." After all, it wasn't her fault that her husband wanted killing. Was it?

"Dao. Dao . . ." She tried it softly, approving, "I like it. Dao Marik."

The pavilion was empty, lit only by the reflections of ripples from the pool. The fragrance of coreliae wafted through the silk with occasional phrases of far music from an orchestra somewhere, and Sheila touched her hair with a voluptuously studied gesture, evidently under the impression that she was irresistable. Given other circumstances, Marik mused, she might've been right.

"Are you really a Han person—Dao?" Her eyes shone wetly.

"Yes."

"They tell terrible stories about the Han. About the awful ways they have of killing people." She moved in front of him, rested her hands lightly on his upper arms and slid

222

them deliberately to the flat planes of his shoulders. "Do you kill people in awful ways, Dao?"

He regarded her with cool tiger eyes, impersonally. "Is there a pleasant way to kill people, Mrs. Mallory?"

She rested her forehead on his cheek, while he stood like stone, remembering another pavilion, another woman.

"The Emperor," Sheila whispered. "They say he had a thousand slaves. Is it true?"

"A thousand, thousand slaves. But you must remember, Mrs. Mallory—"

"Sheila."

He hesitated. "Sheila. Our word for slave does not carry the same connotation as yours."

She slipped her arms around his neck and tipped her head back, her face close. The scent of her perfume was heady, and a faint trace of alcohol and musk blended with her breath.

"I can think of worse things than being slave to a Han," she whispered, "provided he was the right Han." She pulled his head down and kissed him tenderly, expertly, several times, but Marik was moved only to a pang of loss, an old and intense ache. He firmly, gently, disengaged her arms and held her away a bit.

"I think that may be an imprudent gesture, Mrs. Mallory, no matter how well-intended."

She laughed, a trifle shakily, and lit a cigarette with trembling fingers. "I take it you people don't kiss very much."

"We don't kiss very many."

"Touché." There was a niche in the pavilion wall, a place for statuary, and she leaned back into it, took a long drag at her cigarette, watching him, and shivered delicately. "Tell me about the Han."

A safer ground, a welcome distraction. He gazed down history. "Briefly, then. We'd a civilization tens of thousands of years old. Gods of our own. Empires had risen and flourished and fallen and decayed. Then we achieved peace. Men lived in the fern forests, on the veldt, along the seashore, asking nothing, requiring nothing. We had our arts, our gods, our families. There was joy, and peace, and great simplicity."

"Sounds like paradise," she replied, half-derisively.

"We had no serpent."

223

"What changed it, then?" she mocked softly. "If it was so joyous, what did you do?—discover money?"

He glanced at her sharply, his voice tightening from musing to crisp narrative. "The Earthlikli discovered us. They took everything, as your saying goes, that wasn't nailed down. Our ores, our artifacts. Our young women."

"Native aliens?" Her nose wrinkled in repugnance. "Ugh. How could they?"

"I believe the term is miscegenation."

"And those native women had Earthling children?" She shuddered. "How horrible!"

"Yes, it was. Their children must have looked to them like monsters. Too many fingers, round pupils, pink or yellow skins instead of the normal green." He smiled at her discomfiture. "Many young girls threw their infants off the chalk cliffs."

Her face turned up at him, no longer yearning, but sagging, disgusted, older than it had appeared. He realized for the first time that she was just a little bit drunk.

"And that's what you are," she muttered. "A native woman and some damned bum of an astronaut . . . And I thought . . ."

"I know what you thought. I know what you think now. And you're still wrong." He touched the edge of her mind, felt the chaos there, the half-realized dreams and hungers, the petty feuds, saw himself as she had seen him, not in Federation but in Einai uniform, of gray suede and mailed helmet, with a viith slung across his shoulder, like a knight in her childhood's imaginings. He let her become aware of his mental presence just enough to taste the alienness, the frightening sense of his being. Then he focused his attention (anger, bitterness, loss) on the space between them and let a tiny globe of incandescence grow until it burst, smashing like a piece of fine crystal. Sheila shrank gibbering against a wall.

"That's what I am," he said.

He stepped out of the pavilion and almost collided with Paul Riker.

"I thought I heard something break, Marik," Riker said. "Everything all right?"

"It is now, Captain," Marik answered coldly. Riker eyed the pale, unsmiling Sheila who emerged unsteadily from the pavilion without glancing their way. "Anything I should know about?"

"The lady discovered that she had made a mistake, sir." He caught sight of someone in the crowd. "If you'll excuse me—" He was quickly lost to view.

Riker was relieved. So the lady discovered she'd made a mistake, eh? He grinned inwardly. And Marik had had the good taste to turn her down. He'd shown a certain gallantry, too; he hadn't embarrassed the indomitable Sheila in public, if, indeed, Sheila could be embarrassed. Riker had his doubts about it. He remembered, with a twinge of chagrin, his own first romantic encounter with Pooky Mallory's man-eating wife. He'd been a mere Ensign, and the old man had caught them kissing on the terrace and made quite a joke of it, telling it everywhere. It was a full year before his shipmates stopped ribbing him about it.

Now, of course, Sheila was more than a joke. She'd become a full-blown weapon in the hands of her cherubic husband. Careers and political deals (and once, the future of a continent) had risen or fallen because of Sheila Mallory, and Marik was well out of it—but Paul Riker would have given a month's pay to know what had happened.

A young Xhole boy carrying a belled flambeau glided among the crowd, striking the shaft of the torch intermittently and making pleasant music. It was the dinner summons, and Riker joined the others who were making their way through the salon and thereby into the banquet hall. Marik had not yet returned, which was unlike him, for he knew they'd be seated at one of the high tables and the inscrutable alien was a stickler for Protocol.

Riker waited until last, glancing around the deserted pool area; but Marik was nowhere to be seen. The Captain gave it up and followed the last remnants of the party crowd inside. Marik would turn up. He always did.

Paige stood in the doorway, only half-at-attention, for the banquet was starting (with an interminable invocation that had the Krail squirming and coughing politely) and no one was paying the slaves much attention. Later, when the Masters required assistance in getting out of the hall with a measure of dignity, the slaves would be a welcome

225

necessity; at the moment, they were extraneous to the feasting and conversation.

Remembering his earlier spartan ration in the Xhole kitchens, Paige studiously ignored the aromas of roasted meats and wine bouquets, looked away from the tempting translucence of delicacies shimmering in silver. At one of the high tables a seat was empty, and he wondered idly who it belonged to. Some overstuffed politician, he decided, out making Policy Decisions—or time with the ladies —when he could have been feeding his face. His mouth tightened against a smile.

Paige's slavery had been hard on him, had made him cynical and obedient to a fault, had taught him to hate. It was a new feeling, this hate, and all-pervading. He wondered sometimes whether it had seeped into the matrices of his bones, between the interstices of his very viscera; or if it was not, perhaps, only superficial, a protective veneer that freedom could peel away, leaving him whole again. It was an interesting mental exercise, and such exercises helped make his slavery more tolerable.

As it was, his lot was better than it had been under Beq nom-Pau. Good, plain food had put flesh back on his rawboned frame, rest and the relative ease of personal servitude had erased some of the lines marring his face. Scars healed. But slavery chafed his soul, made him restless. And reckless.

Four times he had tried to escape, and four times Aper ser Nalm dispassionately had him punished ("Nothing personal, Paige, no vendetta here; merely a reinforcement of the learning process"). Paige refused to learn. After his last attempt Aper ser Nalm had affixed a shock collar to Paige's neck, the ultimate restraint which could control or kill the wearer at his owner's will. Only the Master could remove it; an attempt by anyone else generally resulted in the death of both slave and would-be rescuer. Since the first demonstration of the shock collar, Paige had become—exteriorly, at least—a model slave. But they couldn't stop him from hating. Nothing could stop that.

A brightly-garbed waiter bearing a large tray of crystal goblets murmured in apology and Paige stepped back into the corridor to accommodate him. The heavy door swung shut between them and Paige was left standing alone in the corridor staring at it.

226

Alone in the corridor.

Alone.

He blinked. It was that easy, then, a polite sidestep, a few words, and he was beyond sight of Aper ser Nalm—he fingered the collar gingerly—if not beyond his reach.

He glanced up and down the hallway. Well-lighted. Silence of deep carpet. No guards. There should have been guards here, would ordinarily have been, but the presence of armed guards would have implied the expectation of trouble, and the pacific Xhole had asked that the State Banquet be kept as non-military as possible. The principals agreed to forego their guards and elected to wear ceremonial weapons to the table instead, much to the distress of their hosts. A saber was a saber, after all, no matter how ornate the scabbard; and a viith, with or without the jewelled rhyming inlay, could still eviscerate a man in two easy strokes. Not much wonder the Xhole were unhappy; but it left the corridor clear of guards.

Paige felt vulnerable and uncomfortably empty-handed. He could've used a weapon, just anything, not necessarily one of the ceremonial jobs. Even a short length of chain would have been better than nothing. He would have been inordinately grateful for the blocky utilitarian security of an ordinary gun.

There was an access hallway halfway around the shallow bend of the corridor, a long passage that led outside, through a series of porches and arcades, to the launches.

Voices behind him, approaching.

He gained the hallway and flattened against the darkened wall, while the staccato conversation of a pair of Krail soldiers followed them quietly down the hall and was submerged in a muted collective cacophony as the door to the banquet hall was opened, closed.

The silence hurt his ears. He waited a moment longer. No sounds of pursuit. He hadn't been missed, not yet, at any rate. He moved off down the hallway, starting toward the doors. There, at the end of the darkened passage and beyond the open portals, a broad green, the fine benediction of lawn sprinklers, and—freedom! He moved faster, trotting eagerly. Freedom. It was a taste on the tongue, a singing in the blood. His sandals pounded on ear drummed on heart beat on stone.

The breeze drifting in through the open portals was

227

cool and heady, and he hesitated in the arcade of a sculptured porch. Not fifty yards away a sleek two-man launch stood poised against the stars. He made a little breathy laugh of exultation and leaned both hands on slim fluted columns. He was free! All the elements of escape were here, so smooth, so beautiful, it was as though someone had planned it. His ears came alive, his skin became sentient, individual hairs prickled at the back of his neck. *As though someone had planned it.*

Behind him, shadow disengaged from shadow, a hand fell on Paige's shoulder. He whirled, face to face with a blur of blue uniform and slit pupils; but by that time the metal had slid cleanly in, out, of his vitals, weakness spread fast, oh, fast, and he crumpled to the floor puzzled and pained, and the high dark walls closed up and around and . . .

His assailant stood looking down at him with expressionless gray eyes. "I'm sorry," said Dao Marik.

The banquet hall was large and sumptuously furnished, with tasteful pieces of statuary and greenery spotted around the perimeter and couches intricately carved and upholstered in colored silks in the planetary colors of each people present: the black-and-red of Kraili; Earth's blue-and-white; Eisernon's green-and-gold; and of course, their host's colors, the familiar red-on-gold of Xholemeache. There were rich viands from each world represented, and live musicians played anthems and ballads from both Federation and Krail planets.

The Xhole had alternated their guests so as to prevent (for example) a tableful of Krail legionaries from throwing insults, however guarded, at a gathering of Federation starmen. Separating them, it was felt, would put the newly resolved conflict on a safer, one-to-one basis, and perhaps leave room for the beginnings of understanding. The Xhole, however, were famous for their racial naiveté.

Mykar Sharobi, Priyam and Chief of Staff of the *USS Hope,* was bored stiff. He disliked banquets, mainly because he saw no purpose in sitting down with people for whom he had no respect, to eat food he had no taste for, while discussing subjects in which he had no interest. This gathering, despite its galactic significance, was no exception. It was a common saying among his cronies that old Mike wasn't happy unless he was up to his elbows in somebody's guts, which was a close, if crude, approximation of the truth. Sharobi himself would have been the first to admit it.

The Krail seated across from him, a diplomat by the name of Aper ser Nalm, who headed the Krail delegation, said clearly, "Isn't that so, Priyam?" and Sharobi reluctantly dragged himself back to the present.

"I beg your pardon?"

"The good Reverend here was arguing against permitting the Einai 'heathen' —I believe that was your word, Reverend, sir—to belong to the Federation. I suggested that you would be able to discuss the Einai more intelligently than I."

The exquisite young girl at his elbow—the Gruk Senator's daughter, Sharobi guessed—looked charmingly disbelieving; and Aper ser Nalm, flattered, murmured a comment for her ears alone. She blushed and lifted a pretty shoulder, fluttering her fan.

Sharobi, ignoring this byplay, considered the Reverend Kaiser's pompous expression and refrained from saying the things that sprang to his mind; instead, he folded his interlocked fingers on the table around his plate and grunted, "In what way are the Einai 'heathens', Reverend?"

"First of all," he began ponderously, "they do not acknowledge the veracity of the Holy Writ—"

Marik slipped into his place, making a brief chom-ala to the others. "My apologies," he murmured, chiefly to Riker, who made a mental note to find out where he'd been—and why. Marik had been behaving strangely all evening. A Xhole waiter appeared immediately and began serving him.

"Please—go on," Marik's tone was sincere, and the Reverend Mister Kaiser colored, clearing his throat uncomfortably.

"Very well. To continue: the Einai are true heathens in several ways—" he ticked them off on his fingers "— first, they have built no temples or churches. They support no standard faith. They do not acknowledge the Lord; in fact, every other word they speak is a reference to pagan gods, whom even they admit do not exist! That, Doctor, is the hallmark of the benighted savage!" He nodded once to punctuate his remarks, scowling pugnaciously at Marik, who was busy with his fish course.

"That benighted savage is one of the best Science Officers in the Fleet!" Riker interposed, somewhat testily.

"Just how many Einai have you met, Mister Kaiser?" Sharobi inquired politely, and Marik glanced up. He knew that silky tone only too well.

"I had a mission at Palau, Doctor, for several years. And while many of the natives would cheerfully come to sing—"

"We *are* fond of singing," Marik interjected quietly.

"—none would remain for the sermon. Not one!"

Aper ser Nalm chuckled. "I wonder why?" he asked. the Gruk girl, who struck his arm playfully with her fan.

Sharobi folded his arms. "So you left."

The Reverend cleared his throat. "I was recalled," he admitted, and added quickly, "It wasn't the Church's idea! It was the provincial Protector! He decided we were robbing his people of their cultural heritage, or some such nonsense, and demanded that every offworld mission in the Protectorate be taken away except the Franciscans, out near Melungeon. Seems they were teaching the natives a new way of farming." He forced a dry laugh which no one shared. "How to plant cabbages upside down, no doubt!" He laughed again, genuinely this time, for he thought the joke rather good; but he faltered to an embarrassed halt when he realized that he was laughing alone, that not one of the aliens seated with him (nor the Captain, he suspected) understood or appreciated the reference, and he was left with a blunder on his hands, and no place to put it down.

"You see," he tried to explain, "there's this story about Saint Francis—" He trailed off gratefully as the waiters began removing dishes and replacing them with the next course, wildebif sizzling on charis-wood, with garnishes of truffles and feathery louvi. The aroma floated up and filled their heads.

"The trouble here," Sharobi theorized, cutting himself a healthy chunk of succulent steak, "is that you don't understand the Einai—"

"Don't understand them! My dear fellow, I've written a *book* on them!"

"—because if you did, you'd know that the Einai are a very religious people. It's possible that Priyam Marik could explain that to you—defend them, if you like."

"There is no defense against heathenism," Reverend

Kaiser announced didactically. Marik laid down his utensils.

"Then permit me to make several statements about my people, sir. You say we build no churches or holy places; if we call no place holy, it is because for us, all places are holy. If, as you say, we do not find God in your Book, understand that we find Him at the end of a stylus, under an electron microscope, uncurling with a growing fetus or a fern frond.

"Yours is a narrow God, who can be imprisoned in a building to be visited once a week, or left in a Book, for reference. Our God is here. Tadae is alive—now!"

Aper ser Nalm laughed softly and shook his head in exasperation. "Gods!" he muttered. "You people and your Gods!" He drew his pulsar, a lethal, hand-sized thing whose shape inferred its function (one need not know what a shark was to instinctively sense its terror) and weighed it in his hand. There were sharply indrawn breaths from nearby tables and several Federation men half-rose from their chairs, reaching for sidearms; but Aper ser Nalm merely displayed the weapon.

"Here's a god for you, if you must have gods. Omnipotent, irrevocable, pitiless and final. It has the power of life and death over peoples and planets, and requires nothing of its disciples but courage." The Gruk girl avoided his eyes. "That's the kind of god real men understand!"

Sharobi stopped in mid-bite, not lifting his head, and Marik turned toward the Krail with uncommon interest. Riker was wearing the same broad grin Marik had seen on his face when, in a waterfront bar on a nameless planet, the two of them had had to fight their way back to the ship. His hand rested lightly on the pommel of his elegant sword.

"I don't suppose you'd care to debate it, would you, sir?" he suggested, and their Xhole table host quickly signaled the waiters to pour more wine, evidently feeling that things were getting out of hand. He leaned forward anxiously.

"Will you try some of our poor wine, honored sirs? It was made by an ancient process, aged a thousand years, waiting for the day of peace." It was an open plea, and the Krail bowed insolently, putting away the pulsar, as he accepted it.

"By all means, let us drink to peace." He raised his goblet to Sharobi, to Riker and to the Senator's daughter, who dimpled, and drank it in one draught.

Sharobi, who was much more familiar with the Xhole's renowned cellars, sipped his wine slowly, waiting for Aper ser Nalm's inevitable reaction. It was not long in coming.

The Reverend Kaiser, however, being made of the stuff which prompts martyrdom, was not one to be eclipsed. He slapped his hand on the flat of the table as conversation resumed around the hall, making the Gruk girl jump nervously.

"This episode of the pulsar is a classic example illustrating my point, Doctor Sharobi, concerning the worship of false gods!" Sharobi muffled a grunt under a hastily-contrived cough as the fellow buckled down to familiar rhetoric. "Whether a gun!—or an idol of burnished obsidian!—" (he intoned) "—or simply the demonic name of the graven image!—the calling upon of false gods to witness speech is the absolute hallmark of a pagan and godforsaken people!"

"By Jove," Marik observed quietly, "I believe he's right."

The Reverend's face turned the color of louvi, but he had the good grace to laugh with the others, all except Aper ser Nalm, who was wearing a most peculiar expression. Riker stared shamelessly.

The Krail nobleman had picked up his eating tools to cut a segment of wildebif, when his arms sank against his will to the table. His eyes focused intently on something quite close and visible only to him, and he swayed rhythmically where he sat. Sharobi hid his grin in his wine cup and Marik watched with a scientific detachment that was beautiful to behold. He, too, knew the Xhole wines. The Xhole host hovered solicitiously, trying to help, but Aper ser Nalm could only croak, "My slave . . . "

A tall, icily blond Krail officer approached, snapping his fingers for the nobleman's slave, and flanked by the most malignant-looking youngster Riker had ever seen.

"I am Commander Beq nom-Pau," he announced. "What's happened here? If the Overlord's been poisoned—"

Sharobi pushed back his chair. "Nothing so dramatic, Commander. He's had a little too much to drink, that's all. Let's get him to a quiet place where we won't upset

232

everybody, and we'll give him something to ease it off. Marik, give me a hand here."

"Let me help," Riker insisted, getting one of Aper ser Nalm's limp arms over his shoulder. Sharobi grabbed his other arm and Marik sent for his medikit as their table-host led the way to a private antechamber. Beq nom-Pau looked around impatiently.

"His slave. Where is his slave?" People glanced from one to another, there was a buzzing murmur of excitement and several people were getting their wraps when Reverend Kaiser took the situation in hand by standing up to explain politely that the Overlord had been 'taken slightly ill' but would be fine, and that everyone should go back to his dinner and enjoy himself, which his gentle and frantic Xhole hosts appreciated no end. Under the commotion, Beq nom-Pau tossed Charvin the Master Control for the shock collar and snapped, "Find Paige!" Charvin saluted and hurried away.

The orchestra launched into an enthusiastic rendition of a work by ancient Earthling composer, whom the Xhole introduced as Jawf Phyllis Oussa. Everyone settled down and enjoyed the composition, and peace was restored.

Sharobi, Riker and Beq nom-Pau stood around the couch where Marik was treating Aper ser Nalm for what their table host, with his stilted English, had described as his overdraught. Riker thought the juxtaposition of ideas was funny, but Marik shot him a fishy stare, managing to say everything by saying nothing, and Riker subsided.

Aper ser Nalm began to come around as Marik pulled the leads out of his arm. "Wh-what happened?" he asked thickly, trying unsuccessfully to sit up. Marik laid a hand on his shoulder.

"Lie down, sir."

"I don't unnerstan'—" He wiped his face with an unsteady hand.

"You drank yourself under the table, Overlord," Sharobi told him. "Priyam Marik put you on the pump for a few minutes, to assist your body's dialysis of the alcohol, and gave you a healthy jolt of caffeine. You should be feeling pretty well in a few minutes."

Charvin, the Krail youngster, stepped into the room and crossed excitedly to Beq nom-Pau, saluting slickly. "We have found the slave called Paige, sir," he reported.

233

"Where is he?"

"Dead, sir. On the terrace, Commander."

Sharobi and Marik exchanged a knowing glance, and Sharobi ordered, "Take us to him." Charvin led the way with the others following close behind. The Xhole table host, wringing his hands, hurried away to find the Vice-Chancellor, and Riker remained with Marik. Aper ser Nalm made a feeble attempt to join them, but Marik restrained him.

"You'd better lie still, sir. You want to be well enough to sign those documents tomorrow. The Peace Charter and the rest." The Overlord resisted for a moment, then sighed.

"You're right, of course. For some reason, I'm very tired. I think I could sleep."

Marik put away his hypo, which indicated a loss of a quarter grain of morphine. "By all means, sir," he assented, "try to get some sleep."

Riker leaned against the wall, his arms folded, saying nothing until the Overlord's deep, even breathing indicated that the drug had taken effect. Then,

"What's going on, Marik?"

"Going on, sir?" He folded the heart/lung device neatly and slipped it into its packet.

"Come on, let's have it. You and Priyam Sharobi are up to something, I want to know what it is."

A series of changing expressions flickered across Marik's face, and Riker could see him weighing his words carefully. He turned away to finish packing his medikit, and said slowly, "I killed a man. The slave called Paige. I killed him."

Riker stared in disbelief, shaken. "But—why? I could understand the duel with Vartik, but this? Did he jump you, did you mistake him for someone else?" He was grasping at straws, and he knew it. Marik was perplexed by his distress.

"No, Captain. I lay in wait for him and took him by surprise. He had no idea that I was there."

Riker felt stunned, as if someone had hit him a blow. He began to pace up and down the room, slowly, unaware that he was pacing at all. "There'll be an inquest, of course. Thing like this, happening at the peace talks." Thoughts crowded in, the memory of Marik's feline stalking, during the duel with Vartik, the swift whipping of the shun-daki disc, the legends, the stories, the rumors. People murmuring that you could never really trust an eye-eye, you could live with them a hundred years and eat out of the same dish, but when the chips were down, they'd cut your throat as soon as look at you. He stopped and stared into Marik's impassive face. *And yet . . .*

"I don't know what this is all about," he muttered, "but whatever it is, I'll do everything in my power to help you." Marik's eyes warmed.

"You already have, sir."

"He's dead." Mykar Sharobi stood up and regarded the Krail Commander, Beq nom-Pau, with obvious distaste. "Looks like it could have been heart failure."

The group stood around Paige's inert body (now covered with a cloth, for the features were beginning to stiffen), the Xhole table host visibly upset, the Vice-Chancellor pale and unsmiling, the Krail and Earthlings evidencing stages of concern that varied from Charvin's mild interest to Reverend Kaiser's patent disgust. Beq nom-Pau rubbed his chin.

"A pity," he remarked. "He was a valuable servant. And an intelligent one." He leaned down and unashamedly removed the shock collar from the body—being careful to clasp the Master Control while he did so—and handed it to Charvin. "Analyze."

"Good sirs, this is most unfortunate, most unfortunate indeed," mourned the small, blue-skinned Xhole Vice-Chancellor. His natural shade had paled to the miserable tone Marik always described as 'cold Earthlik'. "Rest assured, Commander, if there is anything Xholemeache can do to make restitution—"

"For a slave?" Beq nom-Pau smiled coolly. "You are too generous, Vice-Chancellor. The galaxy is full of slaves."

"I wonder if I might take the body, then," Sharobi interjected heavily, "since you seem to have no further use for it."

"Does the *Hope* rescue dead slaves, Priyam?" nom-Pau's query dripped ice and suspicion.

"We autopsy them. Could be some kind of viroid took your lad out. If it was, we've got a nasty job on our hands. There are delegates from four systems here tonight."

Beq nom-Pau searched his face distrustfully. Did the devious Saubagi half-breed intend to score a propaganda coup with a dead Erthlik slave? Not likely. In any case, he had removed the collar. It was Sharobi's word against his own. Sharobi stared back steadily, but there was no reading that dark gaze. It was mesmerizing, like peering into a dark well, or into space. He was conscious of the Vice-Chancellor and other dignitaries watching him, and he tore his eyes away and forced a tense smile.

"With our compliments, then, Priyam. You understand that we regret his having been a member of your own species." Sharobi nodded shortly but made no comment. He seemed anxious to get it over with.

"If we might prevail upon our excellent guests to return to the Great Hall," the Vice-Chancellor coaxed, "we have arranged an humble entertainment—" They followed him gratefully down the hall.

A pair of residents, dressed as orderlies, arrived with a stretcher and helped Sharobi heave Paige's rigid body onto it. They moved quietly, quickly and without words, men doing a routine task, draping the body, guiding the stretcher down the corridor and out onto the terraces.

A lone caretaker squatted by the sprinkler controls, adjusting the spray, and looked up incuriously as they trundled by.

"Good evening, Honorable." Sharobi nodded shortly.

"Evening." They made as to walk on, but the caretaker laid a gentle hand on the stretcher and it hovered still.

"One has died?"

"Yes. Look, we've got to be—"

He cut off Sharobi's protest with an upraised palm. "A psalm for the dead. It is customary, is it not?" *Good Earthenglish. No mere caretaker this. Security, perhaps, or even a spy. It wouldn't do to have him get suspicious.* Sharobi's eyes narrowed, but he bowed.

"By all means, friend Xhole," Sharobi purred. "A psalm."

The Xhole threw back his head and called, in a clear and piercing tenor that rang like struck silver:

"Oh, Chu'l Kerai-ist! Hearken unto the sound
My voice, hear the prayer of your servant!

236

For they have taken away my strength, my hands
Are as water.
My eyes are shut with the sight of death,
My breath has journeyed from me.

My voice shall cry out—no more—
My works walk after me, alive.

Oh, Chu'l Kerai-ist! Hear me and take me
Home!"

"He will sleep better now," the caretaker said, covering
his head and exchanging the four ritual bows with Sharobi. The medics moved sedately away with the body, Sharobi trailing behind solemnly, until the caretaker was lost
around the far corner of the chateau. Then Sharobi un-
covered his head and barked, "Let's go! Move!"

One of the men raced ahead and yanked open the aft
lock of an ambulance-skimmer, hoisting out a MAX, and
extended the slab of the already activated machine.
Sharobi and the other men rushed Paige's body to the
MAX, peeling off his tunic as they hurriedly tied him into
the systems.

"Punch a complete blood transfer and let's pump some
oxygen into him. We don't need anoxia. Is he open?"

"These veins are pretty good. I don't know how patent
the rest of them are." The resident slipped the needles in
easily.

"Code in a little heparin, just in case." The resident
hid his smile. Heparin. What an old-fashioned guy a genius
could turn out to be. But he answered smartly, "Yes-
sir," and coded in the heparin.

Their hands flew at their work, and within moments
Paige was tied in and being transfused, his heart massaged
for him, his lungs functioning reluctantly under an automatic Bennet valve. Muscle relaxants flowed in with fresh
blood and his skeletal muscles softened, slowly losing
their rigor and falling into more natural positions. The
EKG readout on the compak gave a weak, voluntary *bleep*
as Paige's heart hiccoughed on its own, and began a spo-
radic, arrhythmic blipping as the skimmercraft gunned its
engines, leaped off the runway and climbed for the *Hope*.

Hennem-mishli hadn't wanted to come to this farce of a banquet and, because she'd been having difficulty with the pregnancy, would not have been there had Beq nom-Pau overriden the doctor's meek suggestions that she stay at home—in bed!—and insisted that she come. It had been a bad idea. Aside from the fact that she felt not at all well, as evidenced by dark smudges under her moat-gray eyes, nom-Pau had refused to permit her to wear her habit, but instead ordered her maid (who spoke no Einai) to dress her in the tightly restrictive Krailim national dress, which compressed the pregnancy so stringently that even though she was almost at term, her garb barely hinted at her condition. Nor was physical discomfort the only problem.

It was humiliating, to say the least, for the Commander to lead her around from table to table like a prize brood mare, exhibiting tangible evidence that she'd produced an heir. Adding to this humiliation, he'd refused, too, to let her wear the symbolic Blue Face, the pale dyeing of the lower face that signified the acceptance of the child, but not of the father; without that symbol, she might've been any common tramp. Several of nom-Pau's acquaintances had eyed her disrespectfully and smilingly commented to nom-Pau in Krailan about her; while she did not understand the language, their meaning was abundantly clear. One of the women openly giggled, hiding her face in her veils.

She was inordinately grateful when nom-Pau, having momentarily exhausted his enthusiasm for his progeny in favor of conversation with his compatriots, deposited her unceremoniously beside the gigantic fireplace and disappeared. She sank down on the hearth, miserably uncomfortable, and watched the embers glow and recede, thinking of Kles and the Death Dance he'd made for Dao —and of Dao. Inevitably, of Dao. Without him, she felt small and lost, as if she would never be able to find her way home again, if, indeed, there was a home to go back to. Without Dao, even that was questionable.

There was a mindless titter from a nearby table, and Hennem-mishli caught a knot of Krail women staring at her, whispering and simpering rudely among themselves. Angry tears filled her eyes and her fists tightened in impotent rage. If Dao was here, she thought hotly, he'd take care of them for me! She turned away from their giggling.

If only Dao had never died! She'd show them all!

The logs blazed up with a roar, as of applause, but died back again quickly leaving only ashes.

The Banquet was slowly breaking up. The cloakrooms were opened and servants moved about obsequiously here and there, carrying various outerwear, for the night was chill.

Riker and Marik, as Protocol required, were making the rounds of the remaining dignitaries to say their goodbyes, pay the ship's respects, and assure everyone, as Riker put it, of their fervent hope for everlasting peace to reign forever throughout the galaxy, amen. It was a tedious procedure, he added, as an afterthought, but it was the price of the meal. When Marik refrained from commenting about the meal—and its price—Riker, whose dress boots were a little tighter than he was, remarked that it cost more to feed the Krail than to fight them, to which Marik retorted mildly that the Captain was overdoing the drunken Commander impersonation, but if he felt it was essential to his mental health, Marik would go along.

"I *would* appreciate it, sir," he stipulated, "if you would tell me *why*."

Riker chuckled wickedly. "War games, Mister Marik. I guess I wanted to see just how you'd act if I got really nasty sometime—and you had to bail me out."

Marik flashed him a sidelong glance and remarked that the way to play that particular game was to get nasty—and find out. Riker grinned drily, and Marik asked, "Who's next on the list?"

Riker consulted a hastily scribbled pony and sighed, "Commander Beq nom-Pau and his lady." He noticed that Marik was favoring his leg and added mercifully, "Look, if you want me to handle this and you could rest—" but Marik declined respectfully, on the grounds that nom-Pau, being less perceptive than the Einai, might be unable to distinguish war games from the real thing.

It was in this mood of dry banter that they came through the arches into a large room where the greater proportion of Krail guests had gathered, eating and conversing in their staccato native tongue.

Riker inquired of a subordinate and was told that the

239

tall man, there by the fireplace, was Beq nom-Pau. "The one," he added significantly, "with a taste for Einai confections."

"What's that supposed to mean?" Riker demanded testily, but the Krail only shrugged and went back to his companions with a knowing grin.

Riker craned his neck and could scarcely see him among the guests, so with dogged determination, he started making his way through the crowd, attracting a few curious glances, Marik trailing him by several yards.

Nom-Pau turned as he approached and gave a good imitation of a welcoming smile. "Commander Beq nom-Pau?" He nodded and Riker extended his hand. "Paul Riker, sir, Captain of the USS Skipjack."

Nom-Pau shook the proferred hand perfunctorily, bowed briefly and gestured at the others. "My honor, Captain. Allow me to present Armsman Dan sun-Co, Dirk Powys, and my lady—" he led her into the circle "—Madame nom-Pau."

The voluminously-veiled woman gave him a quick, startled glance and hesitantly offered Riker her hand. The warm, green-peach gold of her skin was welcome among the throng of snow faces, and under the dark, upswept wings of her brows, her lashes were little black fans lying modestly on her cheeks. Riker caught her cool fingers and held them, struck by her exotic beauty, until the little fringed fans lifted to reveal a gentle gray gaze that searched his eyes, as if asking what sort of a man he was; and then, evidently approving, joined the perfect lips in a tremulous smile. She murmured, in a throaty whisper, "Mekka som iki, Kappen-shan."

Riker bent and kissed her hand, saying, "Madame," and wondering if he could have been mistaken about the mute appeal in those almond eyes, the feeling that she was asking his help—but for what?

Then Marik stepped out of the crowd, and before he could present him to nom-Pau and his exquisite lady, Marik halted abruptly, blanching, and the woman's expressions flickered from hope, though disbelief, exultation, horror, the black-fringed eyes widened and she crumpled senseless to the floor in a flurry of excitement and helping hands and staccato mutterings; but Marik reached her first.

He lifted her tenderly in his arms and, his back against the massive stone of the fireplace, swept them with the icy blaze of his eyes.

"Who is responsible for this?" he challenged, deadly quiet, and nom-Pau stepped forward, diplomatically taking his arm.

"Perhaps she would be better off in a quiet place, chomshan," he suggested in Einai, and after lingering a moment more Marik followed him to a dim-lit sitting room, where Marik laid her gently on a velvet couch and loosened the veiling about her throat. He quickly checked her pupils, her pulses, her respiration—

His hand encountered the stiff bindings that encased her, mummy-like, from ribs to thighs, and he flashed a furious glance at nom-Pau. "Who bound her like this?"

"Our physician," nom-Pau answered silkily. "Her condition, you see."

Marik saw. When he lifted his head, his face was so pale as to be frightening. "She is not wearing the Blue Face." *The Blue Face, that would signify a transplant.* His voice was dead calm.

"Nor the habit," nom-Pau smiled, sensing triumph in the wind.

Marik rose to his feet and regarded the unconscious Shimshen with an unreadable stare. Without lifting his eyes, he asked evenly, "The child?"

"Mine!" boasted nom-Pau, clapping his shoulder fraternally. "They tell me it is a son." The Einai's pallor was rewarding, but he managed a creditable bow that took the edge off the Krail's enjoyment.

"Congratulations, sir," he rejoined formally. "My best wishes to you and—your lady." He paused. "Your physician should see her—immediately. She is not at all well." A stiff bow. "If you will excuse me—"

Nom-Pau answered Marik's bow with an elaborately mocking one of his own, but it was doubtful whether the Einai noticed it, or indeed, saw anything at all.

Riker's penetrating brown stare invaded his eyes as he stepped back into the crowded room. "Everything under-control, Marik?"

"Everything, Captain," Marik replied steadily, and Riker glanced around at the Krail who stood about in watchful knots, muttering ominously among themselves.

241

"Let's get out of here, before this thing blows up into an incident."

Marik followed him out wordlessly, stood silent, as Riker made their last few formal goodbyes, numbly promised to contact Sharobi in connection with his upcoming surgery.

They were in the skimmer, headed back for the ship, before Riker broke the silence.

"Beautiful girl, Commander nom-Pau's lady."

"Yes." The curvature of the planet arched away to infinity beyond his impassive profile.

Riker hooked his elbow over the back of the seat, twisting in his straps, and warmed to his subject. "It was as if she recognized us, you know? She was just smiling, like people will at a party, to be friendly—and then she recognized us. But I don't know how." He paused, and when it became clear that Marik wasn't going to offer any information, he persisted, "Do you?"

Marik chose his words slowly and carefully, his opaque, gray eyes staring into opaque, gray screens staring back.

"Madame nom-Pau is called Hennem-mishli, 'Wheat-in-the-Wind'. She is an Einai of Imperial heritage, the granddaughter of Priyam Oman Shari-Mnenoplan."

Riker laughed in delighted surprise. "Then you do know her."

Marik's voice was almost inaudible. "She is my wife."

The physician came out of her room wearing a worried frown, plucking nervously at his neck as Beq nom-Pau, who had been pacing the sitting room, crossed to him menacingly.

"Well?" he demanded.

The physician cleared his throat. "No change, Commander. She is still in labor. The child is large," he explained apologetically, as if it were due to some lack of foresight on his part.

Nom-Pau made a sound of impatience with tongue and teeth. "It has been more than a day!" He took a turn around the room. "Is the child well? Has she injured it?"

"It is sound so far," he hedged, moving unobtrusively out of striking range, "but there is still that narrow pelvis—"

"I will have my heir, alive and well," nom-Pau ground

out dangerously, "if I have to kill her!—and you!—and the Imperator himself!"

The physician glanced nervously at the Sentinel on the wall hoping the pickup—as they frequently did—had garbled that part of the message. Listening voluntarily to that kind of treason could be worth a man's head.

"The child will be well," he promised, oiling the waters, "by the Fist of the Imperator!—or I will take my own life!"

Nom-Pau, pacing again, lifted his head to warn him that he had better deliver a healthy child—and promptly! —or nom-Pau would save him the trouble.

In the inner room, on a vast white bed, a snow field, that dwarfed her already fragile body, Hennem-mishli lay gray with exhaustion, barely breathing. She had been in labor these thirty hours, and while various servomechanisms saw to the child's safety, no such consideration had been made for the woman who was involved only because no machine could gestate a child. But she knew, as the physician must, that if she died before the child presented, no servomechanism in the galaxy could save it. Krail babies were notoriously fragile.

The pains had stopped. There had been none for more than an hour, for she had no strength left to have the child. The hot bricks the physician had ordered banked around her, to ward off the chill of the snowstorm that raged just outside the windows, served only as comparison to her cold flesh, and scarcely stirred her sluggish blood. She lay and thought wearily of the child.

She had always thought of it—and at it. Throughout the pregnancy, she recalled, with the misty euphoria of extreme shock, with the enemy's innocent son curled sleeping in her womb, she had thought gentleness at it, and love, and contentment. She had sung softly to it, low, kindly lullabyes she knew it would hear as a murmuring susurration, and subconsciously remember. It would be a Krail—but it would be born of an Einai, a Han—and that could make all the difference in the world. For she'd loved it.

She knew what she had to do. Every Shimshen was a midwife, and Hennem-mishli had seen her share of difficult births. *When the child's head is greater than the*

243

diameter of the bony canal, the Abbess had lectured, *it is sometimes wise to have the mother leap from a modest height and so force the head, through simple physics.* She had seen mothers die from this treatment—and she had seen babies live. It was worth the chance.

She lay waiting, feigning sleep, until the physician stepped into the sitting-room, presumably to reassure Beq nom-Pau; and then she lifted her frail tonnages of hand, arm, head, groped the needle-inputs out of her side and, panting hard from the exertion and covered with a film of cold sweat, she swung her legs over the side of the bed, stumbled to the door, and locked it. The room darkened and she clung to the wall, feeling the pain surge, the wall shake as the physician knocked politely, and then more excitedly, on the door. There were voices.

She made her way across the room, supporting herself on chair back and tables, to the frosted window, laid her cold cheek against it—*ice crystals recalling fern forests*—and fumbled weakly at the latch. With strength compounded of sheer will, she flung the long casement open —*they were pounding on the inner door now*—and tottered into the howling storm, the frigid wind whipping her thin nightdress about her legs, making a banner of her dark hair. She stumbled to the edge of the unprotected terrace, head swimming, numb even to the frozen whip of snow against her cheek, the ice carpet under her bare feet, and looked down.

The embankment was a sheer seven-foot drop. It should be enough. The child must live, *it must!* Deliberately, not thinking of Dao, and his abandonment of her (for then she surely would have died) she stepped off the edge of the terrace into a well of agonized impact, and the child's sudden furious crying, and blessed oblivion.

Ten minutes later, with the door askew on its hinges, the physician informed Beq nom-Pau that he had a fine, healthy son, born in the snow as a result of the Shimshen's fall—he dared not call it a leap.

Nom-Pau, viewing the child squalling silently in its plastex incubator, smiled inwardly, reflecting on the power it would bring him. "His name," he announced softly, "is Lan, 'storm-born'. Nom-Pau Lan. Let it be so entered." He signed the documents and thumbprinted them.

The physician trailed him to the door, grateful that his

life had been spared and hesitant to anger the proud
father: but as nom-Pau opened the door, he ventured,
"Commander, what of the woman?"

"Woman? What woman? Oh, the— Did she survive?
What splendid animals these people are!" He shrugged
indifferently. "Well, we shall see. We shall have to see."

It was Aper ser Nalm who came up with the idea.
They had been drinking heavily, celebrating their col-
laboration on the birth of their mutual heir, when ser
Nalm lifted a finger to his nose and tapped it.

"I have it, nom-Pau! By the Fist, it's the best idea I've
had all year!" Beq nom-Pau slowly put down his unsteady cup and patted its rim to settle it.

"Very well," he invited tipsily, "say on! Tell us what it
is you've got!—if it isn't contagious!" He snickered into
his hand, and ser Nalm joined him.

"What I've got," he confided elaborately, "is a place to
get rid of your Einai woman!—unless of course," he
lowered his voice "—you want to keep her around for,
uh—"

"Absoluely not!" nom-Pau defended hotly, breathing
fumes in his face. "The Einai are not even human!
—they are human-appearing animals!—an'mals! Shockin'
sugges'tion . . ." He refilled his cup and drained it in one
draught. "I am a moral ind'vidual, Noble!"

Ser Nalm made an overhand, placating gesture. "Al'
right, al'right, have it your own way." He smiled drunk-
enly, like a death's head and leaned forward confidentially. "I know a planet—with a sentient race on it—that
needs a Shimshen!" He waved his arm. "That Federation
Council—*knows*—that you've got her!" At nom-Pau's expression of amazement, he nodded emphatically. "Oh, yes.
And they want to *assign* her—as a race mother—or some
such—to an emerging 'people'." He made an upward-
spiralling motion with his fingers. "Their religon, or whatever."

"You're drunk," nom-Pau told him, "and boring, too."

"Truth!" the Noble insisted, refilling his cup, and nom-
Pau's. "Now, I know of this planet"—he began to chuckle
softly—"where we can drop her like a stone—and be
rid of her!—permanently!—without arousing the Federation!"

"And since when," nom-Pau demanded suspiciously,

245

"are *you* so int'rested in mollifying the *Fed'ration?*" He banged his cup emphatically on the table. "I couldn' care less about the Fed'ration! I say to everlas'ing *doom* with the Fed'ration!" His face was puffed and swollen, his tongue thick. "Since when are *you—*"

"Its sun," ser Nalm chortled softly into his cup, *"is going nova."*

Nom-Pau closed his mouth and blinked a few times. He looked blankly at ser Nalm, into his cup, and back at ser Nalm, who nodded, highly amused.

"The sun—" he repeated stupidly.

"—is going nova. In nine months, give or take a week."

They began to smile, and it became a chuckle, a chortle, a guffaw, a roar! They howled! The laughter became so raucous that the sentry outside the door found his lips twitching with it, and had to review the entire Rulebook with mnemonic precision to keep from laughing aloud.

When the merriment had finally died down, nom-Pau wiped his eyes and choked, "What a fabulous trick, Noble! What a com-uppance for the pious Federation! And fire is such a *clean* solution!"

"Isn't it?" ser Nalm agreed jovially, uncorking a fresh bottle and filling nom-Pau's cup yet again. "You must try some of this Marsala. It's really excellent!"

"Welcome back, Lazarus."

The words pulled Tom Paige up from darkness, back to life and light and sensation. He opened his eyes and he was lying on a bed in a clean, pale green hospital room, with indefinable Earthling smells and—he turned his head drowsily—the inevitable white-tuniced nurses whisking by in the corridor.

Lazarus?

Memory flooded back and he sat up quickly, wincing at his stiff muscles, and grabbed his flat belly with a cautious hand. No wound. There should have been some connotation of injury, a scar, some mark—

"Wait a minute—" He looked up sharply. The small group of men standing at ease around the room smiled at his confusion. One of them, an obvious crossbreed built like a bison about the head and shoulders, casually tossed him a pair of fatigues with a medical patch worked in-

246

to the left breast. Paige caught them cleanly and inquired, as he slipped into them, "What's going on?"

"You're aboard the *USS Hope*," the crossbreed said without preamble. "I'm Mykar Sharobi, Chief of Staff. These people are Doctor Alexander Meng"—the Oriental lifted his hand like a ballplayer—"Artie Michaels, who claims to be the surgical resident around here; show him who you are, Big Artie"—Artie, a bespectacled, wiry youngster with a wide, white grin, reached forward and shook Paige's hand warmly "—and Rabatfiliakrin Tayen, our Minsonai orderly."

Paige put his hand into Tayen's huge palm, squinted up at the two-inch canines shining in the Minsonai's grin, and mumbled, "Glad to meet you, Charlie."

"Good to see you breathing, Doc," he replied affably.

"Everybody decent?" Two nurses, one with large, expressive, brown eyes and the other with a crown of redgold braids, stuck their heads in the door and entered. "The two Annas," Sharobi grunted. He indicated the brown-eyed one, "Anna Bunt, better known as Kraut Annie, and Anna Derenthal, our Supervisor of Nursing." The two Annas smiled and nodded, busying themselves at the food service slot. Sharobi regarded them with a jaundiced eye. An aide could have dialed Paige's food; but evidently the two Annas wanted a look at him themselves. He found it hard to understand how two such exemplary nurses, such intelligent and efficient people, could bring themselves to act like a couple of *women*.

Paige tried to stand and found his knees weak and wobbly. Big Artie helped him sit and advised, "Better take it easy for a few minutes, Doctor. We gave you quite a slug." Paige, mystified, shook his head, passing a hand across his eyes.

"I don't know, I'm—I'm still confused. Last thing I remember, I was on the Vice-Chancellor's terrace, and somebody gave me a jab right in the belly—"

"Needle," Meng interrupted in his precise Earthenglish. "We administered a massive dose of curare, plus fifteen minutes worth of hypox to keep you oxygenated while you weren't breathing."

"We knew you'd been taken prisoner. These things have been circulating around the Black Market for a while." Sharobi tossed him a sheaf of drawings signed merely *'Mennonishan'*—Mennon's Man—expertly done, of himself and Charvin and the Shimshen and the slaves on the airstrip. Sharobi stabbed a stiff finger at a head study of Paige and grumped, "With that collar around your neck, there was no way to rescue you—as long as you were alive."

"So you killed me."

"Priyam Marik killed you," he corrected. "We needed someone who could get a needle into your inferior vena cava on the first try, fast and quiet. Marik filled the bill."

"You could have let me know."

Big Artie grinned. "How?"

"Once they thought you were dead, it was a simple matter to get Noble Aper ser Nalm out of the way, so that Beq nom-Pau could replace him at the, uh, death scene." Sharobi grinned sourly. "Ser Nalm might've gotten suspicious, he's got a devious mind; but nom-Pau has a reputation for being direct. We knew he'd give us your body; and odds were he'd remove the collar from a dead slave."

Paige rubbed the back of his neck and pulled his twitchy smile. "Sounds pretty iffy, Priyam," he ventured. "You're lucky you got away with it."

"Not as lucky as you are," Sharobi informed him succinctly. "Derenthal, you want to get Doctor Paige something to eat?"

"It's already on its way," she informed him complacently, and the chute made a low 'pop' and deposited a tray on the bedside table. The smell made his mouth water, and he stammered, "I want to thank you, sir, and everybody else who—"

"Don't muck it up with a lot of sloppy sentiment, doctor!" Sharobi growled. "I've got a proposition for you. Your outpost is finished. You're not needed there anymore. A Federation team is going in and setting up a provincial clinic. Modern buildings, roads, landing strip—" Paige's head flashed up, his mouth quirking wryly.

"Who's going to build it?—the landing strip."

They looked curious, puzzled. "Why—robotracks, of course. Why?" It was Michaels who asked the question. Paige shook his head.

"Just wondering." It was impossible to explain why he'd

248

asked, even to himself. To cover his embarrassment, he pulled the plastex hood off of the tray and viewed his dinner with a mixture of emotions. Thick, sizzling steak, running with pink juices, a mealy baked potato with its edges turned back *so*, wallowing in sour cream, and a garlicky, wooden bowl filled with crisp greens and snapred radishes and cucumbers that smelled like a Connecticut summer.

"Anyway, to continue," Sharobi grumped, "we have an opening on staff here, if you're interested. We pay pretty well, and you get a teaching/learning experience that's the best in the galaxy. And with your competence in jungle medicine—"

The knife slid across and into the tender meat, slicing off a healthy wedge. The fork speared, lifted. Sharobi's voice persisted, rough and comfortable as a wool blanket, and an unaccustomed lassitude swept over Paige, a relaxing of the bitterness and hate that had made a hard core inside him. The fatigues had been worn before and had the comfortable feeling of home and habit. They wanted him here, on the *Hope*. He was free.

The meat melted between his teeth, but a knot had tightened his throat and he couldn't swallow past it, or speak; so he just kept chewing, and chewing, and chewing, not caring that his face was wet, or that the others were grinning at him, or that Sharobi, without waiting for him to accept the job, gave him a rapid-fire list of duties two men would be hard-put to complete. He just sat there with that happy grin on his face, chewing the same piece of meat, while the others joshed him and poked each other and generally let him know he was among friends.

After a while, he got down, not only that bit of meat, but seconds of dinner, and dessert.

Chapter VI

"To the Gryphon, the Sky;
To the Ramper, the Sea;
And the Gift of Free Choice
To my Brothers and Me . . ."

(Fragment of a child's rhyming book
found at the ruins of Allampaila,
Eisernon, c. 1341 G.F.T.)

The ship first appeared as a warning blip on Marik's screen, an infinitesimal mote that enlarged quickly to a visible target.

"Unidentified vessel off the starboard quarter, sir," Marik commented unemotionlessly. "Coming up fast."

Riker turned his Command Post. "Put it on visual. Send 'Routine Patrol' and our registration, Miss Jen. Request identification."

The forward screen blazed on, evincing the presence of a sleek, black, unlit ship swiftly blotting out the stars.

"Vessel coming abeam of us, sir," Marik's cool voice announced. "A Krail *prao*-class gunboat, from the look of her."

"Patch me in," Riker ordered. Jen's fingers flew over her console and he touched the com control. "This is Captain Paul Riker, of the *USS Skipjack*. We are on a routine Federation patrol and consider ourselves in neutral space—"

"Her deflectors are going down, sir!" M'Benga rumbled suddenly, and Riker snapped, "Evasive action!"

The ship shuddered as a blast from the Krail's gunnery hit her a glancing blow amidships even as she veered, and

250

Riker barked, "Sound 'Battle Stations!'" He hit the com stud. "This is the Captain! Red alert, red alert, this is the Captain, all hands go to red alert!"

The klaxon squawked, a deafening repetition, and M'Benga directed, "Damage Control party to berthing compartment 03-102-14. Check for *Charlie* fire. Damage Control to 03-102-14. Sickbay, stand by."

On the screen, the Krail gunboat completed its forward trajectory, made a wide, sweeping turn and appeared to hover for a moment; then:

"She's coming about, Captain," Marik noted. "Headed right for us."

"Forward torpedoes, stand by!" Riker said quietly, his eyes on the screen. *The ship was a fragment, a jot, a speck of motion—*

"Torpedo room by, sir," the reply ricocheted back.

"Torpedoes aft!" *—a chip of blackness afloat on the Deep.*

"After torpedoes standing by, sir," came the eager, metallic voice. Riker glanced at Marik, who reported evenly, "Laser banks armed and ready, Captain."

"We'll want a five-second burst." He sat slowly, tense and poised, watching the screen. "One more time, Miss Jen. Send 'Routine Patrol' and our identification."

"Aye, sir," she answered, complying, but the console began to jar with the lethal, sub-audible reverberations of the Krail's resonance transponder, and Jen clutched her sensitive Xhole ears, trembling. The vibrations pulsed inaudibly, quivering flesh and bone, straining eardrums. It shook cheeks and eyes and hearts, and even Marik winced and clapped his hands over his ears.

Riker catapulted out of his chair and was across the Bridge in two strides, slamming it off. "Mister Rutledge," he clipped, wheeling on him, "Come to heading 218 mark 3. Flank speed. Let's take it right down her gullet!"

"Flank speed it is, sir," Rutledge acknowledged, and yawed the ship around on a collision course with the Krail vessel, while the image on the screen grew from fleck to miniature to model, and still they hurtled toward it.

"Make ready to dive," Riker murmured at the screen.

"Ready," came the cool, steady, inhuman voice.

The Krail gunboat swelled, grew, bloomed up like a malignant black flower, devouring stars.

"Hold it . . ." Riker eased them, his eyes fixed on the screen. "Steady as she goes, Mister Rutledge . . ."

"Captain," M'Benga warned uneasily; but Riker murmured again, "Hold it, hold it . . ."

The Krail ship was upon them, a phantom, a devilfish, a looming, black kite that would surely wreck them, vaporize them with the impact, and scatter their molecules to vast infinities of space—

"*Fire!*" he shouted, and, an instant later, "*Dive, dive!*"

The klaxon squalled, the ship plunged, and the disintergrating Krail gunboat passed so close overhead that Mahmut Busaidi, who was in the repair crew, confided later to M'Benga that it had sheared off several docking stanchions and left an irregular, six-foot-wide streak of black paint along the hull.

The *Skipjack* levelled off and Riker said, "Let's have a look, gentlemen."

M'Benga, switching the screen on, grumbled, "You sure do take some chances, Paul, I'll give you that." And Rutledge, who almost never ventured an opinion, concurred that he *had* cut it a bit close, hadn't he?—for an officer and all that. Miss Jen just sat trembling, eyes shut, palms pressed together at her nose.

The screen showed an infinite panoply of stars, without a trace of a shadow. "Sensors?" Riker queried, and Marik rechecked his findings.

"Metallic debris, some hard radiation; an occasional bit of organic flotsam." He looked up. "Its combined mass would approximate that of the gunboat, Captain."

Riker steepled his fingers and stared at the screen without seeing it, puzzling over the Krail attack. What was a gunboat doing away out here, alone, and why would it attack without provocation, almost a year after the Peace Charter had been signed? True, it could conceivably not have heard about the Xholian Truce, or might've been a renegade—or even had a deaf Captain and an insane crew!—but he discarded these conjectures as absurd. The Krail were too efficient to misinform their people, and so totalitarian that if the Imperator made a proclamation, everybody had damn' well *better* know about it!—or else!

Besides, the ship was new, and carried one of the
252

dreaded resonance transponders. There were reputed to be only a few of them in the galaxy. Why would a gunboat—out in the middle of nowhere—be carting one around, unless—

"Marik," he queried slowly, "how many transponders would you say there are in this sector of space?"

"One less, now," M'Benga grinned, and they laughed a bit, while Marik absently touched the scar on his cheekbone and rubbed his fingers individually against his thumb, thoughtfully. "There are the two that were known to be on Krau; one the Erthlikli destroyed at Minsoner's Lunar Base IV; and the one that was on Eisernon, near Bex-elakli." Of course, he added, there were several aboard Krail ships-of-the-line, "But they're not in this sector, sir."

"And this wouldn't be one of those."

"Not likely, Captain."

"Could it be the one from Eisernon, Paul?" M'Benga suggested. "They got away with that one—didn't they?"

"So they did," Riker agreed grimly, turning his attention back to the screen. "This—*attack*—makes me wonder just how much else they got away with!—that we don't know about! Mister Marik," he ordered briskly, "I want a return course plotted!—to wherever it was he came from!"

Marik handed him the coded chip. "If you will forgive my anticipating your order, sir—"

"Any time, Mister Marik," he grinned. "Mister Rutledge, bring her about. Let's see just what it is they don't want us to find!"

The ship looped gracefully and rolled, *metal splinter, silver needle, minnow, flashing in the Deep, a*nd darted back across the scattered molecules of the destroyed Krail gunboat, toward it's enigmatic Point-of-Origin.

Captain Paul Riker leaned back in his command chair and, without turning from the viewscreen, asked softly, "How does she look, Marik?"

"Much like your own star, sir. A yellow dwarf; eleven planets one with four moons, two with a single satellite each." He spun his chair to face Riker. "What makes this star uncommon is the fact that within an estimated

253

twenty-four hours, it will shift from its present ninth stellar magnitude to a plus-one magnitude nova."

"The birth of a bigger and better star." Riker lifted his brows. "Interesting!—but not enough to provoke that attack! There's got to be something more, something we're missing! We'll scan these planets one by one, and see what we can dig up. What's our nearest margin of safety?"

Marik calculated quickly, talking in a preoccupied murmur as he worked. "Since the nova will vaporize the majority of its planets—" he finished his mathematics and looked up sharply "—I suggest we retire the ship to three AU's."

Riker thumbed his com stud. "Power Deck, stand by for warp to three AU's. Marik, we'll hold her here until you've finished the Index."

"Aye, sir." Marik turned back to his station and began the exacting task of adding new Space to the computer, while the others waited, holding the ship suspended, like a gigantic moth, in the glare of the swollen sun.

The planet called by the starcharts Q-131-d was in a geological stage comparable to Jurassic Earth; but the shifting sun, like insanity amok, pounded its continents with monster hurricanes, shrugged mountains and heaved waters into mighty *tsunamis* and river bores, probed its vitals with scorching electric fingers and tornadic suctions. Torrential rains harrowed its grasslands, roared in scalding cataracts down fresh gutters carved of mountainsides, and cascaded, steaming and muddy, onto the plains below.

One of the planet's sharp, young mountain ranges, honeycombed with crosscuts and bubbled caves, galleries and rills, held the only remaining life. In one of the large main caverns, which gave off of a score of tunnels, there was gathered perhaps a hundred upright, flat-muzzled, man-sized saurians with quasi-human faces; and in the middle of them, a small and gentle Shimshen sat at her communications equipment, coolly pleading for help.

"Teklif! Teklif! Hemson ki mynon so?" her voice continued, *"Mayday! Mayday! How do you read me?"*

The ground trembled and shuddered, and one of the smaller saurians shoved its flat little head under her elbow and squeezed its eyes shut, hissing softly with fear. She

254

paused just long enough to stroke it calm again, before taking up her monotonous—and probably hopeless—appeal.

"Teklif! Teklif!" she begged, "Hemson ki mynon so? Teklif, Teklif, hemson ki mynon so? . . ."

Riker sat staring at the looming star in his viewscreen, contemplating it abstractly, with no reaction. The intercom signalled and he touched it lightly. "Bridge."

"Power Deck standing by for warp, sir." Engineering's voice was metallic and distant, *and Riker had a fleeting memory of a summer's day on Zerev, when he had lain as a child among a field of clover and let his electronic nursemaid call him and call him, while he watched the llanas wheel high above, and smelled the sleepy, musty scent of dry grasses . . .*

"Index completed, Captain." Marik's brisk declaration snapped his yawn shut with a twinge of embarrassment, and he ordered, "Screen off. Prepare to warp." He would have given the order in the next breath, but Communications came alive as Timmoni Jen sat bolt upright, the pseudo-Roman ruff of fur bisecting her head quivering with excitement, her eyes wide.

"Captain!—Something—" The turn of a dial and a woman's voice, heavily interspersed with static, became audible.

". . . teklif! Hemson ki mynon so? . . . Teklif, teklif! Hemson ki mynon so? . . ."

"Too much interference for subether," M'Benga ventured, trying to place the language, and Miss Jen shook her head.

"Not subether, First Officer, sir," she corrected in her singsong syllables. "We have voice contact from bright-side of Planet Four, this system."

"Krail?" M'Benga wanted to know, and Riker spun his chair, his eyes blazing with excitemnt.

"No! *Einai!* What's she saying, Marik?" he demanded; but Marik was already at Communications.

"It's a distress signal, Captain." He flipped the toggle and made a few quick, minute adjustments that brought the voice in clearly. Then he cut in.

"Son-ili *USS Skipjack.* Son-ili *USS Skipjack.* Ki Mynon hem-zetli. Ki mynon hem-zetli. Fen tu kelec imm?" *Identify yourself.*

Riker's orders crackled like ice. "Lock onto that radio source! Activate surface scanners! I want to know what's going on." He slapped the com. "Power Deck! Disregard warp command. Program for standard flyby Planet Four and set up an observation orbit!"

M'Benga wheeled on Marik. "What's an intelligent—"

Her voice interrupted. "Zo-ili Hennem-mishli, Shimshen-al-Eisernon. Hemson so an-an starship klin?" *I am Hennem-mishli, a Shimshen of Eisernon. Permission to come aboard?*

Mishli! He bent his head and they could not see his face.

"—what's an intelligent life-form doing down there? Doesn't she realize this star's going nova?"

"She knows there is a danger, but not what it is." To Riker, he added, "She asks permission to beam up and talk to us."

Riker nodded shortly. Into the com, "Transport Sector, personnel one to beam up. Sickbay. Anderson to Transport Sector."

Marik lifted a hand and deliberately set the toggle. "Alai," he said softly. "Temteg: alai. Mok." *Granted. Out.*

Riker was waiting for him at the lift, and it whisked them down its hollow, metal gullet past the many levels of light, to the Transport Sector and Hennem-mishli.

The beam shimmered and she was there, small and slender, her robes iridescent in the diffuse light. The lower half of her face was painted a delicate blue in the familiar Shimshen caste-mark, and her hair was a glossy, dark fall down her back. Marik stepped forward, stiffly military, to help her step down from the grid, and she looked up as if at the sun, vulnerable and warm, and gave him a misty smile. In another moment she might have flown homing to his arms.

"Chom-ala, Dao," she whispered, hands patterning the air.

But Marik's formality was merciless. He answered her chom-ala smoothly, with a slight, deferential bow, his face an expressionless mask. "Shimshen." He indicated the Captain, who came forward, smiling, and took her hand. "Zo-ili Captain Paul Riker, ze komandt."

"Welcome aboard, Shimshen," Riker murmured, kissing her fingertips. "The *Skipjack* is yours."

She made a swift chom-ala, pulling her hand away from his without appearing offensive (although Riker rejected later that the *handkuss* being a strictly Earthling custom, she'd probably thought he was going to bite her) and murmured, "*Dom* Paul Riker. Chom-ala. Sint kaeli so an-an starship klin." It was clearly a compliment, and Riker flushed with pleasure.

"Uh, thank you." To a crewman, "Get Translators." And when the amulet was resting on the green-shaded hollow of her throat, he continued, "This way, Shimshen. We can talk more comfortably in here. Marik."

"Captain." Marik's tone was as stiff and unyielding as his posture. "I still have work to do on Index correlation, sir—"

"You'll come along with us," Riker retorted flatly, cutting him off. "That's an order, Mister. Neal." Anderson regarded first, Marik, and then the Shimshen, with narrowed eyes, thought quietly for a few minutes while they ushered their gentle guest to the conference room, and then suddenly clamped his pipe in his teeth, grinning faintly to himself, like a man who'd just made a pleasant discovery—or a workable plan.

The conference room, compact to begin with, seemed smaller because of the number of personnel who'd been summoned into it. The Shimshen sat at the center table, flanked by Riker and Marik, with M'Benga, Anderson and Hayashi, the Engineering Officer, ranged around the sides. She leaned her folded hands on the table and said, without preamble, "I need your help, gentlemen."

"You sure do!" M'Benga averred, and Riker interrupted to ask how she'd come to be there in the first place.

"I was assigned to Q-131-d by the Federation Secretary of Human Development, at my own request, and sent here in a drone launch."

"Who suggested this race to you, Shimshen?—rather than another?" Riker was keenly, grimly, interested.

"Why—Commander Beq nom-Pau, for whom I had gestated a Transplant, according to my vows."

Riker and M'Benga shared a brief glance. *A Krail, who sent her here to be incinerated by a sun.* Scuttlebutt, rumor, embellishment, had a little different story about Marik's exquisite Shimshen—and Beq nom-Pau—and there was an uncomfortable shifting of feet, a clearing of several throats, and Riker prompted, "So—when the child was born—you came here."

"There is an emerging race here, Captain. They call themselves the Ungt." Her tone became soft reminiscence. "I was to function as Race Mother, teaching—and doctoring—and guiding them—until they had the basic concepts of social cohesion and morality, based on the Decalog. Then, like other Shimshenli on other worlds, I would have left them; and my name would have become history, legend, fable, and forgotten. Now," she sighed, resting her head tiredly against her palm, "that's changed. This solar disturbance has been killing the Ungt, the conditions are unbearable . . ." She lifted her head wearily. "Of a race of possibly forty-eight thousand, only ninety-four individuals survive. Something is terribly wrong—not so?"

"Your star is going nova." M'Benga was flatly candid, a cool, black monolith. "In less than twenty-two hours, all but the outermost planets will be vaporized, and those left will be uninhabitable for several millenia."

Her hands flew to her face in horror. "Then we must get the Ungt off the planet! To leave them would be more than murder!—it would be genocide!"

Anderson glanced up from filling his pipe. "I'll buy that."

"Well, while you're buying it, Doctor," Riker growled, "give some thought to where we're going to put them up!—because this sub doesn't have the sheer physical space required to accommodate ninety-four more people! Assuming they *are* people!"

Marik spoke. "What is the designation of the Ungt?"

"Saurians. Oviparous, cold-blooded oxygen-breathers."

"Animals, then," Riker pointed out. "Reptilian animals that still lay their eggs in warm sand."

"They are intelligent, Captain! They learn so quickly, so well!" She clasped her hands decorously—desperately —on the table before her. It was the only outward sign of her agitation, and even the usually perceptive M'Benga missed it, and grinned fraternally.

"A dog learns quickly and well, Shimshen. He'll lick your hand and fetch the stick and jump through a hoop! But that doesn't make him intelligent!"

258

She turned to Marik for help. "I do not understand 'dog'".

"A lesser quadruped, native to his planet."

"Ah!" She smiled. "The Ungt *were* animals—yes. But they have come a long way. The same solar flares that have troubled the planet for half a century have caused an accelerated mutation among the Ungt. They already have a primitive social structure, a written glyphlanguage —and they no longer eat their children."

"So they no longer eat their children!" Riker toyed with his stylus, a bit caustic. "Well!—that's something to recommend them!"

Marik's head came up quickly, but Hennem-mishli was unmoved.

"Agreed. All races began as predators, as cannibals. Without Atreus and Thyestes—would you have also had Aristotle? Perhaps not." She paused, catching her full, lower lip with a white edge of teeth. "You won't let them just—die?—Captain Riker?"

He thought about it for a moment, conscious of their eyes on him. "No. I won't just let them die!—but neither will I risk my ship and my crew for a race that might still be no more than animals. Mister Marik, Doctor Anderson and I will beam down to surface with you. We'll meet the Ungt, run our own tests—and if we determine them to be intelligent life-forms, we'll proceed with the rescue. Otherwise—"

Marik came to his feet in one lithe, silent motion. "It is inconceivable," he said softly, "that a Shimsen could make a mistake regarding the intelligence of emerging life-forms. Such a suggestion is highly offensive to the Shimshen—and to me."

Riker got to his feet, too, thinking fast. His first impulse was to inform the haughty alien that he'd jolly well have to live with it!—if he was so damned touchy! Then he rethought the situation and addressed the Shimshen directly, although he was talking to Marik, too.

"I'm sure the Shimshen realizes my responsibility to my ship—as well as my regard for her station."

"I would welcome your meeting the Ungt, Captain." She smiled into his eyes companionably. "They are a most remarkable people."

"Good!" Riker approved. "Marik?"

If he hoped for some warmth, he was disappointed, for Marik replied curtly, "Time is short. Permission to beam down?" At Riker's nod, he turned on his heel and left quickly. The others rose and followed him silently out of the conference room.

They beamed down into a small cavern far inside the mountain range, the stale air and stifling heat intensifying a claustrophobic unease at knowing that tons of rock shifted above them. There was a faint, reflected light from a larger cavern some distance down the slick-walled, rocky gallery, and the Shimshen started toward it, confidently leading the way. The others followed, the Captain and Anderson stumbling over obstacles their Erthlikli eyes could not see, and Marik privately blessed his night-sight and lent them a hand. There was a dull rumble far above and powdery debris filtered down on them through a thin fault overhead as the mountain stirred.

"You will not notice, please," came the soft voice floating ahead of them, "that the Ungt have a certain natural scent. They are extremely sensitive."

Anderson barked his shin painfully on an outcrop of sharp rock, grunted an epithet he hoped the Shimshen missed, and made his entrance hobbling into the large, brightly-lit cavern, which was stagnant and heavy with the rank, reptilian odor of the Ungt. Anderson got a whiff and choked as discreetly as possible.

"Intelligent they may be," he grumbled at Riker, who grinned. "Sensitive they're not!" He coughed again, and the Ungt saw them.

And they saw the Ungt.

The scaly, half-humanoid faces turned in slow reptilian arcs as the starmen entered, and they muttered occasional, sibilant words of Eisernai, only partially recognizable in mouths never made for subtle nuances of pronunciation. They stood upright, dragging long, thick, scaly tails for balance, their small forearms already well-adapted for using tools. A few articles of household belongings—if they could be called that—stood in untidy piles near the wall, mute testimony to the perseverance of those clumsy three-fingered hands.

The Ungt surveyed the newcomers shyly, hissing and muttering uncomfortably among themselves and huddling close to the Shimshen; but one small, bold female, not yet mated, found Anderson irresistible, and walked round and around him, hissing admiringly.

The doctor didn't notice. He set up his portable testing apparatus (even as Riker and Marik were doing, on their side of the cavern) and tried not to inhale too deeply, or pay attention to the uncomfortable, wet maps of perspiration at his armpits and back. The air was so still. Even the slightest breeze would have been a boon, but the air hung motionless, and you waded through it as through a hot gel. He passed a hand across his face and glanced up as if he could see the sun growing outside, and wished for the briefest moment for the cool woods of Michigan II, for pine and mint and Mackinaws.

The Shimshen went to the center of the cavern, lifted her hands and said, "I call upon the Ungt to hear me."

They turned to her, trusting as dogs, with a kind of primeval innocence.

"These are the skyfolk" (the wide, flat, Roman-bridged noses swung slowly, snuffing the air in their direction) "who will take you away from here to a quiet place, with warm, shallow seas where your children can hatch safely in clean sand. You will become many again." She caught Marik's eye but he looked away, pretending not to have seen her. The months would have fallen away, had he let them.

"But first," she continued, less enthusiastically, "the skyfolk must test you, so they will know how wise you are, and how to make you comfortable on their ship. With the gracious permission of the honored Elder." She ceremoniously hung a Translator around the neck of the big, old bull who waddled forward importantly, and he bobbed and nodded a few times before he spoke.

"Thiss one, being Eldesst," he drawled sibilantly, "givess mosstt good Sshimsshen permisshin to tesstt." There was a lot of bobbing and ducking and nodding, presumably the Ungt's way of applauding, Anderson decided, and promptly tripped over the little female's scaly tail. She kept circling him again and again, dogging his every move and tripping him with monotonous regularity as she scuttled underfoot. The victim of an instant mad crush, she kept poking her muzzle under his arm, examining papers meaningless to her, sniffing his stylus and beaming into his face.

"Oooh, Sshimsshen," she breathed happily. "You bringing back beaussiful male to caverness!" She popped up directly into Anderson's vision at close range. "You liking Ank, sskyfolk male? I pretty, yess?"

Anderson allowed tactfully that yes, she did have a certain aura about her, which earned him a dirty glare from Marik, a grin from Riker, and the announcement from Ank that if he really liked her that well, she would be happy to build the nest herself, a suggestion that Anderson, wiping his dripping brow, vetoed with great vigor.

They got down to testing in earnest. Halfway through the procedures, the heat became so oppressive that the Shimshen had to help the females wash down their little ones with water, to prevent dehydration, and Ank, visibly wilted, sat on the floor in everyone's way and panted pathetically.

By the time they were ready to beam up, most of the saurians had disappeared into ancillary passages and Marik, who had a mind for such things, recalled that although there were numerous females cradling translucent, soft-shelled eggs against their chests—when they'd first arrived—he'd seen no eggs at all for the past several hours. He started to inquire about them, but dismissed it at the time as unimportant. He had no way of knowing that for the rest of his life, he was to bitterly regret not having asked.

On the *Skipjack*, Communications officer Timmoni Jen sat contemplating the forward viewscreen, on which the sun grew and swelled even as she watched. She was alone but for M'Benga and two crewmen standing watch, all of them drawn to and mesmerized by the visible changes apparent on the screen, and when her intercom signalled, she moved as though drugged to answer it.

"Bridge. Lieutenant Jen."

"Powder Deck," snapped Hayashi's flat metallic voice. "I'm getting a drop in coolant ratio, and the McIvors are beginning to heat up. We've got to get out of here! Let me talk to the Captain."

"He's planetside, Chief. They're still testing."

"Can you raise him for me?"

She shook her head as if he could see her. "Ship-to-surface frequencies are jammed. Sorry."

"You're sorry!"

The com went dead as he slammed it off and Tang, one of the botanists on Marik's service, came onto the Bridge and looked around worriedly. "Not back yet, eh?" Jen shook her head and he snicked a bit of impatience between tongue and teeth.

"Listen, things are getting pretty hot back in Hydroponics. We're going to have to install extra cooling coils under the tanks or we're going to lose a lot of valuable produce!"

"I'll see what I can do." She flicked a switch. "Environmental Control. Can we bring down the temperature in the Botany Section? It's very important."

"Negative, Bridge." There was concern in the hurried tone. "We need all the coolant we've got. Half our hull is facing that sun!"

One of the younger crewmen, who'd been watching the sun on the viewscreen, murmured, as in a dream, "And it's growing . . . you can almost see it grow . . . and grow . . . and . . ."

"You're relieved, crewman!" M'Benga's order was a dash of cold water in the face, ice down the back. "Notify your replacement!" The crewman rubbed his smarting eyes and came back reluctantly to reality. He focused on the fascia chronometer, blinking.

"—but, sir, there's another hour—my watch—" he swayed.

"Now, crewman!"

He left, sleepwalking, past Tang, who stared through him, defeated, disgusted. "Six tanks, Simon. Six lousy tanks. It's taken me months to grow those cultures." He passed a tired hand across his moist face. "Well—I'll innoculate some fresh specimens and flash freeze them for cloning. Maybe I can save something."

M'Benga sobered as he turned back to the viewscreen. "As long as we save the ship, Doctor," he muttered. "Just as long as we save the ship."

Log entry. By the hand of Paul Riker, Captain, USS Skipjack. 10 May 1225 G. F. T.: We have completed the testing of the Ungt, who may or may not be intelligent beings. Neither the Medical Section, Mister Marik, nor I have been able to determine the exact extent of their development, and upon that factor depends all of their lives. We will leave the final decision to the computer's metal objectivity; but whatever the decision, it must be made quickly, for the planet is rapidly becoming untenable for any lifeform. And my ship can no longer remain so near the nova without suffering intensive damage. End log entry. Riker clear.

At precisely 1500 hours, Riker and Marik strode into the unearthly sunlight that filtered into the Bridge as if through the skin of the ship. Riker thrust a recorder at the crewman manning Marik's station.

"Feed this information into the computer and get me an answer yesterday." He sat back at the Command Post. "Marik, set up a screen field."

"Aye, sir."

"Polarize all ports. Jen, get me a complete geological report on Planet Four."

"Ionization completed," Marik reported. "Screen field intact."

"I want a reading on all particle emission, including hard X-ray, and a running report on climatic conditions on the planetary surface, to a depth of two miles."

"Noted." Marik glanced up from his console. "Suggest spot check on personnel for radiation absorption."

"Good!" Riker touched his com. "Riker here. All hands whose ticket exceeds five Roentgens, report to Sickbay immediately. Section Chiefs check in at ten-minute intervals."

The intercom piped. "Power Deck."

"Riker. Go ahead."

"Skipper, I'm having trouble holding her. The engines are heating up real bad. If she goes critical, we'll make our own nova."

Riker hesitated. *But if they are more than animals—* "Give me another couple of hours, Chief. Then we'll pull her out."

And in the bowels of the ship, Hayashi slammed a hand against the intercom, cutting it off. "If she'll hold up another couple of hours!" he retorted hotly; but the mute blank screen only revealed his own angry reflection, and in the background, that of his sweating techs, slamming home a few more damping rods.

High above, on another deck, Neal Anderson was conducting a personal ships-tour for the Shimshen, with Ank scampering along behind them, her claws making soft, scratchy, skittering sounds on the smooth deck. Hennem-mishli sighed and paused outside of the Botany Section, running her fingers lightly along the bulkhead. She glanced up shyly, with a self-defensive little smile and shrug.

"I am very comfortable aboard your so-beautiful ship."

Anderson grinned at her and said, around his pipe, "This time we'll keep you here, Shimshen, where it's safe."

"No." She laid a light hand on his arm, and he looked down and drowned in the gray moats of her eyes. She dropped her lids and brought them up again, and her pupils, little cat's pupils, dilated with the intensity of her feeling. "Only if the Ungt come, too, Doctor. They are entrusted to me." Softly, "They are like my children." *Dark smudges of shadow under her eyes, and a wistful droop to the corners of her mouth.* Anderson removed his pipe and pursed his lips thoughtfully.

"Shimshen—how long were you signalling for help before we read your mayday?"

She lifted a pretty shoulder and shook her head, disclaiming details. "Hours. A day and a night—and perhaps another day, I'm not certain . . ."

He nodded sagely. "We'd better get you some sleep, little lady."

"Not until I know what will become of the Ungt."

"Nonsense!" He took her elbow and gently ushered her into a nearby stateroom, beautifully furnished and somehow vaguely familiar. "I'll find an empty berth for you and you can get a couple of hours' sleep. Do you good." He sat her down on a sleek divan and tucked a cushion beside her. "Wait here, I'll be right back." She started to protest again, but he jabbed his pipe stem at her and ordered, "Sit!—and wait!" and she subsided, smiling ruefully at him.

The door shut behind him, and she was alone. For the first time in many months, completely alone, her precious burden of responsibility lifted, answerable for the moment to no one but herself. She covered her eyes, not permitting herself to think or remember, and slowly relaxed into an attitude of utter fatigue. Her shoulders slumped wearily and she rested her forearms in her lap, touching her eyes, her mouth, with an unsteady hand. The tiredness crept upon her and she felt her muscles go loose and heavy, relinquished her weight to the sturdiness of the divan, and rejoiced in the sweet, cool, silkiness of the fabric against her cheek, as she rested against it. *Soft. Unbelievably soft, and she was so tired . . .*

Hennem-mishli, Shimshen to the Ungt by order of the Galactic Federation, slept the deep, untroubled sleep of a little child.

Behind her, on shelves along the far wall, stood various artifacts, among them a bronze takkat set, a large, faceted gemstone, and a carved-wood shun-daki rack with two scarlet, silk tassels looped over the top of it.

Now that the first step of his plan had been executed, Neal Anderson, inordinately pleased with himself for a man who was meddling in someone else's affairs, closed his eyes and calmed his thoughts. He was trying to remember a technique he'd half-learned at a beer party one night, during his student days on Eisernon (when a tipsy Einai—who was later found murdered—told more than he should have about the legendary Han), and gingerly at first, then with more confidence, he sent mind-touch to Marik, probing, feeling for a weakness, and he concentrated on the Science Officer's injuries with every bit of medical knowledge he had. Although he was in no way a telepath himself, Anderson was willing to make a sizeable bet that by amplifying Marik's constant discomfort, he could give him abundant reason to seek the solitude of his own stateroom. He'd had no idea it would be such an effort.

Paul Riker sat slumped in the Command Post, regarding the sun, glaring back at him through the viewscreen, as he would a belligerent antagonist, and with a sudden movement of his hand, snapped it off abruptly. "What about that surface report, crewman?"

The crewman jumped. "Coming in now, sir." He read sketchily from the scanner, "Planet Four is roughly comparable to Earth's Jurassic and Zerev's Chereni periods. No polar caps to speak of, widely-distributed shallow inland seas, abundant subtropical foliage. There's only one discrepancy, sir."

Riker spun his chair, waiting expectantly.

"There's no discernable life. There are plenty of animals—saurians, a rough version of Earth's archeopteryx, even a few small mammals—but they all register as dead. Not one life-glow, sir."

Marik turned from his station. "Radiation increased by twenty-one percent over initial report."

"Increase ionization field to two-thirds."

A crewman appeared at Riker's elbow, deferentially handing him a tapeslate. "Captain, here's your answer from the computer. A complete ethnobiological report, complete with a breakdown of saurian intelligence levels, individually and collectively."

Riker skimmed the tapes quickly, seeking his answer: *Are the Ungt human—or animal?* He found what he was looking for, read avidly for a moment, and then slapped the tapeslate against his palm.

"Stalemate! They're borderline! Too intelligent to be animals, and not advanced enough to be classified as true humanoids."

"Then it's your decision, Paul," M'Benga told him, and Riker tossed the tapeslate into the crewman's hands.

"My decision!—do I save my ship and leave an intelligent race to sizzle in its own sun?—or do I jeopardize the lives of everyone aboard to rescue a bunch of clever animals? *Just when does a being become human?*"

"A most fascinating dilemma, viewed objectively," Marik observed. He forcibly closed his mind to the insistent mind-touch, the nagging suggestion that urged him to rest his aching leg, that drew his nerves out thin, stringing them like wires around the scars, wrapping them, keloid and screaming, around the shaven raw edges of bone. Perspiration beaded his forehead and trickled down his spine, and he locked his teeth. Whoever was doing this to him knew his art well, could pry with invisible fingers at the clamped lid of his Pandora's box, the remembered dungeon inside his mind. He fought it off, wondering at the chasms of time and little deaths that could bridge a comment and its reply.

"Assuming it *can* be viewed objectively," the Captain retorted caustically, and Marik heard him as though at a distance. The pain in his leg rose in volume and in pitch, and he clenched his hands to keep them from gripping his thigh.

"If you will excuse me," he heard his voice say evenly, and he entered the lift, barely limping at all. A hum, and he was gone.

Anderson's grating thoughts followed Marik down corridors, through hatches, making him aware of his pain and his pride, so that he would of necessity seek the shelter of his own quarters, and the privacy to suffer alone. But he would not, Anderson reflected, with the comfortable smugness of a man blatantly meddling in someone else's love-life, *going to have much time to suffer; and certainly not alone.* Anderson had seen to that.

Marik stumbled gratefully into the privacy of his quarters and leaned hard against the wall, gripping his leg with both hands while the ache rose and swelled and after a while diminished enough to permit him to limp over to the cabinet and pour a bowl of tarangi. He started toward the divan with it, but *she* was there, curled softly in sleep, tendrils of dark hair caressing her throat. The edge of her teeth showed wet and white, and her mouth was crumpled childishly against the pillow.

Anderson engineered this, he thought, *Anderson, with his fine antennae sniffing and sensing the dying dreams, the withered and faded memories that lay moldering in the corners of his mind. Anderson, breathing Autumn-evening pipe-smoke on them, stirring them to a semblance of life, spinning them in whirling, heart-pounding eddies, until the dreams got up and danced away to the music of their own cadences, and Marik knew they had never been dead at all.*

He leaned against the cabinet watching her sleep, sipping the tarangi and feeling its warmth flow along his limbs and ripple under his hide, until the bowl was empty. Then he lifted a chukuri down from the high shelf and, seating himself cross-legged on a broad, low table, he began to play a polyphony that spoke of ancient and forgotten things: of fallen stars, and ruins overgrown, and promises. The strings wept softly into the stillness.

Her eyes opened, *dream-stippled, thoughtpocked, petal-glazed,* and her dimples deepened and disappeared. Her voice was fuzzy, drowsy, and very dear.

268

". . . The Lay of Masiosh . . . It's been so long . . ." She sat up quickly, an inspiration of silk, remembering. "Oh. —the Ungt?"

Marik bent his head over the chukuri, executing a difficult chord. "He's not yet made a decision."

She stood up, arranging her robes uncomfortably, acutely aware of his physical presence; and she crossed to the shelves where his trophies were tastefully displayed, absently touching one or two of them, a carving from Gham, chant-discs from Monastery, that whispered of alien stars when she laid a hesitant finger on them.

A large, faceted red gemstone caught the light and she held it near her face, intent upon its touch, while Marik regarded her pensively, his fingers searching out and plucking the myriad stiff bass rods of the chukuri.

"A tactile stimulus," she murmured delightedly. "It feels like . . . like . . ."

"Like music sounds to him who hears it," he assisted quietly. "To each, different. I traded my rations for it on a planet whose name I've long forgotten. It is yours, may it please the Shimshen."

"You are very kind."

He inclined his head in acknowledgment, watching the strings as he played. A small pulse began to beat, steadily, under his jaw.

"I think you have changed—Dao Marik." Softly.

His voice was grimmer than he had intended. "Everything changes, Shimshen."

She closed her eyes. "You didn't call me, 'Shimshen' at Pal-alden-Shali-Rho—or when you sat in my grandfather's pavilion and learned your sciences—and I wore the Blue Face, even then."

"And you wear it now." Bitterly, "But in between?" The chukuri cried out.

She whirled on him, wounded, her fingers pressed against her lips, hoping for some sign of warmth, of compassion; but his hand on the chukuri was clenched at the horn, and the line of his body was taut and hard, a harsh curve from the folded legs to the angle and set of the head, bent over the instrument.

She shook her head childishly, her eyes brimming. "Have you never forgiven me?" she murmured brokenly.

For answer, he deliberately got up, sauntered across

the room like an injured panther, and put the chukuri
back on its high shelf. Its strings lightly stung the silence,
trembled the air between them and faded, breathless, as
she whispered, "I think you do not hear me—or see me
—any more."

"I see you." He braced his hands tensely against the
shelves, his tone flatly declarative. "In the deeps of space.
In the heart of every sun." He turned the gray blaze of his
eyes upon her. "I hear you—in the vast, open places that
have never seen light—and in the distant music of a
thousand, thousand stars."

"Oh—Dao!" *Blushed, warmed, melted.*

He gathered her hungrily in his arms, burying his face
in the cool, dark, silk of her hair, and heaved a deep,
shuddering sigh of relief. Her arms slipped around his
neck and he could feel the racing of her hearts; and when
she trustingly, eagerly, lifted her face (warm shimmer-
frost, petalpeach, sundark) he kissed her cheeks, her eyelids, her brow, and found her mouth with a fervent passion
that stirred them both, and they clung together like lost
children.

After a rapturous moment, she drew back reluctantly,
patting his cheek with a soft palm, and snuggled her
head against his chest, while Marik stroked her hair and
caressed her cheekbone, her chin, the line of her brow,
with the tips of his fingers and told her—in a husky
whisper—of his agonizing search for her, from Sum
ChiT'ath to the farthest reaches of the galaxy.

"Wherever the ship made planetfall," he said unsteadily, "I thought, 'Here, surely here, I'll find her.' Day—and
night—I looked for you, asked questions, bribed beggars
and thieves . . . Palaces, monasteries—" his arms tightened
protectively "—alleys, morgues . . . Gods, what an empty
universe it was!"

"And then you found me—at the banquet—with that
dreadful Krail!" She shook her head sympathetically, her
teeth tightly-locked behind parted lips, her eyes swimming. "Oh—Dao!—How awful for you!"

"How awful for *me?*" he echoed in a pained murmur.
"How awful for Hennem-mishli!—to be alone—among
the enemy!—and bear his child!" He crushed her to him
as if to shield her from the past, defending her against his
own aloofness. *"I wasn't even there!* T'ath help me, I

270

thought you loved him!" A soft cry of anguish, *"I left you there!—alone!"*

She laid a light hand on his mouth, and kissed him lightly. "I'm here now—with you," she whispered, and he held her close, with a terrible resolve.

"And that's how it's going to stay, Mishli. I don't mean to lose you again!—for the rest of our lives!"

"Not for the rest of our lives," she agreed, and he bent his head and kissed her again, tenderly, their dual image reflected minutely in every facet of the scarlet gemstone.

Paul Riker was uncomfortable. Although the climate control was set at maximum (he'd checked twice with Environmental Control) the Bridge was hot and humid. His tunic stuck wetly to his back and perspiration trickled beside his ear, intensifying his annoyance. Even the Bridge personnel were beginning to wilt noticeably, and Timmoni Jen, that paragon of self-righteous military decorum, sat slumped in her chair, her usually-stiff head-ruff drooping sadly over one convoluted ear. Riker was on the com when Marik came onto the Bridge.

"—then find him!" He glanced up, saw him and snapped. "Relay that!" On his feet, he continued crisply, "We're going down."

"Then the Ungt are intelligent!" Marik exclaimed, and Riker spread his hands.

"We don't know," he said simply. "And because we don't know—because I don't want to bear the moral culpability of walking away from a drowning man!—and because *I—just—don't—know!*—when those inhuman-looking, dependent, inconvenient creatures turn into *people!*—we're going down! Any questions, Mister?"

"One, sir."

"Well?" He stared up into Marik's sober face, and the alien grinned boyishly.

"What took you so long?"

Riker stifled a sour smile and politely inquired what the hell Marik had to grin about!—with a planet to be evacuated—and a sun threatening to incinerate the ship! To which Marik replied drily, seating himself at his console, that it was his unbounded faith in his superiors that made his yoke so light. Riker turned and studied him with more than passing interest, reflecting that Marik was, at

271

this moment, warmer and more responsive than he had ever seen him. It was obvious that he and the exquisite Shimshen must have resolved their differences, and he realized, with a sudden burst of insight, what mental agonies Marik must have suffered, wondering whether his beloved still breathed. He tugged himself back to the present with an effort, for the riddle of Marik was interesting, and the heat made the least exertion sticky and unpleasant.

"Screen on!" The planetary surface glared up at them, bright and burning. "Planetary report."

M'Benga read it out calmly, his dark face shining with sweat. "The inhabited face of the planet has rotated to darkside, sir. We receive no life-glow from the western hemisphere. Planetary survey scanners register intense surface heat, heavy beta and gamma ray bombardment, and in increase of hard X-ray."

"Radiation levels?"

"Increase of thirty-seven percent over previous report," Marik said evenly. "Increase of sub-atomic particle bombardment, both to the surface and to us. Q-131 has shifted to sixth magnitude over the past three hours."

Riker asked quietly, "How long do we have, Mister Marik?"

"It's now 1605 hours. At 1800 hours, we'll reach our limit of endurance. Escape will then be impossible, sir."

"Not quite two hours." He wiped a runnel of sweat from under his chin. "Time's running out. All ahead one-third, Mister Rutledge. We'll ship for darkside and stand in the shadow. Buy a little time for our cooling units, anyway."

"Helm, aye." There was an unheard vibration, a throbbing not quite felt, somewhere under the boots, and the image on the viewscreen changed, darkened, rested the eyes with a wet, burning relief, as the massive ship fell lazily around the planet.

"Mister M'Benga, break out the skimmers. Volunteers only. Extend a search-and-rescue over the entire eastern hemisphere. Pick up anything that moves. We warp at 1800 hours." He hit the com. "Sickbay: rig for emergency, gentlemen. We're bringing up the saurians."

"Sickbay, aye," said the little metal voices, and Riker wheeled on Marik.

"They'll be needing you," he said quietly. Marik met his eyes in surprise and dawning comprehension—*he knows!* —and Riker nodded curtly, creaking the thrall. "Get with it, Mister."

"Yes, sir." The lift swallowed him whole, and sighed.

Across the Bridge, M'Benga rumbled, "All hands. All hands. Volunteers for search-and-rescue report at once to Skimmer Pods for launch at 1610 hours. All hands. All hands—"

The intercom piped and Riker touched it to silence. "Riker."

"Power Deck, Skipper. My cladding's beginning to break down! I've got one radiation leak and I'm waiting any minute for another! We've got to get out of here!" Hayashi sounded dogmatic and anxious.

"Negative, Power Deck! I need two more hours! Use individual personnel shielding until we can pull out. How do you stand on coolant?"

"With two McIvors overheating," shouted Hayashi, trying not to shout, "how do you think I stand!—sir!"

"Do the best you can, Chief."

M'Benga turned slightly from his station. "Captain, skimmers report full complement."

"Brief them and get them down." He sat watching the sun gleam malignantly over the edge of the planet, hating it, and M'Benga's voice was *the dull murmur of bees furred in yellow and brown, muttering and chuckling among the tall grasses, and the strong light of Zerev bathing his face with summer.*

"M'Benga to skimmer crews: one minute to launch. Planetary condition red. Repeat, red. Imperative skimmers avoid brightside. Use tractor beams only, to apprehend saurian personnel. *Skipjack* warps at precisely 1800 hours, this date. Any skimmer not present will be considered lost and will be abandoned. Questions? Mark! —five—four—three—two—one—hack!" A pause and Lieutenant Jen lifted her head.

"All boats away, sir."

The Bridge was hushed and tense. Now, for the first time, they were fully aware of the fraility of the silver minnows that had spewed from the Skimmer Pods, thin gray seeds catapulted into the atmosphere, (too hot), the radiation (too hot), and the men inside them, betting

273

their breakable, glass bones and their boilably-juicy bodies and their puny, electric-spark brains against the uncaring planet, the merciless sun, to save another race that could break and boil, too, and be dead in the savage sunlight.

M'Benga turned to Jen, the worry eloquent in his eyes, and she nodded gently, as to herself.

"If you employ gods, Mister M'Benga," she ventured primly, "now is as good a time as any to petition them."

The darkside of Planet Four was in colossal turmoil, riven by earthquakes, spouting up great boiling geysers and huge growing brambles of electricity. The swamps steamed with scalding mists and bubbled thickly, and the flight of skimmers, darting luminous across the night sky, left tracks of radiation, as in a cloud chamber.

Inside Skimmer Five, two young crewmen, Takahashi and Busaidi, skittered along close to the surface, primitive treetops slashing at the underbelly as they buzzed the swamps. A tiny, blue light flashed on the control panel and Busaidi tapped it impressively.

"Life-glow!" He coded a few factors into his board. 'Locked on! She's all yours, Tosh!"

"There he is! Okay, baby, come to papa!—he maneuvered a pair of sensitively balanced rods on the panel before him "—got him! Okay, Busaidi, my lad—to the hunt!"

Busaidi pulled his face into a caricature of an early Earthling (Ancient Civilizations 301), dragged in his chin, showed his upper incisors, drooped his eyelids and generally managed to look like a hairless, black gopher with a bad allergy. "Righto," he sputtered haughtily, and Takahashi squinted at him, grinning broadly.

"I give up!—are you the Lord High Chamberlain?"

"Tut, tut, my lad," Busaidi informed him, "I'm Phew-Bah, the Lord High Anything Else! (Introduction to Drama, 112)," he added, in his own voice, and they laughed, listening to their rescued saurian bump and hiss in the after lock, and veered away toward the horizon.

In Skimmer Eight, two more crewmen, Danny and Amelie, skinned through a narrow mountain pass, standing the skimmer on its stubby wingtip as they sheared close to the rock face. Three little blue lights flickered on their control panel, and Amelie pointed.

"Regardez, Dannee. Glow-worms." He smiled warmly

274

at her and they set off together after the lives that flickered on their panel.

Keller and Sikh, in Skimmer Three, fought back panic as first their communications and then their control systems failed. Sikh wrestled the stick but there was no response, and the air whined past in a rising shriek as they plummeted toward a mountainside, St. Elmo's fire playing fretfully along the hull.

"Keller!" Sikh's voice was not his own.

"Mayday! Mayday! Skimmer Three, coordinates as follows: forty-one degrees, three min—"

A sudden borealis flared above them and Sikh, blinded, lost control. The craft twisted, spun and crashed spectacularly on the mountain, debris scattering in glowing fragments along the rock. Keller, thrown free by some freak of his ejection device, fell headlong, his null-G bakpak only partially effective in the fierce magnetic fluctuations around him. He screamed as he fell, burning and smoking. He was still screaming when the Transport Sector locked on to him and beamed him aboard in the whisk, the wink, the caught half-breath of time between impact and death.

On the Bridge, Timmoni Jen came alert. "I have a Mayday, sir."

M'Benga, monitoring the operations from his station, reported quietly, "Life-glow of Skimmer Three extinguished."

Jen put down her earphones slowly and blotted her wet face with her sleeve. "Disregard."

"One up and safe," piped the Transport Sector, and Jen made a little, shivery breath and covered her face with her hands. Riker stared into the viewscreen at the swollen, blazing sun that was beginning to show around the curvature of the planet, and it hurt his eyes. He rubbed them tiredly. *Great God,* he thought unaccountably, *what business do men have meddling with the Infinite?* He chuckled inwardly, then, remembering the old saw about the rocketmen who believed that if God wanted men in space, He would have equipped them with stabilizers.

"Captain, message from Skimmer Five."

"Put it on." She flipped a toggle and Takahashi's voice

came in loud and clear, occasionally interspersed with static. He was in high, good humor.

"—and Busaidi in Skimmer Five, checking in. Everything here is go, it's a plum of a job, and we will expect turkey and bonbons upon our arrival back at the pods."

Jen cut in, bewildered. "Say again, Skimmer Five. We do not read 'terket and bonbons'. Say again."

There was subdued laughter and Busaidi chuckled, "Disregard my insane friend, Lieutenant. We're *go* on all counts."

"Understood 'all is well', Skimmer Five. Onboard environmental conditions?"

Inside the Skimmer, Takahashi winked at Busaidi and said, in heavy, Old-Earth dialect, "Vell, idt's hodt. Ja. Wery hodt."

"Undt vet," Busaidi assisted.

The communicator made a strangled sound. "Say again, Skimmer Five," it pleaded decorously. "I do not read you, say again?"

"Idt's hodt und vet," Takahashi shouted merrily, while Busaidi curled up in the seat convulsed with glee, one hand extended quivering atop his head in mimicry of Lieutenant Jen's furry ruff in extreme agitation.

M'Benga cut in. "Save it for the girls, hotshot. What're your conditions?"

"Hot and humid, sir," the reply snapped back somberly. "We have so far apprehended seven saurians, sir."

"Bring 'em in."

"Aye, sir." Takahashi sounded crestfallen, and even the Captain pulled a slow grin, and wagged his head.

"Wait a minute, Tosh! Look!" Busaidi pointed to the board, where one by one the blue-burning life-glows blinked out, leaving the board dark. The Japanese jumped from his seat and cracked the aft hatch, wincing at what he saw. He came back looking queasy.

"They're dead. Every one of 'em, Bu."

"But they were fine when we picked 'em up!"

"Radiation." Takahashi gave a brief, involuntary shudder. "They were—burned. They—" He shook his head as if to negate what he had seen.

A life-glow burned on the panel as suddenly a dying, groaning reptile staggered out of the scalding mist, lifted its scaly arms to the Skimmer like a child wanting to be

276

picked up, then stumbled and fell into the simmering morass.

"It saw us," Busaidi said tightly. "It saw us and wanted us to help it."

Takahashi stared straight ahead, expressionlessly. "Prepare to jettison cargo." And as his friend looked askance, he repeated himself, his cracking voice betraying him.

"Dammit, Bu, prepare to jettison the stinkin' cargo!"

Busaidi pressed a stud and the hull telegraphed the swift slick sliding of metal hatches somewhere aft; another stud and a series of irregular thumps as the cargo bays swung wide and spilled their contents to the water smoking below. Then the skimmer lifted light and free. Takahashi and Busaidi did not speak, nor had they need to do so.

Sikh's body had beamed up from the wreckage, snatched up at the moment of impact, the split-second of death; but the Transporter had been a fraction of a millisecond too late. They tried anyway to save him. Compressed air whisked the emergency sled down to Sickbay, where Marik, Anderson and a team of nurses and technicians labored to bring Sikh alive, to resuscitate and recirculate and bring back to awareness that which had been a man. But at last they trooped wearily out of the operating room, the doctors silent, the others talking together in subdued tones.

"I almost thought we could save him, Marik," Anderson ventured, fumbling for his pipe. "You're a helluva surgeon; where'd you study?"

Marik peeled off his gloves and contemplated a reply. "I studied privately," he said at last, tossing the gloves into the chute. "From childhood. Under Oman Shari-Mnenoplan. He was a—"

"I know who he was! Migod, everybody in the galaxy knows who he was!" He wagged his head and whistled. "So—you knew Shari-Mnenoplan!"

Marik's eyes dilated, glittering blackly. "I knew him."

Anderson waited, with keen interest, for him to continue; but when it became evident that the inscrutable alien wasn't going to divulge any more information about himself—or the old Master—he coughed and said awkwardly, "Your report mentioned fertile eggs."

Marik nodded, shrugging out of his greens. "I'll set

up the incubators." Anderson watched him limp away. *If I ever have a son,* he thought, but cut the thought off as irrelevant.

Amelie could not raise the *Skipjack.* She shook her head at Danny and blotted her wet face with both palms. "*C'est* impossible. Too much static. We have to wait."

"Better turn up the cooling unit, hon."

She checked the dial. "They're up to the maximum now, cher."

He swept his forehead with a quick thumb and wiped it on his pantsleg, pointing in the same gesture at the board. "Life-glow!" He banked toward the coordinates set by the onboard computer. "That'll make six. We'll bring back every half-dozen."

"Bon. I'll go pass by the cargo hatch and make sure they're okay, non?"

She had started to crack the hatch when Danny shouted, "Amelie! Don't touch that hatch! Dog it, quick!"

She slammed it shut, hitting the automatic locking mechanism, and leaned against it, indignant. "Dannee! You scared me!—what's wrong?"

"Come look at this radiation gauge. Those lizards are too hot to count!" The Geiger counter roared and one at a time, the blue lights flicked out. The cabin was hushed but for the fierce buffeting of the wind. Danny peered over the side as they banked again, and saw only steam and darkness, through which showers of luminous particles rained down like jewels, like fireflies, like delicate and deadly wasps.

"That's what it's like out there," he whispered, cradling her cold, moist hand, and tipped his head toward the hold where six saurians lay dead. "That's what it does to you."

As they watched, the radiation gauge crept up another notch and hung there expectantly.

Dawn sprang up in the east like an apparition, the giant sun's corona revealing a landscape of nightmare, where tatters of mist and steam streamed across the shields, and great branches and logs and gouts of vegetation howled as they whipped, flung, dragged across the land, caught, held, and were tossed again. Radiation rained tiny suns onto the hull and interfered with communications.

Takahashi spoke quietly. "There's not one left alive, Bu. We'd better check in."

Busaidi began his efforts to raise the *Skipjack*, while in his ears rattled the static of the encroaching sun. It was exactly 17:0.

The ship was hot, its hull glowing mothwing white in the glare of the growing star; and inside, even with Climate Control set on maximum cold, crewmen moved in slow motion, wet and exhausted. Tunics hung limply on flagging bodies, and the bridge was livid with sunglow. Timmoni Jen looked up tiredly from her panel.

"Skimmers Two and Six are down, sir. Survivors of Six request beam-up."

The intercom stud. Riker thumbed it numbly. "Transport Sector: two to beam up." He eyed Jen's board grimly. "Only two?" She nodded, brushing weakly at the film of moisture on her face, but before he could release the com, an urgent voice cut in.

"Break! Skimmer Eight."

"Go ahead, Eight."

"Sir, we report no survivors on the surface. All dead in the marshes, sir. Everywhere you look."

"You're certain."

"Aye, sir. The only survivors would be in the caverns, from what we see here."

The com piped, "Transport Sector. Two up and safe, sir."

Jen's head came up. "Captain, Skimmer Five reports no saurian survivors. Requests orders."

"Give me a reading, Simon." Riker wiped his wet face.

M'Benga licked his lips with a dry tongue and advised, "There is a strong penetration of secondary particles into the atmosphere, hard X-ray bombardment and a drop in radio frequency." He blotted his slick face. "This is Marik's department, but it's my guess that we've got a severe disturbance coming up. You'd better get this ship out of here, while you still can."

"Captain, Skimmer One reports no survivors."

"Skimmer Eleven, Break! No surviving saurians—"

"Maximum screen field, Mister M'Benga." Riker's voice sounded dry and raspy, and he was annoyed that it should. He cleared his throat and hit the com stud. "Riker to all boats. Riker to all boats. Abandon search-and-rescue. Re-

279

peat, abandon search-and-rescue. All boats will rendezvous at the central mountain range and collect saurian personnel for beam-up——"

A series of jolts shook them hard, knocking Guns off his feet, and the light heightened perceptibly, smarting the eyes and searing the skin. The shell of the ship seemed almost transparent, and the unearthly radiance filtered through it onto the bridge, dimming, then growing again. Marik's station hummed, chattered, roared with life, computers begging to be heard, *incomplete data, inefficiency, overload, data, please, incomplete data*—

"Fluctuation in the ionization field!" His hands flew over the console, soothing the hysterical machines. "I can't sustain the field, Paul!" Little, metallic voices whispered and chittered through the com and somewhere a man screamed thinly before the second jolt hit the ship. M'Benga stopped reluctantly, his hands still. "The screen is down, Captain. Now we're as vulnerable as the saurians."

On the Power Deck, gauges rose sharply, and a spray of steam spurted explosively from a huge pipe joint and clouded the room, flooding the floor with scalding water. There were shouts to 'man those pumps', while a wildly rising whine raked the eardrums and technicians dove for the damping mechanisms. Steam felled a crewman who was lost in the thick, hot cumulus that shrouded the deck, and another technician slipped and sprawled trying to reach him. The raw energy pulsing through the walls of the McIvor engines was almost visible, and the Chief roared "Damp those piles! *Damp 'em!* but his voice was lost in the melee of human cries and the rushing of steam. *"Shut down the reactors!"*

Three technicians started for the banks of levers and Hayashi fought his way to the intercom. "Power Deck, skipper!" he shouted above the din. "The piles are going critical! She's going to blow wide open!"

Riker leaped to his feet. "Sound GQ, Jen! The piles are going!"

"Oh, my God!" M'Benga moaned, and Guns muttered something in Russian and crossed himself.

Riker thumbed the stud and announced, quickly, coolly, "This is the Captain. Condition Red. All hands prepare to abandon ship! All hands prepare to abandon ship!"

Klaxons blared a warning as the lights began to dim, and crewmen raced down corridors still pulling on shielded, self-contained suits and helmets, standard emergency gear for shipwreck in space. Others hurried to shut down delicate machinery and still others fitted protective, self-locking shields on the animal cages in the biolab, so that even the experimental animals might survive.

In the surgery, standing over the puffy pink-and-yellow grotesquerie that was crewman Keller, Neal Anderson and Dao Marik were busy with the infinitely delicate work of removing masses of cooled flesh and replacing it with identically calibrated strips of tissue-thin synthon. Anderson moved aside as Marik reached for the medicomp and worked out the intricate, complicated chemical miracles that would turn synthon into human tegument.

The alarm sounded with regular mechanical panic and nurses and assistants ran to secure patients in space-tight cylinders. No MAX's, these, but they would insure maximum safety and decontaminated surroundings until the danger was past. Anderson ordered his people to the lifeboats, and glanced at Marik questioningly.

"It would kill him," Marik's voice was very calm and detached as he released into the synthon an infinitely small, carefully measured dose of DNA that corresponded exactly to Keller's own DNA pattern. The synthetic tegument swelled slightly and was subtly changed as the DNA flowed through it cell by cell, and it grafted to the fascia, taking on the fine-grained, tell-tale reality of true skin. Freckles popped out on it, and a mole that had been burned off grew back as they watched. One square centimeter of true flesh, restored. Marik lifted his head for a wipe, and Anderson, cutting another tiny patch of frozen synthon, muttered preoccupiedly, "Miss D'Anjou, shut that thing off, will you?" She ran to stop the alarm at the manual switch, and the silence was deafening.

A moment later, lifting his head to rest his stiffened neck, Anderson caught the warmth of approval in Marik's eyes.

But the rest of the shop was an anthill, a beehive of activity. Crewmen and junior officers crowded the lifeboats and strapped snugly into accleration couches, for there would be no grav-grids on the lifeboats, no illusion

281

of a solid, planetary mass under the boots; there would be only the starry abyss. The junior officer on each boat initiated the sequence that readied the engines, polarized ports, swung the outer hatch away, leaving them poised on the brink of the Deeps. Then he lay back, thumb hovering at the launch stud.

The Power Deck crew worked frantically at the damping mechanism, the banks of gauges and levers and rods, the actual physical shielding. Steam sprayed wildly and several technicians, faces puffed and red, were whisked to Sickbay in the tubes. Those remaining labored harder to fill their places. The Chief's normally-yellow skin was bright orange and his oblique eyes were swollen almost shut, but he managed to stay on his feet, outworking all of them, scorching his hands on red-hot pipe fittings, shouting orders over the noise and confusion. Now he straightened hopefully.

"Stand by to rotate neutron reflectors!"

Hands flew, programming the rotation of the giant reflectors, and another of the technicians staggered from the heat, fainted and slid to the floor. She was left lying there for only a moment (the precious moment without which they all would die).

"Rotate One and Three!"

Hands spun dials shrouded in mist, depressed levers slick with steam; and gauges hung dangerously in red margins, watching with shattered, glass eyes. Inside the mammoth machines, massive neutron reflectors moved with elephantine deliberation, ponderous slowness, presenting their absorbant hindsides to the radiation.

"One and Three absorbing!" The technician's voice was flat and heavily-accented, but the excitement in it was universal.

"Rotate Two and Four!"

Again, the giant reflectors did a collosal about-face, while crewmen waited tensely in lifeboats to explode away from the mother-ship, and medics in an operating room found no time to wonder whether each breath might be their last.

Then, throughout the ship, lights began to blink off, electronic equipment hushed its hum and chatter. Air vents exhaled weakly, breathing their last, and in Astrogation the big computers faltered, wavered and winked out, one by one.

The reflectors completed their rotation. Gauges hovered, hesitated and grudgingly began their slow and steady descent. The Power Crew peered at them blankly for a moment, wordless in the hot, stifling darkness of the Engine Room; then they shouted gleefully and swore and pounded each other on scalded shoulders, laughing and crying all at once. Hayashi stumbled over to the wall com, pressed the stud with the uncommonly precise finger of a veteran drunk, and leaned on the burning bulkhead.

"Power Deck. We've got her closed down, sir. She won't blow."

On the darkened Bridge, Riker closed his eyes gratefully, holding back the surge of relief that threatened to engulf him: then he answered evenly, "Well done, Mister Hayashi."

"Sir, we'll be without power until we can make repairs. All we can give you is emergency standby generator."

"How long?"

"I don't know, Skipper," answered the weary intercom. "It looks pretty bad from here. Maybe a couple of hours, if we're lucky."

Riker took a deep breath and let it out slowly. "You don't have a couple of hours, Chief. You don't have an hour. It is now—" he consulted the fascia chronometer "—seventeen thirty-two hours. I want this ship on standard power, capable of warp speeds, at eighteen hundred hours."

"Sir!" The com exploded in a metallic travesty of indignation. "Skipper! —my techs are beat! Half of 'em are in Sickbay! We'll never make eighteen hundred!"

"You make it, Mister Hayashi," Riker said softly, in a most deadly tone. "Eighteen hundred hours. You make it."

The automatic release on two huge ports had triggered, and now the Bridge was lit by the far stars on the one side, and by the nearer malignant glow of the sun's corona on the other. Riker shielded his eyes with his hand and gave the order to secure from general quarters. As M'Benga's bass-string voice made the welcome annunciation, Rutledge turned to the Captain diffidently.

"Orders, sir?"

"We wait," Riker said.

283

There was an observation port on the starboard quarter near the operating complex, and Dao Marik stood somberly contemplating the stars. He was still wearing his surgical greens, his mask hanging limply around his neck. They had saved Keller and most of the others, and when suddenly there were no more emergencies, Anderson had sprawled out on an empty examining table and snored. Marik had homed for the stars.

The corridor was empty and starlit, and Hennem-mishli appeared noiselessly in the far angle. He lifted his head, and the sight of her was cold water in the throat after a sultry day, rain after the long drought. Her robes whispered of silk.

"It is permitted?"

He scarcely nodded, and she came to the port beside him and stood riding the slow revolution of the ship, while the planet hove (oh, slowly) into view. An angry rim of brilliant light seared the horizon, casting strong shadows across her face, and they watched little running snouts of light, like lava, silhouette mountains, engulf valleys, sheet across plains.

Marik slipped his arms around her and she leaned back trustingly against his chest, folding her arms lightly over his. The rim of light grew, glaring and inexorable, with a terrible, awesome beauty.

"It makes a very bright light," she ventured quietly. His arms tightened protectively.

"A very bright light," he agreed. Her hair breathed of musk and jasmine.

"When your voyage is over, Dao—what then?"

He smiled and rested his chin on the top of her head. "I'll remember a pavilion at dawn, with memlikti singing in their golden webs—and a new Shimshen learning to play her pipes. I'll think of it—and when my voyage is over, I'll come looking for a place called Pal-alden-Shali-Rho—and a Shimshen called Hennem-mishli."

She looked up at him and smiled, more with her eyes than with her lips, and he regarded her with a brooding affection; then they stood silently together watching the brilliant light as inch by inch it blotted out the stars.

The Bridge was hot. Hot and dry, as an oven is hot and dry, or a bit of metal in the sun, insignificant and

284

burning. When she spoke, Lieutenant Jen's voice was weak and sick.

"Trying to register a message from the surface, sir. On emergency standby generator."

The stud was wet with sweat. "Riker. Keep it short."

"Skimmer Eight, Captain, at the rendezvous." He paused. "Sir, it's the saurians. I tried to explain to them about the beam-up, as ordered, but they panicked. They're scattered all through the caverns, and there's miles of tunnels back there. Some of them even ran out onto the surface."

Riker passed a hand over his eyes to clear them. "The Transport Sector's out of commission, Eight. We're adrift, barely holding orbit. Return to the ship." He rang off and sat regarding the com with something like distaste. "Simon, call off the search-and-rescue."

"The Shimshen will have to be told," M'Benga offered. "If you like, I could—"

"Thanks, I'll talk to her." He smiled grimly, without mirth. "The privileges of rank, Mister M'Benga." To Jen, "Get me Dao Marik."

The intercom piped. "Observation Port, Sickbay." The cool voice of Marik made into silver, into bronze. *Into brass*, thought Riker, irritably; then, "Riker. Is the Shimshen with you?"

"Yes, sir. Something wrong?"

"I have a tape she'll want to hear." He pressed the playback, rerunning both the Skimmer report of the Ungt's panic, and his own order abandoning the search-and-rescue mission. The tape ended in a monotonous *click, click, click,* and there was no sound from the Sickbay. Riker could only guess at her reaction.

"I'm sorry, Shimshen," he apologized lamely. "We'll be lucky to get the ship clear in time."

"I will go down to them," her small voice begged unexpectedly. "They trust me, they'll listen to me. I'll make them return to the cavern before the ship leaves—and we can save at least some of them!"

"Skimmer Twelve is still in its pod," M'Benga interjected quietly. "I can easily—"

"No dice, M'Benga!" Riker flared. "I've already lost four men, three boats and a lot of valuable time down there in that hell-hole! I'm not risking one more life! Not yours, not hers, not anybody's!"

Hennem-mishli's voice on the intercom was gentle and final. "I couldn't save my own child—or the sixty thousand children who died with her, Captain. Now—if I cannot save the Ungt—I will have lived for nothing."

"Not all races live by the same standards, Paul. Not even all members of the same race, or species." M'Benga was frankly pleading, showing compassion Riker never would have suspected of him. "Look, there's nothing I can do here—nothing!—until the McIvors are reactivated. But they need her down there, Paul! Let me take her down."

"And if I refuse?" *If I forbid you to boil and burn and wither?*

"You cannot refuse, Captain," said the cool, imperious voice of the Shimshen, and suddenly she was alien, with purposes far beyond his ken. "No Shimshen may be held against her wishes. You will permit me to leave."

Riker measured his words, calibrated them and weighed them to the milligram, dealing them out flatly. "You're right, of course, Shimshen. You have my permission to leave; but I must point out that you will find it most difficult to pilot a skimmercraft alone. Riker clear."

The intercom went dead and Hennem-mishli turned to Marik in despair.

He was smiling.

Skimmer Twelve slipped smoothly out of the pod, lifting like a thing alive as the hatch clamped tight behind it and left it poised in space. Marik pointed her nose down and felt the old exultation return, the freedom and danger of the calculated fall toward the looming planet, the easy pitching to an acute angle for entry and—yes, there it was, the slight, significant shudder as the craft entered the upper reaches of the atmosphere, the old familiar red glow, filling the cabin and narrowing his eyes. He glanced at Hennem-mishli.

Her face was a flame, a torch, a lamp, her dress incandescent. The glow made her cheeks ruddy and filled the dark fall of her hair with dull red embers. Her eyes shone lambent and golden.

"We will save them—won't we, Dao?"

He made a small adjustment on his control panel and

286

flashed her a confident smile, but did not reply. There was nothing he could have said.

The air became denser and more turbulent and the skimmer occupied Marik's whole attention, yawning and pitching perilously before he dropped it in a powered dive several thousands of feet to relatively calmer air. The radio signalled and he touched the throatset of his helmet. "Marik. Skimmer Twelve."

"By whose order do you commandeer one of my boats, Mister?" Riker's tone was cold and smooth, like a weapon.

"You gave the Shimshen your permission, Captain." He cut back the speed expertly and felt the skimmer's graceful response. "Your skimmer is in uncommonly good condition, sir."

"You get my—commonly good skimmer back to its pod, Mister," Riker ordered icily, "—fore I have your head on a pike!" Static crackled the ears.

Marik did a slow barrel roll, banking for the major continent off in the distance, and Hennem-mishli took a long, audible breath and closed her eyes, her fingers digging into his thigh. He levelled off apologetically and touched his throatset again.

"Sorry, Captain. Unable, repeat, unable. For all the good reasons your First Officer gave you a while ago. These 'children' have got to live."

The radio sputtered static for a moment and then burst into speech. "—as she gets them calmed down, —get her —ack here, ——stand? 1800 hou— Marik!" Between bursts of static, Riker sounded angry. Angry and concerned.

"Acknowledged. Twelve clear."

A wide, molten arc of light crested the horizon as far as the eye could see, and the little skimmer darted down to surface between savage bolts of lightning and roiling shreds of steam that boiled up and condensed and fell torrentially only to steam up again. Hennem-mishli pointed with a little exclamation at a second craft, Skimmer Nine, flitted past, climbing steeply in the opposite direction.

"Wish them well," Marik said grimly. "They're climbing into turbulence."

They banked sharply and the caverns were dead ahead. Skimmer Nine never reached the *Skipjack*. Wavered

287

lines of force caught it up and held it waiting, weightless, for an instant (its crew threw defensive arms up, against the blinding glare) then Skimmer Nine exploded violently, its fragments falling in luminous arcs, in burning parabolas, falling in slow grace like dying fireworks.

The Power Deck was a vast cavern, sweltering hot and dimly-lit by bobbing hand torches. Its crews swarmed over the skeletons of the monster machines like ants, carrying bits away with them. Riker paused in the half-light at the foot of the ladder, his tunic clinging wetly, uncomfortably to his skin.

"Mister Hayashi!"

Hayashi peered through the gloom. "Captain! It's hard to see you, sir—"

Riker stood gazing at the mammoth bulk of the McIvors as if they were sentient and stubborn. "It's now 1750 hours, Chief," he said in a soft undertone. "Where's my ship?"

"Sir!—we're doing our best!"

Riker whirled on him in a fury. "*It isn't enough!* I can't warp this ship on your good intentions!"

Something broke inside the Chief. He pitched down the heavy tool he had been carrying and shouted into Riker's face, "What more do you want! My men are dropping like flies! There's live steam in there!—and hot residue!—and no room to work, even for a gang of Xhole, if I had 'em!—which I don't!" He pushed his face pugnaciously at Riker's icy calm and yelled, "Right now it's a hundred and forty-six degrees Fahrenheit under those engines—."

Riker's head came up cleanly and his voice carried sharp and clean and quiet, so that everyone but those men deep inside the McIvors stopped to listen.

"And the center of that nova out there approaches thirteen million degrees Kelvin! Enough to vaporize a planet. It's near edge gets here in ten minutes. Ten minutes, Mister Hayashi. That doesn't leave you any time to belly-ache about your little problems." He started for the ladder, then turned back, still grasping the rung. "Get on it!" he commanded sharply. "I won't be Master of a Flying Dutchman!"

288

Skimmer Five was in trouble. Busaidi managed to hold her fairly level, but that was about all. She lost altitude quickly, slipping down toward the boiling swamp, the air shrieking past in a monotonous rising whine, and it was with great difficulty that Busaidi held her nose up.

"No use, Tosh. She won't respond! We're gonna have to belly in."

"Check!" Takahashi made a few last-minute entries in his tapes and braced himself for the shock.

It was not as bad as they had expected. Initial impact was a jolt, but they did not break up; instead, they skied boisterously through a sweltering, log-filled sump, snapping their landing gear and denting the underbelly, slewed over a half-submerged strand of melting sand, brought up sharply against a crumbling mudbank, and settled slowly in the simmering morass, shaken but unhurt. Takahashi wiped cold sweat from his lip, gingerly massaged his stiff neck, and drew an uncertain grin.

"You okay?"

"Sure." Busaidi clasped his hands to keep them from shaking and pressed them against his eyes, letting his breath out in a soft *whoosh*.

The Japanese tried his communications equipment but found every band blanked out with static He flipped switches and turned knobs and dials, but heard only the cellophane crackling of the atmosphere, the endless crunch of a billion autumn leaves under the flung weights of a million autumn children. He snapped the switch off and sat back irritably, trying to control the little nagging fear growing at the back of his mind. Busaidi raised his head.

"How bad?"

"Oh, we're in terrific shape," Takahashi drawled. "The cooling unit's out. The radiation shield's down. And I can't raise the *Skipjack*—we're getting a periodic blank-out of hailing frequencies from that damn sun."

"Try a shorter wavelength," Busaidi urged. "We can't stay here."

A trickle of boiling swampwater ran slowly along the floor.

"It's all static, chum. No good." Breathing was becoming difficult and Takahashi loosened the collar of his tunic and pulled it away from his throat with a clumsy

289

hand. "Maybe . . . later. Give it, uh, give it a few minutes, huh?"

Outside the thin plexiglas ports, the swamp bubbled lavathick, an ooze of mud and penetrating stench, chopped and pocked and sheeted with monsoon*deluge*hurricane, each blast of wind shuddering the Skimmer a little deeper into the mire; and the first tenuous fingers of bizarre light that pierced the flying scud scored their skins like acid, corrosive and barely simmering on the hide.

Takahashi, numbly studying his hands to keep from meeting his friend's eyes, came alert, recognizing the telltale swollen bronzing of his skin and tried to joke it away. "Hey, look," he said, off-handedly. "Me with a golden tan! Can you beat that?"

"I can match it," Busaidi replied soberly, his eyes bleak. He extended his arms, and there was an uncomfortable quiet.

Takahashi's voice was hoarse. "Must be getting close to 1800. . . " He leaned back against the headrest and panted lightly.

" . . . Tosh?" Busaidi blotted a patch on his arm where blood seeped scarlet through the unmarked black skin. "You know what I'm thinking? . . . I'm thinking we've just about had it . . . "

They were dehydrating quickly now, covered with sweat, dry-mouthed, semi-conscious. Takahashi rolled his head toward Busaidi, who was bleeding in several places, and made a grimace intended as a smile. ". . . funny you should mention that, chum . . . " he croaked.

The Manual Destruct button glared at them in red from the control board, commanding their attention, silently coaxing the swift pressure of a thumb that would end the heat and the pain and the thirst. Takahashi tried to grin again, but didn't make it. He shook his head 'no', quickly, slightly, his eyes pleading wordlessly past lips swollen beyond speech. Busaidi was almost inaudible.

" . . . I'm not . . . 'n any rush . . . " He rested his forearm on the panel and leaned his head down upon it. Takahashi was already slumped unconscious in his seat, his skin blistering visibly where the intermittent rays of the sun touched it.

Then everything was still except for the constant buffeting of the hurricane howling outside.

The mountain caverns were vast, dark and deserted, and footsteps echoed, voices reverberated, in their vaulted expanses, making Marik and Hennem-mishli speak in whispers as they entered the main tunnel opening. Marik took her arm warningly.

"Be quick, Mishli."

She nodded. "They can't be far. But Dao—" her hand was light on his arm "—stay out of that passage." He saw a sloping shaft so dark its blackness was virtually tangible. "It's their burial maze, and only the Ungt know how to come out again."

They split up, each into his own tunnel, keenly aware of the solid rock that separated them and of the danger (even here, especially here) of seeing sudden actinic light that meant the sun had licked up the planet (too soon!) like some great fiery toad (*beetle-world, mothship, and my beloved*). Marik ran faster.

Hennem-mishli followed an old trail down, down into the mountainside to another, smaller cave sometimes used for councils in the past. She hoped desperately that even now they would have met to discuss this new turn of events, and would allow her to talk to them.

The cave was empty, but she caught the first sharp scent of the Ungt, and stepped confidently to the center of the cave, hoping they wouldn't see her hands tremble.

"I am Hennem-mishli, Shimshen to the Ungt," she announced clearly. "I call upon the honored Eldest to show his head without fear." Her words bounced back from the hot, wet rockwall, and the tunnel openings stared at her with open mouths.

She waited patiently.

Marik caught the unmistakable scent in his own corridor and flattened against a wall, hearing the furtive, scraping footsteps approaching. When it was near enough, he began to whistle softly through his teeth.

A flat saurian head peered curiously around the corner and Marik grabbed it—*pounce!*—and—restraining it with some difficulty, half-carried, half-dragged it back to the main cavern.

Hennem-mishli, too, had found her saurian. There was the *skitter-scuff* of clawed, scaly feet and a large old male put his head out of a tunnel, gazed at her with suspicion and then grunted recognition. The rest of him slowly followed and he waddled up to the Shimshen with dignity and something akin to pride. "I am Eldesst," he hissed. "I sshow my head wissout fear."

"I look upon the Eldest with awe," she replied, in ritual homage; then, dropping it, "Where are the people, Eldest? We have to leave! Get them—quickly!"

The Eldest hissed angrily, with fear, and his spiny ruff lifted at the neck and laid back uneasily. "Not leave! Sskyboat not ssafe for Ungt! Sskyboat kill!" He came closer, confidentially. "Sstarman ssay beamer-light taking Ungt apart in ssmall piecess!—pick up up!—put on sskyboat! Not liking ssmall piecess! Ungt sstay here!"

Hennem-mishli stifled a compassionate smile and knelt to look into his face. "Wisely said, Eldest," she complimented graciously. "Only the Elders can speak so well; the young make even truth seem frightening. Even among the starmen, you see, this is so . . ."

He squatted down on his haunches to listen to her.

Outside, the sun came up.

Marik had torn great ropes of wiring from the servos, and used it to truss up two young male saurians for beaming up; now he was using the last of it to immobilize a determined little female who had no intention of going anywhere!—least of all to the *Skipjack*. Marik had time to think of gentle Ank, aboard the ship, who was no trouble at all.

He placed the little female against the stone wall and got a nasty bite on the hand for his trouble. He'd gripped it with a smothered exclamation, when suddenly there were footsteps, humanoid and hurried, racing down the tunnels toward him. Marik flattened against the rockwall and caught the intruder as he came in; in one blur of smooth, easy motion, he pinned him, a thumb against his jugular vein.

Then Marik recognized him: a crewman, one of the support personnel. He was soaked with sweat and breathing hard. "Sir," he croaked. "Sir, Skimmer Five—"

Marik released him abruptly, holding him erect until he caught his breath. "Skimmer Five—?" he prompted.

"Mister Marik, sir, we found 'em! The crew of Skimmer Five. Takahashi and Busaidi, they were mired in the swamp. We dragged 'em out with our tractor beams, but they're hurt bad." He trotted toward the narrow tunnel he'd come from, talking in short spurts, breathlessly, as he ran. Marik followed hard on his heels.

"Are they viable?"

"I don't know, sir. You can decide for yourself."

Takahashi and Busaidi were sprawled on the bare, rock floor where Danny had left them. Amelie was sponging their faces with water from the skimmer's vacutank, but she was doing little more than assuaging her innate mother-instinct.

Marik examined the crewmen quickly, compassionately. Both were semi-conscious, suffering from heat-stroke and severe radiation burns.

"We never would of found 'em without our sensors, sir. We caught their life-glow on the way back. Locked on, and there they were." Danny was trying hard not to look at them, not to be shocked before Amelie. Probably his first encounter with a sun, Marik surmised, turning back Busaidi's eyelid. *Hippus reaction. Brain damage.*

"Quel!" Marik muttered, and got to his feet. "Get these men back to the ship immediately," he ordered.

"But—the skimmer's only a two-seater, sir," Danny protested. "And I can't put these men in the cargo hatch!—they'd die!"

Marik examined Takahashi, who was tossing his head from side to side in a spasm of agony. "You take this man and pilot vessel Eight," he told Danny, and to Amelie, "This one will occupy vessel Twelve with you. If you follow him"—he tipped his head toward Danny—"you stand a good chance of getting back to the *Skipjack*."

"But what about you, sir? And the Shimshen?"

Marik made no answer. Instead, he extended a hand, fingers widely outspread, close over Takahashi's face. He held it briefly; then, as one gesture, pressed both his jugular veins hard and fast, and rapped him smartly, center forehead, with the inner side of an index finger.

Takahashi underwent a transformation. His face relaxed its tight grimace and went slack. His body settled in a loose, easy attitude, and his ragged, shallow breathing levelled off into slow, deep slumbering breaths. Danny stared.

"How—how did you do that?" he blurted.

Marik lifted Busaidi in his arms and started toward the

293

skimmers. "Help me get them into the boats," he ordered over his shoulder. "The sun is coming!"

The Eldest was almost finished speaking, but nothing more he could have said would undo the truth and ease the bitter ache of failure that weighted the air.

" . . . sso you ssee, Sshimsshen, only a few of uss, like Ank, can sstill lay eggss that bear young. All ozzers have been touched by sze ssun." He swung his head toward the tunnel mouths. "Szey will never come out of sze tunnellss. We wissh to sstay and die wiss our world." He gazed at her, then, with the fires of intelligence burning behind his eyes and in his brute face. "Becauss of you, we die wissout fear."

She stroked his head. "Only a few left to save? Surely I should have been able to do better than that . . . " She caught her breath, hope flooding her hearts. "The eggs! Eldest, the eggs, sixty of them, more than enough for a new colony! Where are they?"

"Ssomewhere in tunnellss, Sshimsshen. For ssafety."

"With your world about to die?" she chided gently.

He shrugged apologetically for his people. "They forget," he explained.

"Where are they? Can you take me to where the eggs are?"

He shrugged again. "*I* forget."

"Never mind. I'll find them." She fled down a corridor, only half-hearing the Eldest's warning.

"Sshimsshen, do not go. Iss danger, in tunnellss!"

Above her, as she ran, the rock stirred and shifted mightily, and the floor heaved under her feet.

Riker stood by the port, watching the two skimmercraft, vessels Twelve and Eight, lift through the sunglare and slide through the ship's open, inviting docking hatches. As they disappeared into the adjacent locks, he started for the Hangar Deck, glancing at his chronometer. *1750.* Marik would have to be officially reprimanded. Ten minutes was cutting it a bit too close.

Danny and Amelie helped the crew chief heave Takahashi and Busaidi out of the skimmers and into the emergency sleds, and felt the weight of responsibility lift from their (oh, tired and aching!) shoulders as the familiar hiss of air sped them to Sickbay. Amelie clung to Danny tightly and sobbed, while he patted her awkwardly.

"Oh—Dannee! It was so awful!"

"It's all right, honey. Shush, now. Hey, shush, it's okay
—" He braced up as the Captain stalked into the Hangar
Deck and glanced around. "Sir!" Amelie straightened, too,
somewhat tardily, sniffing.

"Where's Mister Marik?"

"Still on the surface, sir. He ordered us to take two
crewmen up. I asked him what he was going to do, but—"

Riker whipped out his communicator and locked onto
Marik's band. Static spat back at him. He tried again,
wrenching at it in his anger and concern.

"Captain," Amelie apologized, "we tried to make him
come with us—"

Riker didn't bother to turn around, but barked, "Dismissed!" He tried Marik's band again and gave a short
exclamation of satisfaction as it piped.

"Marik here," said the communicator evenly.

"Skimmer Twelve is back without you, sir," Riker informed him in a cold fury. "How do you explain that?"

"Two crewmen required immediate medical attention.
Without it, they would have died." There was no apology
in the answer, and Riker was angered. Marik might at
least have had the good grace to sound repentant. He
stiffened and his tone was crisply military.

"I can afford the loss of two crewmen if I must, sir;
I cannot afford the loss of my Science Officer!" He paused
and continued in a most caustic growl, "When I get you
back here, Marik, I am personally going to tear off your
hide!"

He cut the communication off and began climbing again
for the Bridge, ladder after ladder, past Astrogation (too
Dark), past the (too hot) marshy stink of the Botany
Sector, past the Biolab and the cloying sweetness of mam-
malian dead reaching into the ladderwell and clung to him.
By the time Riker reached the Bridge, he was trembling
violently from head to foot, his vision obscured by a
tenuous dark mist he kept trying to rub away. He reeled,
supporting himself with one hand against the bulkhead,
and looked for his people.

They had collapsed, each at his station, from the heat,
and the damnable ports would *snap open, admitting the
worst of the heat and glare and . . .*

He shook his head hard, wiped his dripping face with

an open hand, and stumbled toward the Command Post.

He almost made it. He reached for the wavering com stud, but the ship's gravity tugged at him, drew him down, the floor spread wide to catch him and he fell far, far, far until he hit the floor with a sick smack. Then it was dark.

It was dark in the tunnels, too, and Hennem-mishli frantically prayed for clearer night-sight, or a torch, or even (blasphemy!) for a tiny crack in the rockwall to light her way. She found no living Ungt—though once she fell across a saurian, recently dead—nor had she found the precious eggs.

And the sun was coming.

Marik's frantic search for her seemed hopeless. He sent mind-touch and she cried back at him, *here, Dao, here!* But in the labyrinthine tunnels, where was *here?*

"Mishli!" he called, at the top of his lungs. "Mishli! —zarik tu kelec imm?" *Where are you?* But there was no answer.

Faint light in the distance, at the end of the passage, and he ran toward it, stumbling a bit on rubble, and ran headlong into the full glare of the sun. He made a smothered outcry, flung his arms up before his face and fell back into the safety of the cavern, staggering far back into the darkness, the blessed, protective darkness. When the bibbing, smarting white blotches disappeared, he lowered his scorched hands, the sleeves of his tunic still smoking thinly. His face felt burned and stiff, too, but there was no time, no time even for the pain. He took a clean breath and ran back for the fork in the tunnels.

"Hennem-mishli!" he shouted again. "*Mishli!* Zarik tu kelec imm?" Spent, he mumbled in Earthenglish, "Where are you? . . ."

The Power Deck was alive with heat, with work, with hope.

"Hey!" The shout froze them all, and one of the engineers stuck his head out of the belly of the engine, his face split in a wide grin. "Hey, Chief, we got it fixed! Godalmitey, we're gonna make it!"

Hayashi jumped to his controls as engineers and techs fled the engines, and roared, "Stand by to rotate reflectors!" To his Mate, he barked, "Either we'll start her up again, or we'll blow the whole ship!"

The Mate jumped, grinning. "What've we got to lose?" he yelled, all his teeth showing white. "Go!"

"Rotate One and Three! Rotate Two and Four! Clear that water away, Hansen! Move!" His hand hovered over the automatic cutoff, ready to reverse the process should he have misjudged. "Stand by for fusion!" He took a deep breath, closed his eyes and hit the stud.

He had not misjudged. Hayashi's beloved engines boomed to life with a slow, dull rumbling that became a comfortable, even roar. Lights began to flicker on all over the ship. Ports snapped shut, polarized. The sluggish, fetid air, heavy with myriad scents of man and animal and machine, began to stir, to eddy unseen, crisscrossed with currents of fresh, cool air from the ventilators. In Astrogation, the big visual computors and sensory mechanisms twitched on and resumed their various analyses and readouts as if nothing had happened. Crewmen began to come around, to move and waken and take up their duties, and in the Biolab, technicians made notes of how many small, furry things had died and would have to be replaced, thereby unconsciously giving substance to their belief in their own survival.

Riker came awake at the foot of the Command Post, a painful welt burning at his temple, and he got up as his staff started to move, getting to their feet unsteadily. No one was badly injured. He leaned against the Post and touched the com.

"Damage Control. Riker. Give me a readout."

"We're on standard power, sir. Severe damage to five sectors: Hydroponics, 87 percent; Biolabs, 45 percent; Transporter, 50 percent—"

Riker came alert. "Hold it. Transport Sector. Recheck data for me. How many grids are operative?"

There was a pause. "Three, Captain."

"It's enough." He rang off, checked his chronometer and grabbed a stunner.

"M'Benga—it's now 1754. If I'm not back by 1800 hours, you're to warp to our next starfall and bring them the data we've collected here." He rechecked the stunner's charge. "I'm beaming down for Marik and the Shimshen."

Her search had been fruitless, futile. After the frantic race against time and the sun, she'd lost. There were no

297

eggs; or, if they existed—they must exist!—she'd never find them. And she'd endangered Dao and the Earthlikli aboard the ship— Her head lifted quickly. Had she heard something, something?

Marik called again. "Mishli! Zarik to kelec imm?"

Her face lit up. "Dao!" She started for his voice. "Dao? Zo-ili an-an son!" *Here I am.* She heard his uneven footfalls light on the passageway and ran to meet him; but she was unprepared for the sight of his face, raw and scorched down one side, or his blackened and charred tunic. She touched his cheekbone gently.

"I'm sorry," she whispered, and Marik would have answered, but the rock, the mountain, the planet shuddered, throwing them off balance. He grabbed her arm.

"Come on. Quick!"

They raced through shifting, writhing rock for the main cavern and the three surviving saurians.

Riker beamed down into the cavern, giving the bound saurians only a perfunctory inspection. A humanoid had tied those knots; Marik was still somewhere in the vicinity.

He flipped his communicator, while above him, the stone ceiling crackled ominously and showered dust and rubble down upon his head. He ran for the tunnel mouth and crouched in its safety.

"Marik!" he snapped into the communicator.

"Here," said the com, short of breath.

"The ship is on full power. Bring the Shimshen and let's get out of here! We have about four minutes."

"Negative, Captain," said the cool metal voice (*damn the man!*). "Hennem-mishli has not yet found the unborn Ungt."

"Then I'm coming in after you!" Riker plunged into the depths of the tunnel, trying to get to them before the sun boiled the rock into lava. He stumbled over a mummified saurian and plunged on blindly.

"Negative! Negative!" protested the communicator gripped tightly in his hand. "The roof is about to collapse! Your footsteps could—"

The tunnel trembled, echoed, roared as the ceiling of the burial maze fell in, throwing him under the protection of a jutting ledge and pinning his arm to the sidewall with a huge shard of rock. He tried to jerk free but the effort made his head spin. Dust settled slowly about him and he could see, dimly outlined on the floor, some dozens of crudely embalmed saurian mummies. *Well, Riker, if you have to be killed, a cemetery—even an Unget cemetery, is appropriate.* Wet warmth trickled off his numbing fingers and the ground stirred again, and flexed.

"—going on?" the communicator insisted. "Captain! —what happened, can you read me?" His communicator, lying open among the dust, sounded desperate.

He made two tries before he could get the words out. "The roof—You were right, Marik, I'm—my arm, it's—it's pinned—"

"I'll be right there!"

"Negative!" Riker barked, gritting his teeth as he inadvertently jarred his arm. "Negative, Marik! Get *her* out of here!—Marik!"

Somehow, Marik was silhouetted in the tunnel mouth. He clambered over bodies and debris, digging his way to the Captain (*and a wayward bit of his mind promised Oman Shari-Mnenoplan that this time, Marik would save the life he was trying for*) and the Shimshen, assisted by a bulky, old male saurian, helped clear away the rubble. The old saurian scuttled in to help Marik and between them they lifted the shard of rock off Riker's arm and held it up while he pulled free. Finally, Marik half-supporting him, sacrificing gentleness for time, Riker gained the tunnel, his knees buckling under him. His arm was a mess of torn flesh and bone splinters, and Marik bound it quickly with the Shimshen's sash, while she ran back for the Eldest; but the ground shook and spilled her into the debris and she made a sharp cry. Marik half-turned for her, and her face was alight, incandescent. In her two careful hands she cradled an Ungt egg.

"They're here!" she exulted, digging for them. "Oh— my Dao!—they're right here!"

The Eldest's voice rumbled from just beyond her. "Ssooo. Remember now. Iss here. Life wiss deass."

He dug with both clawed hands and pulled out a crate of fertile eggs as another tremblor rocked the caves; Marik shouldered the precious cargo and between him and Hennem-mishli, they supported Riker for the last few yards into the main cavern.

"Come, Eldest!" Hennem-mishli called, but the old saurian had disappeared into the tunnel's blackest hole, and a moment later, as they scrambled for the cavern, the tunnels were buried under tons of fuming rock, and a thin, brilliant, actinic line of light showed far up in the ceiling of the vault. Riker slumped against a wall, indicating the saurians bound against their own hysteria. "Where are the rest of them?"

"Only these are left," the Shimshen replied quietly, "possibly sterile, too."

"It's just as well." Riker stopped to catch his breath, ignoring the trickle and drip, trickle and drip of blood coursing down his arm. "We can only take three at a time anyway. Transporter Sector damage." He flipped his communicator with his good hand and was annoyed at its trembling. "Transporter Sector: three to beam up. Saurians."

They shimmered away like heat waves on a summer afternoon, mirages to fool the eye.

"Now us," Riker breathed in relief. "We've got one minute until warp. Shimshen."

She shook her head 'no'. "I can't go with you, Captain Riker." They turned to her, unbelieving, and Marik started toward her.

"Mishli!"

"There are only three places—and no time." She placed the crate next to Riker, begging Marik to understand. "You, Dao—and you, Captain—and the infants, the eggs. All there is left. Many lives—against one."

"Come *now*—Shimshen!" Riker snapped, with all the authority he could muster. "Marik!" He gestured 'come' with a tip of the head. They paid him no attention, each realizing the truth at last.

Marik's face was gray. "Don't ask this of me, Mishli. *I won't leave you again!*" There was a deep, muffled roar as other tunnels collapsed, far inside the mountain, and a new, stray shaft of vicious sunlight probed the cavern and shorted out a servo. Marik touched the Shimshen's face gently. "Go with the Captain, Mishli," he urged. "I'm staying here."

"Marik!" Riker's stunner was fixed full on Marik. He was swaying where he stood, but his aim was commendable. It wavered not at all. Marik tensed to spring, but the Captain brought the stunner up quickly on the Shimshen.

300

"It would be a mistake, Mister." He took a ragged breath and continued, "She has the right to make a choice. You don't. The ship needs you. The crew, the technicians . . . the remains of the Ungt. I won't let you kill yourself. Not for her, not for anyone."

The rumbling grew, making the cave walls shudder.

"Paul!" It was hate and agony and the wrenching ache of loss, and the nearest to pleading that Marik would ever come.

"Not for anyone," Riker repeated, and flipped—or tried to flip—his communicator with his mangled hand. Miraculously, he made it.

"Transport Sector: rig for split beaming. Personnel two, cargo one."

Hennem-mishli gazed up at Marik and he drowned in the drowning gray eyes. "Forgive me, Dao. It's my choice, you see; my place to be. Sixty eggs—sixty thousand children . . ." The tears spilled over and became bright traces down her cheeks, but her face was calm with serene purpose. "When you are out there, where it is very deep," she whispered, "think happily of the pavilion at dawn . . ."

". . . and the memlikti singing in their golden webs . . ." His voice was tight and his fingers gripped her slender shoulders. *"Hennem-mishli!"*

"Transport Sector rigged for split-beaming, sir," announced the communicator briskly, impersonally.

"To the Gryphon, the Sky . . ." Hennem-mishli placed her palms together and opened them out gracefully, making a farewell. "Chom-ala, Dao." Softly.

Marik made the gesture. "Chom-ala, Shimshen."

"Three to beam up," Riker barked. "Make it fast!"

She pressed her palm tightly against Marik's—their old childhood 'forgive' gesture—and drew back slowly, hands, palms, fingertips, as he shimmered away to nothing and only their fingers touched—and were gone.

Marik appeared on the Transporter grid, his arm still extended, bemused, still feeling the pressure of her fingertips. Riker, staggering down into the arms of concerned crewmen, said *"Warp! Move!"*

Marik sprang down, raced for the lee port on the Bridge, and stood staring out at the rapidly fading planet, its diminishing star. Sudden light flared against his face,

301

briefly glossing the Bridge, and the mighty ship rolled just a bit before it stabilized. Marik watched the planet disintegrate in flames, and somewhere in one corner of his mind, he heard Ank mourn.

"Oohh, Misss Jen! . . . Bose my heartss iss ssad!"

"We are all sad, small-lizard-Ank," Jen answered primly, gently. "But at least the Shimshen saved your people. Come," she said, "come."

Sound faded and Marik stared fixedly at the sun, which was swiftly becoming a brilliant new star in the blackness of space.

A hand fell compassionately on his shoulder, but he did not turn around.

"Marik?" The Captain's voice, full of sympathy without pity, asking forgiveness without apology. Marik's eyes swam and ran over, and still he did not move. When he spoke, his voice was calm, even, and well-controlled.

"It makes a very bright light," he said.

AVON ⬖ MEANS THE BEST
IN SCIENCE FICTION!

Brian Aldiss

CRYPTOZOIC	V2362	75¢
NEANDERTHAL PLANET	V2322	75¢
STARSHIP	V2321	75¢

Ursula K. Le Guin

LATHE OF HEAVEN	14530	95¢

Zenna Henderson

HOLDING WONDER	N445	95¢
THE PEOPLE: NO DIFFERENT FLESH	V2344	75¢
PILGRIMAGE	V2312	75¢

Roger Zelazny

CREATURES OF LIGHT AND DARKNESS	V2362	75¢
LORD OF LIGHT	N187	95¢
NINE PRINCES IN AMBER	V2444	75¢

Wherever paperbacks are sold, or order directly from the publisher. Include 15¢ for handling; allow three weeks for delivery.

AVON BOOKS, Mail Order Department
250 West 55th Street, New York, N.Y. 10019